YOU MADE YOUR BED

Thank You Kathy
for your support

Sincerely

Marleen
Turner

YOU MADE YOUR BED

Darleen Turner

Library of Congress Control Number:		2010916087
ISBN:	Hardcover	978-1-4568-0429-9
	Softcover	978-1-4568-0428-2
	Ebook	978-1-4568-0430-5

This book was printed in the United States of America.

To order additional copies of this book, contact:
Xlibris Corporation
1-888-795-4274
www.Xlibris.com
Orders@Xlibris.com
88152

ACKNOWLEDGEMENTS

---•---

I would like to thank all my siblings. If it weren't for you, I would not have all the memories that I hold so dear to my heart. My memories are what gives me the imagination that I need to be able to write my story. So a big thank you to Raymond, Edmond, Antonette, Eugene, Emily, Paul, Emile, Therese, Catherine, Mickey, and Susanne.

Thank you to my husband, Dennis, for loving me for who I am and believing in me, making me feel like I can accomplish whatever I set out to do. Thank you to all my children for not laughing at their mother, for wanting to put her imagination into a book. So thank you, Tina, Jason, Sherri, Cole, Clint.

Thank you to all my grandchildren, Victoria, Patrick, Kayden, Lacie, Saxon, Tavaius, Jaydyn, for just loving Grandma.

Thank you to my two daughter-in-laws Leslie and Kayla who help me with my lack of computer knowledge.

I would also like to thank Steve, Terri, and the production staff from Xlibris for their effort and assistance.

The biggest thanks has to go to my mom and dad for teaching us to be strong and independent and for loving all of us. We all miss you both very much, and we pray that God keep you safe so we can meet again.

Your loving wife, mother, sister, and grandmother,

CHAPTER ONE

It was an early spring day. The sun was bright and warm; it seemed to wrap its arms around you and hold you in its embrace, making you feel strong and safe. The new flowers had such vibrant colors to them and such a seductive smell that this gave such an uplifting gait to one's walk. This was the time of the year when all new and fresh sprang to life. The grass was letting the brown shawl that had seen it through the winter start to fall. And it too reached for the sun, and it seemed to be saying, "Hey, can you see me now?" Even with all this, I still seem to have an underlying feeling that something was wrong; I could not shake it. I could not get enough sleep, and I had no energy. I was thankful that my sister only lived six blocks from me. She worked at the liquor store and would have today and tomorrow off, and we usually got together for coffee on our days off, but not till later in the day. She will be surprised to see me, but I do know she will be up as she has five kids and a husband to deal with each morning. But I was feeling restless and thought I would pay her an early visit. Just as I was to knock on the door, Louise opens it. I do not know who scared who the most. She was about to throw her garbage out, which I almost got in the face.

"Woo, Charlene, and good morning to you. You're up and at it early. Thought you would have slept in for a while yet."

"No, I wanted to see you before you left to do your errands this morning."

"Oh yeah, what's up?"

"Well, for starters, I would like a cup of coffee as I am out till payday."

"I have just put on a fresh pot, so you're in luck there. Sit down and tell me what's on your mind."

"I don't really know what it is, but I have not been feeling quite right. It's nothing that I can put a finger on."

"What do you mean? Charlene, you sick or something?"

"I'm tired all the time like I can't get enough sleep, and I have absolutely no energy. Have you tried doing someone's hair with your eyes half closed?"

"I can't say I have. Have you been eating enough? If you don't have coffee, what else you don't have?"

"Yeah, I've been eating OK. Sometimes it does not stay down, but I am eating."

"So how long has this been going on?"

"How about that coffee you told me, I could have."

"Coming right up. Now tell me, Charlene, how long?"

"I don't really know for sure, a month or so."

I no sooner got half my coffee down when it was coming back. I made a mad dash to the bathroom; thank goodness it was so close. After a few minutes with my head in the toilet, I felt like there was nothing left inside me.

"Charlene? Charlene, are you all right?"

"Yeah, I will be out in just a minute." Wiping my face and rinsing my mouth out to get rid of the foul taste, I looked into the mirror and saw what I thought was a very flushed face. Like I had been in the sun too long, which of course I had not been. I felt my forehead, and I did not have a fever. But I better get out of here before Louise gets worried.

"Here, Charlene. Sip on this apple juice slowly! You said this has been going on for a while. Have you been to see a doctor about any of this?"

"No, what do I have to see a doctor for? I probably have the flu bug. Spring is a good time to catch it."

"Spring is a good time to catch a lot of things."

"What is that suppose to mean?"

"Well, how much weight have you gained and how sore are your boobs and when was your last period?"

"Just wait! Wait one damn minute. Are you saying what I think your saying?"

"Well, Charlene. When was it? Your last period?"

"I don't know. I haven't thought about it. I have never really paid any attention to it!"

"Then I suggest you best figure it out as close as possible. Charlene, I'm going to the city next month to see my gynecologist, and I think it would be a good time for you to come with me and get a check up if you haven't been to see a doctor here yet."

"I have not been to see a doctor, for I did not think I needed one. By the way, what the hell is a gyno? Or whatever you called him."

"It's a woman's doctor and a very good one. I had him when I had the twins."

"I'm sure I'll be fine."

"Come on, Charlene. Humor me, we have never been to the city together, it could be fun. We could do some shopping and have a nice lunch out somewhere different than here in Stony Creek."

"I can't shop, Louise, as I have to save for my hairdressing school."

"Then come and get a good check up at least."

"I will see, but right now, I will go and let you go do what you have to do today. Perhaps I will have a little nap."

"Charlene, you book off for the fifteenth 'cause I'm going to make you an appointment today."

"OK, OK. When is it?"

"The fifteenth of next month."

"If I'm up to it later, I will come back for coffee. It's such a nice day, or at least I thought it was."

"Now come on, Charlene, don't be like that. It could always be worse!"

"I guess you're right. I can't see how right at this moment, so I'll catch you later." The flowers did not seem to smell so damn sweet now nor was the sun keeping me as warm as it had done earlier. Pregnant! How the hell can I be pregnant. I can hardly pay rent and feed myself once a day on what I make; there's no way I can afford a baby. Besides that, I live in a damn attic of this old lady's house. Christ, I don't even have a bathroom of my own. Maybe Louise is wrong. Please, please, God! Show me that she is wrong.

I have to go in through Mary's back door to go up to her attic. She is always sitting at her table, reading her Bible. If she sees me, she'll want me to stop and have tea with her, which I usually do as she is very sweet and lonely. She always wants to feed me and help me in some way. Sometimes the cookies have filled the empty hole I have had, but today, I think they might just come back, and I would not want that to happen. I know she has a son as I have seen him with her, and when he's drinking, he's mean to her. I don't know if she has a daughter.

She tells me, "You're a good girl, deary! I'm glad I can talk to you. I don't know what I would do if I didn't have you to vent to." She goes to church, rain or snow, so I wonder what she'd say if she was to be told I'm pregnant. She'll be so disgusted with me she'll tell me that I will have to move out. All was quiet, and somehow, I missed her as I slipped up to the attic. I made sure I was extra quiet and stepped just right on the stairs as they had a squeak in them when you stepped on them just the right way.

My mattress sat off to one side as I didn't have a bed, so it was on the floor. The floor way only plywood, so it was warm from the heat below; it kept my bed warm. My clothes, what I had of them, were stack in boxes lying on their sides, which gave me shelves to keep them from being wrinkled. I liked to be clean and very tidy to go to work. As a child growing up in a family of twelve, it was hard for our mother to keep up with the laundry. So we weren't always clean and tidy back then; sometimes we were embarrassed at how we looked. I have become obsessed with my appearance. Becoming a hairdresser also teaches you how to apply makeup and what to wear with what.

I also had found a small wooden box that someone had thrown out, which I picked up and used for a night table; my lamp and clock fit just right on it.

I spend a lot of time reading my books on hairdressing. Once I get my journeyman's license, I will make a lot more money than I do right now. My schooling will be paid for, but I have to save for living in the city. I will be there for four months and that alone scares the heebie-jeebies out of me. I have never lived in a big place in my life, and you hear of all the terrible things that happen to people in those bigger centers. I'm hoping to live close by the school.

I'm apprenticing at the CLIP and CURL on Main Street. Right now, I don't make a lot of money, so I've learned how to buy groceries that go a long ways, such as macaroni, dry soups, breads, cereals, crackers, and eggs. It has taught me how to stretch a little food and money a long way. It doesn't leave me much to go out on, and by the sounds of it, I went out one time too many. Leaving home at an early age and not been taught a whole lot about living on your own has made things very interesting for me. Perhaps if I would have left home on better terms with my mother, I could call her now and again and get some help, but as it is, I'll have to figure it out on my own. My mother always said, "You make your bed, you lie in it." So once you were gone from home, there was no going back. There would be no help from there either.

I'm OK with eating once a day. I haven't lost weight, and I usually feel great. But, if there's a baby, I have heard people talk about how much they eat when eating for two. If I'm pregnant, what will happen about my job? Can I work right up until I have the baby? What will I do about school? Who would take care of the baby after or while I'm in school? I fell asleep thinking of all the what ifs and how I would feed and clothe my baby. At first it was easy as I was breast-feeding and was able to keep the baby wrapped in a blanket, but then my baby started getting smaller and smaller, and it cried all the time. What was happening? What was I doing wrong? This was all happening because I couldn't afford to eat more than once a day and that was not enough for my body to produce the nourishment that my baby needed. My baby had become so small that I had to wrap it up in a tissue and kept it in my pocket. Oh god! I have to do something before my baby dies; I started running to Louise's. I was running and running, but I wasn't getting anywhere.

"Charlene, hello there, Charlene, are you home?"

Louise's calling me woke me up from my horrible dream. "Just a minute," I said as I tried to get my wits about me before I answered the door.

"Hi! What are you doing here?"

"You said you might come back, and seeing how you weren't in a good state of mind when you left this morning, I thought I would come check on you. You look like you've seen a ghost. Are you all right?"

"Yeah, I was napping and had a real stupid dream."

"Well, come with me. We're going out for a late lunch as my husband won't be home until real late."

"Oh, thanks, but I can't."

"Why not, Charlene? What's keeping you here?"

"Money! Louise, I don't want to spend more than I really have to right now."

"I asked you, so I'm buying. Now comb your hair and come with me please, Charlene!"

"All right, All right."

Even at four in the afternoon, the sun was still warm, and it made me feel great to be alive. Louise had brought her car as she was taking me to the corner café where her oldest daughter worked. Her daughter was only six months older than myself; she always calls me Auntie Charlene. People would laugh about it but never really knew why she would call me that. It was just a standing joke between us. So Crystal brought our sandwiches and a few fries with a glass of milk.

"Gosh, Louise, I don't think I can eat all of this."

"One thing about it, Charlene. You can take it home. It doesn't need to be warmed up." That was a good thing because all I have is a hot plate, which works OK for what I need to cook.

The next month was hell especially when food smells would upset my stomach. I spent a lot of time running to the bathroom. It was a good thing our boss was a drunk; it was easy to pull things over on her.

"Beth, we can't keep this up. Liz is going to figure it out sooner or later."

"Charlene, wait until you have seen the doctor. Then for sure you will have to tell her."

"All right, but this is getting harder to do every day. You can't keep covering for me."

"I can and I will, so let it go for now. Charlene, after your doctor's appointment, you'll have to decide."

"Decide what, Beth?"

"Liz, will want you to give the baby up for an adoption or have an abortion."

"Are you kidding me?"

"I am not the last girl she made get an abortion, and they paid for it. She will want you to do the same, that's a promise."

"I don't know if I could do that! Have an abortion, I mean."

"That is something only you and your doctor should decide."

I met Louise at the bus depot at 5:30 AM. Louise would not take her car to the city; it made her very nervous to drive around so many people. She said this way she could enjoy herself as well. Once we were on the bus we slept a little longer or at least I tried to. I mainly laid my head back and kept my eyes closed so I wouldn't have to answer all Louise's what ifs. Yet I knew if there was anyone I should and could talk to, it was her as she has already been down this road alone. But guess if I'm pregnant, I'll have a lot of time to ask questions. Louise is twenty-three years older than myself and now has five children. So she should know what she's talking about. I wonder what she will think of me after today. She always tells me I look as fresh as a daisy.

"Charlene."

"Yeah."

"Have you told Mother yet?"

"No, I didn't want to until after I've seen the doctor."

"Why? Do you think I'm wrong, Charlene?"

"Not really as much as I want you to be wrong. I guess if the doctor tells me, it will be real then."

"I suppose so, but I have been there, trust me you are, and no, I am not playing doctor. I just know the signs, that's all."

"Thanks!"

"You going to tell the father or have you already?"

"No, I don't think so. He doesn't have to know."

"Why the hell not? He has a responsibly towards you and the baby."

"That might be true, but I wasn't enough for him before. I sure don't want him back because I'm having his baby."

"You telling me he's with someone else now."

"Yes, he has been for quite some time. He told me he was going out of town to work and then I saw them together, and I knew they were more than friends and she's not his sister either. I also saw his mother, and she made sure she told me how happy they are and she hopes no one will get in their way."

"But, Charlene!"

"No! I said I don't need him now or ever."

"He should have to pay you, Charlene. It wouldn't kill him to help raise the child he helped create."

"No!" I said. "I don't want to have to answer to anyone about the baby. So can we please drop it now?"

"OK, OK, calm down. We'll talks about it another time."

"No, we won't. There's nothing to talk about, do you understand!" Two hours and a cab ride later, we were ten minutes late but still had to wait. Louise was the first to go in, and after fifteen minutes, she was back out.

"Boy, that was quick!"

"I was just getting my results from last time and my prescription refilled."

"Is Charlene Green here?" a lady asked from the desk.

"Yes, that's me."

"Hi! My name is Bella, and I am going to be your nurse for today, OK? Would you please come with me now."

"Charlene, did you want me to come with you?"

"Thank you, but I will be OK."

"I will be waiting right here for you. Good luck!"

"Thanks. I'll need it, I think." The hall I followed Bella down seemed to go on forever. The light green paint made me think of the hospital, and it seemed to be closing in around me. I was getting a little short of breath as I was beginning to panic.

"You OK, miss? There is nothing to worry about. You're in good hands here. You have one of the best doctors in the city." As she opens the door to the examining room, the window was open, and a burst of cool air hit me; it felt so damn good I just stood there taking it all in.

"Please get undressed and put on this gown."

"What for? Isn't the doctor just going to talk to me?"

"Are you not pregnant?"

"I don't know for sure."

"Well then, put this on, and the doctor will find out for sure now, won't he?"

"Do I have to?"

"Yes, and I suggest you hurry up now because he won't be long."

I broke out into a cold sweat as I hurried to get the gown on and get myself covered back up. There were so many name snaps on the arms it was hard to tell where they all went, which side belonged where. I was just getting on the table or bed or whatever it is called when a knock came on the door and the doctor came in. He was an older man just starting to go gray on the sides, but I also noticed that he was a very nice-looking man for his age. I could feel my face turning red, so I tried looking away from him just as he reached out and took my hand in his. Man, are they ever soft. I think they were even softer than mine.

"Hello, Charlene. I'm Doctor Gage, and I sure hope I can help you today. I see by your chart that you think you may be pregnant."

"Yes, I do, or I should say, my older sister thinks I am."

"Who is your sister?"

"Louise Palmar."

"Oh yes, I just saw her. In fact I have delivered some of her children. So she could very well be right about you."

"How old are you, Charlene?"

"I will be twenty-one in August."

"Is this your first time pregnant?"

"Yes, it is."

"You never had a miscarriage or an abortion?"

"No, never!"

"All right, I want you to lie down and put your feet up in these stirrups. I've been told they're cold and uncomfortable and you will find it a little embarrassing, but it is the only way we have of being able to give a thorough examination. I'm sorry, but this is the best that I can do."

As I lay there with my legs stretched apart and the doctor seems like he got his face right up in my privates, you could say embarrassing was an understatement. I could feel him inside me and whatever he was using was also cold. He was talking away like I do this all the time. I sort of blocked him out and was trying to keep my mind on the pictures that they had stuck up on the ceiling. I knew some of them, but some were out of my league. I was sure that if I were pregnant I'd be getting to know more about my anatomy. Some of them made me a little queasy.

"After I'm done with you, Bella will take some blood from you and weigh you. Then I will be back in once I have some answers, and you and I will have a chat, all right!"

"OK."

"Now you can get up and get dressed." And with that said, he was gone. A faint tap came to the door, and Bella came in with her little basket of goodies.

"OK, Charlene. Are you ready for this?"

"As ready as I ever will be." She took my blood and weighed me just as the doctor said she would.

"Here are some small booklets for you to be able to read."

"What are they on?"

"Your pregnancy and on birthing. There is a lot of info in here for you. You don't have to read it all right now, but it will answer a lot of questions you may have, and there may not be anyone around to answer them for you. These books are right on the money as far as the information goes."

My head is spinning as I bend over to put on my shoes. I stumble just as Dr. Gage comes through the door. He catches me before I hit my head on the end of the table.

"Bella, please get her a glass of orange juice and a muffin. Sit down, Charlene, until you have had the orange juice. It will help you get your senses back."

"Thank you. I just can't wrap my mind around the fact that there really is a baby! I keep thinking this has to be a mistake. It can't really be happening."

"I'm sorry, Charlene, but it is true. There is a baby. If you want the father to come in while I chat with you, that would be OK with me. In fact he should be here to understand what is all to come. There is a lot involved with having a baby."

"No! No! He's not here with me."

"Oh, and why is that?"

"It's just me, that's all."

"Are you telling me you're having this baby on your own? You are having it, right?"

"What do you mean by that?"

"You're not wanting an abortion or anything like that, are you?"

"I don't think so. I can't see myself having an abortion if I don't need to."

"Why would you? You are healthy, and there is no reason why you can't have a healthy baby. Will your sister be helping you?"

"She says she will."

"Then that's all you need. As time goes on, you will need more help. I want you to come back next month so I can do an ultrasound. At that point, we will be able to tell you when your baby is due and also if there are twins."

"Twins? Are you for real!"

"Well, Charlene. There are twins in your family, and you are larger than you should be at this time."

"It can't be twins."

"Why not, Charlene? Anything is possible. I also want you to stay in touch with your doctor in Stony Creek as well."

"My doctor?"

"You do have one, don't you?"

"No! I have not needed one."

"You do now, and I will give you a name of one out there who I would trust with my daughter. He has eight children of his own, so there won't be much he won't know about babies."

"All right, this ultrasound, is it safe?"

"Oh yes! It was a real blessing when that was invented. It in itself has saved a lot of babies as we can tell early if something is wrong. Right now, you are due at the end of December. The ultrasound will tell us exactly when. Now do you have any question for me?"

My head is swimming with the news about maybe twins. Questions? I am numb right now and couldn't even think of one to ask.

"Here is the name of the doctor out there, and if you need anything before I see you again, call him. I am going to send him all the information on you so it won't be a surprise when you go and see him. I want you to make your next appointment on your way out and please let my girls now that you are to be booked for an ultrasound. Take care of yourself and the little one or ones, and I will see you next month." With that said, he was gone. My mind is on overload and twins keep going over and over in my mind. Oh my god, TWINS!

"Charlene, Charlene, are you all right? Are you ready to leave yet? We can go for lunch and do some window-shopping before we leave for the bus depot."

"WHAT!"

"Are you ready?"

"I just have to make another appointment, then we can leave." It only took about five minutes to get all arranged for the next trip, but it seemed to take half an hour.

We were sitting at the table in this little side café. It was a beautiful place all done in antiques, which made me think of the farm we had been raised on. But that thought was short lived as it was taken over by the thought of twins again. It seemed to me every word on the menu said "Twins, twins, twins."

"Charlene, you haven't said much since we left the doctor's office. In fact you look like you are on another planet, is everything all right?"

"All right! Sure just ducky."

"Come on, Charlene, What is that supposed to mean? I've come this far with you, so spill it. Was the doctor hard on you because you are going to be a single mom?"

"No. He never said too much on the subject."

"OH! Really, no questions about the father?"

"No! And it's not a big deal. I wanted to just get up and runaway. Could we just drop it for now, please?"

"Sorry, Charlene. I didn't mean to upset you, I just thought—"

"I know, I know. It's not you, can we order now, please."

"Sure!"

We had both ordered just a light lunch and ate in silence for some of the time, then for some reason, I just blurted out, "TWINS. He thinks I'm having goddamn twins."

"Oh, that explains your mood. You didn't want one but now maybe two. Is that why you have to come back?"

"Yea, he wants to do an ultrasound. He said he will be able to tell more then."

"That will be good, and you know it could always be worse, Charlene. He could have told you that you have cancer that you can't live with, but twins, you can."

"Perhaps you're right, Louise, but twins, what the hell will I do with twins. It's going to be hard enough with one never mind twins. One on my own is going to be a challenge."

"Charlene, you're not alone. Remember that you have us, and we have been down that road with twins. You know what, one is a blessing in itself. Two is totally a blessing from God, and if he didn't think you could handle it, he wouldn't give them to you to mess up. The girls and I would love to help you."

"Thank you, but it's not up to you. It is my problem."

"Maybe not, but you are family, and that makes them family which makes it our problem as well. That's what families do, Charlene. When the going gets hard, we step up to the plate and make it somewhat easier. Do you really think we would just sit by and watch you struggle when there's a baby or two involved?"

"No, I guess not. How am I going to afford twins when I can hardly afford to feed myself? I don't have a good place to call home. I don't think living in the attic of someone's home qualifies as a proper living condition to raise children."

"Maybe not, Charlene. But they would be dry, warm and, most of all, with their mother who will love them more than she realizes possible."

"If someone was to report me, I would lose them as sure as we sit here."

"Charlene, we would not sit by and watch that happen."

"Thank you, but once again, it would not be your problem. What about my hairdressing? What will I do about it?"

"You will have to put it on hold for a while. You can always go back to it after the baby is born, and a lot of women do."

"But I can make real good money once I have my journeyman's ticket. Just maybe I should do the smart thing here. It would be better off for all."

"Charlene, just what do you think would be the smart thing to do?"

"To adopt them out or perhaps an abortion."

"You really think that would be a smart thing to do, Charlene. Either way, you will pay for the rest of your life. To adopt them out. Every time you saw twins, you would wonder if they're yours. If you did not see them, you would always wonder where they were, are they really being loved the way you would have loved them. Every special day that would come along, you would wonder: their school years, their weddings, and what about their babies. Would you not want to be their grandmother? It does not matter which one of these options you choose, you will be sorry for the rest of your life. It would be a heartache that you would never get over, Charlene. In the end, it would kill who you are. Remember, Charlene, you are a fighter. You always have been. I know you can do this, and with a little help from us, you will do just great, Charlene. Please don't go do anything stupid that you will regret."

"STUPID! I already have done the stupidest thing a girl on her own could have done, and that was to believe in someone."

"That may be so, Charlene, but what is cannot be changed now. You just hold up your head and keep faith in yourself, and it will see you through, with help from your family. Please! Charlene, promise me you won't do anything without coming to me first. Remember, Charlene, you have been chosen for whatever reason to be their mother not some stranger who has been picked out of a few, and it would break your heart year after year."

"You don't think it will break my heart if I'm not able to take care of them and I lose them to someone in the end."

"We would never let that happen, Charlene."

"How can you say that, Louise when I most likely won't have a job when Liz finds out?"

"We will help you so long as you are honest with us and let us know when you need help. Don't be so damn proud. Pride is a good thing but don't let it get in the way of good judgment."

"You say you will help, but what about Ted? What is he going to say?"

"Ted will be just fine about it. After all, they are a part of a bigger family than just us."

"But!"

"No BUTS, Charlene! Now let's finish up so we can go window-shopping. We still have two and a half hours before we have to catch the bus. So just relax. All the worrying in the world won't change anything that is to be, OK? Let's take it one day at a time."

"OK." Our lunch went by great and mine even stayed down, which was a plus. We left the little café and walked up and down 119th Avenue; we only went a couple of blocks either way as there were so many shops here that we did not have to go to any malls.

Buy the time we had left and gone back to the bus depot, my feet were telling me they had had enough. So we sat down with a cup of tea and waited for the bus.

"There sure was a lot of nice things you could buy for a baby if you had a place to do it in."

"You know, Charlene, you can make any place a home by fixing it up. It does not have to cost lots of money all the time."

"I know, but I don' t even have a bathroom of my own, never mind a room for a baby."

"Maybe not right now, Charlene, but no one says you'll be there forever. You keep it very clean, and I think it could be cute all fixed up. If your landlady doesn't mind, I would help you. I think we could have a lot of fun. Come on, what you say! Want to?"

"Really, you would want to do that!"

"Sure, paint and wallpaper are cheap, and in no time, you'll have a very cute place. We can look in the secondhand stores for furniture as I know you're not a person who likes new things."

"I think people throw out things they can get a lot of use out of for some time to come."

"That's why they throw it out. Because they get tired of it and want something new. They say one person discard is another person treasure. We could probably get a lot of very nice things, so we will start to check it out on Saturday. Another place is the take it or leave it. There you don't even pay. You just take it home, and I've seen very nice things been taken there and dropped off. We might have to let them know what we are looking for, and the people there will set it aside for us."

"Really, I did not know there was such a place or I have been down there." Once we were on the bus, it left me two hours to daydream, and that's just what I did. One thing about daydreaming, you can be wherever you want and you can have whatever you want. It can be a wonderful time, until you get disturbed.

"Charlene."

"Yea, Louise, what is it?"

"You going to call Mother now that you know for sure."

"Is there really a hurry? What is she going to do other than put me down, tell me how stupid I am? It won't really matter to her one way or another."

"Perhaps not, but it will give her reason to believe that you are trying to hide it from her if she hears it from someone else. That in itself will piss her off and make it harder for you to deal with her."

"I know, I know, but she is the last person I want to deal with right now. I can already hear her saying, 'Well remember you made your bed you must lie in it, and don't be bringing it here and thinking I am going to take care of it 'cause that is not happening.' As if."

"You're right. I have heard it all at one time or another. But the longer you put it off, the harder it gets. You want to be one step ahead of her on this, trust me, OK? If you phone her and she starts getting nasty with you, you do have the option of hanging up. That's a good thing about the phone. She will get nasty, and there's no doubt in my mind. She will tell you that getting pregnant's not the way to hold on to any man. All you have done is show him how easy and cheap you were, and they usually leave you with the kid. Mother's words not mine."

"See. That's why I do not want to call her. Let me get over the shock first. Maybe in a couple days, I will be able to handle her."

"All right, Charlene. But don't wait to long."

"I won't, I promise."

"I won't say anything when she calls, not until you have told her, not because I'm ashamed of you either. I've been there. I know you feel ashamed of yourself, no one knows that better than me. But, Charlene, don't be so hard on yourself. We all make mistakes, and we have to just move on and learn from them. If someone asked, Charlene, I don't want to lie about it as in time you won't be able to hide it very well."

"You're right, and you shouldn't have to lie. It's not like there's anyone else there other than Jacob to tell her, and we both know he won't do that."

"Jacob, I had not thought of him until now. Maybe it's because he's been out in the bush working, but now that spring is here, he should be coming in for spring break up. I can't think of what he might have to say about it."

Jacob is my second youngest brother that lives at Louise's and sometimes sleeps on my floor, depending how much he has had to drink when he comes over. We get along pretty good and hang out now and again. Wonder what he would do if he knew the baby's father was one of his friends. Once I met his friend, I stayed more to myself than going out, but that didn't get me anywhere other than we were not seen downtown, so no one will know who the father is, so I won't have to worry about anyone telling him. I will just have to watch where I hang out now. I sure won't be going to any bars, so that in itself should keep me away from him. I just laid my head back and closed my eyes.

Today has been such a roller-coaster ride that my head was starting to hurt. I wanted no more talking just peace and quiet, Louise must have thought I had fallen asleep as I heard no more from her until we were only minutes from home.

"Charlene, wake up. We're home, and is it even nice out still?" It was five thirty and suppertime, but I wasn't hungry as we had a late lunch. You want to come for supper, Charlene?"

"No, thanks anyways, but you know what I think. I'm going to walk home from here."

"Are you crazy? It's a long walk."

"I know, but you're right. It is very nice out, and I don't have to be home for any one time. This will give me a chance to see other yards and the flowers that are blooming. I will take my time. I will be OK."

"Are you sure, Charlene?"

"Yea, I'm sure, Louise, and thank you for all you have done for me. Thank you for being there today with me. You know you're more of a mother to me than a sister, right?" Hugging her just did not seem like it was enough. I wanted her to feel the love I have for her and for her to know just how deep it went. She maybe my stepsister but never once did I ever think of her as less than a full-blooded sister.

"You know, Charlene, everything will work out all right. You'll see. Call me, or better yet, stop over, OK? Remember, I love you, Charlene."

"I love you too, Louise, and thank you once again."

"My pleasure, and you don't have to thank me. That's what sisters do, OK?"

"OK." She climbed into her car and was gone. The walk home was pretty. I saw a lot of spring beauty.

I was so relaxed that I was not paying any attention to my surroundings or even to where I was.

CHAPTER TWO

"**H**ELLO THERE!"

God, how I could be so stupid and walk this way. It takes me right past the baby's grandmother's place, and he is there a lot.

"Hi."

"You just out for a walk, are you?"

"Yes, it's such a beautiful day."

"That it is."

"Would you like a glass of iced tea?"

"No! I mean, no, thanks. I'm on my way to my sister's for supper, so I best not stop today."

"Oh, all right, another day then."

"Sure, see you, bye for now." I didn't think my legs were going to start moving. Sort of stumbling, I finally got walking at a good pace as I was scared that her son would appear. I was a little shaky the rest of the way home, and seeing Mary out in her garden wasn't what I wanted right now either. Damn it, I'm just not having any luck right now. But I should have known she would be out in her flower beds as she spends a lot of time out there. She has shown me pictures of her flowers all in full bloom and her gardens are fantastic. People drop by and buy flowers right out of her garden for their wives' birthdays or their anniversaries. She calls the money she makes off her flowers her mad money. When I asked her why, she said it was because every time she's mad at her son, she comes out and spends time with her flowers. She also tells me that flowers do a lot better when someone talks to them. Who am I to argue with her? She's the one with the beautiful gardens. I don't think I have ever seen as many different color of roses in my life. The blue rose has to be my favorite one. They are highlighted with a dark navy blue around the edges and a soft dusty blue over all the rest; on the very edge, they are white. Their smell is strong enough to scent a room with only a couple of flowers, yet not to strong that you can't stand them for too long. She told me I could have the first blue ones that bloom this year. She tells me that they stand for tranquility, which stands for peaceful, calm, and to reduce tension. Boy, do I wish I had some now.

"Well, hello there, deary. You were up and gone early this morning. Did you plan on getting all you could out of such a beautiful day?"

"Yes, Mary. I have had a very full day and a long one. I went to the city with my sister."

"Oh, that was nice, deary. Did you do a lot of shopping?" she asked as she looked down at my hand that were empty.

"No, I didn't, Mary. My sister done some, but I didn't have what it takes to be able to shop. You know that green stuff that people are so tied to."

"Yes, I do, and the cities not a place to go empty-handed. So what all did you do besides window-shop."

I wasn't ready for this. Not right now. How was I going to tell her that this good girl isn't so good after all? I'm going to find myself out on the street soon, I just know it.

"Come on, deary! What it is? I was just going to go and have some iced tea. You want to join me?" She takes me by the arm, and we walk up the path to her back door.

"Is Sam home, Mary?"

"No, he won't be in until tomorrow. He had some meeting to go to."

That was good. At least I didn't have to worry about him overhearing what we were about to talk about.

Mary washes her hands and takes the dirty apron off before she makes our iced tea. She places two different kinds of cookies on a plate like she always does as she likes to see me eat. She tells me all the time that I'm too skinny. But I'm not, I'd tell her. She feeds me these goodies anyway. They are usually ones that she has made from scratch as she tells me. So they are delicious and very hard to turn down. Mary would be very hurt if I refused her baking.

"Now, deary, tell me about your day."

I try to speak, but nothing comes out. My throat feels dry and as if it has swollen shut. So I take another sip of iced tea and try again. Still nothing comes out. I shuffle in my seat. I clear my throat once again before I begin.

"Mary, I had to go to the doctor today." There wasn't any other way to tell her except straight out right.

"You did? Are you sick, deary? What is it? Is there anything I can do to make you feel better? What did the doctor say?"

"Mary there is nothing you can do, and as far as what the doctor did say, he tells me I'm pregnant."

"Oh!" she says as she slips on to her chair. "For sure, deary, sometimes they're wrong, you know."

"I'm sure, Mary, and so is the doctor."

"I see, and how far along are you?"

"The doctor figures about three months. But I have to go back next month, and he'll do an ultrasound, and that will tell us when for sure."

"I have heard of those things. It's something new since I have had my children."

"He says it's safe, and they use them all the time."

"What are you going to do now, deary?" Oh, she sounded so disappointed. I was breaking her heart. The last thing I wanted to do was hurt Mary.

"What do you mean, Mary?"

"You going to have the baby or what? There are so many young girls having abortions today, it's not funny. Some put them up for adoption, but not as many as there are choosing what they think is the right thing to do."

"As far as an abortion, I won't be doing that. That's for sure. Adoption is another story, and I can't say it's for me either. My sister says neither one would be a good answer for me. She thinks I'll pay for the rest of my life mentally, and she's probably right."

"I'm glad to hear that someone has already talked to you about those choices. They are not for everyone. Some girls can make that choice and go on like nothing ever happened. But you don't strike me as that kind of girl."

"Thanks, Mary. But you probably didn't think I was the kind of girl who would get herself into this kind of a bind either."

"Things happen, and today it is more common than it used to be, or I should say, it was hidden more back when I was younger. But you know, deary, adoptions are not always bad. For the young mother or the baby, every situation is different. After my husband and I had our fourth son, we were told I could not have any more children. It broke our hearts as we had hoped to have a girl one day. My husband had surprised me by asking if I wanted to adopt a girl. I guess adopting a girl wasn't as hard on me as adopting a boy would be on him. For they always want their sons to carry on their blood. So anyways, we did put in for a girl when our son was only two months old as we thought it would take a while to get one. As it happened they found us one within one month's time. She was even close to home." Mary goes off into outer space, and I can tell that her memories are playing back in her mind at this time. I didn't really want to bother her, but I really wanted to hear how it turned out. For I always thought she didn't have a daughter. I see tears start to form in her eyes, and I reach over and take her hand.

"Mary, it's all right. I'm sorry I brought it up."

"That's not it, deary."

"Then what has upset you so?"

"The week before we were to go pick up our daughter, my husband was killed in a car crash coming home from work. So they wouldn't let me get her. They said it was going to be too hard for me as it was with the four boys I already had. Being a single parent, I didn't push it as I didn't want to make waves and perhaps they would take my children away from me."

"I'm so sorry, Mary, for all your loss and heartaches that you have been through."

"Thank you. So the dream of having a daughter died with my husband. That is until you came along." Now the tears are flowing from both of us.

"Thank you for saying that, Mary. I was afraid that you would want me to move out when I told you I was pregnant."

"Can't you see, deary, God has sent you to me. I need a daughter in my life, and you and your baby will need someone to help you as you will need someone after you go back to work to babysit."

"You would want to do that?"

"Oh yes, I'd love to."

"Mary, that's really nice of you to say that, but it would be a lot of work and very hard on you."

"Oh please! Won't you let me be a grandmother even if it's only pretend? No one would care, and it sure wouldn't hurt anyone. Unless you are going home to be with your mother! This I would understand as I would want my daughter to come home."

"No, Mary. Mother won't want me home alone or with a baby. She will only tell me, 'You made your bed, now you have to lie in it.'"

"She won't help you, deary?"

"No, not a chance."

"What about you're dad? Surely he will say something to her."

"No, and I won't make life hard on him. He would try and do things for me if I lived closer but not this far away. Mother calls the shots most of the time. She is very hard-nosed, and I guess it from how they were raised. Once you quit school and move out, there is no going back. For a visit and that's that, end of story."

"That might be so, but I think you should call them and let them know. Then they have the option to say come home or not."

"My sister thinks I should tell them before anyone else does. If I don't, she figures, Mother will think I'm trying to hide it because I'm ashamed of what I have done. I am ashamed, but that's not why I don't want to call them. I know she will make a big stink about it either way. So I just want to put it off as long as I can."

"You can call them anytime you need to."

"It's long distance."

"I never did ask you where they live. I just took for granted that they were around here."

"They live in BC in a small town called Red River."

"I have heard of that place. My sons go out there and go house boating. They say it's a very nice place to go for holidays."

"That it is, but I never liked living there. I feel too closed in with the mountains so close. Jasper is as close as I like the mountains."

"Anyways, that doesn't matter. You still have to call them whether it's long distance or not and tell them about the baby."

"Or babies."

"What does that mean, deary?"

"The doctor told me he thinks I'm having twins." Mary jumps up and runs around the table to me. She is hugging me and laughing and crying all at once. "Oh my god, oh my god!" is all she can say. Then she stops and says, "This is a real blessing sent from God." How she was meant to be there for me. After a couple of minutes, as she wipes her eyes, she looks at me with such concern.

"What is it, Mary? What's wrong?"

"Oh deary! You can't stay up in my attic."

Now my tears started to flow. I knew it would come to this sooner or later.

"But please, Mary. Just for a little while until I see what is happening with my job. After tomorrow, I might not be able to afford your attic, and I promise I will move out as soon as I can." I'm sobbing so hard now I can't make out what she is trying to tell me.

"No no no, deary, that's not what I am saying. Calm down now and listen to me. Here now wipe your eyes and get a hold of yourself. This is not good for you or the baby, or babies! I'm just saying the attic was good for you but not to have little ones up there. It's not really what you would want to call home for them."

"I know, but just—"

She cuts me off. "The basement suite is coming empty at the end of the month. That's only two weeks away, deary. Why don't you have a look at it. I was going to put the ad in the paper tomorrow. But I will wait to see what you think."

"A basement suite, I can't afford that, Mary!"

"Never mind that right now. Let's go have a look at it as the men that live there are gone for a few days."

"Where is this basement suite you're talking about, Mary?"

"It's right here. I have one. Come now and I will show you."

I followed Mary downstairs, and all was clean smelling until she opened the door.

"Boy, it sure smells in here, Mary."

"Yes, but that is something that is an easy fix. These men have been in here since my husband died. They were friends of his, and I think they thought they should watch over me for him. But now, their work is taking them away." I was thinking that if they were watching over her, they sure let her son push her around a lot.

"Come in and see what you think."

"It doesn't really matter what I think. I can't afford a place like this." It is a two-bed. Kitchen and living room are one big open space with no carpet, which by the look of the floor was a good choice on Mary's part. It has its own bathroom, which also has room for the washer and dryer that are in it. A place like this would be great but just a dream. As I'm walking through it, I'm thinking of what I would do with it if it were to be mine.

"Well, deary, what do you think?"

"It would be great, but I won't have the money for something like this until after I get my license."

"Who said anything about money?"

"If I'm going to adopt you and the baby, so to speak, then let me be the mother you need and the grandmother your baby will need in replacement for a place to live. I would let you move upstairs with me, but Sam would not like that." Sam is Mary's youngest son, and from what I have seen of him, I wouldn't want to share a living space with him.

"Mary, that's so sweet of you, but you can't afford to give me a place to live without being paid."

"Yes, I can. I can do whatever I wish as my husband left me very well-taken care of. I will never have to worry again. In fact it's more than I'll spend with the amount of time I have left on this earth. That's why Sam is still living at home. He still works, but he knows what was left for us, and I think he was always scared that I would be lonely enough if he moved out that I would have married again. So, deary, I don't need any money for this place. I know if George could talk to me, he would tell me I'm doing the right thing."

"Maybe your son will want to live down here."

"He has already told me he's not interested. It's not good enough for him."

"Well, I think it's great, and if you really are sure about this, then yes, I'll take it."

"Good. Now let's go back upstairs and celebrate with a fresh glass of iced tea."

"All right, let's do that, Mary." On the way back upstairs, I had to pinch myself to see if I had died. Did I just get a nice place to live for no money, and someone who wants to take care of my baby so I can finish my hairdressing? How real is this? Who is going to believe it? But then why do I need to tell anyone besides Louise?

This was like winning the lotto for me, even better as I get a mother, and my baby will have a grandmother, which I have never had in my life and never will. It will get hard to get used to as I have always paid my way even if the attic only costs me seventy-five a month. I still paid my own way.

"What will Sam say, Mary?"

"Who cares? This is between you and me, and if he doesn't like it, he can move out of my house any time. He might complain, but it will only be to hear himself, and it won't be the first or the last I'm sure."

"I don't want him getting mad at you over me. I have seen what he does to you when he's mad."

"You have?"

"Yes! And I don't like it."

"He only gets that way when he has had too much to drink. But you are not to worry about him, OK?"

Mary fixed us our iced tea, and she seemed to be off in her own little world as I was in mine. I had daydreamed about having a room to fix up cute for the baby. I never thought it would be so soon. Two weeks would go by fast; I'll have to watch in secondhand stores to pick up some things or perhaps check out that place Louise was telling me about. The take-it-and-something place.

"Deary, deary, are you with me? Here's your iced tea."

"Oh yes, thank you. I was just thinking of the things I'll need to get for the basement. Seeing how I don't have anything."

"The things for the baby are all you'll need to worry about."

"Why's that, Mary?"

"Everything else comes with the basement. Those men came with just their clothes on their backs."

"Wow!" This can't get any better. If my mother could see me now. I know she would find fault in what I'm doing. Instead of saying, "Good for you, girl, I'm glad for you," I know she would make me feel so guilty that I would probably turn Mary down on her offer. So I don't think I will be telling her of my good fortune any time soon.

"Deary, we can shop for the baby as it gets closer to the time as you will know if you are buying for one or two. We can paint and wallpaper any time you want to, after all it is spring. All should be fresh. What do you say, deary, are you up to it? I mean, having a mother so close." I take her in my arms and hold her close to me she feels smaller than she appears to be.

"Mary, you have taken a horrendous day and turned it into the best day of my life. I don't know how I will ever repay you for all you are doing for me."

"No one said anything about repaying. Just letting me be part of your life and your baby's life is all the pay I'll ever need. I believe God and/or my husband has sent you to me. So please, no more talk of money, all right?"

"All right."

"Promise me that you will speak no more of money, deary."

"Promise."

"All that matters is that we need each other, and somehow, we were brought together, so let's enjoy it."

"All right, Mary."

While I was still holding on to her, she looks up at me and says, "Deary, can I ask you something? You can tell me it's none of my business if you want, and I'll understand."

I knew this was coming; it was just a matter of time.

"Yes, Mary. You can ask me anything you want. I think you have earned the right to know whatever you want."

"Where is the baby's father? Will he want to live here?"

"He lives here, Mary. No, there's not a chance in hell, pardon me, that he will be living with us. He made his choice that didn't include me or us."

"I'm sorry to hear that. What does he say about the baby?"

"Nothing. I haven't told him nor do I plan on it."

"But, deary, he has an obligation to you and the baby."

"That may be so. But I don't want to answer to anyone about the way I'm living with my baby. Besides, I wasn't enough for him without the baby. I sure don't want him because of a baby."

"I understand, but it could be hard for you down the road."

"I'll have to cross that bridge when I get to it."

"Is he with someone else?"

"He was the last time I talked to his mother. She made sure to tell me how happy they were."

"Does she know about the baby?"

"Not yet. But if I stay working, she'll know as she gets her hair done through our shop."

"You're a proud girl, and I am very proud of you and how you are going to do this on your own. But I do think financially he should be helping you and that's all I'll say about it."

"Thank you, Mary. I can't say I'm not scared because I am. But I have taken care of babies before. I know that when it's your own, it is a lifetime commitment. After all, I have made my bed. Now I must lie in it alone if need be."

CHAPTER THREE

I also know that my baby will not know its grandmother very well. She will stay at her distance as if she would catch something if she got too close.

I laid my head down as it was hurting, and I fell asleep and ended up dreaming that my mother and I had gone shopping for the baby and all the fun we had that day. We were going to shop until we drop, she told me. I was so happy; it was the greatest day of my life, but I was awakened by my alarm going off. I didn't want to let my dream slip away. Please let me hold on to it just a little while longer. Getting up and getting ready for work, I couldn't get the dream out of my head. I thought that maybe it will stay with me and get me through whatever lies ahead. But for now, I must go to work, and I pray that this day goes by fast and well. I couldn't wait to have this day behind me. I found it to be quite a bit cooler today than yesterday. It could just be my nerves as I know I am uptight and my stomach is in knots and it feels like today will be one of those days where nothing is going to stay down.

Liz can be very sweet when she wants something from us, but she can also be a real bitch if you cross her. So far I hadn't been on that side of her. When she gets to drinking, there's no telling what will happen. She drinks every day after work, which I guess is all right as she is on her own time and, most of the time, is not hurting anyone else but herself. She will send one of us over for her bottle as she does not want anyone to know that it's for her, even though they do know as it's been the same for years. She is my sister's sister-in-law. She might be a drunk, but she has been very nice to me; she is paying for my hairdressing with the understanding that I stay working for her for five years once I have my ticket, which I do not see a problem with as I do need a job and I will already have my clients built up there, so why would I go somewhere else. I found that so long as you were on time, clean, and presented yourself well, Liz never complained.

Sometimes she seemed to be off in her own little world, and us girls would laugh and joke about her dreaming about her next drink; and if she ever knew that, she would fire our asses.

I got to the shop around eight thirty as I never liked being late nor did I like having to go straight to work the minute you come through the door. I found it much nicer to be able to come in have a cup of coffee and catch up with the other girls on what was happening. Liz always came in around nine as she never had appointments until nine thirty.

"Good morning, Beth."

"Yeah, same to you, Charlene. And how did it go?" Beth never said anything around the other girls as she was the only one who knew anything.

"The answer is yes and in December."

"So today is tell-all day, Charlene!"

"Yes, it is, and that's not all there is!"

"Oh, really! Better or worse? If it can get any worse for you, I don't know."

"No, Beth, if anyone has bad luck on top of bad, it's you. I myself would like to keep it that way, if that's OK with you."

"Oh, thanks a heap."

"You're welcome anytime, dear friend."

"Now that I brought you your coffee fess up there, partner."

"You want the good or the bad first?"

"Might as well be the bad first because then maybe the good can wipe it out."

"Good thinking."

"Doctor tells me he thinks I am having twins!"

"Twins! Are you shitting me?"

"Twins? Who's having twins?" Carrie, one of the other girls coming in, asked.

Beth just points to me—"She is!"—as she heads out of the coffee room.

"Oh my god, Charlene. How did that happen?"

"How do you think?"

"Yeah, but you're not married."

"No, duh, is there some kind of a rule that I missed out on."

"No, but . . . Well, what are you going to do?"

"I won't know for sure until my next trip back to the doctor."

"Charlene."

"Yeah, Beth."

"Liz will be in right away, and I think you should wait until the end of the day to tell her. And Carrie you keep your mouth shut!"

"Hey! Mum's the word."

"That's what I was afraid off."

"Come on now, Beth. You think you are the only one who can keep a secret?"

"This is something Charlene is going to have to deal with herself. It is between her and Liz, and they should be alone to talk about it. So you have your ass ready to get out of here as soon as you're finished today. We do not hang around for drinks with Liz. You got it?"

"Yeah, yeah, Beth. I hear you and Charlene. You know we are with you whatever you decide."

"Thanks, guys."

Liz comes in and she is in a foul mood; she went on and on about the cop and how her husband wasn't speeding. He's never

had a ticket in his life. There's not a better driver around as far
as she is concerned, which we just shake our heads about as we
know he drives drunk most of the time. But other than that, the
day went by pretty fast as we were all busy today and didn't have
many breaks. Come the end of the day, all the girls were gone
before I knew it. No one said good-bye or "See you tomorrow." I
guess they didn't want to get tied up with Liz, so it was easier to
just disappear. I was in the coffee room cleaning it up for the day
or just killing time.

"Hey, Charlene. Where did everyone go?"

"I guess they had other things on the go tonight."

"So it looks like it's just you and me tonight. So how about
fixing our drinks as I cash out. I shouldn't be long."

"All right, I can do that." So I get her vodka and orange juice,
and I get myself just iced tea as orange juice will bother my
stomach if I drink it too often and seeing how I just had some at
the doctor's office yesterday, I best not touch it today.

I was just setting down our drinks when Liz came back.

"You know, Charlene. I can see your clientele is getting quite
large. At this rate, you will be making the same as the other girls
when you're done school as your percentage goes up once you
have your license. This makes me very proud of you, Charlene.
I could tell from day 1 that you were good at this. In fact you
are a natural. You will go a long way and maybe even take over
my shop when I'm ready to retire. Some people can take all the
training in the world and still not be good at it. In fact I don't
know how some of them get their license. So here is to you and
your future." She lifts her glass up to me and so I raised mine
back.

"Thank you for saying so, Liz." But now how do I tell her the
good news.

"What's with the iced tea, Charlene? Are you sick or
something?"

"Not really, not that way, I'm not."

"What do you mean? Either you are or not."

Here goes everything, my dreams everything!

"Liz. I have something to tell you, and you're not going to like it!"

"Then you might as well tell and get over with."

"I am going to have a baby in December."

"What the hell have you done that for? Remember you're going to school in five months." She takes a big swig of her drink and is turning red in the face. I trust you know what you have to do. You do, right?"

"I didn't plan for this to happen."

"Girls your age never do, so do you need money? We can give you what you'll need. You can pay us back once you're back to work."

"I just need my paycheck that I have coming."

"Yes, it's all ready, and that surprised me that the girls all left without theirs. But now I know why they all left like they did."

"Here is your check."

"Thank you, and I must get going as I am meeting my sister for supper."

"All right then. We'll see you when you get back. But take all the time you need."

The sobs came harder with every step. I'm glad I wasn't meeting anyone, but I had to tell her something so I could get out of there before I broke down in front of her. I basically knew what she wanted as Beth had already told me. I had just hoped that seeing how we're almost family, she would have been somewhat different. Walking home gave me time to think of what to do. In between sobs, I tried to think, but it was harder than I thought. I think I will go see my sister in Calgary for a few days; maybe by then Liz will have had time to rethink what she wanted me to do. I haven't been to see Marie in sometime. She is my sister who is only two years older than I. We have had a lot of good times together. We have worked at the same jobs. We have rented together, had the same friends, and partied together. Somewhere we finally parted ways, and at first, it was hard not having her around. But we grew in different directions, and she became a big city person while I stayed a small-town girl. She won't like this either, but she will help me figure out just what I should do.

Mary was waiting for me with tea all made as she knew what today was and she figured it would be hard on me.

"Oh, deary, it didn't go all that well I can see." I guess she could see. My eyes were red and swollen from crying so hard all the way home.

"Come now and sit here," she says as she hands me a warm face cloth.

"Wipe your face and drink your tea. It will make you feel better."

"Thank you. How can people be so insensitive to someone else's feeling? Liz didn't even ask what I wanted to do. She just told me what I had to do."

"Oh really!"

"Well, in a roundabout way. I think she does it that way so you can't blame her later. When you become sorry for the choice that you made."

"Are you sure Liz meant it that way?"

"Oh yeah, she asked me if I needed any money. They would give me what I needed, and I could pay them back later. Liz also told me to take all the time I needed and to call her when I was ready to come back to work."

"What did you tell her?"

"I told her thanks, but I had enough of my own money."

"So now what? What are you thinking of doing! You're not going to do what she wants you to do, are you?"

"Mary, I am not going to have an abortion, but I am going to go to see a sister of mine that lives in Calgary. I have not seen her in some time. Perhaps with me going away for a few days will give Liz a chance to rethink what she is asking of me. If you do not mind, that is. I just want to go for a few days, Mary, do you understand?"

"Yes, I think that might do you some good. For you have had a couple of heavyhearted days, deary, and it is not good to be so stressed out at this time in your life. You should be enjoying your pregnancy as it will go by very fast. How will you go to Calgary?"

"I am going to take the bus."

"You have enough money on you?"

"Yes. Liz paid me today, and it will only cost me fifty dollars."

"Then I guess that's all settled."

"Mary, it is OK. I will not be gone too long."

"When you get back, we can start to paint downstairs."

"Oh Mary, I won't be gone for two weeks!"

"Maybe you won't be gone that long, but the men are moving out on the weekend as their job starts earlier than they thought it would. They also paid me for one more month even though I told them that they didn't have to. But they said they knew it needed a real good cleaning and a painting."

"That was very nice of them, eh, Mary."

"Indeed it was. I couldn't have asked for better renters between you and them. I have been blessed. So now we can do whatever you want downstairs.

"Mary, that is your money. You should spend it on something for yourself."

"This is for me as well. I feel very excited about the whole thing, I can hardly wait to get started."

"All right, Mary, if that is what you want. We'll start as soon as I get back. I should only be gone three days as my sister works a lot and I'll get bored sitting around waiting for her."

"You take it easy and try not to worry about too much. Things will work themselves out."

"I will, and thank you for the tea. I feel so much better now. I must go and pack a bag as I want to catch the five thirty bus tonight."

Mary hugs me as if she wasn't going to see me again.

"Mary, I will be back, I promise. You make me want to come back. You have become a big part of my life. I don't know where I would be without you. I feel as though life is worth it again, and things could always be worse, thanks to you."

"You have given me just as much. You make me feel alive, I have not felt like this since my husband died. This makes me want to get up in the morning, and I go to bed with a smile on my face. I also thank God each and every day for bringing you to me. He knew that I needed you as much as you need me. So go now before you are too late for the bus. Call me if you need to, and I'll pray for you always."

"I know you will, thank you, and I will see you soon." With that I was gone up to pack. As it was, I should have taken a cab as I was cutting things close.

I had just enough time to get my ticket, a juice, and a sandwich before getting on the bus.

Once I was settled on the bus and we had headed out of town, it hit me like a ton of bricks. *You dumb ass, you didn't call Marie to see if she would be home.* She often went away as she worked different shifts, so she was coming and going all the time. I guess I will call her when we get into the city, and perhaps I've just taken a bus ride. Oh well, I had nothing but time on my hands. I did call her once we were in the city. She said all was great as she had the next four days off. I did not go into details. I thought I would tell her more when I got there. For now, I just told her I had a few days off and wanted to see her. I had one hour layover in the city, so it was a good thing I had brought a book along. So I went back on the bus and got into reading. I knew I could only read for a short time as I got motion sickness when I read while traveling; this was OK, for when it was time for the bus to leave, reading had made me realize how exhausted I had become. I just put my book away and laid my head back, and before I knew it, I was fast asleep. I woke up to the driver saying, "We have a two-hour supper stop here, and for those going on to Jasper, your bus will be leaving from gate 12. Those of you who are staying, I thank you for traveling Greyhound, and I hope to see you again. Please do not forget you baggage up top." With that said, we pulled into the terminal, and all got off the bus. I still had my juice and sandwich that I had bought, so I thought I would just find a quiet place to sit and eat it while I waited for Marie to arrive. That did not happen as she was standing just inside the doors, waiting for me.

"Hi, Charlene. How the hell are you?" she says as she hugs me. "It's been a while."

"Yes, it has been some time, and I am just fine, thank you."

"Supper?" I ask as I lift my sandwich up for her to see.

"Let's get the rest of your bags, then we can find a real café and have a sit-down supper."

"What? You don't like my offering of supper?"

"Looks too much like what I had for lunch. So no, I don't, sorry."

"Marie, this is it for bags," I tell her as I pat my backpack.

"You travel light."

"It has all I need."

"All right then. I'm just parked around the corner. With my luck, I probably have a ticket by now."

"Still pushing it, are you?" Marie never likes been told where she could or couldn't park, so over the years, she has had a few fines to pay. You would think that after all this time she'd give up the battle.

"Who the hell are they to tell me when I will be done doing what I have to do?" To our surprise, there was no ticket.

"Well, I'll be damned. Someone must be sleeping on the job today," Marie says as we climb into her car, and we pull away.

"There's a small café about four blocks from here. I know you will like it as it is all done in antiques and colors that are all you."

"Sounds great, maybe it will give me some decorating ideas."

"What do you need decorating ideas for? Are you not in the attic anymore?"

"I won't be when I get back."

"Oh really, where are you moving to?"

"I get to move into Mary's basement suite. I'm so excited about that. I will even have my own bathroom and washer and dryer. All the furniture comes with it."

"Super, Charlene, what is that going to set you back each month?"

"Nothing."

"What? Nothing? How come? What did you catch the old lady doing that she wasn't supposed to be doing?"

"It's not like that, but it is a long story."

"How long did you say you were here for?"

"Three days or so"

"Then get talking."

"Well, in exchange for letting Mary babysit and be an adoptive grandmother, I get to live there free."

"OK, but what does her being someone's grandmother and all have to do with you?"

"Because she wants to be my baby's grandmother."

"She what?" she exclaims as she looks at me like I have two heads.

"Look out for the red light!" I yelled.

"Oh shit." And Marie slams on her brakes. Now we are in the middle of the intersection, and people are honking their horn at us, and some are giving us the finger.

"Marie, do you think we could get out of the line of traffic before we become accident victims."

"What the hell do you mean your baby?"

"Just what I said."

"Are you shitting me?"

"No, Marie. I am pregnant."

"It sucks to be you." She has a lot of Mother's ways, but she usually comes around. "Holy shit, I have to get parked. Good thing that café is just up here."

Once we were inside, the waitress took us over to a corner booth. Now I am not sure whether that was just luck or if she could see the distress on Marie's face.

"Could I get you ladies something to drink?"

"Yes," Marie says, "I'll have a light beer please!" The way she was acting, I was sure glad that we were stuck back out of view from anyone.

"All right, Charlene. When is the baby due?"

"It is due at the end of December."

"Do you still have a job?"

"I did have when I left, but I don't know if I will when I get back."

"Was your boss not happy with the news?"

"You could say that. She told me to have an abortion."

"Are you going to do that?"

"I thought about it, but no, I am not. Louise says I'd be sorry for the rest of my life, and it is killing a baby!"

"I believe that too, but for some, it is a better way to go."

"But you can always adopt out. Why kill it?"

"I think the girls know that after they have carried it for nine months they're going to give it up in the end, so they decide to get an abortion right away. But you know, Charlene, that you are almost too far along now to have an abortion, so what was your boss thinking? It would be dangerous for you now."

"What will she do if you don't have an abortion, fire you?"

"I don't know. I never took the time to ask her."

"Holy shit, Charlene."

"Would you quit saying that!"

"Sorry, I don't know what else to say! You sick in the mornings?"

"Not every morning anymore."

"What did Mother say when you told her about it?"

"I haven't told her yet."

"Charlene, you know it won't be pretty when you do tell her!"

"When is it any time I have to deal with her?"

"I know, I know, what is with the animosity between you two all the time? The last time you two were together, I remember tea being thrown in someone's face. Charlene, have you ever asked Mother what you did to piss her off so much that she doesn't let it go."

"I always think I'm going to next time I see her, but the visits don't last long enough. I usually end up leaving in a hurry."

"Marie, do you think I could have been adopted?"

"I never heard that from anyone, but why don't you ask one of the older ones, for you and I are too close in age for me to recall Mother being pregnant with you."

"I've always felt since I was about ten years old that I never belonged there. That she never wanted me. I can't say I really want to hear the truth."

"Do you really think you are, Charlene?"

"Well, look at me, I have reddish hair the rest of you don't!"

"Yeah, I guess I never thought of that before."

"Maybe I should ask Louise, seeing how Mother should have been pregnant with me at the same time, since how Crystal and I are only six months apart. Can we order now? I'm hungry."

"Oh sure, Charlene. Is there anything that bothers you to eat?"

"No, that's pretty good now too." So we ordered our supper, and I told her all of what Mary wanted to do for me. The fact that I get to move into the basement suite as soon as it's painted and all cleaned up and how we were going to start that as soon as I got home. We are also going to go to secondhand stores and a place there Louise was telling me about called the take it or leave it, and I guess you don't pay for anything you take from there. Louise says people take new things, and if we let them know what we are looking for, they would set it aside for us. She said she would take me there on Saturdays."

"Sounds like a good idea to me, and when we're done supper, we'll go down to the one mall and see what we can find for the baby."

"OR BABIES"

"WHAT!"

"I haven't told you yet. The doctor thinks I could be having twins."

"Holy shit, Charlene."

"Marie!"

"Sorry, Charlene. What if it is?"

"Well, with all the help Mary wants to give me and Louise and the girls, I should be OK."

"Louise hasn't told Mother?"

"No, she said she wasn't telling her."

"Hey! Don't look at me. I'm not telling her either."

"Coward."

"You're right, and I do not envy you for that task."

"Marie, I don't have money to go shopping right now."

"That's OK. I don't have a lot, but I can buy a few things right now to help, and I will help out later as well. It might not be much, but I will help, and I'll buy in yellow and white. We can't go wrong then. Perhaps someone will have a baby shower for you and then you will get all you need in the right color."

"I never thought of that."

"Charlene. What about the father? Is he going to help you?"

"No, he's not, and that's how I want it, end of story."

"All right, I'll say no more."

"Thank you."

We spent the next three hours oohing and ahhing over everything; we even laughed at some of the things people might really wear on their babies. The baby furniture was unbelievable; the only thing was some of it wouldn't last too long before they grew out of it, and for the money, it would be such a waste. The one crib I really liked was done in an antique white, and the carvings were just out of this world. I could see it done up in a white baby eyelet layette. I have always felt that newborns should be in whites only. You can sterilize whites with bleach. The same as I don't think you should wash their clothes with ours. I was starting to feel a little heavy on my feet. I know I'm tired by now; it has been a long day, and once in a while, I'd get a pain that would make me stop, and Marie must have seen the frown on my face.

"Charlene, are you all right?"

"I keep getting this sharp pain now and again. I think I've done too much walking."

"Tell you what, I'm going to pay for what I have picked out and then I will get you back to the apartment so you can put your feet up. How's that sound?

"I think that would be great, thanks."

It was a good thing she had an elevator in her building. I don't think I could have done stairs. Marie had bought a fair amount of baby things; she kept saying, "Oh, look at this," "Oh, you need to have this," and "This is too cute." So for someone who seemed to think I had done the stupidest thing ever, she was right into the shopping. I guess when I leave, I would be taking my problem with me, so what did she have to worry about, so she might as well enjoy the part she could. She always plays the role of being a real bitch and yet she could be so kind and caring. She and I have been through a lot, and this will only be one more milestone for us.

"Marie, if you don't mind, I would like to have a nice warm bath before we go over all the things you bought."

"Sure, Charlene. I will get you some towels and some soap as I had to buy some today."

"All right, thank you."

"I'm going to make us some tea while you're in the tub."

"That sounds great." Oh, sitting in the tub and not having to worry about hurrying because Mary might need the bathroom or maybe Sam would come home at that moment and need the bathroom, this was so relaxing. I thought perhaps I would fall asleep. The lavender soap that Marie gave me made me feel totally calm. I can't remember when I felt like this; it too has had been quite a while.

"Char. Charlene."

"Yeah, Marie, come in."

"Just want to let you know our tea is ready."

"As much as I don't want to get out, I will"

"I can bring it to you in here!"

"Thanks, but we were going to go through what you bought."

"I know, but we could do that tomorrow if you have had enough."

"No, that's OK. I'll get out."

"All right."

"Some of these are so damn sweet you would want to wear it on the baby all the time."

Isn't that the truth? So we went over all the things she had bought and talked about names, and I told her I hoped for a boy. I didn't think I would want to raise a girl on my own. The mint tea had tasted so good I decided to get another cup. I started across the living room, and I felt something warm running down my legs and didn't think too much of it, just thought I hadn't dried very well somewhere.

"OH MY GOD, CHARLENE, YOU'RE BLEEDING!"

"What the hell! What do I do, Marie?"

"Charlene. Get your shoes on. I'm taking you to the hospital."

"Do you really think I need to go there?"

"I can't say for sure, but that's where I'm taking you, now hurry!"

"Damn, I forgot my purse, Marie."

"Well, you shouldn't need any money."

"No, but I will need it for identification."

"If they can't bring you up in their computer, I can run back and get it once they are taking care of you, OK?"

"All right, Marie, I'm scared!"

"That makes two of us, but just try and stay calm, Charlene. It's a good thing I'm not far from the hospital. When we get there, you stay in the car while I go get help." We pulled up into emergency entrance and Marie went in to get help, and she and a nurse came out with a wheelchair.

"I can walk. I don't need any wheelchair," I say to the nurse whose name tag said she was head nurse and that her name was Elenor. She said, "I think you will just park yourself right in the chair and let me push you where we have to go."

"All right." So I climbed into the chair, and she takes me up to maternity ward. She turns to Marie and tells her that she can go fill out all the information that they need. So Marie leaves us to go to admission.

Elenor asks how long this has been going on.

"Well, we went to that all-night mall and was there for about three and a half hours. I started to feel it then, there just uncomfortable."

"When did the bleeding start?"

"Not until we got home and I had a warm bath then sat down to have tea."

"Is it a bright red or is it dark almost black or is it on the pink side?"

"It's not red. Red, so I would have to say more on the pink side."

"Well, I think that's a good sign, but we will let the doctor decide, all right? He'll be in right away. Are you feeling faint at all?"

"I feel all right. Even the pain is easing off since I got off my feet."

"Hi, I'm Dr. Fielding, and I have asked for the nurse at the station to bring me a portable ultrasound. That way we don't have to move you anymore. I want to see what's going on inside and make sure the baby is all right. Your sister brought me up to date before I came in. She was telling me that you were out shopping for quite some time after you have worked all day hairdressing, so this could just be a stress call, but I want to make sure."

"How long will that take?"

"Not long, Charlene. Would you like your sister to come in? She sure is welcome too."

"I'd like that, thank you, Elenor"

"Not a problem. I will go get her now."

"Hi, Charlene. How you feeling?"

"Not as bad as I was. They're going to do an ultrasound."

"Yes, the doctor told me he had ordered that along with the needle."

"What needle?"

"This one," Elenor says as she came around the curtain.

"What is it for?"

"It is to stop contractions. This is somewhat early for them, so we want to stop them as soon as possible," Elenor told me. "One good thing about the needle verses the pill, it works a lot faster. Are you OK with needles?"

"Yes, I am if that's what it takes."

"Good girl, now roll over and give me your left hip please."

"Here, Charlene. You can squeeze my hand."

"Thanks, Marie. Oh damn, that stings."

"I'm sorry. I should have warned you about that. It will only last a minute or so."

"Now here we go," the technician says as she puts the warm jelly on my stomach, which almost made me pee myself. All of a sudden, we could hear a *kerswoosh, kerswoosh* it sounded like horses running underwater.

"What's that," I asked.

"That, my dear, is the baby's heartbeat. Although it is faint, it is nice to hear."

"Oh sweet. It sure sounds funny"

"Have you ever talked to someone underwater? You sound funny as well."

"I guess, hey." The technician moves her wand around and around on my stomach and does a lot of measuring and a lot of punching in on the keyboard of the machine she is using. After about ten minutes, she seemed satisfied with what pictures she had taken. "Now I will give these to your doctor, and he will come see you. Here is a towel so you can wipe the jelly off."

"Thank you."

"You're welcome, take care."

"That was not so bad now, was it, Charlene?" Marie had asked as she came up alongside the bed.

"Could you see the baby from where you were standing, Marie?"

"No. I could see the movement of the spot where the heartbeat was coming from, and that wasn't really clear either. We should have asked her to show us more or explain what she could see."

"Next time, we won't keep our mouths shut."

"I could only hear one heartbeat."

"Me too."

"That's good for me though, right?"

"Yeah, Charlene. It is, yet in a way, it would be exciting to have twins, don't you think?"

"I suppose other than the fact that I will be alone with them most of the time and I think it would be hard. What do you do if they are both hungry and crying at the same time?"

"You have been blessed with two boobs, Charlene, for a reason."

"Yeah right, you don't think it has something to do with balancing us off. Wouldn't we look funny running around with just one?"

"Not if that's how all of us were born." Just then Dr. Fielding came in.

"Sorry, but I heard part of your conversation, and I have to say myself I prefer the look of two." We both went red in the face, and he just laughed.

"Now, miss, the ultrasound is showing a small tear in the wall of your uterus, and if we keep you off your feet for one week, it will heal on its own, and you should be OK. Will it be a problem of staying here for a week as I see you are from out of town and also a hairdresser? So you will be worried about your job as well."

"Staying is not a problem."

"All right then. I will let the girls know at the front desk that you are not to get up for more than the bathroom, and no bathing. Sitting in hot water can bring on the bleeding again. You may have short showers, warm ones. Any questions?"

"What is causing the tearing?"

"You have gotten pretty large for as far long as you are, and the stretching of the uterus to such an extent has made it weak in that spot. The good news is that it will heal now that we have you off your feet." The weight you are carrying right now will only be increasing, so you want to make sure this heals very well right now."

"Will I be able to go back to work?"

"You should be able to for a while, but that is something you and your doctor will have to watch as time goes on. I will be sending him a report on you and all that we have found and what we have done for you, all right?"

"Were there twins?"

"Not that we could see. I had thought perhaps you were pregnant with twins because of your size and perhaps you were going to lose one. That I have seen happened. But no, there are no twins in there. You may not get overly large, but you will grow for a while yet then it will seem like you come to a standstill. Is there anything else you want to know?"

"I cannot think of anything right now. Marie, can you?"

"No, I think you have covered it all."

"Then I will leave you ladies to your discussion of the women's anatomy. I really hope you don't change it too much as I'm partial to the way it is. Charlene, I will check in on you tomorrow." That said he was gone.

"That was a little embarrassing, wasn't it, Char?"

"Just a bit, so now what do we do? By this time, it is just after one AM."

"Well, I think I'll go home and get some sleep, and you had better do the same, and remember, stay in bed. I will be back later, and I will bring you some books to read as well as some playing cards."

"That sounds great, and Marie, I'm sorry this had to happen."

"Don't you worry about it. I'm glad you weren't alone when it happened as you might have waited too late to go to the hospital." With that she hugs me good night and was gone.

Elenor came in shortly after. "OK, miss, it's time we shut out your lights and you get some rest, and don't think we won't be keeping an eye on you. We are pretty good watchdogs around here. Good night. I will see you tomorrow afternoon, unless you need something before I am off shift, just remember to ring this bell."

"I will, thank you and good night." Elenor left, shutting off the light as she went out the door. I laid there in darkness for quite some time, thinking about all that happened; it felt like I had been here in Calgary for days already. I was feeling a little let down that there were no twins as I think I was getting used to the idea. I had said twins so many times that I was believing that there were going to be two babies. Oh, come on, Charlene. You best count your blessing that there is only one. Someone is surely looking out for you. You didn't want one, never mind two. But that thought has gotten a little easier to bear with all the help I will be getting from Mary and Louise. Oh damn, Mary. I must see if Marie will call and let her know what has happened, for she will be very worried in three or four days if I don't show up. I fell asleep and had a very good one. It might have been short, but I do feel rested as they bring my breakfast into me.

"I could sit up at the table."

"Doctors orders, you are to stay off your feet as much as possible. This is our job so just enjoy."

"Thank you." This was a bigger breakfast than I have eaten in months, so I had no idea if I could eat it all. In the end, I had eaten half of it. When the nurse came back for the dishes, she was surprised at what was left.

"You're not a big eater, miss."

"No, I'm not." I wasn't about to tell her that I hadn't been able to afford to be a big eater.

"Remember you are eating for two now. Do you want me to leave your fruit dish? You can always pick at it through the day."

"Yes, please. That would be OK, thank you. May I have a shower after this?"

"Sorry, not for twenty-four hours. The doctor wants you to wait on that. However, I will bring you a basin of warm water so you can sponge bath."

"Thank you." I guess that was surely better than nothing; after all, I did bath at Marie's last night, and I don't need to shampoo my hair.

"Miss, I would like to check for any bleeding."

"All right."

She lifts my gown and pulls the pad they had put on me last night down somewhat.

"This doesn't look too bad at all! The one thing with this, the quicker you are to stay off your feet, the better it gets. But I have seen where women have come in way too late and in the end they lose their baby."

"That would be terrible."

"It sure is."

Knock, knock. "Can I come in?"

"Sure," the nurse said. "And who might you be?"

"I am Char's sister."

"That's good 'cause now you can watch that she doesn't get out of bed. She is to wash up in bed for the next twenty-four hours."

"I can do that. Is she giving you a hard time?"

"No. I think she understands how serious this can be."

"Here, Charlene, I brought you a book on baby names, and I brought us cards to kill the day."

"Thanks, Marie, but you don't have to spend your days off here. I am a big girl now, you know. So you don't have to hold my hand as you probably have other things you want to do on your days off."

"Nothing that I can't do next time. Besides that, you came to visit me, and it's not your fault you ended up in here. But seeing how you have, then I guess this is where we will visit."

"OK then. Marie, if I give you Mary's number, would call and let her now as she will be waiting for me in a couple of days?"

"Yeah, sure thing."

The rest of the day, we went through the baby names and couldn't believe what they had in there that they thought people would call their kids. Like Marie said, it was scary but a lot of those names are used. That evening we played cards for a while. The day seemed like it had gone by pretty fast, but that's one thing about Marie and I; we can always find something to talk about. We even went back to the first job we had together and how much fun we had back then.

"Charlene, do you remember the first time you had to use a tampon and what a disaster it turned out to be?"

"Yeah, well someone should have told me that the cardboard had to be removed that had to be the longest day at work ever!"

"Talk about walking around like you had a stick up your ass. I couldn't help but laugh."

"Do you believe in what goes around comes around?"

CHAPTER FOUR

"Yeah, whatever. You know, Charlene. We never got to talk last night, and there was something I wanted to tell you."

"Oh really, what's that."

"I'm getting married."

"What? When?"

"In September, the long weekend out at Mom and Dad's."

"Are you serious?"

"Very."

"How did you talk Grant into that?"

"I didn't. I'm not marrying Grant."

"Who then?"

"Gary."

"His brother! Are you for real? Since when did you guys start dating?"

"Well, it's not like we haven't known each other for some time."

"Yeah, but to marry his brother! Why what happened to you and Grant?"

"I got tired of him knocking me around."

"He used to knock you around?"

"Yes, and it got to where I started to sleep with a knife under my pillow."

"You're joking."

"No, I'm not, and Gary found out, and he beat the living hell out of him and told him he had better not come close to me ever again."

"I still can't see why you would marry his brother."

"Charlene, remember what you just asked me a while ago about believing in what goes around comes around."

"You're marrying his brother to get back at him or to get even? Marie, that is the stupidest thing I have ever heard of. Does Mother know about this upcoming wedding?"

"Yes."

"What does she say about it?"

"She must be fine with it as she's making most of the arrangements for me. But you have to remember that they knew Gary a long time as he used to go into their store all the time, and she said that she knew he had eyes for me then. They never did like Grant."

"What about Dad? What does he say?"

"You know Dad. He just grunts."

"Marie, are you sure about this?"

"Oh yeah. It will be fine."

"That's not why you marry someone."

"Not you maybe. But the bastard's going to pay."

"But, Marie, in the end you're only going to hurt yourself. There has to be another way."

"Ladies, would you like some tea or coffee before visiting hours are over?"

"It's that time already. Sure we will have some, thank you."

So we get our tea and coffee and drink in silence for a short time.

"Marie, I wish you would think about this some more. I don't think this is a smart thing to be doing. It could screw up the rest of your life."

"That's not for you to worry about. You have enough on your plate."

"It's late now, so I best get going before they throw me out."

Hugging me, she starts to leave. "Marie."

"What?"

"Please rethink what your about to do."

"I will be fine, now go to sleep. I will see you tomorrow." Then she was gone, leaving me lying there in deep thought about the biggest mistake she will be making. Who in their right mind marries out of spite? Marie has always had the attention of men, and I am not sure why as she can be very snippy most of the time. If I were a man, I would get the feeling that to her I was nothing but dirt under her feet. She has always came across as if she were better than anyone else. She was Marie, and there was no other. I had thought she was like this because she was not sure of herself, and it was a way of preventing herself from being hurt by anyone. I feel that there has been something in her past that has hurt her to get what some people thinks as a chip on her shoulder. Sometimes she can be so sweet. But a lot of the time, she would sooner chew your head off than to talk to you.

Over the years, I have been able to read her, and I have learned that at times like these, you cut your visits short or your conversation if you are on the phone; either way it's not going to be a good one, so you might as well get out of it as painlessly as possible. So I also know that she is very stubborn and strong minded, and when she makes her mind up, you're not going to change it. That way, we are very much alike. So I guess if she plans on going through with this marriage, then I will just be available when the walls come tumbling down. Over the next few days of her coming and going, we had talked about a lot of things, and every time I tried to bring up her impending marriage, she would change the subject, so it was to no avail to continue.

Things had gotten better for me; the bleeding had completely stopped, and the pain also was gone, so they let me out of the hospital. I was to stay at Marie's two more days before heading for home just in case things were to start all over again once I was up on my feet.

Of course, Marie was back to work, and the days were long waiting for her. She would call me on her breaks and on her lunch hour; we spent most of her lunch hour on the phone. I don't know how, but we always had lots to talk about. Marie has become very into the baby scene; she always comes home with something for the baby. There is a shop right by her work, so she says she can't just go past it without stopping before coming home. Marie had to give me one of her suitcases to put all the baby clothing in.

"You might have come empty-handed, but you're not going home that way."

"You had best stop soon, Marie, or there won't be anything left for me to buy."

"Trust me, Charlene. There's lots left to buy now and later, you'll see."

Today I am heading back home, and I am feeling sad about it as we have had a good visit in spite of the hospital stay. I wish that she and I could live closer, but that will never happen as she is a city girl at heart, and I am a country bumpkin. It is strange how that happens we grew up in the same house, had the same parents, yet in so many ways we are all different. I suppose that's what makes life interesting, and believe me, in our family with twelve kids, it has been anything but dull. This has been a mine, his, and ours combination, also another story in itself, which I won't get into right now.

Marie and I sat at the bus depot having our last cup of tea together while waiting for the bus.

"Charlene, are you sure you're ready to go home?"

"Yeah, this has been nice, Marie, and wish it could go on, but I must get home and see what lies ahead of me there. I don't know what is really happening about my job, and I am excited about getting moved into the basement."

"Don't you go and overdo it while moving. You should see if Louise will help you."

"That's a good idea. I really only have my clothes, some books, and what you have bought me, along with my bathroom belongings, which still doesn't add up to much. Mary will want to help."

"Charlene, I was meaning to talk to you about that."

"About what?"

"Mary's son. You said he pushes her around when he's drinking. You better be careful that he doesn't think he should be able to do the same with you now that Mary's going to be involved with you more."

"I would call the police if he ever shows up at my door drunk. One thing about the door, it has a peephole, so I won't have to open it to him."

"That's good so long as there's not a time he catches you outside your door."

"I will be careful as there has always been something about him I haven't liked, and that was before I saw him pushing Mary around."

"Marie, do you think you will be coming out my way any time soon?"

"Yeah, Charlene. I will be coming out and checking on you and the little one as someone will have to keep a closer eye on you."

Marie has a car, so it's easy for her to come and go whenever she wants, not having to wait to catch a bus at just the right time, plus the wait-overs take up a lot of time. By the time the layovers were done, she would already be where she was going. In the long run, she gets more visiting time than I do riding the bus.

"I best be getting out to the gate, seeing how they have already called it once."

"I will walk you out to it and help you with these bags."

"OK. Thanks."

Once we were out there, the driver took my bags and put them under the bus.

Hugging each other, we could tell that neither one of us wanted to say good-bye.

"Hey, I will be all right."

"I know, Charlene, if there is anyone who will do all right on her own with a baby in tow, it's you. I just wished I was closer to help, that's all."

"I will have lots of help by the sound of things, so don't worry."

"I will come out as soon as I can, Charlene. Take care, will yea. I'll see you soon."

"I will." And with one last hug, I turned around and got on to the bus; it was not crowded as it was off-season yet for the holiday season. I took a seat on the side where Marie would be standing so we could wave good-bye to each other. As the bus pulled out slowly, I could see her wipe a tear from her eye. I knew she was doing that as so was I. She's not such a hard ass as she would like people to believe.

For the rest of the trip, I read and dozed off and on; we did stop in the city and have one hour for a supper stop, which was good to be able to get out and stretch your legs. I really had to use the bathroom. There is one on the bus, but I find it really hard to pee when I'm moving, and it has such a foul smell.

After the supper break and once we were back on the road, I had taken a seat right at the front; no one was there, and I know from past experience that the driver will talk to whoever is in the front seat as it is difficult trying to talk to someone way at the back. I was right; we were not too far down the road when he started to talk.

"Are you going far, miss?"

"No, I am just going to Stony Creek."

"Are you going home for the holidays?"

"No, I am going home. I have been down visiting a sister in Calgary."

"Had a good visit, did you?"

"One of the best."

"How long have you lived in Stony Creek?"

"I have only lived there a year. I am from BC."

"What part?" I was beginning to feel like we were playing twenty questions although I did not mind it was breaking up a boring ride.

So I told him where I was from, and he said he had been out there and hopes to go again; he and his family had a very nice time.

It was still bright out when we pulled into Stony Creek although it looked windy here. People were coming and going at the bus depot as it is also a café. The driver was busy unloading the baggage. I was standing in line waiting to pick mine up when a hand was put on my shoulder. To my surprise when I turned around, there was my brother.

"Hi there, where you been?"

"I was down to Calgary to see Marie."

"Oh, and how is she?"

"Great, and when did you get in from the bush?"

"Just now. I was just going in to have something to eat. You going to join me?"

"Sure, if you will give me a ride home after?"

"Deal."

"All right then!"

"You going to have something to eat, Charlene? I'm buying."

"Well, I should be seeing how you're buying. That doesn't happen often, but I will just have iced tea please."

"You sure?"

"Yeah, we had our supper stop in the city, so that hasn't been that long ago."

"Guess, eh. So how is your hairdressing going? You must be about ready to go to school, aren't you?"

"Good! Liz tells me my clientele is about as big as the other girls, so once I get my ticket, I'll be making real good money. Trust me, I can't wait!

"Good for you, and who said you wouldn't be able to do anything without all your schooling."

"One thing about hairdressing, you only need grade 10, and they will take you."

"That's great, so it's all working out for you."

"Yes, it is."

"Charlene, are you still up in the old lady's attic?"

"Yes, I am for a while yet. I will be glad to move."

"You plan on moving before you go to school?"

"Yes, I can move right away."

"Where are you moving to?"

"Mary has a basement suite that she's letting me move into as soon as the painting is done."

"Right on, how many bedrooms?"

"Two bedrooms. The kitchen and living room are one big room, and there's a washer and dryer in the bathroom. It is so big."

"Maybe I can rent with you. You won't need two bedrooms, and it will help you with the rent."

"Maybe. We will have to see what Mary says."

"That would be cool. It would be better than the hole I am in at Louise's."

"It would be that all right, but at least you have had a roof over your head, the same as I have in the attic."

"That is true, but I would sooner be in an attic than where I am. The only reason I stayed there was because I am never home. But if you have two bedrooms, we might as well use them, and I can help you out at the same time."

I don't know what to say. I know he will find out sooner or later, and right now, I want it to be later. I have seen where he sleeps, and I wouldn't want to sleep there. But I also want the two bedrooms. I also don't know if Mary will let him stay there for nothing like she is me. Guess she could always charge him for some rent; he's right about not being around very much. I suppose we could see about getting one of those sofas that make into a bed for as often as he is around.

"When are you going to be able to move?"

"Not until Mary has it cleaned up and painted. There were two men in there, so she has to wait until they are moved out."

"Let me know what you find out. Now that I am home for a while, it would be nice to move into something a little better than where I am while I have the time."

"I guess that would be nice for you." I should not have asked for a ride home. What if he sees Mary and asks her about it before I get a chance to talk to her. I don't want to screw this up and maybe she will think I am just taking advantage of her and her kindness. That I will not do, so I would ask her if he could rent a bedroom from her. I guess she could also offer him the attic. He would wonder why he could not live with me. At that time, I guess I will have to tell him he is going to be an uncle.

"You ready to go, Charlene? I have paid the bill."

"Yeah sure, could we stop somewhere so I could buy a pint of milk?" I only buy a pint at a time, for I have no place to keep it.

"Where do you want to stop?"

"Doesn't matter. Anywhere is good. The gas station is more money but is on the way."

"I know you're short of money, Charlene. I will buy you some milk."

"Thanks, but you don't have to. I have money." Marie had slipped one hundred dollars into my pocket when we hugged. I found it when we stopped for supper. I must remember to call and thank her.

"Hey! That's what big brothers are for."

"Thanks."

"Besides if we rent together, I will have to buy my share of the groceries as well."

"True." We get to the gas station, and when Jacob gets out, I let go of the breath that I didn't know I was holding. Now what?

CHAPTER FIVE

W e are about to pull up to the side of Mary's house when I see her getting into a truck. I have seen that truck there before but have never asked her whose it was. Jacob was driving slower than usual as the winter has left some pretty big potholes in our streets. So if you didn't want to lose the bottom of your vehicle in these potholes, you slowed down. I was glad for that as I wouldn't have to go into any great details right now.

"Thanks for the ride home."

"I will help you with your bags, but I won't stay. I would like to get to Louise's and have a long-awaited bath. My back has been hurting for the last few days, and we only have showers at camp."

Jacob had packed my bags up all those stairs, which I was grateful for as I did not want to end up back in the hospital and I did not want to have to ask him to carry them. He would have known something was up because, after all, I am a farm girl, and we don't need anyone carrying our bags for us. I was surprised that he had even offered, but I was not going to make a big scene out of it.

"Maybe I will see you after work tomorrow."

"OK. Thanks again for the lift."

"Don't mention it."

I didn't have a lot to unpack, but I did want to make sure my clothes for work were not all wrinkled up, and once that was dealt with, I would wash up and go to bed. I was tired. Tomorrow could be a trying day. I also want to leave one hour earlier so I can take my time walking as it is a long walk. I'm thinking I should make arrangements with a cab to pick me up in the mornings. I will still walk home at night I have more time then.

I also know Mary will be all excited to start downstairs as I am. Except right now I just want to sleep, and that's what I did. I'm sure my head was not on the pillow too long before I was sound asleep. The ringing of my alarm scared me half to death as I haven't heard it for a while, so not knowing what that sound was right away had my heart beating so fast I could hardly breathe. Once I was calmed down from that, I felt great.

Turning to go down the sidewalk, I spotted Mary in the window; she must have heard me upstairs. She had a big smile on her face and was waving at me. So I smile back, and waving, then—I don't know why I did it—I blew her a big kiss. She just laughed at me and waved harder. So I carried on my way, feeling like I had the world on my side and what a feeling that was.

After what I just went through in Calgary, I felt lucky to be here and pregnant. I can't believe I'm thinking that way, but I am. I hope that Liz is in a good mood; everything else has fallen into place. Now all I need to know is that my job is secure. Then I will be laughing. I couldn't wait to see Beth and tell her I was moving into the basement suite. She would always tell me, "Char, you can do better than this." No one seemed to understand that I needed to save my money for the city. Up until now, the attic was good enough for me. I had no furniture to worry about and very little personal belonging, so what did I need more then the attic for. Sure, my own bathroom would have been nice and to have a stove and fridge, but I have proven to myself if to no one else that you can make do with a little. When I was still at home, we did not have indoor plumbing, and we still had a wood stove, so maybe I do have to go use Mary's bathroom. And I have to use a hot plate; it is still better than what we had at home.

Getting into work with plenty of time to get my thoughts in order before Liz shows up was going to be great. The girls were starting to show up one after the other, and things were starting to liven up, and my peace and quiet would be no more.

"Well, hello, Char. Liz didn't tell us you were back."

"She doesn't know. I just got back last night, Beth."

"How did it go?"

"It was scary for a short time, but all is under control."

"That's great, and you feel good?

"Yeah, I feel pretty damn good in fact."

"Oh really, why is that?

"You won't believe it, Beth, but I am moving."

"You are? To where?"

"Mary has a basement suite in the same house, and it's empty. She says I can move into it!"

"Right on, Char. That will be better than where you are."

"Yes, you can say that again." Just then Carrie comes in.

"Good morning, Char. It's nice to have you back. Hope all went well."

"Thank you, and yes, it did."

"There have been a lot of ladies asking about you, and Liz told them you would be back next week, so she will be surprised," Beth says.

"I didn't know how long I was going to be laid up."

"No, guess not. It's different for everyone," Carrie says as she starts to make coffee for all of us.

We could here noise out back, so we all knew Liz was here. As she came around the corner, she stopped dead in her tracks.

"Well! What a pleasant surprise, Char. It's sure nice to see you back, how are you?"

"I'm good, thank you."

"Are you ready to go back to work?"

"That's why I'm here."

"The ladies have missed you. They tell me it's not the same here without you."

"That's nice of them to say, Liz, but there was someone here just as good as I am to do their hair."

"Oh yeah, we took care of them, but they told us we don't do it the same as you. You have spoiled your clientele, Char, and it would be hard for anyone to take your place."

"Thank you." Over the time, I have spoiled my clientele. I remember their birthdays and anything special that is important to them. Then they know that I do listen; they're not just a number but are real people. A few had just popped in today to see if Liz had heard from me. So they were surprised as well. It ended up been a very nice day after all. I had been worried about nothing. Liz seemed to be totally at ease with everything, and she never brought up the baby once, but then, neither did the other girls, which I found to be strange.

Oh well, I guess it's old news; they had asked how I was, and seeing how I am just fine, there was no need to go on.

At the end of the day, all went as usual. Liz sent Carrie over for her bottle while the rest of us finished cleaning up. I was feeling it; you could tell I had been on my feet all day. I wasn't in pain, but I was tired and looking forward to lying down.

Carrie came back with the bottle, and Liz had her get all our drinks ready.

"All right, girls, and here's to a great day." She raises her glass up to all of us and the girls back at her.

"What's up, Char.? Are you not having a drink?"

"No, thanks."

"Why not?

"I've heard that they think alcohol is not good while you're pregnant."

You could have heard a pin drop; the girls all looked at me like I had two heads, and Liz choked on her drink that she had just taken.

"What?" Liz asked. "Are you still pregnant?"

"Yes, I am."

"Then what did you go away for all last week?"

"I couldn't take the pressure you were all putting on me, so I went away to get my head straightened out and to decide what it was that I wanted to do. While I was gone, I had complications and ended up in the hospital. But now all is fine, and I can go on."

I hear Beth and Carrie say, "We have to go now, see you tomorrow. Char, you want a ride?"

"Yes, please, give me a minute to grab my things." It was pretty quiet in the shop. There was nothing being said about anything. The three of us had left together, and once we were headed down the road, Beth spoke up first.

"You do know, Char. That you surprised all of us, eh."

"I never said how long I was going to be gone, so I don't know why you're all surprised."

"That's not it, Char."

"What is then?"

"Char, you're still pregnant!"

"Yeah, so."

"Liz told all of us that you had gone for an abortion."

"You're joking!"

"No, she's not," Carrie piped up and said.

"I never said I was having an abortion. In fact I didn't say much to Liz about it. She had said that she knew I would do the right thing and asked me if I needed any money. I told her I didn't need any money, then I left. I hadn't even told her I was going to Calgary to see my sister. I thought that if I were to go away for a couple of days, then she would calm down and rethink what she was asking me to do. So this morning I thought she'd had a change of heart and that's why she was so calm."

"With you being gone for over a week, she just took for granted that you had had an abortion," Beth told me.

"I hadn't planned on being gone that long, but I ended up in the hospital and had to stay until the doctor felt it was safe for me to be on my feet. Otherwise, I would have been back by Monday."

"I can see she's not happy with your choice, Char," Carrie says.

"She's probably still sitting there drinking, and tomorrow, none of us will want to be there when she comes in to work."

"I am sorry about that. She shouldn't be upset with anyone other than me. But she will get over it. She will have to because I am too far gone to have a safe abortion unless my pregnancy was harming me, which is not, and the baby is also fine."

"Char!"

"Yeah, Beth."

"So you know you're only having one baby?"

"Yes, they had to do an ultrasound in Calgary, so now I don't have to wait and wonder."

"Did you find out if it's a boy or girl?"

"No, I don't want to know."

"It would make it easier to shop."

"Perhaps, but that's taking the surprise away and all the excitement."

"Well, talking about excitement. Tomorrow should be really exciting."

"Why do you say that, Carrie?"

"Well, Char, you don't think Liz is going to drop this, do you?"

"It's done. Nothing she can say will change my mind."

"She won't see it that way."

"Guess, we will see."

"All right, we'll see you tomorrow, Char."

"See you tomorrow, and thank you for the ride."

"You're welcome." And the girls drove away. Surely Liz will let it go, seeing how I have made my choice. I suppose she could always ride my ass now to give it up for adoption. That won't happen either as I am getting used to the idea of having my own baby. It will be great to have someone to love, who will love me back for who I am, not for who they think I should be. Sure, it might be tough sometimes, but I am not the first to have a baby on my own. Besides Mary is more than willing to help me. How can I go wrong? Think of an angel.

"Hello there, deary," she says, hugging me like a mother should hug their daughter. "I was so worried about you after your sister called. I didn't know what to do for you. So I went out and bought us some paint, the not-so-smelly type so you can paint too. I asked if someone pregnant could use it, and the girl mixing it said yes that it was safe. I picked up a soft yellow and a soft mint green.

"That sounds great, Mary."

"What is it, deary? You sound so sad."

"Well, Liz was upset today because she thought I had gone away to have an abortion."

"Oh no, are you all right?"

"Yeah, I just don't know what to do if she asks me to give the baby up."

"I think if she gets too pushy about it, you should just quit until after you have the baby."

"You really think that would be smart after getting this far with my hairdressing?"

"Yes, deary, I do. You can pick up your hairdressing later. You are going to be off for some time anyways."

"I know, but I was hoping to work for as long as possible."

"That would be nice for you, but the stress is not good for you."

"I will see what tomorrow brings. Now would you like to show me the paint you brought, Mary?"

"Deary, the colors are so soft, and we can go down to the store on Saturday. I would like to show you the wallpapers they have. My favorite ones are the teddy bears and then there is one with soft clouds of all the baby colors. There are also what they call borders, so you can mix and match. There is one baby's room done up to show, I think you will love it."

"All right, Mary, we can go on Saturday." I never worked on Saturdays as Liz is my trainer, and she doesn't work Saturdays unless she has a wedding.

"What happened to you, deary, when you went to see your sister?"

"The doctor told me I have gotten big at a fast rate, and it caused me to get a tear in my uterus, so they treated me and took an ultrasound, and I had to stay off my feet until the bleeding was stopped, so now I am fine."

"Did he tell you whether there was one or two babies?"

"Yes, he did, and I am having only one."

"So long as all is OK with you and the baby, I will take one, that's better than none."

"Mary, that's so sweet for you to say."

"I am sorry that you will be a single mom. I am being selfish when I say I am glad for me. I am so excited to be part of this with you." She comes and gives me a hug. I don't think I have been hugged so much in such a short time. It is a great feeling to know someone cares enough to hug you. I hope I am free with the hugs to my baby as it gets older. Just because we get older, it doesn't mean we don't need hugging anymore. You know I cannot remember the last time my mother has hugged me and told me she loved me. I don't even remember being hugged as a wee child, but surely, she loved me enough to hug me then. Why do parents stop hugging their children? Is it because the child gives off the vibes that they're not huggable, or is it because parents think they're too old to be hugged? Either way, it is not right. A hug makes all the difference to one's day. I think I will post a big note for myself telling me to be sure to hug my child every day for the rest of my life; something so simple can make a big difference.

"Mary."

"Yes, deary."

"I saw my brother last night."

"Is that who brought you home when I was leaving?"

"Yes, he has just gotten back in from working in the bush all winter. It was lucky for me that he had just gotten to the bus depot when I did, so he gave me a ride home."

"Where does he live?"

"He sleeps in the basement at my older sister's, but it is not a finished basement by any means. So he had asked if he could rent with me, seeing how I would have two bedrooms."

"But, deary, you won't be paying to live here. But I don't want to be free living for anyone else."

"I understand that, so why don't you come up with a price for him."

"You also wanted a bedroom just for the baby, so if he moves in, then what would you do?"

"Well, seeing how he is away so much, I was thinking about finding a sofa bed. That way, we all would still have a nice place."

"Then he knows about the baby."

"No! I haven't told him yet. There just wasn't the right time."

"All right, deary, if that's what you think you would like to do. I will think about it as it is probably a good idea for you to have someone around as much as possible. As you know I spend a lot of time doing things for the church. So you tell him about the baby and what you have to offer him and see what he has to say. If he is still interested, then let me know."

"Thank you, Mary. I will."

"Have the men moved out from downstairs?"

"Yes, they moved out the second day you left, so I have been down there cleaning for you."

"Oh Mary, you shouldn't do that on your own. Seeing how I'm getting it rent-free, I should at least clean it."

"Don't you worry, deary. There is a lot to clean. The walls all have to be washed before we can paint; otherwise the paint won't stick very good."

"We will also take off all the trim. That way we can paint them a different shade, then the rest. I have seen it done that way, and it looks so nice, if that's OK with you, Mary."

"Yes, I have seen that too. It's a good idea."

"Promise me, Mary, you will wait until I can help you now. Tomorrow after work, I will start washing walls. I get home early enough."

"Are you sure you should be doing so much?"

"The doctor didn't say I had to stop living."

"Well, we will take it easy just in case."

"That sounds good to me."

"What did Sam say, Mary?"

"He said he didn't give a damn what I did with the basement, not that I cared. Anyways it is my home to do with what I want."

"That might be so, but I don't want to cause you any grief. I must go now as my brother was picking me up for supper. So I would like to change out of my work clothes and wash up a little. I might even get a nap in before he gets here. That will depend how hungry he is as to how soon he could be here. I will talk to you tomorrow, Mary."

"Yes, deary. Have a good evening."

"Thank you." As it was, I did have time to clean up, and I had a half-hour nap before Jacob picked me up.

"You want to go to the Silver Dollar to eat?"

"Sounds good to me."

"How did work go today?"

"Same old thing. You know what Liz can be like."

"Unfortunate with her drinking doesn't make it any better."

"You got that right."

"What do you want to eat? The special looks good today. I think I will have that."

"I think I will too." So when the waitress came over, we had ordered two of the hot beef sandwiches.

"Except I will have potato salad with mine instead of fries please, with a glass of milk."

"I will have coffee with mine," Jacob says

"So, Char, tell me are we going to rent together?"

I had hoped we could eat before that was brought up. "There is something I have to tell you first."

"Yeah, what is that?"

"I am pregnant." He spit his coffee out.

"Oh christ, Char, are you kidding me?"

"No, I am not."

"What the hell did you go and do something so stupid for?"

"I didn't just go do it because I wanted to. It just happened."

"Who the hell is the father?"

"What does it matter?"

"I will kick the bastard's ass, that's what matters. So who is he?"

"I'm not telling you." I wonder what he would really say if he knew it was one of his so-called friends. Would he just laugh about it then, or would he still feel the same?

"Did you tell him?"

"No!"

"Why not? He has to pay for his fun; you don't get a girl pregnant then not help with the cost."

"I don't want him involved."

"He has the right to know, plus he has a responsibility, financially."

"That's all easier said than done, but he is with someone else now, and I just want to be left alone to raise my baby."

"Char, that's crazy how you going to do that?" I don't want to tell him about the deal I have made with Mary, but maybe then, he would get off my case about the baby's father.

"Please, Jacob, just let it go. I am telling you because I will need the two bedrooms in the basement suite."

"Yeah, I guess, eh."

"But I thought we could find a sofa bed, and you could use it. There is room for a dresser in the living room so long as you keep it tidy."

"You're sure there is room?" Just then our supper came, so we waited for the waitress to finish doing what she had to do before we carried on.

"Oh, this looks delicious, and it smells good to."

"It sure does!"

"Why do you sound so surprised, Char?"

"Just the look of this place, I was scared of what we were going to get. I hope the kitchen is cleaner than the rest looks."

"What you don't know won't hurt you."

"I suppose, but you could end up with food poison."

"Just eat, don't think about all that. Char, have you told Mother?"

"No! Are you kidding?"

"You know she's going to blow a gasket right."

"Why do you think I have not told her yet. Besides it won't mean a thing to her one way or another?"

"When is it due?"

"The end of December."

"Maybe you will have a Christmas baby."

"Maybe, as I have learned anything is possible."

"So you won't be going to Mom and Dad's for Christmas this year."

"I wasn't going to be able to anyways with my hairdressing school. I don't have enough money saved for both."

"I'll probably be out in the bush again."

"That will suck, to be there two years in a row. Not going to Mom and Dad's this year was hard, it just wasn't Christmas. To me I feel like Christmas hasn't come yet. Even without gifts, it's nice to see everyone and just have a good time. I imagine that with a baby, I won't be going too far either."

"Well, if I am around and go out and you're able, I will take you with me."

"That would be nice. We will just have to see."

"Anyways what about rent? What did you find out?"

"I wanted you to know about the baby first because I thought maybe you wouldn't want to once you knew. So if you still want to, I will ask Mary and see what she says, and I will let you know tomorrow."

"Sounds good. Have you seen Louise lately?"

"No, why?"

"She was asking about you this morning. She was surprised to hear you had gone to Calgary. She said you hadn't told her you were going."

"I had decided at the spur of the moment to go and didn't have time to tell her."

"You do know that was a dumb thing to do. You should let one of us know where you are going in case something was to happen."

"Yeah, sorry. I will go see her on my way to work tomorrow."

"How long are you working till?"

"I hope as long as possible."

"How is Liz taking the news?"

"Not great. She was upset at me when I came back from Calgary, and she found out I had not had an abortion."

"That's what she said?"

"Basically. Now as far as she is concerned, I should be putting it up for adoption."

"But you're not, right?"

"No. So she will just have to get over it already."

"Thanks for supper. It will be nice when I have a stove and a fridge of my own."

"What do you have in the attic?"

"Nothing really. I use a hot plate, then I take my dishes down and do them at Mary's. I only eat once a day, so it hasn't been that bad. I buy nothing that I have to worry about using up right away. I am sick of soup, but it has kept me full. You can't go wrong with soup and crackers. I am glad to be moving into the basement before summer. I think it could be hot up there and then some of my food choices would have to changed as I don't think butter would stay so great. Right now, I keep it and the pint of milk I buy at the window along with anything that has to be on the cooler side. This has worked fine for me."

"What about mice in the attic?"

"I have been very lucky about that. I was scared at first with my mattress on the floor and all."

"Char, you don't even have a bed?"

"No, just a mattress, but it's great. It's not like I am sleeping right on the floor."

"That's worse than being on the farm, at least we had beds."

"But this is warmer, so I am not complaining."

"Well, I have to hand it to you. I can't see many girls living like that."

"Like Mother would say, 'You make your bed, you lie in it.' It has done me no harm, and I haven't put anyone else out. I am doing it on my own."

"That's the truth. Now I guess I should get you back so you can get the sleep you two need. What do you do at nights, Char?"

"I read the hairdressing books. I also have one that has all the questions that they will ask on my exam, so I have been studying it. There is a lot to learn. I'm sure I could almost be a doctor when I'm done."

"Really!"

"Yes, we have to know a lot about our anatomy. Some of the parts are hard to say and remember. I don't know what all we will ever use, but to pass the test, you have to know it all. So I draw myself these people and put name to their parts. It helps a lot."

"It sounds pretty damn boring to me."

"It might be, but it's something I have to do. Besides what else am I going to do?"

"I guess, eh, but once you have the baby you won't be so bored."

"No, I won't be, but that's a long ways off yet."

"I still think you should get help from the father."

"Drop it, OK?"

"I will find out, and his sorry ass is going to pay one way or another."

"Please just leave it alone." Don't they understand that these people have money and maybe they could take the baby away from me? I won't change that I will never tell anyone. There is no way anyone can make me tell. I will just say I don't know if I need to. It will make me look like a slut, but if it means not losing my baby to someone, then that's what I will do. In time I would tell the child when it's old enough, and hopefully, I will be set up and the child old enough no one will take it away from me. I can only pray that in the end, the child won't hold it against me. But who would love this baby more than I do. Perhaps I won't be able to give it everything I want to right away. But once I have my license, I'll do better than most girls. It looks like I will have a nice place for us to live, and yes, that's because of Mary's big heart. I will be able to clothe the child and feed it well with me not having to pay rent.

The love I am sure Mary will give to it will more than make up for the grandparents it won't know. It will have uncles to take the place of a father, so it's not like there won't be men in its life. Besides if it's a girl, most men will put it on ignore anyway. So maybe I should be hoping for a girl even though I would like a boy first. I think it's nice to have a big brother to look out for you even if we give them a hard time about it. I would hope to have a girl some day along with other children. I think having a big family would be great. Perhaps it's because I come from a big family, and it's been fun; never having a dull moment makes me feel this way.

CHAPTER SIX

O n the farm, we always had things to do and had lots of room to play and, we had each other so no one was lonely. Or at least I don't think anyone was. I do know that some of them couldn't wait to get off the farm. But us younger ones weren't. We were quite happy there. There were so many things that had taken place on the farm like my sister Anna, who is four years older than me, bailing off the horse and breaking her arm when she was in high school.

One winter we were all sick with colds, and Mother was steaming us a couple at a time in the big armchair. When our youngest sister jumped out from there and was scalded so bad that when mother pulled her pants off a lot of her skin from her legs and tummy came as well, it was a scream like no other and one you never forget. It was something you would hear in a horror show. Bev was in the hospital for a very long time.

Our father and mother had both fallen gravely ill at different times, which made it very hard on everyone.

I myself had suffered a lot with abscess. Mom used to heat up pickling salt on the stove and put it into a brown paper bag, which we used as a potion. It always broke the abscesses, and in no time, we felt good as gold. This one time, Mom treated me for the abscesses, and it spread through the whole left side of my face. My whole left side swelled up from the top of my shoulder to the top of my ear. I had terrible earache and headache and ran a very

high fever. Mom had to finally take me to the doctor. I knew by
the look on the doctor's face I was in trouble. Mom knew it too.

"I'm afraid she has got Erysipelothrix. You might have brought
her in too late. I will give you this, and we can only hope for the
best." We left there in silence. But I couldn't stand not knowing
what was wrong with me and what did he mean it might be too
late.

"Mom, what do I have? What was that big word he said?"

I was in grade 5, but that was a much bigger word than I had
ever used. She pulled no punches when she told me.

"It is a sickness that pigs get, and it is very deadly. You have
caught it from the decaying tooth that you have."

"Will I be OK?"

"I can only hope so. But by me putting that heat on, there I
made it even worse."

I was terribly sick for a very long time. I missed a lot of school,
and when I did go back, I had a relapse, which is what the doctor
said. I somehow pulled through. One thing we had to say about
our mother, she was a very good nurse/doctor. We also had an
old lady who would help Mom with us when we were sick.
Everyone called her the witch doctor. But she really was a nurse.
As if that was not bad enough, later I tobogganed off the barn
roof and damn near killed myself. Of course, Marie was with me
that day, and all she did was laugh at me. One time, I damn near
chopped my finger while chopping wood. The whole thing was
just hanging there, and Mother tied it all up good enough that it
grew back together the way it should have. I have a pretty good
scar, but I still have a finger.

For the amount of time we would cut ourselves outside on
broken glass and step on nails, it made our mother a pretty good
doctor, for we lived too far away to go to the doctor every time
something happened. When we needed an ambulance, our father
used to take us in the truck as far as town and then we'd be loaded
into the ambulance and taken to the town that had a hospital.

Our youngest brother Mark, but we called him Mickey, being born not so healthy and that had kept mother away from the farm for a very long time; in the end, the doctors sent her home with him and told her he was not going to live. Mother had brought him home to die. To everyone's surprise, Mother nursed that sick baby to grow up and be strong and healthy, and at the age of six, he had fallen quite a distance out off a tree and broke his leg in a couple of places, one being high in the hip. He started school on crutches. That leg never was the same length as the other one. As well, he was a little slower in learning, but he was not stupid. He loved to fix anything and had a very jolly disposition; he never let anyone upset him. He was also a big tease, which sometimes the rest of us found annoying. He never meant anyone any harm; Mickey himself loved life to the fullest.

Moving to BC for us was a real adventure, for neither Mickey nor I had gone anywhere for a holiday of any kind. Not like the other kids as our parents were going out to BC and looking for some place to buy and where to buy, they would take the other kids with them. Mickey and I stayed home to milk the cows, feed the pigs, haul in the wood, and the water. We did not mind as we loved the farm. We had not been anywhere to know what we might be missing. It was not a big deal when we did not go with our parents.

We were to leave that spring day after school with our big brother Jacob. Moving as the summer was just to begin was a great time to get to meet the kids and to get to know the town in which we were to be living.

It was also sad for us not to be at the farm when it was sold, but we thought that maybe our parents thought it would be too hard on us to see our pets sold to other people. Mickey and I did not know that was the plan that we were to leave with Jacob after school that day so it did not leave us much time for thinking or feeling sad. It almost seemed ironic that we never had a holiday from the farm, but we were the first to leave it while it was being sold. Yes, we were sad but excited as well; after all, we were going where we had never been before. We heard all of them talking about the mountains, but it meant nothing to Mickey and myself. So going someplace new with Jacob made it easier and more fun. He had been there before, so all along the way, he was able to tell us what was what.

We had stopped for supper, and Jacob had told us his eyes were sore. We did not know why, and he never said anything. But earlier that day, Jacob had been in town watching someone do some welding, and when you do that, there is a good chance of getting what is called a welding flash. This is like a burn to the eyeball that you don't feel right away. As time goes on, the pain is so bad that you have to go to a doctor, and they freeze your eyeball till it heals.

Jacobs's eyes got really bad as we traveled, and it got to where he was crying in pain; neither Mickey nor I knew what to do. Then Jacob asked us to guide him over to the side of the road and then we were to get us some help. Mickey and I did not know how we were going to do this; we did not know anyone out here in no man's land.

"I want you two to get out and flag down someone so they can take us to the nearest hospital," Jacob had told us.

Mickey and I just looked at each other; we knew that we were scared, so there was no pretending.

"Who are we suppose to stop, Jacob?"

"I don't care, just stop the first damn vehicle you can."

"All right, come on, Mick." As we opened the truck door and stepped outside, we slid way down the side of the road. That's how close Jacob had gotten to the edge before he stopped.

"Holy shit" was all we could say; we were both so scared. The mountains were all around us; they seemed to be wrapped in hoods, which made them look like the grim reaper.

"Charlene, I'm scared," Mickey finally says as we're trying to climb back up the side of the bank.

"Me too, what are those big black things?"

"I don't know, but I don't like them." Of course it was the mountains, but we had no idea. They seemed to be closing in on us although they were not moving, but we felt they were. We finally get to the top of the bank and then started waving for someone to stop; it must have taken another half an hour before this man in a small car stopped to see what was wrong.

"Hey, kids, what's wrong?"

Mickey says, "We don't know. Our brother needs a doctor. He told us to get him some help."

The man walks up to the window, and you could tell he was not so sure of what he was going to find. Jacob is rolling around on the seat in pain.

"Hey, man, what's wrong?" he asked Jacob.

"I got welding flash today. I need a doctor. I can't see anything."

"Let me help you into the car, and I will move your truck to a safer spot. You're pretty close to going over the edge here, and someone could hit you as well."

"Thanks, man." The man did what he said he would do; then, we were on the road to a place called Golden. He said that was the closest hospital. That's when Mickey and I found out about the welding flash and what it was. We sat in the backseat and listened to them talk in between Jacob moaning with pain. Mickey and I were still scared as this guy drove like a maniac; we thought a couple of times we were going over the edge. The roads out here are not very wide. We finally got to the hospital, and once the doctor had tended to Jacob's eyes, he had us phone our oldest brother Richard that lives in Spruce View to come and get us. We slept on the chairs in the waiting room until Richard got there, which was about three in the morning. For Mickey and I, our adventure had started out pretty damn scary and one we would never forget. The mountains did not look so scary in the daylight; in fact all they were, were large rock, which we came to enjoy climbing later in our move. They no longer wore hooded caps or gave us the feeling that they would swallow us alive.

This was to be the summer like no other. The summer of 1969 was a start of a whole new life for us. In the end, it was a very busy summer in which we met a lot of new people. We learned how to swim like all the rest and spent most of our days in the river. We still had to haul water and wood, and besides helping in the house, there was not much to do as chores now that we did not live on the farm. We missed the farm for a long time especially the animals as we all had our own pets. We talked a lot about them to our new friends and told them of all the fun we had living on the farm. Some of them wished they could have that experience of living on the farm. This in many ways made us wiser to the world around us as we lived in a small town now and got to learn their way of life. In the end, we were the richer ones and with all the knowledge that we would learn. It would take us further in life than just staying on the farm or just living in town. We had settled in quite well, and that's one thing they say about children being so resilient. We were able to pick up and move on without being too disheartened.

Our summer turned to fall, which was almost still summer, and then winter came; it was not as hard as the winters in Alberta. We did still get snow, not as much, but we still had winter. Spring seemed like it came really fast; it got warm and the flowers started to bloom. Before we knew it, it was summer again, and we were going to enjoy it to the fullest, for now, we were just like we belonged here. It was like our family got much bigger. Everyone's parents were our parents, and I guess that's how it is in most small places. No one had to worry about their children. Everyone looked out after you if you were in there neighborhood.

The summer once again was hot, dry, and beautiful, so we spent a lot of time at the river. Everything was lazy, laid-back summer, and our father had put in running cold water so that was one more thing we did not have to do. Life seemed to be at its best; in fact, we did not think it could get any better.

The one thing Mickey and I still do was bottle picking, which was our time together when we would talk about a lot of different things. The one thing that was on his mind was the new school he was going to this fall. Our parents had taken him out of the public school and found one that would train him to be a mechanic as he was very good at hands on but not so good at paper. He was so excited about this, for he got picked on a lot in school. Not because he was mentally handicapped but he was slower than normal. This was due to his troubled birth. Our mother never told us what was the problem, and we never asked, for it made no difference to us, for we loved him for who he was. Mickey was always there for us, and he would do anything you wanted him to do. We also did not let people use him. Mickey was so easygoing that some people thought it was smart to use him for their joke.

"Char, Char, are you awake?"

"I am now. What's up, Mick?"

"Remember we were going bottle picking today!"

"Yeah, what time is it?"

"It's five AM. But I want to go see Robert today first. I will call you when I'm headed back home and you can meet me halfway, how does that sound?"

"Great, I have to do my laundry today anyways before I go anywhere."

"All right, I will call you later." With that said, he was gone. So I rolled over and went back to sleep for a while. Mickey was always up very early; he said he could never sleep. But then he was in bed early as well. It did not matter what we were doing or where we were, he would just disappear at 8:00 PM. At first, some of our friends would get mad at him, but that never bothered him, and they finally accepted that. That was Mickey.

Mickey and I were only two years apart, so we grew up very close and were used to doing things together. Living in this small town and with our parents having the country store, we met a lot of people and had a lot of new friends in our lives, and we were starting to do a lot more things differently, and we started going in different directions. I know this was bothering Mickey as well as myself, but we also knew we had to let go sooner or later, and his new school would start us on that road. I worried about who would watch out over him at school and see to it that no one picked on him. Our parents had told him and us it was on a trial basis, so if it did not work, he could quit at anytime. We all knew this was a very good opportunity for him, and we let him know that we supported him 100 percent. Mickey was so happy, so we were happy for him.

The day went by fast, and before I knew it, it was going to be too late to pick bottles, and Mickey had not called yet. I had tried to call him a couple of times and had gotten no answer. He was usually pretty good at being where he said he would be and really good about his time. He never made anyone wait for him. Mickey always seemed to get a lot out of a day. He rode his bike all the time; even when his friends would walk, he rode slowly beside them. It was like he was cramming all that life had to offer into a day. The next day would be the same he did not sit still. Mickey saw nothing but the good in everyone, and he saw all the beauty that surrounded us from the worms to the smallest bug. He would pick them up with such ease as not to harm them and say to us, "Look, guys! Is this not a beauty?" and set it back down as though his life depended on its safe return. When we got home, he always told our parents about whatever creature he had discovered that day. Their reply would be "Yes, that's something."

It was later that afternoon when Mickey had called the house and talked to Mom.

"Where are you?" Mother had asked him.

"I'm still at Roberts. I have been helping him and the neighbor haul hay, so we would like to finish up before I come home."

"All right, but you be home before dark as you don't have lights on your bike," Mom says to him.

"I will, Mom."

Hanging up the phone and returning to her chair at the end of the table, she had just sat down when the phone rang, so Mom got up to answer it.

"Hello." Then she started to scream like I have never heard Mom do before. So I grabbed the phone from her.

"HELLO! HELLO!!"

"Mark shot himself!"

"WHAT? Robert, what did you say?"

"Mark shot himself!"

"How bad is he hurt, Robert?"

"Mark shot himself." And the line went dead. Robert had hung up. Marie heard Mom screaming and came in from the store to see what had happened.

"Char, what the hell is wrong?"

"Robert said Mickey shot himself and hung up!"

"Go out and get Dad!" So as I went to get Dad, Marie called the police and the ambulance; they were both six miles in the opposite direction then where Mickey was. He was six miles the other side. Marie waited at the store with us so she could take the police to where they were. Our parents had left and gone to where Mickey was.

Mark Allan was his real name. But we all called him Mickey Mouse when he was a new baby. Mom had said it was because he was so small when she brought him home to die. The name Mickey just stayed with him.

Once the police came and picked up Marie, I was left with our youngest sister Bev, who was crying out of control. As there was a room between the store and her bedroom that had a lock on it, I grabbed her by the arm and shoved her in there and locked the door. Then I went and locked the store door and sat and waited for our parents to come home with Mickey so we could see where he was shot. He knew how to use a gun; we were all taught that on the farm in case of a bear or cougar or anything that would bring danger to us. I was telling myself that he was going to be OK. After all, he knew about guns. So what did Robert mean when he said Mark shot himself? That was impossible. When you know how to use a gun, how do you shoot yourself? So I had myself convinced that Robert did not know what he was talking about. About an hour later, our parents came home. When they came through the door, our father was holding our mother up. He looked just as grim as our mother did.

"Dad, what is wrong with Mom?"

"Where is Mickey? Is he OK?"

Dad guides mom over to her chair and gets her down. Neither one was saying anything. I have never seen them look like this ever.

"Mom, Dad, what is wrong?"

Mom finally speaks in a voice I don't recognize.

"Where's Bev?"

"In the spare room"

"Get her," Dad says; he sounds like Mom. They have become strangers.

"OK," I say and I run and unlock the door and tell Bev, "Mom and Dad are home. They want you to come out." We go back to Mom and Dad together, and we did not notice, but we were holding hands very tightly.

"Mommy, where is Mickey," Bev asked.

"He is dead," she said, and she sounded like life had left her as well. Bev began to cry out of control once again, and this time all I could do was take her in my arms and hold her as tight as I could. Neither one of our parents moved to console us. My tears were flowing pretty heavy and fast, but Bev needed me like never before. Our mother was sobbing so hard that she could not keep her head up, and our father sat there like he was in no man's land.

"Dad, where is Marie?" I asked.

"She will be coming home with the police when they're done."

"What happened, Dad? How did Mickey get shot?"

"The police will tell us more when they get here. They wanted me to get your mother out of there after Mickey died."

"Mickey was still alive when you got there, Dad?"

"Yes, he was for a short time. He was in no pain nor did he know we were there. He died in our arms." The tears are rolling slowly down Dad's face. All of a sudden, he looked very pale, and he looked like a very old man.

"Charlene!"

"Yeah, Dad"

"Would you make your mother some tea? I really think she should have something."

"Sure, Dad. I can do that. How about you?" He gets up and goes into our living room and slips into his big arm chair that he watches TV from.

"Dad, are you all right?" I asked as I take Bev in there and put her on the sofa beside Dad so I can go make the tea he has asked for.

"Yeah, I will just sit here and wait for the police to come. There is nothing else to do."

I was not finished making the tea when Marie came through our back door with the police. The police had decided to park at the back of the house so the neighbors would not all be coming over right away to see what was wrong although I felt like I could have used someone's arms around me right at this minute.

"Here, Char, let me help you." She sounded so sure of herself and not broke up at all. How can that be; does she not care that Mickey is dead, or had Mom and Dad been wrong, and Mickey was OK?

Of course, I was too young to know that she was dying inside but had to hold it together as she could see our parents were in no shape to do any of the arranging. Marie poured tea for all of us including the police while they sat there and told us how Mickey had not shot himself. It had something to do with where the gun was and the story that Robert had told them. The police told us that it was more like a "I dare you" thing between two boys that went wrong. There would be no charges laid to the boy because of his age. His mother might get a charge for not having a loaded gun locked up.

"That little son of a bitch better not show his face around here," my dad said to the police.

"Now, Henry, it was a terrible accident, and two wrongs won't make it right." The sad thing about this is that Robert was Mickey's friend from Alberta; they had gone to school together there as well. Our parents were also old friends. Mickey was so happy to find out that they had moved only six miles from us. Now all friendships would be destroyed after so many years.

The funeral was all arranged by Marie, and she had to do all the calling of all the family. It ended up falling on Mother's birthday, August fifteenth. When all was said and done, nothing was the same, Mother's birthdays for sure. For some reason, we were not to talk about Mickey in a good way or bad. It was like he never existed. Sharing our memory should have helped us get through the grieving. Our parents became stonewalls and total strangers to each other. They were there but only in bodily form. The laughing and fun times came to an end. The groups that used to hang out at our place for Christmas never came this year. Our home became a tomb, and it was then that I decided I was not going back to school. I wanted out of there. I would be sixteen on the thirtieth of August. Marie and I had talked about it and so we started to look for a job. We did find one at the laundry mat in Spruce View. So we moved into a motel, and we worked very hard and got along so well no one knew we were sisters. Of course, we started to party a lot, and I started to date. This was all very exciting to me, having a great time. We went to see Mom and Dad now and again but not much had changed. Our little sister was still at home. But man did it feel good to laugh again. We new Mickey sure would not mind seeing us have a great time. Although our mother had tried putting a stop to it many times but to no avail. Marie and I stayed in Spruce View for one summer and one winter, then she moved on to Calgary, and I stayed behind for three more years and worked in a bakeshop that also had a restaurant on it, so I learned two trades in one. After my three years, I then decided that I wanted to do something a little different, so I took a trip out to St. Paul, Alberta. I had a brother living there, and I thought I would surprise him, so that I did. I stayed with Jeff for two weeks, and of course, they partied a lot there too, so I guess Marie and I were not so bad because we partied. Our mother tried making us out to be terrible girls, and she kept saying we were going to find ourselves in trouble. I had no idea what she was talking about because right now we were having a hell of a lot of fun. Guys seemed to really like me even now that Marie was not around me. I always felt that they were nice to me or wanted to be my friend just so they could get to know her. After all, she was the pretty one. I did not think I had much going for me with my reddish hair, and I had a real bad overbite. I was somewhat shy because of it, but I also like to joke around and tease. I could be a real clown when I needed to be. I met this guy at Jeff's place that seemed to be really into me. He was very good looking and that sort of made me wonder why he would be interested in me. He could have his pick of girls, I was sure of that. He was also a very nice guy, so what was up, I never got to know because the night after I told him I was moving on to see my older sister, he committed suicide. That threw me for a real loop. I had asked Jeff why. He told me he had not been happy for a long time. In fact, he thought I had made him laugh more than they had seen him laugh for some time. I was feeling pretty down as I wondered if Dave had taken his life because of something I had done. To this day, I have never found out. So I had stayed on a few more days so I could go to Dave's funeral before leaving and going to my sister's place in Evansview.

I once again got on the bus, went to the back, and slept until we got to the city. There I got off and had an overnight wait, and my sister was only one and a half hours away. I called her, and Anna told me she would come pick me up. I wandered around, went to the bathroom, and tried to wake up and then I found a corner near the bathroom that I put my suitcase down and I sat on it and be damned if I did not fall asleep. That's where Anna found me when she came looking for me. I must have been a real sight.

"Char, Char, come on, wake up. It's time to go home." I damn near jumped out of my skin when she grabbed me by the arm and gave me a shake.

"Oh, please don't shake me. I have a headache."

"Were you partying last night?"

"No, I must have slept with a kink in my neck."

"Well, I don't think suitcases were made for sleeping on, you fool."

"Thanks for the update."

"Have you eaten today?"

"Not yet."

"Then come, I will buy you lunch. Maybe that will take your headache away."

"Maybe."

My sister had her two little ones with her son, Lee, and her daughter, Ann. They were both nice-looking kids and well behaved. Lee was only a couple months old when Mickey was killed. That was our first time seeing him. Now he was about four years old, and they were such sweet kids.

"How have you been, Char? I haven't seen or heard from you for some time."

"I know and I am doing fine. I have talked to mother now, and again, she says you do a lot of partying!"

"No more than anyone else, but I think Mother thought we should stay and live in that tomb longer, and I just could not stand it anymore. It was like we all died with Mickey."

"That bad, eh!"

"Yes, some time when you're talking to Marie, ask her what it was like!"

"We wanted to live the way Mickey would want us to."

"Mom and Dad, they don't sound so good, Char."

"I know, but there is nothing we can do except wait for them to decide when it's been long enough."

"Yeah, I guess. Hey, I want to go out and see them this summer. Maybe you will come with me?"

"Anna, I would just sooner wait. It was hard getting out of there once."

"I guess I should have stayed longer after the funeral and helped you girls out, but Marie seemed like she had it all under control."

"She did and never complained, but when I decided to leave, she said she was leaving with me. I think she carried all she could. We were not allowed to live anymore. It was like laughing was a sin. Mom had phoned to the bars in Spruce View where Marie and I were hanging out to get us kicked out, but that never happened. After all, I was dating a guy whose mother worked there, so she was not causing me any trouble. Oh, by the way, Ron says he may come down."

"That's OK. Are you staying for a while?"

"Yeah, I want to get a job and maybe a place to live on my own."

"OK, I can help you with that. I need a babysitter for a few days, for mine has to go in for surgery. The restaurant is looking for help on Main Street."

"That's good. I will check it out, and maybe be able to start there after I help you out."

"Are you sure you want to help me first?"

"Of course, I will. That's what sisters are for, remember?"

"Great. Settled then. Come on, kids, eat up so we can head for home."

"OK, Mommy," Lee answers. The kids did not finish all their lunch but then they had a pretty big order, so Anna got the rest to go. Once we were on the road going home, it did not take long before they were both sound asleep. I had told Anna how my visit with Jeff was. She and Jeff did not get along to well as he was always feeling sorry for himself, and she gets ticked off at him because you can change your life if you want to. Instead of blaming everyone else for things that go wrong in your life, take the bull by the horns and do something about it. If you don't, no one is going to do it for you.

I also told her about Dave and how sad that made me. She told me it must have been something he had been thinking about doing because he had not known me long enough for me to make that kind of impact on him. That made me feel better about myself, I guess.

I babysat for Anna, and I also went down to see about that other job, which Lyn agreed that I could start after I helped Anna out. We also found a small yellow-and-white house to rent for four hundred a month, which Anna said she would help me get. So I did that. Ron showed up the next week, and we just started living together; it seemed so natural, and it came so easy.

Ron had gotten a job on a paving crew and so we were happy, or so I thought. We lived like that for four months; then one night he tells me he is leaving. I never said anything, and I did not ask why or when. I just let whatever was to happen happen. I guess I had felt all along that it was too good to be true. Ron and I had been dating since I had moved to Spruce View. But it was on again, off again; he was not one to be tied to any one person, but oh, how I loved him so. I tried not to make a scene and to pretend I was cool about his decision although it was breaking my heart. The next morning when he left for work, I knew he would not be back that night. The song by Freddie Fender was playing when he left. (I'll be there before the next tear drop falls.) I tried to stay for a while, but in the end, I just could not. I had talked to Anna about it, and she thought that maybe a move would be good for me to do. So I decided to try Stony Creek as Louise and Jacob lived there even though I was getting used to being alone. So I packed all what I had, which would be my clothes, and Anna took me up to Stony Creek. After a couple of days, I had found a job at the Clip and Curl, which was one of the oldest hairdressing shops in town. So they were busy all the time and always needed girls. I had also found a place to live, Mary's attic.

"You know, Char. If this does not work, you can always come back."

"I know, but I would like to try this. Maybe then we can work together. Thank you for all your help. We hugged one more time before her, and the children headed for home. I was a little nervous, and I did not know when for sure I would be seeing her again.

CHAPTER SEVEN

Today I must leave early so I can stop and have a coffee with Louise. I have so much to tell her since the last time we were together, which feels like months.

It once again is a beautiful day, and I do know what lies ahead for me now, and I have been able to make plans; this gives me such a fantastic feeling, and it is nice to know I have my own home. This is great, a new home, a job that I want to work at, and make it a dream come true. Anna and I have talked about working in a hair shop together for some time now, so here is my chance, and also a baby to love. How can things get any better.

As I get close to Louise's, I see her cleaning her living room as her big window faces the sidewalk. I sneak up and knock on her window. I am sure she almost wet herself.

"Hi, Char," she yells with a big smile and waves me in.

"Hi yourself."

"Do you have time for coffee?"

"I sure do. That's why I am here."

"Great, how have you been? I heard you had taken a trip. I had come down to the shop a couple of times and no one seemed to know anything. I finally saw Jacob one afternoon, and he told me where you went."

"I am sorry about that, Louise. I decided at the last minute to go and see Marie, more or less to give Liz time to cool down, and then I was having problems, so the doctor there put me in the hospital until things got better. Now I am just fine."

"So how was Marie?"

"She's good. She is getting married the long weekend in September."

"Well, they have been together for a while now."

"No, not really."

"Why do you say it like that?"

"Marie is not marrying Grant."

"She isn't?"

"She is marrying Grant's brother Gary."

"You're kidding, right?"

"That's exactly what I said. I even tried to talk her out of it but had no luck."

"So why is she?"

"Something to do with revenge from what I could get out of it."

"Isn't that a stupid reason to marry someone?"

"I asked the same question, and she just said, 'Maybe for someone else.'"

"Guess all we can do is wish her luck."

"You know, Louise, what I can't understand is why Mother is all for this."

"She is?"

"Oh yeah, she's making most of the arrangements because they're getting married out there. Marie said mother was busy hand-sewing the beads onto her veil."

"Then I guess they must know more than we do, Char."

"Guess so."

"Now tell me what is new with you."

"A whole lot, like I am moving."

"Moving! To where?"

"Into Mary's basement suite at the end of the month or when we have it cleaned and painted."

"Good for you. See I told you, you wouldn't be living in the attic forever. What is she going to charge you to live there?"

"You better sit down."

"That bad, Char?" she says as she sits down sort of hard onto her chair. "Why would you do it then?"

"Louise, I don't have to pay rent for the basement suite."

She chokes on her coffee and says, "I didn't expect to hear that! How come? What is the rest of the story?"

"As you know, Mary has four sons, and I have found out that she never had a daughter, and none of her boys want to be parents. So she asked me if she could be my adoptive mother and the baby's adoptive grandmother. In return for letting her share our lives, she will provide us a place to live free of rent. Mary also wants to babysit when I am ready to go back to work."

"Well, Char. Is she sure she can afford to give you a place for nothing?"

"Funny I asked her the same thing. She told me she did not need the money as her late husband left her very well taken care of."

"Then I guess as the saying goes, *Don't look a gift horse in the mouth.*"

"Louise, what the hell does that mean?"

"I don't know, but don't shoot the messenger"

"So how big is the basement suite?"

"I have two bedrooms. The living room and kitchen are one open space, and the bathroom has a washer and dryer in it, so that makes me happy."

"That's one thing you won't have to buy."

"I won't have to buy anything other than what I need for the baby's room. It comes with everything."

"It is about time something went in your favor, Char."

"I feel like I have won a jackpot. I do worry about Mary's son that lives with her as I have seen what kind of an asshole he can be to Mary. She tells me he is just like that when he is drinking."

"Char, you be careful around him!"

"Oh, I will. One thing about it, there is a peephole on the door, so if he ever comes around, I will call the police."

"You be sure to do that before you answer the door."

"I will. Don't you worry. Anyways would you like to come over and see the basement suite on Saturday and maybe help us pick out some wallpaper for the baby's room."

"Char, you keep saying 'baby's room' like you know there is only one, do you?"

"Yes, I do as they had to do an ultrasound when I was in Calgary, so they told me then."

"You won't have to go back to the city then?"

"The doctor in Calgary wants me to just be safe and make sure he hadn't missed anything. He told me all was just fine right now, and there was no reason why I couldn't have a healthy baby."

"I am glad that you know now. Do you feel better about that, that there is only one?"

"In some ways, but we had talked about twins so long that I was getting used to it, so in some ways, it was a letdown. But I am just fine with what I know. Everything is falling into place now. I just hope that Liz has come around, or it could be tough working with her. Mary tells me to quit if she is nasty about it and pushes me to put it up for adoption. She tells me I can pick up where I left off."

"Char, she is right about that as no one can take your hours of apprenticeship away, so if you don't finish before the baby, you sure can once you decide to go back after you have the baby."

"Today I will know more of how she feels about it as she was not happy that I hadn't had an abortion when I was in Calgary."

"Are you kidding me? She thought that's what you went for?"

"Yes, so she was some choked. The other girls and I got out of there as fast as we could. We didn't give her time to go on a rant about it."

"Liz will just have to get over it, and if she says anything to me about it, I will tell her so."

"Thanks, Louise, but you don't have to on my account."

"I know that, Char, but you're not the first, and you won't be the last. If she only knew how many kids her son has running around to different women, maybe she would shut her mouth."

"Really!"

"Yes, and don't you say I told you anything. She can pretend all she wants, but it will give us some ammunition to fight back with, all right? So see what she has to say today, and we will deal with it."

"Will you come with Mary and me on Saturday?"

"Yes, I would love to. What time?"

"I will ask Mary and call you."

"This should be fun. It has been a long time since I have done any shopping for a baby's room. It must be a good feeling, eh, Char, to know the baby will have a bedroom and a nice home. Not that the attic wouldn't have been, but I do know you were not happy with that set up."

"Yeah, I am very excited, and Mary has been so great, she is being the mother that I need right now. I know that you are here for me, and I love you for that. Maybe it's Mary's age, I don't really know, but she does make me feel special. She tells me God sent me to her, and for that, she is grateful. I was so worried about how she was going to react when she found out about the baby. She had totally stunned me with her offer I had to pinch myself to see if I was still on this earth."

"I am so happy for you, Char. And I hope this works out with you and Mary. It will be good to have someone so close to be able to help, and by what you say, you might find Mary almost living with you."

"That is OK. She is so sweet and caring I only hope this won't be too much for her."

"You will just have to watch, Char, and make sure she gets her rest as she is not a young woman anymore."

"I will. By the way, did Jacob tell you he wants to live with us?"

"No, he hasn't said anything to me, but that would be good too. That way, there would be wheels if you need to go to the hospital."

"That's funny because I think Mary said something like that too, except he will have to pay her rent."

"So he should and help you with groceries."

"Jacob said the same thing although he won't be around too much of the time with his job and all."

"Maybe not, we can only hope that he's around when the time comes especially if you go into labor in the middle of the night."

"Well, Louise, I best go to work. I don't want to be late and get Liz off on the wrong foot before the day even gets started."

"Thanks for stopping and catching me up on everything and call me about Saturday."

"I will and thank you for coffee."

"You're welcome, bye." With this I carried on my way; the streets were starting to get busy as the day was warming up and the stores were starting to open. It sure seemed like there were a lot of people out today or had I just never noticed before as I always seemed to have such heavy thoughts, I never really noticed what was going on around me, but today, it just seemed like a day that was full of life; maybe that was a good sign. All I could wish for now was for the same thing to be happening at the shop; here is hoping that all is on an upbeat as the weather is beautiful; the sun is so warm. How could anyone have cold or bad thoughts of any kind? Life is good, and at this moment, I cannot think of anything that I would want to change as I am happy with my decisions.

Then like a black cloud, it hit me; you fool, of course, there is something I would like to change. I would like very much to be sharing all this with my mother and even my father. I know he would be OK with all that is going on; even if he didn't, he would not make me feel any less a person. He would ask how I planned to do it all and say something along the lines like "I hope it all works out for you" as he slips fifty dollars into my hand. Our father is a generous man with a very big heart when it comes to little children, in fact even with the big children. After all, he had twelve of his own, so there must be something about children that he liked to have so many around.

As I approached the shop, I see all the girls have arrived early. I suppose they're all waiting to find out what happened. Will I be staying or moving on? When I enter the coffee room, all went quiet; the girls all looked at me as if I had two heads.

"Hey, don't let me stop you from talking," I tell them.

"It's not that, Char," Beth says. "We're just waiting to see what you have to say. We also want you to know that we will tell Liz we're all fine with the fact that you're pregnant. Besides it has nothing to do with us. We are your coworkers and friends, having a baby won't change that."

"I am glad to hear that as I am not the first single mom and I won't be the last, but it will still depend on what Liz wants, and if she pushes any more, I most likely will be quitting."

"Char, don't say that!"

"I'm sorry, Beth, but I want to enjoy this pregnancy not be nagged about it all the time."

Liz came in, and she was in a fairly good mood. "Hi, girls, and how is everyone today?"

Everyone said, "Just fine, Liz."

"That's good as you can see we have a very busy day ahead of us, and Char, some of yours are doubled booked with you being away you had some that wouldn't let anyone else do their hair, and they really want it done now! So it will take you through your lunch break as well as later into this evening to get them all done."

"That's fine with me."

"Liz!"

"What, Carrie?"

"Char can't do all these alone. Some of them Beth and I can do."

"I don't think so. They're Charlene's clientele."

"That may be so, but it's too much on her feet in one day."

"That has been her choice. Now please get to work."

"Liz!"

"That will be all now, to work, Carrie."

"Don't worry, Carrie. I will be fine. I will take my time, I am sure my ladies will understand."

"That is not the point, Char. Liz knew better than this. She is just being a bitch about it, and you know it. What if your pregnancy can't take it?"

"If I feel any discomfort, I will stop right away trust me. Like I said, I will take my time." The day was very long and busy it seemed like there was no end to women today. One nice thing about it all was that they were very upbeat, thoughtful, and patient; all were very excited about the baby. So I got the low down on names and a lot of what to do's and not to do's; no one meant any harm, and it made my day go by a whole lot easier. I know it wasn't what Liz was expecting. I am sure she figured I would give up and lose my cool and my head and make a real mess of things, but that did not happen.

"Char."

"Yeah, Beth."

"I am staying to help you clean up tonight."

"You don't have to?"

"I know, but I am. I know you would do it for me."

"Thank you."

You could see on Liz's face she wasn't too impressed about the help I was getting although she didn't say anything except "Are you girls having a drink tonight?"

No was the reply from all of them. You could tell by the tone that they were totally pissed at Liz. Carrie and Beth helped me clean up and get ready for the next day. When I looked at the book, I only had half of what I had today. Beth gave me a ride home after all was said and done.

"Thanks for the ride, Beth!"

"Don't mention it. What a bitch, Char. I am sure that was not legal what she did to you today. No one should have to do that."

"It won't happen again. She was trying to prove a point that she has the power over me, and I must kiss her ass to keep my job, but she doesn't know everything, so if she tries this again, I will hand her my scissors and leave and don't you think for one minute that I won't. This baby is all I have, and I won't do anything to jeopardize it. So if it means hanging up my scissors for a while and starting somewhere else, I will. Liz doesn't know that I know that my hours that I have put in can be carried over, and I can continue after the baby is born through someone else. Right now, she thinks she has one over on me, but she doesn't, and she will be surprised when I tell her what I know. So I hope she will lie off because I do not want to quit yet. I would like to work as long as possible.

"We hate the idea of you quitting, Char. It will not be the same without you. But we do understand as a person can only take so much harassment before they get worn down. Liz will be sorry if you go somewhere else as all your ladies will follow you, and she makes good money off of you. It would be very detrimental to her if she forces your hand. But some people can't see past their nose, and in the end, it will be all about how much she has done for you and then you turn around and crapped on her. No one will know about the fact that she tried to make you get rid of your baby other than the ones we would tell, and believe me, I will make sure my ladies know what really went down if that is OK with you, Char!"

"Thanks, Beth, but you don't have to get involved."

"I am your friend, Char, and you have seen my boys and I through some ugly times, so I am in all the way. Unless you do not want me to be?"

"That's not the case at all, but you don't need to be looking for another job because of me. She would most likely fire you if you stand up for me to her. In front of anyone else would even make it worse, so be careful. You have to put yourself and your boys first. I know you're my best friend, Beth, but please don't lose your job over me!"

"You know what, Char. I was looking for a job when I found this one. So I am sure I could go somewhere else as well, and like you, my ladies would follow me. So it's not like starting from the beginning where ladies have to get to know you first and that makes it easier for other shops to hire us because they know we would be bringing clientele with us. I don't think there's too many who wouldn't give us a job, just maybe, Char, we should look together. We would be taking double the money to someone else. Quite frankly, I am tired of how Liz thinks she should run all our lives. She seems to think she needs to know all there is to know about us. The only good thing is when were working here, she wouldn't dare gossip about us, but once were gone we will only be crap under her feet."

"You know I do admire what you're doing on your own, not making the father take financial responsibility for the baby and all. I know firsthand how tough this can get, you have seen me there."

"Yes, Beth, I have, and I always wondered how you did it, so guess now I will find out. The only thing is I don't have rent to pay."

"What did you say, Char, about not having to pay rent?"

"Mary told me if she could be my adoptive mother and grandmother, then she would give the baby and I a place to live. That's how I got the basement suite. She says she needs us as much as we need her. Mary also wants to babysit when I go back to work. Everything has turned out to the better. How can I go wrong?"

"Well, I'll be damn. How could you get so lucky? I'm glad for you, Char, as the attic was going to be a hard place to raise a baby."

"Yeah, it wasn't going to be easy, but it would have kept us warm, dry, and together."

"You're right about that, Char. And other than there is a lot of laundry that comes with a baby, they don't move too much for the first few months so that would have given you time to find something else. This sounds perfect for you!"

"Mary is such a sweet lady, and she is so excited about the baby as she hasn't any of her own. None of her sons want to have families, so I didn't want to break her heart when she made me the offer."

"From what I know of her, she will be good for you. Her son is the only one I would worry about!"

"I don't like him either, and there is a peephole on the door, and I will keep it locked all the time although he never has bothered me upstairs. I guess the longer I am there, the more chance that something could happen. If he ever comes to my door, I will call the police because I have seen him pushing Mary around, and I think, next time I see that, I will call them. I don't know how she will take that, but after all, if she is going to watch out over my baby and myself, I think I have the right, don't you?"

"Maybe you should talk to her about it, Char, 'cause you wouldn't want to spoil a good thing that you two have going now. Perhaps it would cost you a place to live in the end, and that is s pretty sweet deal she has made you."

"You're right. I guess I could just watch, and if he gets worse than he is, then maybe I'll call. I should see about the phone numbers of her other sons. I could tell her it's just in case some time I might have to call them for her, and she's not able to give me their number. I think she would be OK with that."

"You're probably right, Char. I should get going. The babysitter and the boys will be wondering where I got to."

"I'm sorry you should have come in for coffee. But sometimes it seems easier to talk in a vehicle. When I get moved then for sure

you and the boys will have to come for supper, for I will have a
table and the whole nine yards. I'll give you coffee then!"

"Sounds good, Char. I will talk to you tomorrow."

"Thank you, Beth, for being such a caring friend."

"You're welcome anytime." With a big wave, Beth drives away,
and I feel so good after our long heart-to-heart talk. I never have to
worry about Beth talking behind my back; she never does that to
me about anyone else, so I know she won't do that to me. Beth has
to be one of the most genuine people I have met since I moved to
Stony Creek. She lives in a small trailer with her boys, and I think
it is paid for. I think she just has stall rent to pay and utilities of
course. She drives an old Pinto car that is always breaking down
on her. She has been late for work more times than we want to
remember and also has had to have someone go pick her up from
the side of the road because she has broken down. One good thing
about walking is you always know that your feet are working;
you leave at the right time every day and pace yourself and you
do just fine. I know it is easier for me than Beth to walk as she still
has to get her youngest boy to a sitter. Even after the baby comes
and I go back to work, if Mary still wants to babysit, all I have to
do will be to walk upstairs. I won't have to dress the baby up for
outside weather at all. How sweet that will not have to take the
baby out in the dead of winter. Of course, I will have to make sure
Mary has outside clothes in case she will want to go out.

I am so tired after this long day all I want to do is hit the sack.
I know Mary will be waiting for me, and I hope she won't be
too disappointed when I tell her I am too tired to do anything
downstairs. I know she has waited all day for me, but when I tell
her what Liz has done to me today, she will understand.

As usual, she was at the kitchen table reading her Bible. When
I came in, she came to the door right away.

"Hi, deary! How are you?"

"Hi, Mary. I am dead tired tonight."

"You sure look it, girl, why don't you have supper with me?"

"No, Mary, I don't want to intrude on you and Sam."

"Oh, you wouldn't be. Sam won't be home tonight. He has a meeting in the city again tonight. I made soup and sandwich. It's not much as I am not a big eater. How about it?"

"All right, Mary, that will be nice, thank you." So as we sat and had our supper, I had told Mary about what Liz had done to me today, and she got so upset I was sorry I had told her. With tears rolling down her cheeks, she said to me. "Deary, she could have made you lose the baby. My grandbaby. Oh, deary, why don't you quit before she gets her own way? How can someone be so thoughtless to another person!"

"Yeah, well, it is over, and I won't be doing that again. I am also too worn out do anything downstairs tonight. I am sorry, Mary, I know you have waited all day for me."

"Now don't you fret about that. We have lots of time to do downstairs, but your health comes first. Now I want you to finish up your soup, and we will go into the living room and have some chamomile tea."

"That sounds wonderful, Mary."

So I went into the living room, and she has these oversized sofas with the deep cushions, and you just sort of disappear into them, so I sat down and curled my feet in under me, for they felt a little on the cold side, and I pulled the fuzzy afghan that she had made over myself; it had such a relaxing aroma to it. I think it was washed in Ivory snow, so I laid my head back waiting for Mary to bring in the tea.

The last thing I remember was looking at the fireplace that was burning low, which set such a warm glow on the soft colors she had painted her walls; she had used an antique ivory with an old rose boarded. This all went very well with her dark cherry furniture, which was all Queen Ann style. These were some of my favorite colors as well as furniture. I think I have been reborn for I favor the old more than the new. I hope someday my home I am able to do in antiques; this makes a home very elegant and warm.

I must have slept like a rock, for I heard nothing all night, and I hadn't moved a muscle. I woke up the same way I had fallen, still wrapped in the fuzzy afghan, except I also had a hand-made quilt put over me, and the fire was still burning low. I could also smell fresh coffee and muffins, so I knew Mary was up. When I looked at my watch, I was surprised to see it was only 6:00 AM. I only get up this early if I planned on stopping off at Louise on my way to work. I felt much rested, so I got up and wondered out to the kitchen. Mary had her back to me as she was busy taking muffins out of the oven, so I didn't want to startle her, so I stood quiet and still until she put the hot pan down.

"Good morning, Mary. I am so sorry I fell asleep on you last night!"

"Good morning to you, deary, and don't you worry about falling asleep. Your body was needing it or you wouldn't have fallen asleep so fast. I could see you were very tired. I just couldn't bring myself to disturb you. I sure hope that was OK that I let you sleep!"

"Oh yes, thank you! Now I will go up and change my clothes and come back and wash up for work."

"You will have coffee and a muffin with me, won't you? I have it all ready!"

"All right, Mary, but this could become a habit, you best be careful."

"That would suit me just fine, deary. I would love to take care of you and the baby."

"That is sweet, Mary, but at your age you should have someone spoiling you, not you spoiling us. I will be back in a few, OK?"

"All right, I will get out your cup."

"Thank you!" I left and went upstairs. After been snuggled up on that old sofa and the fireplace, my attic didn't feel very homey to me this morning. I couldn't wait to move; maybe I will even talk to Mary about putting in a fireplace. It would have to be gas or electric, for I have no way of getting wood. I would want it to be safe as well. I think hers was gas. I should be able to do that with the money I save on rent, we will see. I hurried up so I wouldn't keep Mary waiting as she must be planning on going out early, otherwise why would she be up so early. It took me about ten minutes to change; it is getting harder to find clothes that fit me now, and I don't have many to choose from, so I best make a trip to the thrift store. I think it is even open today, and it is only one block from work. I will go down on my lunch hour and check it out. These pants will be OK. I will see if Mary has a safety pin that should get me through today.

"Sorry it took me so long, Mary. I am having a hard time fitting some of my clothes."

"You know, deary, I work at the thrift store. You want me to check it out for maternity clothes. I am going in this morning, and today is Two Bags Tuesday for ten bucks."

"What does that mean Two Bags Tuesday?"

"You can take two garbage bags full for ten bucks, and that is putting as much in the bags as possible."

"All right, Mary, that would be great. I will come down on my lunch hour and see what they have there."

"I will look when I get there, and if there are good pieces for work for you, I will put it aside for you. Our maternity clothes don't stay long, for the ladies outgrow them so fast some of ours are on their fifth go around. What would you sooner wear to work?"

"Summer dresses now that it's warm, and I think they would go further than pants. I think the pants will get too tight to soon."

"All right, what size of dress and colors?"

"If they are a shift type dress, which I prefer, then a size 10 will do, and in pastel hospital colors so they're like uniforms. If there are more whites, that's even better. I would like some brighter colors for everyday wear for off work as well."

"I will see what they have. I know we get a lot brought in from the nurses. You know what they're like. They won't wear each other's clothes. After all, they make good money, so if we're lucky, we might be able to get you some pretty nice ones, cross your fingers."

"Oh Mary, that would be fantastic."

"Here now, you best get eating and drink your coffee while it is hot."

"Thanks, and by the way, would you have a safety pin I could get off of you?"

"Sure, how big?"

"Well, how about one to close this cape." I lift my shirt up, and my tummy is sticking out between my pant closure, and Mary just starts to laugh.

"I think I have one to do the trick. I can see why you're in need of some clothes, so you better come see me today."

"Oh, I plan on doing just that." Mary comes back with the safety pin. What it was, was a diaper pin, where the head of the pin slides back down over itself and locks.

"This is an oldie," Mary tells me as she handed it to me.

"I will be sure to get this one back to you tonight, thank you so much." I finished my muffin, and man, they were delicious. I also had two cups of coffee, which means I best go pee now before I leave or I may find myself squatting in someone's bushes along the way. I don't know what the law is about women squatting on the side of the road. I know I see men taking a leak on the side of the road quite often, and I have never saw a policeman do anything about it, and I have never heard of anyone getting a fine for it. But I don't need a fine or a trip to the crow bar hotel.

"All right, Mary, I must go now. Thank you for a great sleep and breakfast, and I will see you at noon."

"Here, deary, I put a couple muffins in a bag for your breaks today, and please make sure you take the breaks you are entitled to. These are healthy muffins. I didn't even put sugar in them. The fruit has enough of its own sugar."

"Thank you again for everything!" And I was off. It was a cooler day today; it almost looked like rain, not that I minded rain. I don't mind walking in the rain going home but not to work; it does a real number on the makeup, not that I wear very much and it is really hard on the hairdo. I have gone into work a few times looking like a drowned puppy. Those days, I'm really glad that I got to work early; it gave me chance to redo my hair before anyone showed up. I will be wishing I think that I wore a heavier sweater. What I don't need right now is a cold. I don't want to take any kind of medications. I know a lot of them are not good to take while pregnant. I want to have a healthy baby; that's why when Louise told me she thought maybe I was pregnant, I quit smoking. I was not a heavy smoker, but still none of it is good for you. It was easy to quit, for it made me sick to the stomach anyways. I have seen women smoke right through their whole pregnancy; it did not seem to bother them at all. As I had thought, by the time I got to work, I was chilled right through. So I got myself a cup of tea and went and sat under one of the hairdryers, not because I was wet. I was just cold. I guess the air is damp today; maybe while I am at the thrift shop, it would be a good time to look for another coat for days like today. Perhaps I should get one that's a little bigger around on me. If I keep growing like this, nothing will fit. I will find myself shopping at the tent and awning place. I have seen a lot of people who should shop there. What is it with people? Are they not able to see how ridiculous they look in what they are wearing? We have seen large people, and I mean, we're talking humongous in something fit for Minnie, and we have seen very small people wearing something so huge on them; maybe three of them could wear it at one time like go figure would you. I was deep in my thoughts when Beth came over and tapped me on the knee.

CHAPTER EIGHT

"**H**EY, GOOD MORNING, CHAR!"
I turned off the dryer so she won't have to continue yelling at me.

"Good morning to you too, Beth."

"Did you get wet on your way down or did you sleep in and had to do your hair when you got here?

"Neither, smart ass! I got cold this morning walking, so I was just warming up."

"So why didn't you call me. I would have picked you up."

"I didn't know first thing that it was this cool out. I was fine until I was halfway here. Guess the farther one walks, the cooler you will get."

"Yeah, and what did you wear?"

"Not enough, that is for sure."

"If it doesn't get any warmer, I will give you a ride home after work."

"Thanks, but I am going to the thrift shop at noon. I will see about a coat along with some clothes that fit."

"I see you are outgrowing your clothes a lot. What is with the pin? Tell me about it.

"The pin is to hold up my pants. Mary works at the thrift shop today, so she was going to put some good things away for me when she got there so I won't miss out on the nice clothes. Today is Two Bags Tuesday for ten bucks."

"I think I will go with you in that case and see what I can find for the boys. They seem to going through a growing spurt and that sounds cheap enough. I will have a look and see what they look like. Maybe I will be lucky. It sounds cheap enough."

"It sounds too good to be true is what it does."

As we all begin our day, no one noticed what time it was until the phone rang, and it was Liz saying she wouldn't be in today. Beth was to sign my time sheet, and we were to cash out. This was totally out of the ordinary for Liz. She never missed a day; she took her business very seriously. We girls always joked about Liz dying standing behind one of her ladies. We also respected her for the fact that her business was a well-respected one here in town and had been for many years. Liz has had her beauty salon for thirty-five years; drunk or not, her business never suffered. Liz also hired very good cosmetologists; if you proved otherwise, she didn't keep you. She gave you a chance to prove yourself, and if you couldn't, end of story. She could be blunt, and sometimes, that hurts, but one thing about Liz, you always knew where you stood with her. She never said to anyone anything she had not already told you. In fact I never heard anything come back to me of what Liz had said about anyone. She was very professional in every sense of the word.

For the most part, she was good to her word, and if she said she would help you, she did. Liz did like to know what was going on in everyone of her girls lives; I suppose that was fair game to a point.

Carrie, Beth, and I stuck pretty close together as we were all around the same age. We had our work stations all beside each other. Elaine, Marie, and Jessie were older ladies, and they stayed to themselves; we were all polite and helpful towards each other; that's how Liz wanted it, but we did not have to hang out together for some of the things us younger ones do would make the older ladies cringe, so a lot of our goings-on stayed between the three of us. They knew I was pregnant but never said anything one way or another, nor did they make me feel ashamed of it either. I felt that they were OK with it; if the truth be known at their age, they probably had daughters who have gone through the same thing, or perhaps they themselves have. It is not the end of the world after all; it is just a baby.

The morning seemed a little off without Liz, but I was confident in what I was doing now; after all, there were still five ladies to help me if I couldn't figure out what to do. Liz is a very good trainer, and she knows her hairdressing skills; there's no mistaking. All is wise and has many tricks up her sleeves to fix many mistakes.

One time, Beth had permed a lady's hair that had been badly bleached at home and her hair turned blue, not a real bright blue but blue enough that it was very noticeable. Beth freaked out more than the client did; not Liz, she just came over calmly and said, "Well, ladies, I will go make us a pot of tea and then we should be able to figure out what to do to fix this." Beth, still in a panic state, started to object.

Liz just said, "Calm down. She is not going to go anywhere until we have fixed her up, make her comfortable, and let her know you have it under control."

Beth done as Liz had told her to. The lady she was doing didn't seem to mind that her hair was blue, she had told Beth.

"It will grow out if nothing will change it."

It was so badly damaged from the bleaching that Beth could not put a color on it, scared it may start to fall out. Liz came back up front with the tea and had us all sit down around the lady and discuss what would be a good safe way to handle this; after all she was concerned as well about her hair falling out. So after some debate and everyone had a suggestion, Liz said to me, "Char, why don't you take the remaining tea and rinse the lady's hair with it!" Seeing how I was the one in training, I did not think anything of it really. I just said, "You want me to pour the tea through her hair?"

"Yes, and just work it through as you would a conditioner for three to five minutes."

"OK," I said, and I did just that. After working it through for a good five minutes, I rinsed it out, and we just looked at it with disbelief. Her hair was a very light brown; the blue was all gone.

"I will be damn" is all Beth's client could say, and that said it all for the rest of us.

It is now noon, and Beth and I are leaving for the thrift shop; the sun is showing through some, but it has not gotten any warmer, or so I felt. I was glad that Beth was giving me a ride. It might only be a couple of blocks, but after this morning, I didn't feel like walking in it again.

When we got there, Mary was so excited to see me.

"Oh deary, I have gotten some very nice uniforms put away for you, and there are some more over here. The girls told me that two nurses came in yesterday and dropped these off. They're just like new just as I said they would be. I put all the white ones aside for you because I know you prefer white for work."

"Thank you, Mary. I would like you to meet my friend Beth."

"Hi, Beth. It is nice to see you again. I see you with Charlene a few times." This has to be the first time I have heard Mary say my name. It sounded so strange coming from her lips.

"Hi, Mary. I want to say thank you for helping Char. Out the way you are, she really needs someone like you in her life."

"I need her too," she says as she slips her arm through mine in a protective way and gives me a side hug.

"I will let you and Mary go ahead and tend to your shopping. I want to go check and see what I can find for the boys. They need everything, so I never know what to buy first, but maybe this way, I can afford to buy a little of all."

"Sure, Beth, and let me know if you need something that's not out here as we wash the clothes as they come in, so we may have it in the back," Mary tells her.

"OK, deary, what else do you need?"

"A coat would be nice today. I got pretty cold walking this morning."

"I guess so. I dressed for it, and I remembered you had left with just a sweater on." I found a lightly lined summer coat in a soft pink, which looked good on me with my blond hair. It was only two dollars anyways, but Mary shoved it into the two bags we had managed to fill, so full we could hardly close them. I would have clothes to do me for a few months if not until after the baby was born.

Beth had also found enough for her two boys to fully fill two bags, so we both left there very happy with ourselves.

"I will need to borrow Mary's iron tonight so I can wear something real nice tomorrow. Liz will be surprised when she sees and hears what I got and for how much."

"I can't believe the uniforms you got, Char. And some you will be able to use after you have the baby; they will still be in style."

"I am glad Mary works there because I would not have known about the Two Bags Tuesday deal."

"Yeah, that was sweet. My boys will be happy."

"I am glad that you came with me. I sort of feel like I have finally done something for you in the way of helping."

"Char, you help me in more ways than you would ever know. The strength that you show gives me the strength that I need sometimes to get by."

"They have that deal every month. I will ask Mary if it is the same Tuesday of the month or if they switch it around. I would like to go more often and check out the baby stuff."

"I am glad I came to I think that would be a great idea, Char. It would save us both a lot of money to shop there. The things I got for the boys were just like new as well. That way, they won't be embarrassed to wear them. I have had people give me their hand-me-downs, and the boys hate it, for most of them are well worn.

"Mary says most of these come from very wealthy families that like to and can afford to spend money on clothes every day if they want to; a lot of them go to the same church as she does, so she knows that the clothes are like new. Some of them have only been worn to church, and there are a lot of children going to that church."

"After seeing what you got today for uniforms, I hope to get some next time as I am in bad need of some as well."

"I will let Mary know. All she needs to know are your colors and what size. Mary will put them aside with your name on them."

"Color doesn't matter with me. Being dark, I can almost wear anything. Size is a little different depending on the style."

"You can always try them on. Nothing saying you have to buy what she picked out."

"That is true, Char." We got back to the shop with time to spare, so I had the muffin that Mary had sent with me. She had wrapped them up so well they were still warm, and they were meal size so I gave one to Beth.

I don't know if it was my imagination or had it really warmed up from the time we had gone to the thrift shop and back to the salon; maybe it was all the excitement over our great buys that warmed us up. I don't really care. I will take the warmth any way I can get it. Once we were back at the shop, everyone wanted to know what and see what we had found. Beth and I had gone through all the good deals we got and then some as we told them what else was there. I was surprised to find out none of the other ladies had ever been there either. I suppose that when you make good money, a thrift shop is the last place you would think about going to shop. I don't think it is advertised all that well; mind you, I have never looked in the paper for it. I just heard of it through Mary. I don't really know who at all would shop there. I suppose people who really are thrifty and then it wouldn't matter to them

that the clothes have been worn a bit. Beth and I had told them
that we were going to go back, and with Mary working there, I
would know when a new bunch of clothes came in and how I
was going to keep check on baby clothes. Babies grow out of their
clothes so fast everything is still like new. Maybe I will be able to
get a crib from there if I let Mary know to watch for one, anything
else in the line of furniture as well. I will keep my fingers crossed;
it would be nice to get all I need at a steal of a price. I am glad
people don't just throw stuff out anymore.

There are too many people that don't have anyone to hand
things down to or storage room to keep it for how many years it
may take before someone needs them.

I know I would like to keep some of the baby's things to use
again and to hand down perhaps to my children when they start
having their own families. I think it would have been neat if I
could have been putting my baby to sleep in the same crib that
I had slept in. Even though our crib would have been very well
used with it going through the last six babies for sure. I think
they used bassinets a lot more when we were babies, perhaps
even more so with my older brothers and sisters. I am not sure
why, other than maybe room was a factor; only people living in
huge houses would have had what they called a nursery. It would
have all the furniture a baby would have needed or the nannies
needed to take care of those babies. I suppose a baby's room today
is also called a nursery. So I guess when my baby's room is done,
I will have a nursery. I like the sound of that. I also hope to have
a rocking chair in there. I remember when I would babysit, it was
so nice to sit in the rocking chair and hold the tiny sweet-smelling
baby close, and you would be gliding slowly back and forth. You
could also fall fast asleep; it was so relaxing. I was told that the
motion of moving back and forth was to a baby like when they
were in the womb, so they found that very comforting. Even as
we get older, in fact I don't think it matters how old we are, to sit
in a rocking chair, we all find comfort in that motion. So perhaps

the baby in us never leaves; it is just put on the back burner until something like a rocking chair brings it back to the surface. When you think about it, rocking is the motion most people used to comfort anyone that's hurt or sick, young or old. I have also seen it done by people that are in distress; they will sit with their knees up to their chest with their arms wrapped around them and rock back and forth to comfort themselves.

So this tells me that a rocking chair is an absolute must as far as a piece of furniture that is needed for the nursery. I must remember to tell Mary about it so she also can keep her ears and eyes open for one. I bet she would love to use one when she babysits.

The day was winding down, and we had all been pretty steady today. The chatter about the thrift shop as well as the rocking chair and anything that had to do about the baby was talked about. Even Elaine, Jessie, and Marie were in on the conversation. I think it was because Liz was not here, and they were able to relax, and we made them feel like they were part of us as a group, and I was interested in anything they might have to say, so we had laughed a lot when they had told us of some of the happening that went on when they were young mothers, and to think they had survived and so did their children. I also heard from some of them how little they had to work with when they had babies. One client said she had to use her dresser drawer to put her baby to sleep in for the first five months until her father-in-law had made her a crib. She said that crib had gone on to be used by other family members as well as neighbors. She had finally put it in their hometown museum when they were looking for items, for all the regulations now concerning the proper spacing in the bars of the crib made their crib unsafe to use.

This day had become a very eventful day in learning, and I know now that no matter what, I will do just fine with my baby.

I already have more than some of these ladies had all the time their children were young. For some of them, it has only been in the last ten years that they even had running water and indoor plumbing. I feel like once I get moved into Mary's basement suite, I will be in a mansion all of my own. I just can't wait.

I think I will be forever grateful to Mary, and I won't dwell on the things I don't have, but I will give all the love I have, and that over all will see us through. We will be warm, clean, and safe, and I know we won't be going hungry with Mary around as well as Louise, and if Jacob moves in, I really shouldn't have a worry in the world, and as soon as I can go back to work, things can only get better. Right!

Beth and I start to pack up the clothes we had bought; we were just getting the last of it tied up when Liz came through the door. Beth and I just looked at each other, for she looked like hell; we have never saw Liz look this way.

"Hi, Liz." we say in unison.

"Hi, girls, you had that much garbage today?"

"No, this is what we bought at the thrift shop," I tell her as Beth takes the first bag out to her car.

"I needed uniforms and clothes that fit, and Mary told me about this sale they were having, so Beth and I went on our lunch break. I got some beautiful uniforms for cheap."

"Well, I sure hope they're not going to make you look any cheaper than your pregnancy is already doing," Liz said just as Jessie and Elaine came around the corner. I must have looked pretty stupid standing there with my mouth hanging open. I could not believe she had just said that to me.

"Liz!!" Elaine snapped at her. "That is totally not called for."

"Well, it is true. When you are a single girl and pregnant, that is exactly what people will think of her."

"That is so not true. Don't you think the man had anything to do with it? Why is it always the girl's fault? You know what it is a person like yourself that always hangs the girl. Is it because they're easier targets, that no one can see past the point that it took two? No one ever says how cheap the guy is. When you think about it, they are the cheap ones. Most of them never fess up to the fact and help out with the baby. They have had their way now, they move on to another. They haven't learned a damn thing because the next girl he is involved with ends up pregnant. But once again, the girl is titled cheap right, Liz, but he has just done that to the girl prior to this one and that's OK with you. I think you owe Char an apology for what you just said. That was a terrible thing to say to her."

"An apology. Did she apologize to me for what she has gone and done after all the time I have spent on her?"

"What the hell does she have to apologize for? She is having a baby not quitting on you. You talk like all her time has been wasted, and it hasn't been. There are a lot of girls who have had baby's partway through their training, and they just pick up where they left off when they come back, and you know it as well as I do. We have seen it many times."

"I am not having a girl like that working for me."

"Now what? You're firing Char because she is single and having a baby? Liz have you been drinking before you came down here 'cause you're talking totally stupid. Or have you just lost your mind. You don't have grounds to fire Char. And she could take you to the labor board. If you do fire her, I hope she does, and another thing, Liz, is if you do, then I also quit!"

"After all these years, Elaine, you're going to quit on me."

"I sure the hell am. If this is how you're going to treat someone who has shown you nothing but respect and has done everything you have asked her to. She is also very good at what she does. You know that Char is a natural at hairdressing? Why would you throw that away?"

"Elaine, please do not quit because of me. I will quit so there won't have to be problems between anyone. Now that I know how Liz really feels, I don't want to stay and work for her. I would have trouble coming in every day knowing that. I would not be comfortable here anymore. So I will clear out my station now.

Thank you for saying what you said and for backing me. You don't have to quit because of me."

"Char, it is not because of you. It is because of the way Liz is treating you. I don't want to work for someone who has lost all passion for life. You need people to back you, not condemn you. I haven't said anything to you, and perhaps I should have. I'm proud of the way you are willing to take this on your own and deal with it. I'm glad you are keeping the baby. I also know that any shop in town would be lucky to have you on their staff. I will give you my phone number, and you can use me as a reference, OK? First check out where I am, and maybe they will hire you as well. I will be up and working in two weeks. I will be putting a write-up in the paper so my clients will know where I have moved to."

"Thank you, Elaine." I was getting my things out of my station when Beth came in. She heard Liz and Elaine still having their discussion, so she just slipped by them and came to where I was.

"Char, what the hell is going on and what are you doing?"

"I'm packing up my station, what does it look like?"

"I can see that, but why?"

"I quit as of now."

"Why? What did Liz say?"

"She was not very nice, and she was going to fire me anyways."

"You are kidding, right?" I just shook my head. "What about Elaine? I heard her tell Liz she was done at the end of the week?"

"She stood up for me and told Liz that if that's how she was going to treat me, then she was also done."

"After all these years of working for Liz, now she quits. It must have been some nasty."

"Yes, it was. But I sure don't want Elaine to quit because of me."

"I think I will quit as well."

"Are you crazy? You have two little ones to think about where Elaine hasn't, and she is going to another shop. I am supposed to find her, and hopefully, I can work with her. This has nothing to do with you. Elaine got into it with Liz, and she wasn't backing down, so Elaine took a stand for what she thinks is right."

"You do know Liz had been drinking before she came to the shop. She probably doesn't mean a word of what she said."

"People say what they really mean when drinking because they don't have the balls otherwise. It does surprise me that Liz would wait until she had been drinking. She always says whatever is on her mind whether it was good or bad. I had thought she was over the fact that I'm pregnant but guess not."

"What are you going to do? No one will want to hire you until you have had the baby."

"I will take a couple of days and think about it. Maybe I will apply for EI."

"There is always that. That is true."

"I could help Mary get the basement suite done now that I will have lots of time on my hands. So maybe this came at the right time. I wasn't going to be able to go to school to finish my hairdressing this term anyways, so I will wait and carry on after the baby."

"Char, you're taking this damn good, too good in fact, are you all right?"

"Yeah, I'm fine. I'm not going to let people put me down and make me feel bad about myself. I am having a baby. End of story. It is not the end of the world by any means. I think if Liz wasn't a drunk, it would be harder for me to take, but right now, I will take that into consideration and let it be. I guess in some ways I was expecting something to come of it. She never did get to say too much as we had all walked out on her when the subject came up after I came back from Calgary. If you remember, I took the quick exit with you and Carrie that night."

"What do you think Mary is going to say?"

"She'll be glad I did what I did. Mary had already told me to quit if Liz got nasty. She said it wasn't healthy working in these conditions."

"Mary is right about that. Now come on, Char. I will help you get loaded and take you home."

"Thank you." Beth and I loaded up the car, and I said good-bye to Elaine, and she had given me her number. Some of the girls did not know what to say. They had not heard Liz, so they did not know what was really happening, so they just watched.

We all took turns at hugging and saying good-bye, and tears were shed by all as we had become a family. I won't say this was easy because it was one of the hardest things I've had to do. I wasn't going to show Liz how much she had hurt me or how belittled she made me feel. I was going to leave there with my head held high, and there was no way I was begging her for my job. I would still have my pride, for I never shot off my mouth, so I wouldn't have anything to be sorry for, not like Liz. I guess this is all part of growing up, and I do want to be a responsible parent.

The drive home was quiet although Beth had said she thought she would still quit. I can only hope that I had talked her out of it.

CHAPTER NINE

Mary was not home when we got there, so we had plenty of time to unload the car. Beth was still pretty upset at Liz, so I didn't want to show my true feelings, for I wanted her to let it go. She couldn't afford to be without a job no matter how sort of time it might be.

"Beth, I will make us a coffee."

"Please, Char. I don't know about you, but I could really use one."

"Just give me a minute to go down and get some water from Mary's. You know I only have instant right now."

"That's fine with me, Char."

"I will be right back." I was feeling pretty shitty for what I had caused at the shop today, and Beth was taking it pretty hard, so I had to think of something to make her feel like what happened was fine with me. Even if it wasn't, I wasn't going to show it now. I had to be strong; I would have plenty of time later for the tears to fall that were sitting right on the edge. I was just leaving when Mary came home. I knew I had to keep moving or she would know something was wrong not that she wasn't going to know in time, but with Beth waiting for me, I just didn't want to take the time right now to talk.

"Hi, deary, coming for tea?"

"Later, Mary, I have company right now."

"All right, I will be waiting."

"Sure thing, talk to you later." When I put the kettle on and turned around, I could see Beth had been crying.

"Beth, what's wrong?"

"I can't believe Liz is doing this to you, and you're going to be having a baby on your own. What the hell is she thinking?"

"Beth, I was going to have to take time off anyways, so what is the difference if I do it now or later?"

"Later, Char. You would have taken the time for the right reason not just up and quit on Liz, so why couldn't she just wait it out a couple of more months or so?"

"To Liz, I was cheapening the shop and going against what she wanted me to do. She made that quite plain for me to understand."

"You're kidding, right?"

"No, I am not. When I told her about the cheap deals we got at the thrift shop, she said, quote, 'I hope they won't make you look cheaper than you already do being pregnant and not married.'"

"That's what she said to you?"

"What did you say to that?"

"I didn't have time, for that's when Elaine got involved, and she put Liz in her place, and I couldn't get a word in. But then Liz had stunned me so bad by saying that. That I must have been standing there with my mouth open because that's when Elaine started in on her. I was thinking at the time she's been drinking and I was going to let it go. Then when Elaine told her she owed me an apology, there was no way that was about to happen. As far as she is concerned, I screwed up and wasted all the time she spent on me. Elaine tried to tell her that it was not wasted, but she wouldn't listen."

"Well, I am telling you right now, if she says anything downing you to me or any of the other girls, I will be out of there so fast. I think I will go around to the other shops and check them out just in case to see what they might have to offer."

"That is probably a good idea, Beth. Just cover your ass, that's for sure. I don't want you to think anymore of it because now it just gives me more time to get the basement done, which I would love to get finished so I can get moved. I have been saving money to go to school, so I know I can feed myself for a while and not having to pay rent is a blessing. So please just forget about Liz."

"You're a better person than I am, Char."

"No, I am not. But there is no use to worry about something I can't change. Like my mother would say, I made by bed, now I must lie in it. I will be OK."

"Well, you know where to find me or call if you need help or anything. Just because you're not working, it doesn't mean you can't come see us and stay in touch."

"I will. But I will wait a while until Liz gets over her madness."

"That's probably wise. I must get going now. Thank you for the coffee, and you will see me soon."

"Thank you for everything, Beth." With that she was gone, so I just sort of sat there feeling numb and going over in my head of the things that went on today, trying to figure out if there would have been some other way to deal with Liz so I still could have worked for a while. Then on the other hand, once I knew what Liz really thought of me, did I really want to stay and work for her? I wouldn't hold the same respect for her that I once had. To tell you the truth, I don't think right now I could look her in the face. She made me feel very humiliated.

I am a fighter, and I will get back on track. Also I will get my license without her help. I already have a nice place to live, and I have good people behind me. Liz is just a stepping stone on my way to the top. I know I will do well and be able to provide very well for my baby, and I'll just wait and see. I thought I'd best pull myself together and go down and see Mary. Let her know what has happen now. I don't think she will mind that I am not working. So I gathered up our coffee cups so I can take them down to wash. It will be so nice when I can just walk over and put them into my sink.

When I got to Mary's door and knocked, I didn't see her. This was strange as she always sits at the kitchen table and reads her Bible. I knew she was in and yet I couldn't hear anything, so I opened the door slowly and just slipped in to see where she was. I saw her sitting in the big chair sound asleep. At least, I hoped she was sleeping, so I walked over a little closer to take a better look. I couldn't tell if she was breathing or not, and I started to get a little unnerved. My heart was pounding a little faster than it should be with me anticipating what might be. Then she moved her hand and had wiped at her nose like maybe there was a fly on it. I had let out a big breath that I did not realize I was holding. I even felt a little light-headed. Turning around, I had decided she must be tired for her to be sleeping at this time of the evening. So I just let her be. After all, I will be home tomorrow. I will have lots of time to catch her up on the news.

Getting back upstairs, I looked around and thought, *Gee what should I do now?* Maybe I will sort out the clothes I bought so I don't have to dig through the bags to get something to wear. I will put the uniforms that I won't be wearing right now into a separate bag and mark it. I sure hope I can use these later, or would it be wise maybe to take them back to the thrift shop. I know when I go back to work I won't be able to afford uniforms that look like these. I think I will just put them away for now. I finished sorting out my clothes and all of them that were too small for me. I also packed away for after the baby is born. Some I most likely won't be able to wear. I guess that depends on how much weight I'll lose after. Oh well, it is only one more bag to worry about. Let's face it. I don't have anything.

I'm sure I have more hairdressing book than clothes. But then I do enjoy reading all about the new styles and how to accomplish it. They show step-by-step, so some of them are not that hard to do. I only wished I had someone to practice on.

Mary! Yes, she has shoulder-length hair and what a woman doesn't like to be pampered. I could do a lot of different styles on

Mary and perms as well; after all, she is giving me free rent, so I should be able to do her hair. "What do you think?" I asked myself as I looked into my hand mirror. Now this is spooky. I am talking to myself in a mirror. How crazy one can get by living up in an attic. But don't you count on me talking to you too long because I am moving out shortly; then you will have to find another lost soul to deal with, but for now, you will do just fine.

I finally got tired enough I fell asleep. My dreams were all over the place; the one that stands out in my mind is of me moving from the attic to a castle. It was beautiful, and my baby had everything. His room was done up so that it seemed like the sun shined in there all the time. The ceiling was in blue to represent the sky, and the walls were in yellow for the sun. The top of the walls and onto the ceiling had big white fluffy clouds. Off to the south, there were big windows, so it let in all the sun and warmth that a baby needed. He had a wooden rocking horse that looked so real sitting off into the corner just waiting for him to get old enough to use it. There looks to be everything imaginable that you might want to buy for a baby. I could see my baby in the crib, which was of antique white as well as the dressing table and the dresser. As well as a beautiful rocking chair that had a baby afghan hung over the back, which looked to be so soft. All the linen was white with tiny blue trim. The room gleamed for the white tile floor was polished to a sparkle like none I have ever seen. I remember feeling in such awe and totally at ease with it all.

But then for some reason, everything turned black and then we were back to a place that was worse than the attic, and my mother was there laughing at me all that time in the background. I could never see her, but I could hear her. She was like a witch that was just in hiding and was always just around a corner. I could never catch up to her. I would call out to her, and she would never answer, just laughs. Sometimes she would be on the right, and the next time, she would be on the left; there were times when she seemed to be a far distance from me so I would run to where I thought she was, but she was never there. Then just before I woke up, I heard her say, "Remember, you made your bed, now you must lie in it."

I was sweating so bad that I had gotten the chills, so I snuggled down under my blankets and tried to get warm while I tried to figure out what my dream was telling me. A lot of my dreams come true, some good some bad. Ones like these always have a hidden meaning or a warning, so now it is something I have to think about and figure out and just what it is that it's telling me.

I wonder if I am having a boy. Could it all have been because of that? Or was it because I am moving into the basement suite, and to me, it is a castle compared to where I live at this moment. Everything else was just to throw me off and maybe nothing bad will come out off it.

Just then I heard.

"Deary, are you in there?" and a faint tapping came on the door.

"Deary, are you all right? You slept in. You're going to be late for work."

"Yes, Mary, I am here. I'm not working today. If you put on coffee, I'll be down as soon as I get dressed."

"Oh, all right, see you in a few." I could hear her going quietly down the stairs; she moved slowly, but she wanted to be sure of her steps at this age. It doesn't take much for older people to break bones. Most of them take a fall and never get back to being themselves; some of them even die. So I am glad that Mary is cautious.

I hurried and got dressed and wiped my face with the baby wipes I keep on hand for the times I don't get to Mary's bathroom. I take a few deep breaths and just tell myself relax; everything is great.

"Knock, knock," I say as I open up Mary's door and slip inside.

"Come in, deary. I have coffee and fresh muffins that I know you like. They are healthy ones, so come sit and tell me why you're not working today."

"I came down last night like I said I would, but you were sleeping in your chair, so I just left you. I figured you had to be tired to be sleeping at that time."

"I am sorry about that. I don't know if it's just the good weather or what, but I have been very tired lately."

"Maybe you're pregnant."

Laughing, she says, "Wouldn't that be something? Now why are you not working? Are you not feeling well?"

"I feel great, Mary, but I guess you could say Liz fired me yesterday." And with that came a crash to the floor because Mary was so shocked she dropped her plate with the muffins on it.

"Damn it, sorry for that, deary. Why did she do that?"

"I understand that she thought I would cheapen the shop being pregnant and not married."

"You're joking, right?"

"Afraid not."

"What did you tell her?"

"I didn't get a chance because of Elaine. I think you have met her."

"Yes, I did. What about her?"

"She tied into Liz when she heard what Liz had said to me, and it was sort of taken from my hands. But not only did Liz fire me. Elaine quit on her because of how she was treating me."

"After all those years, Elaine has been there a long time."

"She has never witnessed Liz treat anyone like this, so she was taking a stand for what she believes in. She is not worried about work, and she said when I am ready to go back to work, I am to go find her. She gave me her phone number so I can keep in touch. Elaine said she would try and get me in where she is working."

"That is too bad, but I am glad someone stood up for you."

"Beth was going to quit too, but I think I talked her out of it for now, anyways."

"I wonder why Liz waited all this time to fire you. Why not right away?"

"I think it is because we were all leaving together and not staying behind to drink with her. So she never had her chance, and yesterday, she stayed home until the end of the day, and when she came in, we could surely tell she had been drinking, so I guess she had had enough to drink to give her the courage that she needed to say what she really meant. She was not nice about it either."

"I am sorry, deary. But like I told you at the beginning, quit if she got nasty. You can always go back later. This is not the end of the world, it is just a baby."

"Thank you, Mary. You're right. I thought about how it would make me feel when and if this was to happen. You know at first she sat me back, and I was a little numb, but this morning, I feel fine. I know I will be fine without her. I am ready to move on now. Thanks to your caring and your support."

"Well, deary, this isn't all that bad because now we can get you moved before you get any bigger and shouldn't be doing what we are going to do. Our little one here," she says as she rubs my tummy "wants his room finished before he comes into this world."

"Mary, why did you refer to the baby as a boy?"

"I don't rightly know. It just felt good, I guess."

"That is strange because last night I dreamt it was a boy."

"They say most mothers know before the baby is born what they are having, if you are really tuned into yourself. I knew all mine were boys, and each time I prayed to have a girl and tried to talk myself into believing that I was carrying a girl. It was never a surprise when the doctor would say, "You have a boy." My heart would sink somewhat for a while until they would clean him up and put him into my arms, then the disappointment would go away. I don't know how some mothers right from the beginning take a dislike to their baby. Whether it's a boy or girl, they are so small and sweet, how can you turn on someone so innocent and someone who you created, so it is part of you. One would have had to lose their mind."

"I feel the same way. But I know it has happened. The one lady I know went into the baby depression in the hospital right after she had her son. She went to the mental hospital while her husband took their son home. That was a few years ago, and she is still there in that hospital. Her husband has been waiting for her all this time and raising their son. He finally took him once to see her when the doctors thought it would be OK. She would have nothing to do with him. She wouldn't even look at him. Her husband had told us that his son was very upset and wanted to know why his mommy didn't like him. Guess he had nightmares for sometime after. I heard he did get a divorce and remarried to a lady who loved his little boy. They said it didn't take long for his son to call her mommy. They have all been very happy since, and he never goes to see his ex-wife anymore."

"That is so sad, yet it turned out great for the little boy and his dad."

"Yeah, it sure did."

"But now on a happier note, deary, let's go get some wallpaper today. I know it's not ready for that yet, but now that you're not working, it won't take long."

"I am up for that. I had a dream about what I would like to see the room look like."

"Then let's see how close we can do it to that. You just have to tell me what you want. Maybe draw it out a little if you think that would help."

"One thing the ceiling was a nice sky blue, and the walls were sunshine yellow. But it also had big windows. There were large white fluffy clouds that were wrapped on to both the walls and the ceiling it was beautiful.

"The baby's room downstairs is not that big, so we will have to use the soft and pale colors. I am sure we can make it just as nice as the one in the dream. If nothing else, it will give us a challenge."

"I think, deary, that you will make it look just like a magazine. We could look through the Sears catalogue for more ideas. They always show their furniture set up in rooms done up."

"That might be a good idea, Mary. Let's go to the store first and look at the papers. You want to right after we finish our muffins?"

"I am calling us a cab, deary. That way we have more time downtown instead of all the walking to get there."

"All right, Mary." She still looked a little tired and that's probably why she wants to call a cab. That's OK; perhaps the heat is getting to her because of her age. I know I wasn't going to make a fuss about walking. It seems to me it gets a little heavier for me with each passing day.

I am told that most women gain only twenty-five pounds. I feel like I have passed that goal already. I will find out in two weeks when I go back to see my doctor. At my last checkup, I had gained ten pounds; the doctor tells me I am retaining a lot of fluid and so when I have the baby, my weight gain will disappear fast. That will be nice if he is right. I don't want a lot of trouble losing it after. I have seen ladies that never lose the extra weight they gained, and they go on and have another baby. They get totally out of shape with no hope of returning to their normal size. I guess I will worry about that at that time.

Mary and I headed out to the stores around ten. We had gone through three flooring places that also carried wallpaper, and when we got to the third one, we hit the jackpot; they always say, "Leave the best for the last," and it seemed like we had. They had such a large variety it was almost hard to pick other than the picture of the room from my dream was still so vivid in my mind. I couldn't shake it, so I thought I would go with it.

There were clouds that you peeled and stuck to wherever you wanted, and there was also a ceiling light shade that looked like a big cloud, so we bought it as well. For the one wall, we bought a wallpaper that Mary was talking about before that had clouds and rainbows that were of all the baby pastel colors. I was happy, and I could see in my mind how the room would look. I could see the furniture set in it as well. I was lucky because I do have that gift of looking at a house or room and redoing it in my mind right down to the smallest details.

"All we need now, Mary, is our blue paint. Seeing how you bought the yellow and mint green."

"Oh! Deary, you don't need to use the green if it doesn't go with what you have in mind."

"Mary, I want to do all the trim in mint green, and I would lighten the drapes to be white eyelet and mint green trim. I will have to get someone to crochet the trim around the drapes. I know you can buy baby wool that is mint green with white going through it."

"Yes, I have seen that. I also crochet, so can I do the drapes for you?"

"If you want to, Mary. I would be honored if you had the time?"

"I will make time, and yes, I would love to make them for you."

"Then that job is yours!" Mary gets this big grin on her face, and I am sure she must have stood up two inches taller. She was so proud of the fact that she was making the drapes as if she hadn't done enough already.

We get our blue paint along with everything else, so we didn't have to make another trip downtown halfway through our work. Mary wouldn't let me pay for any of it. So I thought I would take her for lunch. When we leave the flooring store, I had asked the clerk if we could pick it all up when we were done at the time we would call a cab. The clerk had said there was no problem with that.

"Deary, where else do you want to go?"

"I am taking you to lunch before we go home. After all, we have to eat sometime today. When we get home, we can just go straight to work, and I'm buying."

"Deary, you don't have to do that!"

"I know, but I'm going to because I want to and can. You're always feeding me, and until I have a nice place to cook for you, this will have to do us. Besides this little café has very good food. The girls and I from work ordered from here now and again."

"All right then, sounds like a great idea." So we did just that; we had both ordered an egg salad sandwich with a few fries and large milk. Once we were done, we went back to the flooring place and picked up our supplies and caught a cab back home.

We got right into it, and Mary said she wanted to lie down for half an hour, then she would be right down. I saw no problem with that as I think older people do nap after lunch, and we did have a bigger lunch than she is used to. I also hadn't been around during the day, so I didn't question what kind of routine she had that she would follow. I had told her to come down when she got up as I would still be downstairs. I did not mind being on my own and just doing what I had to do.

First I looked around in her small storage room that she had, just off on the left hand side of the door going downstairs. I knew I need a hammer and screwdriver set and some sandpaper. I found all of what I was looking for and was able to go right to work. I was feeling very good and full of energy.

I started by taking off all the baseboards and window frames. Some of the wood was fairly old and so it cracked a little under pressure. But I knew I could fix them as I had seen my dad do it many times. I would keep the sawdust that would come off of them when I sanded them, and I would mix it with either white glue or wood glue. Then you put it into the cracks let it set then lightly sand them again before you paint.

Some of the baseboards were almost longer than the room that I had to work in. The window frames I kept in one room and the baseboards in another. I also had marked on the back of them which window and doors they came off of so it would be easy to reinstate them. With these older houses, no one room would measure the same around the doors or windows so this will knock out all the guess work. I had also seen my dad do that as they never had new homes to live in. Guess, watching my dad was going to come in handy now. I never gave it much thought at the time Mary was talking to be about doing the work down here, and another good thing is it is not heavy work. While I was taking off the baseboards, I noticed there were some holes in the wall that should be fixed before they're painted. So I went back to Mary's storeroom and found some dry wall mud. I knew I could do that too, and I was having a blast. I figured I might as well do the mudding before I sanded the trims because it takes the mud some time to dry. Mary must have had to do some of this work seeing how all these supplies were here. There were only seven holes most of them were small, but big enough you wouldn't want to just paint over them. It would make it look tacky. There was nothing to do in the room where I wanted to put the baby, so it will be easy to get that room all done. The worst room is the kitchen; it looks like it was damaged from the back of the chair. So I got to thinking I would like to put what is called a bumper board around at just that height and have it covered with material that matches the valance that would be over the antique lace on the kitchen windows. Perhaps I could have a tablecloth out of antique lace as well with a bouquet of roses sitting in the middle. It would be so inviting to want to come sit at this table.

I would like the valance and the bumper board to be done in an antique tapestry of a dark rose and dark green. Perhaps I could get chair cushions made of the same material. This will all come in time.

Mary finally came downstairs; she looked a little flushed in the face. I guess some of us get a little heated when we're sleeping.

"Hi, deary. Sorry, I napped longer than I thought I would."

"That's OK, Mary. It wasn't that hard to get the trim off. I hope you don't mind I went and found a hammer, sandpaper, screwdriver, and some dry wall mud."

"Not at all. I was going to tell you. But it slipped my mind, must be my age."

"With these supplies on hand, you must have had to do some repairs already?"

"With four boys, my husband was always fixing one wall or another. The boys would get in to a wrestling match, and something always got put through the wall. I have a couple small ones upstairs I should fix. Since my husband passed away, no one could take the time to fix what they damaged. There haven't been many wrestling matches since my husband passed away. I think the boys used to try and show their father who was the toughest."

"Well, you know, Mary. I can look at them and see if I can fix them."

"You can do that, deary?"

"Oh yes, and I enjoy work like that. I used to spend lots of time with my dad outside. He has shown me how to fix a lot of things. So if you don't mind, I will look at them."

"Not at all, if you think you can do it and not hurt yourself."

"Come look over here where the table was. There were some pretty nasty ones here."

"There were so. I was going to get them fixed before we painted."

"Tada."

"Wow, that looks like new."

"I just need to lightly sand it when it's good and dry, and we can paint. The walls in here were the only ones I got washed. The two bedrooms and the bathroom won't take long. I just want to sand the trim now that the walls are mudded so I can vacuum up the dust. Then I would like to put a coat of paint on them, and while they're drying, I will wash the walls."

"I will get us the pails we need, deary. I took them upstairs. Don't ask why. I just had one of those moments."

When Mary got back, we got right to it, and within an hour, we had the walls washed. I was excited about that because now I can start to paint. I will start with the ceiling. I want to feather the blue down into the wall about three to four inches, and I don't want a straight line. The clouds I will put up there will come down on to the wall as well.

"Mary, could I get an old cloth from you please?"

"Sure, did you spill somewhere?"

"No, I want to use it to blend the blue into the wall. If you take it and crumble it up then work the paint where you want it, it will look light and fluffy around where the clouds are going."

"All right. I will go get you some. I have them in the storeroom as well."

"Here you go, deary. I never saw that done! Have you done it before?"

"Yes, Mary. I have for a friend's dining room. We were mixing two shades of rose. Edith, the lady I was doing it for, did not want a solid line. I had seen this done on one of those home shows on TV. She had all old furniture that was of red wood, so the rose colors she had picked looked beautiful when I was done. She had put up three layers of ivory lace drapes it looked like it was a page out of a magazine.

"Then I have all the faith in you that you will do the same here."

"So I will start with the ceiling."

"I am going to go make supper. Sam should be home soon."

"That's fine as long as you don't mind me down here alone."

"Not at all! It is your home now. Would you like to eat with us, deary?"

"No, thanks, Mary. I will just make a bowl of soup later. I am not hungry yet." I did not want to eat with Sam or even be in the same room with him. He makes me very uncomfortable. He looks at me as if some day he'll have his way with me, and that will never happen. When Sam looks at me, he makes me feel dirty.

Mary left, and I got right into doing the ceiling, and while I was painting, I am thinking of the steps ahead and how I want this to look when I am all done. The blue went on smooth as silk; the shade was such a baby blue, and it had such a calming effect about it. That, I felt it, would help calm a crying baby easily. I could see me sitting in the rocking chair by the window and rocking the baby gently back and forth until he was sound asleep.

I finished up the ceiling and had my three-inch boarder worked into the wall. It looked great even if I have to say so myself.

I had most of the trim filled and ready for sanding when Mary came back down.

"Do you know it is eight thirty, deary?"

"No way! I guess I just got so involved that I didn't even think of the time."

"It sure is, and you never went up and ate anything, so I brought you down a sandwich. It is not much, but you have to eat."

"You didn't have to do that, Mary. I would have eaten later."

"This is later. Here sit down and eat now!"

"All right, thank you again."

"You sure got a lot done."

"Go and take a look at the baby's room and tell me what you think." I could hear her gasp as she said, "Nice, very nice. I understand now what you were saying about working the extra three four inches into the wall. It sure does make a difference."

"Once I put on the clouds tomorrow, it will all come together. Then the light shade as well."

"Are you going to be doing much more tonight?"

"No. I just want to get the rest of these cracks filled on the trim so tomorrow we can paint them."

"How many you have left? Do you need me to help?

"This is the last one, thank you. They aren't hard to do. The cracks are not that big nor were there many."

"Good, because you have put in a long day."

"My shoulders are starting to tell me that as well. I am glad these baseboards didn't have a lot of groves in them. They would have been harder to sand. My arms are tired." As I worked on the last baseboard, Mary got busy and tidied up. I could see she wasn't moving as fast as she usually does. She always moved with such efficiency; you knew she wasn't one to waste time. I suppose that came with being a mother of four boys. That in itself would keep one on a very steady pace. The boys all seem to be about two years apart, which I think is quite normal when you're having a big family. I know my brother and sisters were all two years apart except us last three; we were only a year apart. Maybe that had something to do with my little brother not being a healthy baby, I am not sure. I also remember the older kids talking about when my little sister was born, how our mother had to wrap her face to shape it. She looked normal in the end.

"I am finished now, Mary. We can go up now. If you don't mind, I would like to have a bath. Perhaps that would take the pain out of my shoulders."

"That's fine with me, deary. Is that the only place you have pain?"

"Yes, Mary. I feel good everywhere else."

"Maybe you should take a break tomorrow. You don't want to overdo things."

"I would like to finish the baby's room tomorrow. Or at least put up the paper."

"Let's see how you feel in the morning. Now come have your bath, and I will make you a nice cup of mint tea."

"Let's go!" Mary is like a mother hen watching over her chicks. But I can't say I mind it because I don't. On the contrary, I really like the fact that someone really cares and is looking out for me. Mary makes me feel like I belong somewhere. I think she would miss me if I were to move, and perhaps, someday that could be a problem. But for now, she can be the mother hen, that's fine with me. Besides that, I can keep an eye on her as well. I don't think she is feeling well, and tomorrow, if she is like today, I will ask her if she has gone to a doctor; perhaps her blood is a little low. I've heard that can cause people to be tired and feeling worn out.

Sitting back in the bathtub felt fantastic; getting my shoulders down underwater was a little tricky. I could not get too far down in the tub; there just wasn't room, but a little was better than nothing. Lying there, thinking about what I wanted to get done the next day was getting me excited almost to the point where I wanted to go back downstairs and carry on. The bath was just giving me the boost I was needing; after all, what did I have to worry about what time I went to bed or got up. I'm not punching a clock right now, so who says nine o'clock is bedtime or seven is time to get up. Guess, it is because my body has been used to those times it could be hard to change them. I got dried off and put on my house coat and went out to have my tea with Mary.

Mary was sitting in her chair, and once again, she had fallen asleep. Boy, she was getting good at this, or she found me really boring company. So I slipped out to the kitchen, and I could see she had made the tea, so I thought what the hell, why waste it, so I poured a cup and took it upstairs with me. The tea had tasted so good I had wished I'd brought the pot. Besides I don't think Mary will be drinking it tonight. But then how long will she sleep and mint tea is good cold as well as hot. I lie down, and I guess I was more tired than I thought as I had fallen asleep pretty fast.

The sun was full and bright, shining in my window come morning. I could hear the birds singing, and that is such a fabulous sound to wake up to; they always sound so cherry like nothing is ever wrong in their world. Perhaps we should all get up singing and chirping in the morning; things might look brighter on those not-so-bright days.

I got up and dressed in record time as I was excited to go downstairs and get going on the baby's room again. Today, I will take down my tea and my coffee along with a couple of cups. I don't want to use what is down there until I wash them really good; everyone has always complained that I used too hot dishwater they can never put their hands into it. Some of this is so that no one should have to dry them; the less they're handled, the less chance of having anyone's germs on them. I have a very weak stomach, so it doesn't take much to turn me off of something. Maybe today, I will take the time and wash up some dishes down there. I know the stove is disgusting as well as the fridge, but what did we expect to find; we knew that there were two men who lived there.

The trim will need only light sanding before I can paint them, and while I put up the wallpaper and light shade, they should be dry enough to put them up. I don't want the thick paint look. I want more of an old worn stain look, so I won't be brushing it on too thick; it is what I call dry brushing. It makes things appear to be warm and used yet beautiful to look at. I am a sucker for old things. I also think they all have a good story behind them if you take the time to find out. Where did it come from? How did it end up here? Most items have been through many families. People will pick them up at secondhand stores or sales and use them for a while, then take them back to the secondhand store. The items are still in good shape, but they just get tired of them and want something new.

I passed by Mary's door and could see into the kitchen but did not see her, so I just carried on my way downstairs and went right to work. It was only nine o'clock, so I would get a good day's work in today. Starting with the sanding of the trim, which only took me about one hour, it took about the same to do the dry brushing, and I really liked the way the trim was looking. With it being real wood, it had discolored some, and in some of the smaller cracks that I didn't worry about, the paint would be a little darker so it had the stain look and not the painted look. I hope to find an old white crib, and I could do the same to it along with the rocking chair. So I must stop at the secondhand store and check it out and let them know what I am looking for. Now that I have to wait for them to dry, I think I will work on the wallpaper.

Digging out the kettle, I decided I would wash it out and put on some water as I hadn't had my morning coffee yet. This kettle looks like it has seen its better days, but once it is cleaned up, it might surprise me. That is exactly what happened by the time I got done with it. I could see myself in it. The only thing was the inside was so built up with hard water deposits that it will take some time to heat the water but then I have lots of time now, don't I?

I was just going into the baby's room when I heard a knock on the door. Thinking it was Mary, I just yelled, "Come on in. I am in the baby's room."

"Hi, Char!"

"Well, hi yourself, Louise. What are you doing here?"

"I thought I would come see if I still had a sister living close by."

"I'm sorry. I have been real busy. I'm excited to get moved in, so I have been staying at this quite steady. But I am sorry I should have stopped over to see you and brought you up to date."

"Why haven't you been to work? I have called down there to see if you wanted to go for lunch, and all they were saying is that you weren't at work."

"Well, to make a long story short, I sort of quit, yet I got fired."

"WHAT ARE YOU TALKING ABOUT?"

"Liz was letting me go. With me being pregnant, it made me cheap, so it made her shop cheap as well."

"Wow. I am sorry to hear that, Char."

"Come, I have put on water for coffee, and now, it is time for a break."

"All right. I sure like what you are doing in here. This looks so calming and peaceful. Just like a baby's room should be. I wished you would have been around to do my kids' rooms when they were all babies."

"Thank you. I really like doing this kind of work."

"It shows, Char. So are you just going to wait until you have the baby to carry on your hairdressing?"

"Yes, I am. Elaine said to go find her, and she would try and get me in wherever she is working."

"Elaine! Why did she quit?"

"Yes, and she sure told Liz off. I didn't have to say anything. Elaine just jumped right in when she heard Liz. I think she has just been waiting for the right time. Elaine knew more of what was going on than I had thought."

"I'm glad someone was there for you, Char. Liz can be a real bitch, and she likes to make the young girls think they can't do it without her. She is good at what she does, but so are some of the others. You will find someone easy enough. You have a good reputation of been a hairdresser. So you will be OK when time comes. I think it's just as well you take the time now until you have the baby. Has Mary been helping you down here?"

"Yes, a little, but I don't think Mary is well right now. So I am trying to do as much as possible on my own."

"What all is left?"

"The painting of the bathroom and in here. As well as I have to wash all the dishes before I can use them," I said that while I was pouring us our coffee. "I brought some of mine down to use right now."

"How about after our coffee I wash up the kitchen, so you can just paint or I can paint and you wash the dishes."

"That would be great, thanks."

"I like the bedroom set, Char. It is old. I have a white lacy bedspread you can have that would go real nice on it and then you just have to add some color down the road."

"That sounds great to me." After our coffee, we got right into, and Louise done everything in the kitchen and living room area. I had carried on with the painting, and it all came together really nice.

Louise took me out to buy some grocery now that the fridge was nice and clean. This was quick because Louise ran me through, and we picked up just the basics. I can add to it another day.

On the way back home, we stopped at her house for the spread and drapes she had to give me, plus she threw in some lavender pillows that were just to be tossed on to the bed as well as a throw rug that goes beside the bed; it also had lavender in it. A couple sets of double sheets and pillowcases along with bath towels and face cloths. She had told me she had her spare room done with these colors, but once she had the twins, she no longer had a spare bedroom so all this was just in her way and taking up closet space that she can now use. It was a good thing she had held on to it all this time, and they still look new. I had told her what I wanted to do as far as the tablecloth and bumper board. Curtains for the kitchen, and she thought that maybe now Mary isn't well, we should do them. She had told me it wouldn't hurt for me to learn to sew. I had to agree.

"Talking about the kitchen, Char. You must need some dish cloths and tea towels. I have a lot of extras, so we will throw them into the bag as well."

"This is great. I never thought too much about these things. I was just using whatever Mary had brought down for us to use." When we got back to the house and got everything packed inside and put away, I made my first meal. It was only a sandwich, but they were tasty. It was so nice to be able to make them on a counter. Once we were done eating, Louise and I made up the bed and finished up with the cleanup from the painting. We also moved what I had upstairs down. Louise did not want me to carry too much. I had told her I didn't have a lot to carry. But she was determined to move me. So I let her as I can't say I wasn't tired from all the painting. It sure went faster when there was someone else helping and chatting as you're working; it made it somewhat more interesting. We had decided that on Monday, we would go buy the material we needed for the bumper boards, and the wood she said she had some at home that her husband would help us plain-smooth before we stuff and wrap them. I was starting to really enjoy this, being at home and busy doing all these interesting hobbies. Mary will be so surprised. I must remember to check on her before I go to bed.

Bed. What a great thought that is; it is off the floor and is done up so cozy looking. Having the toss pillows and rug made a big difference in how the room looked in the end. A breath of spring is what it reminded me of. Certainly a ladies room, it is so delicate and just maybe Mary will let me take some lilacs from her garden.

"Well, Char, I think I have done all the damage I can do today. I just wanted to see if you were all right, and I think you're handling this crap from Liz just fine. You hang in there and come see me now that you're off work."

"I will, Louise," I say, hugging her. "Thank you for all your help today. I wouldn't be sleeping here tonight if you hadn't helped me." I kissed her and held her close for a couple of minutes.

Stepping back, she says, "Knowing you, Char, you would have put yourself in the hospital trying to get it done today."

"I might have."

"I must go now, and I will see you on Monday."

"You bet, and thank you again."

"You're welcome, Char." And with that, she was gone.

CHAPTER TEN

I just tidied up a few things that I had not got put away. I decided to go up and see Mary. It was funny she hadn't been around all day again. It was quiet, and no lights were on anywhere that I could see from the door. I knocked a couple of times, but she never came to answer. I thought perhaps she felt better today and had to go do something with the church. Oh well, she will see my light on; she knows where to find me.

Once I was back downstairs, I decided I wanted to have a long bath, something I haven't been able to do know for almost a year. I always had my bath quickly so I could leave Mary's before Sam got home. Now I will indulge myself. I will dig out my personal bath supplies and spoil myself tonight. I tied my hair up, for it is shoulder length. I threw a bath towel into the dryer so it would be warm when I am ready to get out. Pouring bath bubbles into the tub and running water made me so excited I couldn't wait to jump in.

Laying back into the bubbles, I thought how fabulous this is. This is what it should be like at the end of every busy day. To be able to reconnect with yourself and to put the world on the outside on hold for at least half an hour. This time should be our time of luxury, one that we can enjoy to the fullest. To be able to soak in the tub and escape from the outside pain and disappointments. In here, you could be wherever you wanted to be. There was no end to your fantasy while you laid back and soaked in the tub.

Oh, seventh heaven is what they call this, and oh, how I have missed it. Even at our parents', though we had to heat our water on the stove, we still had our bath time that was our time once we moved off the farm. I suppose if I had felt more comfortable around Sam, I would have been able to relax in the tub instead of rushing in just to make sure I was good and clean. Most of the time, I was finished bathing by the time the water was ran because I would climb in as soon as I turned on the water just to make sure I wasn't in there too long. But like all good things, it must come to an end, for one thing, my water is getting cold, and I have merrpurpls. Don't ask; that's just what we always called our wrinkled-up fingers after you have been in the water so long. My towel was nice and warm, and that made up for the cool water. I got dried off and put on my long fuzzy nightgown. I had not worn this for a long time. But for some reason, it felt right to do so tonight. I cleaned the bathtub and decided to make a cup of tea, and I would take it to bed with me and read a book that Mary had given me called *Little Women*. I have heard it is a good book.

I shut off all my light except the light above the stove; it would work well for a night-light. Climbing into bed was such a joy, and it was so comfortable to be on a bed that wasn't on the floor. Not that the mattress on the floor wasn't good enough because it was. But it was also very hard, and most time, you just couldn't get comfy no matter what.

This double bed was just a whole lot better; what could I say except thank you, Mary, and may God bless you and keep you well.

I snuggled down into the bed and started sipping my tea and reading the book; it was quite interesting, and before I knew it, it was 1:00 AM. Oh my, I best get to sleep, but I best go to the bathroom one more time or I will be up shortly after I fall asleep.

It did not take long before I was sound asleep. Not once did I get up through the night, which is a real surprise especially after drinking tea that late.

The sun was bright through my window. I thought it must be fairly late in the morning. Man did I have to go to the bathroom now. There was no wasting time. This has to have been the best sleep I have had in some time. I sure didn't feel like climbing out of my nest, but Mother Nature was not letting up, and there could be a mess if I don't move it.

I might as well wash up and brush my teeth while I'm in here. This was great; I can do all these things standing here in my nightgown and slippers. I don't have to worry about being too long or running into someone I don't want to see.

Oh Mary, you were an angel sent to me, I'm sure. I wouldn't have the luxury of all this comfort without knowing you. Thinking of Mary, I decided that was first on my list to do today. I sure hope she has gotten her rest, seeing how she has been so tired.

I was trying to figure out what I would wear today. I could wear something nicer today now that the painting is all finished. There wasn't much chance of me doing too much of anything today. So I pulled out this light blue pantsuit that I had picked up at the thrift shop. It was very summery, and it was a maternity one at that, so it fits just right. I don't like things fitting so tight you can see all the bulges and rolls one might have. I might be pregnant, but I want to look respectable and pleasing to one's eyes. I see a lot of girls that are pregnant and wear anything; they don't care that their bellies are hanging out. Most of the young girls wear small tight T-shirts. I personally think that is a disgraceful way of representing yourself.

I am proud that I am having a baby. It might not be smart, but it is, and I will make the best of it, and besides being dressed appropriately will draw less attention to me than wearing a T-shirt that is way too small. Now that I'm dressed, I'll have a yogurt and a banana for breakfast, then I'm good to go. With that I headed for the door to go up and see Mary. Just as I was to open it, a light knock came; thinking it was Mary, I opened it wide, and to my surprise stood Sam. I didn't know if I should shut the door in his face and lock it or just what I was to do. But then he didn't have the mean scary look in his eyes this morning; he actually looked sad.

"Sam! What can I do for you?"

"It's not me," he said.

"Oh what then?"

"It's mom."

"Mary! What about Mary?"

"I had to take her to the hospital last night. She isn't doing too well."

"What is wrong with her Sam?"

"They don't know for sure. They're doing a bunch of tests on her today. The doctor tells me they should have some answers today I have to go back after work to see mom, and I will be able to see the doctor then."

"Well, thanks for telling me. I wondered where she had gotten to. The last few days, she has been so tired and hasn't been coming down. So I was just going up now to see her."

"She wants to see you, and I told her I would let you know."

"I will be able to see her then?"

"Yes, I told the nurse that you would be in because, right now, they just wanted the family to be with her. She really thinks a lot of you and said you were part of her family, and you were to be let in."

I know I turned a little red in the face when he said that, so I hung my head and said, "I'm sorry."

"No need to be sorry. Our mother has wanted to be a grandmother for a long time, and she always wanted a daughter. We all knew that. You have filled that emptiness in her, and we haven't seen our mother so happy about something or anyone for a very long time. So would you please go up and see her?"

"Oh yes! Is there any certain time I can get in?"

"You can get in anytime. They know you are coming."

"Oh!"

"I was pretty sure you would be going once you knew. I hope I didn't take that for granted."

"No, you didn't. I will go right now."

"Thank you, and maybe I will see you after work?"

"Maybe."

"Bye for now."

"Bye and thank you for telling me."

"You're welcome." Then Sam left. I closed the door and tried to think, but Sam sort of threw me off balance. I didn't think he could be a nice person. But then I know that I saw what I saw and how he treated his mother. But he seemed like a different man right now. There is no way you would think he would treat his mother that way and yet sound so gentle and caring about her now. He didn't seem to mind that his mother and I have gotten close. He made me feel like that was a good thing and that they were all glad about the baby and me. Just maybe, I have jumped to the wrong conclusion. Could I have done that? Did I misjudge him? Is he nicer than I had first thought? It is obvious that he cares a lot for his mother. I must go now and see Mary. So I grabbed my sweater in case the weather changes; after all, one will never know. The sun is shining now, but what about a half hour from now?

The hospital is only four blocks from here, so I didn't walk fast, and in no time, I was there. I went in through the front door; an ambulance was there unloading. So I stood back and waited for the doorway to clear. There were a lot of attendants there, so it was of some big emergency. I could not tell whether it was a male or female on the stretcher or whether it was young or old. There did not seem to be too much movement on the part of the patient, but they moved very quickly and efficiently to get the person into the hospital. Once they were inside, then the ruckus started for all the orders that were being called out to do. The staff were moving in all directions, and I understood that it was a young girl who had gone into labor. Then she pasted out; no one seemed to know why. I had heard one of the nurses say her mother was on her way and the door closed.

So I went to the nurses' station to find out where to find Mary, and the nurse told me room 121. Walking quietly and as quickly as I could, trying to stay out of everyone's way because I knew this was too early for visitors. I was just being let in on a special request. It seemed to be that these door numbers sort of jumped all over.

"Excuse me," a nurse asked me. "Can I help you?"

"Yes, please. I'm trying to find Mary's room."

"It is just around the corner on your left. She was sleeping when I was in there five minutes ago."

"Oh well, maybe I should come back?"

"No, she is waiting for you. Charlene, right?"

"Yes."

"It will do her a lot of good to see you. She has been worried about you."

"Worried about me?"

"Yes. She kept saying something about helping you move because, with you being pregnant, you shouldn't be doing it on your own. Her son told her he could help you move and not to worry about it anymore. I can see why he would say that. She is right. You shouldn't be moving anything on your own. Did you get moved?"

"Yes. Thank you, my sister helped me."

"That will make Mary happy. Now go on ahead. She doesn't sleep too long at one time."

"Thank you." Going around the corner, my heart started to beat fast, for I was not sure what I was going to find. I still don't know what is wrong, so you start to get terrible pictures going through your mind. What if she has tubes coming out all over or can't talk too well, what will I say to her? I came to her door, and it was slightly opened, so I just peeked in. I didn't want to go in too far in case I couldn't handle what I saw. I might be wanting to turn around and leave before Mary saw me. She looked the same other than she was sleeping, I think. I slowly let out the breath that I was holding. Isn't that funny how we do that and we don't know it until you start to let it go. I wonder if people pass out that way. Or how long would one hold their breath without realizing that they are.

Slipping into Mary's room and sitting on the chair beside her bed, I was only there for maybe five minutes before she woke up.

"Oh deary, you did come?"

"Of course, I came, Mary. Why would you think I wouldn't come and see you?"

"Some people don't like hospitals."

"That's true, but I wouldn't want to be in one and have no one come see me either. Mary, why didn't you tell me you were sick the other day? I knew you weren't really up to par as you seemed to be so tired all the time. I would have helped you more."

"I knew you wanted to get moved, and I wanted to see you moved, and I'm sorry I couldn't help you more. Sam said he would move you."

"He did?"

"Yes. So just tell him when you're ready."

"Mary, I moved yesterday. Sam won't have to help me. Louise helped, so when you get home, you can stay with me through the day until Sam gets home. We have it all fixed up nice. You can come down and lie around on the sofa and let me wait on you for a change."

"Deary, you got all your painting and cleaning done, and you moved as well?"

"Yes, Mary, it is all done, so stop worrying about it. Louise came over, and we got right into it and got it all done in one day. It doesn't take long when you're organized."

"I can see that." She sounded so weak and tired still. Mary looked a lot older than I thought she was. But then I really never knew her age.

"Mary, what can I do for you? Or what can I get for you?"

"Deary, I don't know how long I will be in here, so I was wondering if I could get you to make meals for Sam. I'm afraid that if I'm not home to make him meals, he will just drink, and I don't want that to happen. It is not good for him."

"But, Mary, what would Sam say? Maybe he would sooner cook his own supper." Never mind, I would sooner he cook his own meals, but I couldn't tell her that. What am I to do? After all she has done for me, now she needs me to do some small favor for her, and I am trying to weasel out of it. How do I handle being around Sam for any length of time? Maybe I could cook up meals ahead of time and just leave them for him to heat up. Yeah, that's what I could do.

"No, he says cooking is for women, so he wouldn't cook anything."

CHAPTER ELEVEN

"All right, Mary. I will make sure Sam has his meals. Now don't you worry about him."

"Thank you, deary. I knew I could count on you."

I thought, *Please don't make this harder on me than it already is.* I guess I can only hope he stays away from the drinking while Mary is in here, but what are the chances of that?

"Mary, is there anything else I can bring you from home?"

"Yes, deary. Would you please bring my Bible. I left it on my nightstand, my hair brush, toothbrush, and some clean underwear would also be nice. Sam didn't give me time to pack anything last night, and I didn't want to ask him to go get me anything this morning. He was so tired, I just wanted him to go home to bed."

"I sure can. I will pick it up when I go home for lunch."

"Thank you. Now I think I will sleep for a little while."

"Sure, you go ahead, and I can go get what you need. I will be back before you wake up." Mary reaches out to take my hand, and this really disturbed me as she felt so fragile. There was no warmth in her hands at all. She pulls me close so she could hug me, and I felt like I could break something on her if I wasn't careful.

She whispered, "I love you, deary." This brings tears to me right now as I hug her back, and I tell her, "I love you too, Mary." It felt so natural to say that to her. In fact I didn't realize it until now that I really do love her and how much. Not only that but I needed her; she had become someone very special to me and would be to my baby. Mary has helped me get through the hard part of being pregnant and alone. She has taught me to be proud of who I am. Being pregnant hasn't changed who I am; it will only make me stronger, she would tell me.

Kissing her cheek I said good-bye, and this good-bye was going to be a very short one. I would hurry home and get back here so that I would be sure to be there when she woke up.

I was just turning the corner in the hallway when I bumped right into Jacob.

"Well, hi, what are you doing here?"

"Well, I went by your place. Some guy leaving for work said you were at the hospital. Are you all right?"

"Yeah, I am fine. It's Mary. She is not well."

"Oh, what's wrong with her?"

"We don't know yet. We should by the end of the day."

"So where you going now?"

"I was just going home to pick up some things for Mary, and I think I will grab the book I was reading. It could be a while sitting here."

"You want a ride?"

"Sure, thanks." This would get me home a little faster than walking, and for sure, I would be back before Mary wakes up.

"I got moved into the basement suite."

"I heard, Louise told me. She says you have done it up really nice and cozy."

"Well, she helped me, and yeah, I really like it. So when are you moving in?"

"Well, Char. I sort of met someone, and she said I could move in with her."

"I wondered where you had gotten to. Hadn't seen you around for a while."

"This girl. Where did you meet her?"

"Believe it or not, she was hitchhiking, and I stopped to give her a ride."

"You're kidding, right?"

"No, and she's a nice person."

"Why was she hitchhiking?"

"She was on her way to work, and her car broke down."

"So are you moving in with her or what?"

"I think, maybe I will try it. If it doesn't work out, then I can always come here."

"Sure, I don't see why not. You might as well come see what we have done to this place now that you're here."

"I plan on it. Are you going right back to the hospital?"

"Yes, I will stay with Mary as long as they will let me or until her son gets back there."

"Then I will give you a ride back. That way we will have time to get a coffee."

"Sounds good to me, just give me a couple of minutes. I have to go and get a few things for Mary, but you go on in and look around." Jacob went into my place, and I went into Mary's to get the things she asked for. This made me uncomfortable going through her belongings. I didn't look at any one thing. I just took whatever was on top when it came to her underwear. The bath products were not so bad. Having grabbed everything, I was headed to the door when I thought, *Shit, Mary's Bible.* Going back into her room to get her Bible off her night table, I saw a picture out of the corner of my eye, so I took a good look at it, and I realized that it was Mary and her husband, so I took it along with me. She obviously still loves him to have his picture bedside her bed after all these years. What that would be like? I can only hope that I could find the same kind of love some day.

"Hi, I'm here."

"I'm in the baby's room, I think!"

"Yeah, this is the baby's room all right. Just need to find a crib and dresser."

"Louise is right, you did do a great job. In fact the whole place looks very good."

"Thank you."

"You ready to go, Char?"

"Let me grab my book and toothbrush. After so much coffee, you can't taste anything else until you have brushed your teeth." I hurried through and got what I needed while Jacob was still looking around. He was quite impressed at how everything looked.

We headed out to the café. Once we were there and had ordered coffee, I had wished we would have gotten it to go. But I hadn't seen Jacob for a while, and he was all excited to tell me about this new girl and the fact that she was from Denmark and how pretty she was. She had taken modeling in Toronto and how well educated she was.

"So I guess we have to say lucky for you her car broke down."

"No shit, eh. What would be the chances of meeting a girl like her walking to work, or I should say, hitchhiking."

"I find it hard to believe that she would hitchhike. I know I sure the hell wouldn't. I know Bev does it a lot, but then we all know she's not the smart one. She's too spoiled to think anything would happen to her."

"Yeah, she's a bit different than the rest, isn't she?"

"Guess that comes from being the baby."

"Baby or not, she should think before she does some of these trips."

"I agree. Anyways Jacob I should get back to the hospital. I want to be there before Mary wakes up. I also want to be there when they take her for whatever test she has to have done today. So when you get settled in with, what's her name? Sorry, I never asked."

"Her name is Elise."

"All right, when you and Elise get it together, bring her over one night for coffee or day whatever works for you."

"We will, Char. Don't forget to go home and get sleep yourself," he tells me as he drops me off back at the hospital.

"Thanks for the ride, and I will sleep." Here or at home, it will probably work out to about the same amount of time. If I were to go home, I would just lie and worry about Mary. Besides, I don't know if any of the boys will be able to spend much time with her. I will see what tonight brings. As I approached Mary's door, I could hear voices, so I slowed down in case she had company. I could always come back if that were the case. Listening a little more carefully, I could hear sobbing. *Who and why?* I thought. Then came a stifled sound as the person said, "Are you sure, Dr. Stevens?"

"Yes, and I am very sorry to have to tell you. Please make sure you get all your affairs in order."

"How long do I have?"

"Just days, I'm afraid. I can't tell you exactly. But we are able to give you medicine that will control the pain. Please don't be scared to ask for it whenever you want or feel you need it. We can't tell how much pain you are in, so you have to let us know. I will be here for you. All you have to do is let the nurse know, and she will call me, all right?"

I heard something that I took as OK, but I could hardly make it out. I was standing there in a dumb state when the doctor came out of the room. It was just sinking in that it was Mary he was talking to. Something was very wrong; my heart was going crazy. I felt like I could not breathe. The doctor put his hand on my shoulder and was asking me if I were OK. I could see his lips moving but not hearing what he was saying.

"Miss, are you all right?" he asks as he sort of shakes my shoulder.

"Sorry, yeah, I will be."

"Who are you here to see?"

"Mary."

"So that explains it." That explains what is what I wanted to yell at him.

"I am sorry if you overheard me talking to Mary. I should have waited until you were with her. You are still going in to be with her now. She could really use someone."

"Oh yes. I just want to catch my breath and my bearing before I go in."

"I totally understand, and if I can be of any help, please call."

"Thank you." I slipped into Mary's room, putting the things that I had brought for her on to the little table that was sitting against the wall, putting her picture I brought right out front where she will be able to see it clearly. I could see she was sobbing even with her back to the door I could tell. Oh God, what do I do? What is wrong? I go over to the bed and touch her shoulder. Mary turns her head just enough to see me, and she starts to cry out of control. I hurried to the other side of the bed for this side was up, and I take her in my arms, and I just sit holding her and rocking her slowly back and forth. We sat like that for a good half an hour. Then her sobbing was getting a little less. Do I dare ask what is so wrong or will this start her all over again? I just had to take the chance.

"Mary, can you tell me what is wrong?" I ask still rocking back and forth stroking her hair. She has beautiful long hair. I did not realize it was so long as she always wears it up in a bun.

"Oh deary, the doctor tells me I have cancer, and I have only a matter of days." She starts to cry all over again. I was afraid this would happen. Except this time, she wasn't crying alone I was squeezing her so tight I am surprised she didn't complain. But then she has other things on her mind right now.

"I'm so sorry, Mary. How can I help you?"

"Just hold me for a while and please don't leave me."

"I'm not going anywhere." So for the next three days, I sat in her room with her. Either on her bed holding her or beside the bed holding her hand while she slept. I read my book.

"Deary, I don't understand. I have always watched what I ate, and I thought I was taking care of myself pretty good."

"Where is the cancer? Can't they operate?"

"I asked the same thing," she answered in between her sobs. The doctor tells me it is through all my organs. He is not sure where it started and if they had caught it early enough they might have been able to do something about it. But now it is too late. He said they were going to run more tests but have decided they don't have too.

"Oh Mary, I don't want to lose you. My baby needs a grandma that lives close and will love it. What will we do without you?"

"I will try and fight this, deary. I don't want to lose you either, and I so much want to be part of your baby's life." With that said, she was falling asleep in my arms, so I just sort of slipped more on to the bed, so I could be resting up against the head of the bed as well so I could hold her while she slept. After a few minutes, a nurse had come in to see if Mary had calmed down. For the last three days, every time she woke up, she would cry until she would fall asleep again.

"They've been giving her a needle since the doctor talked to her so that it would put her to sleep after being given such a blow." A nurse had told me that she will start getting a little better when she wakes up each time. This will be from being kept sedated. She will sort of forget what she is in here for. I asked if they had to do that to her. The nurse tells me she will be kept sedated now until the end.

"Why will she be kept sedated?"

"Two reasons. First, we control the pain as much as we can safely, and the other, it helps keep them calm so they're not all worked up all the time to the end. She will pass in her sleep. She should sleep for a while if you have things you have to do."

"I am fine. I wouldn't go anywhere. If it is OK with you, I will just sit and hold her."

"That is fine if that is what you want to do, but remember you have to take care of yourself as well. And that baby," she says as she reaches over and rubs my stomach. She leaves us alone, then

I lay there thinking how this seemed to come on so quickly. Mary went from being so busy to tired to being told she has a matter of days. I didn't know cancer worked so fast. Then I don't know anything about this sickness. Do I dare leave when she wakes up? What if she passes before I get back? Do I just say good-bye now and stay away? But then maybe it will be many days, and she would be left here all alone. Will the boys stay when they find out? If they do, will they mind if I stay around?

Mary didn't have a restful sleep as she seemed to be fighting to breathe, so I would just stroke her hair and say softly, "Shush, you're fine. It will be OK. Just sleep now, I'm here," as if that was going to make everything right. What stupid things people say at these times. I guess it's for the lack of knowing what else to say.

I must have dozed off as well because I woke up to someone saying, "She has stayed with her all day just like that."

"Just like that? Has she gone to eat at all today?"

"No, sir. She hasn't left her side."

"Thank you." I heard, but I didn't want to move for fear I would wake Mary up. I wondered what time it was. It was Sam who came around the end of the bed. So it has to be after six if Sam is here.

"Hi," he said very softly.

"Hi," I whispered back.

"Mom's been sleeping a while."

"Yeah, they gave her a needle and told me she would sleep, but I didn't think she would sleep this long."

"You haven't had supper. I will go to the cafeteria and get you something to eat as well as something to drink."

"No, I am fine."

"You might be fine, but you're not sitting here with Mom and not eating. We don't need you sick as well. Besides, you have a baby to take care of, so I will be right back," he said all this in such a whisper and gentleness in his voice and the kindness I saw in his eyes. I couldn't believe that it was the same Sam I have been face-to-face with before. When I saw nothing but coldness in his eyes, it sent shivers up my spine.

Have I really misjudged him? But then Mary said he was only that way with her when he was drinking.

"Here, hope you like roast beef and coffee?"

"Thank you. This is just fine," I said as I reached over to take the sandwich and coffee he was offering to me.

"Oh, I almost forgot here." He reaches into his pocket and pulls out some cream and sugar. I forgot to ask you what you take."

"Both, thank you."

"So you know what is wrong with Mom?"

"Yes, she told me."

"You don't have to stay any longer now that I am here. If you don't want to that is."

"I don't mind. But I don't want to be in the family's way."

"My brothers won't be in until tomorrow evening as they are out of town, and when the doctor called me to give me the news, he said I should call them right away. But they have to drive all night to get home, so they are on their way. The doctor had also told me that you were here. I thank you for staying with her all this time."

"She was really upset and had asked me not to leave. Not that I would have anyways."

"Are you not working now?"

"No. Not until after the baby is born of course."

"So I had no place I had to be. That is why I could stay with your mom as long as she needed me to."

"I am afraid that I won't be able to stay long, but I wanted to see her before I went home to do my paperwork for the meeting tomorrow."

"I can stay all night if you wish."

"How about we see what mom wants us to do when she wakes up. I will wait a while yet before I leave. But I do want to go talk to the doctor, so I will do that now while you are still here with her."

"All right, and thank you again for supper."

"You're welcome. Not much pay for babysitting," Sam said, then left to talk to the doctor. Mary started to wake up and seemed to be a little disoriented about where she was or why.

"Mary, you're in the hospital."

"Deary?"

"Yes, Mary. What would you like?"

"See George."

"What do you mean, Mary? See George."

"Pretty soon, it will be time to go to George." Now she has me paying attention because I'm sure George is her late husband. Mary seems to be so calm now. Then she drifts off again.

Sam comes back, and he looks like he has been crying. He tells me the doctor has told him it is just a matter of time, and there was nothing they can do for Mary except make sure she is pain-free and keep her as comfortable as possible. I already knew most of this from the nurse, but I wasn't saying anything one way or another, for I was still praying that perhaps they made a mistake and the doctors could do something to change the outcome.

"I have called the other boys. The doctor has said he didn't think she would last that long."

"I am so sorry, Sam. Do you want me to leave you alone with your mom?"

"Has she woke up at all?"

"Yes, just for a couple of minutes."

"Did she say anything?" How do I tell him what she said? Or would this make him feel better to know she wants to go to his father? Maybe I will wait and see if she talks about it again.

"Nothing that I could really understand."

"She seems to be calm with you there. Maybe you should stay a little while yet just until we see if she will be settled for the night. I don't really want her to be alone. But I don't know if I can do this on my own. It is being selfish on my part to ask you to do this, and I will understand if you don't want to stay any longer. I know you have put in long days with her already."

"I don't mind, Sam. I just don't want to be in anyone's way."

"That won't be a problem as I know Mom really thinks a lot of you, and she did ask for you to come. I'm really glad you did."

"Me too." We sat in silence for quite some time. It must have been a couple of hours at least before Mary made any kind of noise or movement. At this time, I thought I best get out from under her as I really had to go to the bathroom. Funny, I never gave that a thought until just now; maybe it was just the way Mary moved that it put pressure on my bladder. The coffee Sam brought to be had filled me up. So slipping off the bed, I told Sam I had to leave for a few minutes. He seemed a little nervous about being left there alone.

"I wouldn't be more than ten minutes."

"Thank you."

Once I started to walk, I could feel all the kinks in my legs and arms from where Mary was lying on me. I think some parts of me were so numb that's why I couldn't feel any discomfort at the time. Going to the bathroom made me feel somewhat better. While I was in there, I thought I would wash my face and comb my hair. Lying on it all day made me look like I was the sick one.

I was totally lost in what I should do. I know Sam said for me to stay, but is it right? After all, Mary is not my mother. I don't have any right to be here in such a time that it should only be family even though Sam had asked. But it was only because his mother had asked in the beginning. Now she doesn't seem to know where she is or why or who we are. Some of this, no doubt, is due to the medication that they have her on. I feel useless, plus what do you say to people who are losing their mother. It is not like I know a whole lot about Mary that I could talk to Sam about his good memories that he might have of his mother and their life. Where at least when his brothers are here they can reminisce about the past good or bad.

If I leave, will he think I think less of Mary? When all I want to do is show them respect and Mary too. I will go back to the room to tell Sam I will be going home, and if he needs for me to come, all he has to do is phone.

When I got back close to Mary's room, I could hear her. She was so upset, so I hurried in to see what had happened.

"Sam, what is wrong?"

"Oh thank heavens, you're back. I tried to tell Mom you would be right back. But she was convinced that you were gone, and there was no way she was believing me."

"I am sorry. I just thought I would give you more time alone with your mom." I wasn't telling him I was in the bathroom thinking about leaving, but now I guess I have my answer.

"Deary, deary."

"Yes, Mary, I'm here. I'm not going anywhere."

"I thought I wouldn't be able to say good-bye to you." I heard Sam gasp for air, but I didn't want to look at him. I couldn't stand to see the pain on his face.

"Mary, why are you saying that?" She only talked in a whisper and a very silent one so you really had to listen to hear what she said.

"George is waiting for me. He is holding out his hand for me to take. I told him soon."

"Please, Mary, don't go," I say to her as the tears run down my cheeks. I didn't want Sam to see them, so I wipe them away, but they came pretty steady, it was impossible to keep them wiped away, and Sam did see, and he came over and put his arm around my shoulder. He handed me a napkin, so I could wipe my eyes and nose with some dignity.

"I'm sorry, Sam."

"No need to be sorry. This must be really hard on you? Mom told me once that you don't have a good relationship with your mother. She told me that she was being your adoptive mom."

I shook my head. "Yeah, she was being mom and grandma and a very good friend."

"Did she say she saw Dad?"

"She said he was waiting for her."

"Mom has been very lonely since Dad's passing. But she seems to be at peace with this now, which is good because it will make us accept losing her easier, knowing she is with our father."

"Do you really believe that she sees him? Your dad I mean?"

"I've heard that when you are dying, you see your loved ones that have gone on before you. Perhaps that's what makes it easy in the end to die. I was with my mom when her mom died, and she told my mom the same thing that grandpa was calling to her, so she was ready to go as well. Mom has her faith and lived by it and always said that when the time was right, she would leave and not be scared to do so."

"I haven't had much to do with death. My youngest brother died when he was fourteen, and I was only fifteen, so we didn't know too much about death. Neither of our parents went into any details about it nor did we ask. Besides we wouldn't know what to ask anyways."

"Are you scared of death, Charlene?"

"Yeah, I am scared of what I don't know. I wouldn't want to die young." I had not realized as hadn't Sam that he was still standing with his arm around my shoulders. But now that I have noticed, I want to step away but not so that he would really notice. I just don't want it to be awkward or embarrassing for either of us. Then Mary starts to stir, and we both went closer to the bed that in itself broke our contact.

"Mom, Mom," Sam called to her, and she opens her eyes, but they are glazed, and the pupils are dilated a fair amount. She seems to be able to see right through us. It was creepy.

"Sam, is Thomas and Douglas here?"

"No, Mom, they were waiting to come with James."

"I hope they are here soon."

"Sam, I think you should go call them and find out how close they are. Maybe that would make her rest easier if she knew that much.

"You're right. Do you mind staying alone? I will go call them."

"Of course, not." Sam left and Mary seemed to come more awake than she had been.

"Deary."

"I'm here, Mary. What can I do for you?"

"Sam." She seems to be needing to think about what she wanted to say.

"He will be right back, Mary."

"No, Sam says he will take care of you and the baby for me."

"Mary, I will be fine. Don't you worry about me." I couldn't believe this. Here this beautiful lady is dying, and on her deathbed, she is worried about me.

"Sam promised me and will make a good father for your baby. We talked about it." What the hell was she talking about; no way was Sam going to be my baby's father. I can't say I even really like the guy. I can only hope he agreed with Mary because of the circumstances. Is that why he is showing me the nice side of him? Is this all a ploy to win me over? Or is Mary just talking of a dream she has had?

I must try to stay as far away as possible from him. I don't want him getting any ideas. I sure don't want to send the wrong messages.

"Please, deary, say you're OK with that."

"Shush, Mary, it's OK" is all I could think to say. What have they talked about? What plans have been made without me knowing about them? Does Sam think that he is just coming into my life whether I want him to or not because it is something him and Mary have talked about and prearranged? I sure hope this is not going any further because it will make it really uncomfortable for all of us.

Now is this why he has been so attentive? Wanting me to stay with him and his mother? I was deep in thought and did not notice Sam come back into the room.

"Charlene, is something wrong?"

"No. Why would you ask?"

"You seem to be in another world."

"Just thinking."

"My brothers are only three hours away. They have been driving nonstop since they left. I guess they made themselves thermos of coffee and sandwiches so they didn't have to stop on the road other than for pee breaks, which they said they have almost done that on the fly."

"That's good, Sam. When they get here, I am going to leave. There will be enough with you boys that I shouldn't have to be here."

"But Mom will—"

I cut him off before he could use Mary anymore.

"Sam. Your brothers will want their time with Mary, and it is not my place to be here."

"I have talked to them and told them that you're here and what Mom wants."

"What is that exactly, Sam? What is it that Mary wants?"

"Well, you know."

"No, Sam. I don't know. I am your mom's friend and renter that is all. End of story."

"I don't think this is the time to be discussing this."

"Just what are we discussing, Sam?" At this point is when Mary decided to wake up so our discussion was put on hold.

"We will talk later," Sam said to me as he walks over to his mom's bedside. I just stood there looking at him to see if I could read his face. I sure can't believe that he thinks we have any thing to talk about. I watch him take his mother's hand, and he bends over the bed and is talking so softly to her I am not able to make out what he is saying. Mary nods her head in agreement to whatever it was he told her. Then he speaks up when he says to her, "Mom, the boys will be here very soon. I just talked to them, and they're only about hours away."

"That's fine, not much longer" is what I hear from her. What was the secret that he just told her?

"Is deary staying?" I heard Mary ask Sam. He looks over his shoulder at me and says.

"I don't know, Mom. Why don't you ask her?" This forces me to move up closer to the bed and stand beside Sam. A place I don't want to be. Sam puts his arm around my shoulder and watches to see what I was going to do. Of course, what can I do as Mary is lying there, watching us, and she seems to have a very content look on her face. One that almost says she's proud of herself.

"Thank you," she whispers. She reaches out to take both of our hands. I keep my eye on her, but I can tell that Sam is looking at me and waiting to see what I was going to do. I hold Mary's hand until I feel it totally relaxed in mine, then I just lay her hand down on her chest because now I know she is sleeping again. I step back away from the bed. Sam does the same thing.

CHAPTER TWELVE

"I am going to the cafeteria for a coffee while Mary is sleeping," I tell Sam.

"I'll come with you."

"You don't have to trouble yourself."

"It's no trouble at all."

"Don't you think you should stay here in case your mom wakes up?"

"I think she will be just fine for the length of time we'll be gone." How dense is this guy? Can he not get the message that I want to be alone? I left at a quick pace, but before I knew it, Sam was right behind me, taking me by the arm and turning me around quite abruptly.

"Just what the hell did I do to piss you off so badly?" His face was red with anger, and his eyes were so dark and cold just like I had seen them before. The old Sam was back.

"Don't pretend that you don't know, Sam. To use your mother on her deathbed is about as low as one man can go. But then how would you know you have to be a man first of all." Turning around, I left him standing there. I did not go to the cafeteria. I went out of the hospital and just walked around. I knew there was a coffee shop just two blocks away, so that's where I headed. The night air was cooler tonight than it had been, or was it because inside I was boiling and the wind just felt cool to me on the outside. Once inside the café, I did order a large coffee, and sitting over it, I sat remembering Mary, how when I first met her, she seemed to be so full of life, and yet she was so sad. Getting to know her, I knew why the sadness was still there. She had lost a lot. Her husband was her life, and she loved him then, and she still loves him now. Over the years, she was strong enough to go on, and Sam was right; Mary lived by her faith. Her faith was the second love of her life. From what I could see, it had kept her well and gave her the strength to deal with Sam.

Now she seemed to find happiness again just for the good Lord to take her away. With her faith, I know it won't bother her now to know she is dying, for she believes she is going to her husband. Who am I to doubt this? I know nothing about faith and the Bible or about God. I do believe that there is a higher power that we have no control over. Because we have been told that, that power is God. Then so be it.

It is funny how dying people become complacent with the fact that they are dying. There seems to be no more sadness in their eyes nor do they seem to be scared. Perhaps some time during all this, God does talk with us. Letting us know that there is nothing to be afraid of and that he is there to hold our hand and take us on this fantastic journey that we are all told about.

The only thing that really bothers me about all this is the little children that get sick and die when they haven't had a chance to begin. I really hope my baby gets to live to the fullest as well as myself. I want to be able to see my baby grow up and be a parent. But perhaps sometimes, we ask for too much, and we get shut down by the higher power. I'm sitting here in very deep thought when a hand is placed on my shoulder. Taking a deep breath, I knew before I turned around who it was, so I just asked, "Why aren't you with your mother?"

"Because you mean a lot to her, and I shouldn't have upset you so much that you would leave the hospital. Mom was asking for you, so I told her I would come and get you. Do you mind if I sit down with you?"

"It's a free world, do what you please."

"Thanks. That sounds inviting."

"I didn't invite you, remember. How did you know I was here?"

"I went home first, and when you weren't there, I just figured you had come here for coffee seeing how that's what you were wanting when you left the room to start with."

"I don't think I should go back to the hospital now that I have made the break. I think I should just stay away. Your brothers will be here right away, and your mother won't notice I'm not there then."

A waitress had come over to see if Sam wanted anything, and to my surprise, he ordered a large coffee in a to-go cup, which made me feel better because I thought it meant he was leaving.

"What am I suppose to tell her when I go back?"

"I'm sure you can think of something."

"Come on, give me a break here. I didn't do anything that is so bad that you have to be such a bitch about it."

"I guess it depends on what side of the conversation you are on. I am not interested in the plans you and your mother made about me and my baby."

"You know about that?"

"Yes, I know about that!" All of a sudden Sam says, "I'll be damned."

"What?" I asked him.

"Look who is at the counter."

I did, but it didn't make no different to me. I didn't know anyone standing there.

"It's my brothers."

"Really!"

"I wonder what they're doing here?" And just as he said that, the tallest one turned around and saw us. He waved and said something to the other two, which made them turn around. They also waved, and the first one came over to the table. Sam stood up, and they greeted each other with a handshake.

"James, I would like you to meet Charlene."

"Well, hello! Nice to put a face to the person I've heard so much about," he says as he extends his hand out to me to shake. I know I turned red in the face just the idea that I had been their topic at one time or another.

Hi was all I was able to say. Then he and Sam started to talk about Mary and what all the doctors had said and what kind of state their mother was in at the moment.

James was telling Sam that they just wanted to get some hot coffee before going up to the hospital and perhaps a bite to eat. They were getting it to-go. So Sam was waiting for them. The other boys come over, and we are introduced, and once again I turn red, knowing they also had talked about me at one time, either with Mary or Sam.

"All right, are we all ready to go to the hospital?" Sam said, and they were all in agreement. They had turned one way, and I was turned and going out the other door when James called to me.

"Charlene, are you not coming with us?"

"No. I will let you have your time alone with your mother. Perhaps I will pop in later." He turned to Sam and said something, so Sam came over to me and says, "We don't mind you being there. Even the others think you should be. They know how much you mean to Mom. Please, Charlene, just come and be there for Mom." He pauses and then said, "For me too."

"Sam, I don't think—" He cuts me off with a "Please do this for Mom."

I sigh and take on another deep breath.

"All right, but if I get uncomfortable, I will leave Sam, and it won't be out of disrespect for your mom."

"I understand." We leave the café. The other boys were waiting outside, and when they saw us come out together, they all smiled

and waved as they got into their car. They had waited to follow
Sam up to me hospital. The ride there was quick, which I sure was
glad about as Sam and I never said a word to each other.

The nurse said Mary had woken once, and she had told her
that we were just outside to get some fresh air, and Mary was OK
with that; she just nodded and went back to sleep.

The boys stood around talking to the nurse, and she had told
them the doctor would be in around 8:00 AM. It is now two in the
morning. No wonder I am so tired. I take the chair that has been
put over in the corner and sat down. I felt like I could just drop off
to sleep at any time.

I did sort of doze off and on, and I could hear the boys talking
about when they were all young and at home and about all the
tricks they used to play on their mother, and they would laugh.
Their father would give them a talking to about the things they
would do. But he too would have that silly grin on his face as the
boys never done any harm to their mother, but they sure like to
get under her skin from time to time.

I was able to spend time studying the boys and comparing
them to each other. I had noticed they all have the same laugh, and
they are all nice-looking men, not movie star-looking or anything
spectacular, but they were men you could be proud of to have on
your arm. James had a little more in the looks department than
the others, and I think he was more like his mother when it came
to his personality. Just the way he was so gentle with his mother
and the way he talked to her. But over all, they all were easy to
look at. It made me wonder why none of them were married. Then
it struck me. Maybe they are like Sam and can be really sweet
one time and miserable the next. Just maybe, they can't handle
their booze either. Oh well, that's not my concern now, is it? The
boys seemed like they had a lot to say, there wasn't a quiet time
since they got here. I think they must have gone over everything
in their young lives and relived them all. They also talked loud
enough for Mary to hear all they were saying. Did they do this

for her? Did they want her to know that they felt they had a great childhood and what a great mother she has been?

They all felt they had been very lucky because their mother had been home with them all the time they were growing up. They also knew that they could call on her whenever they needed something even once they had become men and gone on their own.

Then James takes his mother's hand and says to her, "The one thing I am sorry I never done for you, Mom, is give you a daughter-in-law and grandchildren. I know you have waited a long time and prayed for the day that would happen. I guess, Mom, you spoiled us so bad, and you were always there for us. We never felt we need to make that commitment to anyone. We didn't feel the need to have someone take care of us. You've done a fantastic job all on your own, and we love you very much for all of it. Thank you, Mom." He bends over and kisses her on the forehead and then lies his head down on her chest. I could see the tears rolling down his face. No one moved, and I did not know what to do.

"James, we have deary" she says in such a fragile voice it was hard to understand.

At that, James stands up, turns, and looks at me as he holds out his hand for me to take. I hesitate at first, then I get up and walk over to the bed, and I reach for his hand.

James draws me in a little closer, so he can put his arm around my shoulder, and looking at me says, "You're right, Mom, we sure do. We have deary!" and he gives me a side hug. I could see Sam watching us and that made me really uncomfortable. The look he gave me was so unreadable that I didn't know what to make of it, and I sure the hell didn't know what to say.

"Would you please excuse me? I have to step out for a little bit."

"I'm sorry, of course," he says as he takes his arm from around me. I left the room without looking at anyone else, and once I was in the hallway, I took a deep breath. I must have been holding mine without even knowing. Looking for somewhere to sit, I found a bench down the hallway to the nursery, sitting there looking at the babies, thinking soon I will have one of these sweet little babies of my own, rubbing my tummy in a soothing way for which seems to be for a short time, when James comes and says, "Do you mind if I sit with you a minute?"

"Of course not," I say as I slide over to make room for him to sit down.

"You have been gone for quite some time. We were getting worried."

"I am sorry. I don't mean to be a bother to anyone. You don't have to worry about me."

"It's no bother at all. What are you sitting here dreaming about? Are you wishing one of these babies were already yours?"

"Yeah, something like that."

"When is your baby due?"

"Not until the end of December."

"You have a little while yet."

"Yes, I do, and it seems so far away. But my sister keeps telling me it will go by fast, so enjoy my freedom while I can."

James just laughs.

"I guess so, eh." We sat there in silence for some time just watching the babies. I noticed that all babies look very much alike. I suppose that you would have to know the parents to be able to tell some of the differences that there were. Some were darker skinned than others, but over all, they looked the same. I was just wondering if mine would look like one of them when James says to me, "Do you think yours will look like one of them?"

I chuckled and he says, "What's so funny?"

"I was just thinking the same thing. Because they all sort of look the same some a little darker than the others, but over all, they're the same."

"You're right. I never noticed that before. But man, what do I know about babies?" he says to me.

"I don't know too much either. But I guess I will have lots of time to learn."

"I am glad my mom got to know you and the fact that you are having a baby. The fact that you were willing to share your baby with her was one of the nicest things anyone could have done for her. I don't think I have heard my mother sound so happy for a long time."

"Your mother is a very sweet lady, and she made me feel good about myself again. She told me to hold my head up. I was just having a baby, and that didn't make me a bad person. If nothing else, it would make me a better person. With her going to church and all, I was so scared to tell her. I thought she would put me out onto the street. Instead she takes me right into her heart. Gives me a very nice place to live, and wants to be part of our lives. I will miss her. She had become the mother that I was needing."

"I am glad that she had that happiness even if it was short-lived. I know that's all she has wanted now for years, and she used to bug us boys all the time about finding a nice girl and giving her grandchildren. We believed that we had lots of time. We would always say, "What's the rush, Ma. We have a lot of years ahead of us. Let us grow up first. I guess it has taken us too long to grow up. Now none of our children will know their grandparents as we knew ours."

"Did you know your grandparents well?"

"Oh yes! We went to their farm every Sunday after church. It was a blast. We would take a change of clothes, so once we got there, we were allowed to run wild and do a lot of things we couldn't do in town. We would always be there till late Sunday evening. In the summertime, we would go out and stay for a week at a time. We never got tired of the grandpas and grandmas. They were great people. It was a very sad day when we lost them."

"How did you lose them?" Asking him that I could see the sadness come over him, and it was a sadness so heavy it was heartbreaking.

"My grandparents all got along very well, and so once they were all retired, the four of them decided they were going traveling. Explore the world, they would tell us. They had done lots of traveling in a short time because when they were raising their families they couldn't afford to travel. Nor did they have the time with the farming and all. We started to call them our gypsies. They were totally enjoying their time.

"Then the summer of nineteen sixty-three. They were caught in a real bad storm down east, and a big truck went out of control and ran over them. They were all killed instantly. This was a blessing because, knowing them, if there would have been a survivor, they would have spent the rest of their life feeling guilty that they had lived."

"That is so sad, James. I'm sorry I asked."

"Don't be sorry. We have our great memories in our heart and minds. How about you? Did you know your grandparents?"

"My mother's parents used to come to see us once in a while, but I don't ever remember meeting my dad's parents. My mother's parents were not nice people, so we did not care if they come around or not."

"How can you not be a good grandparent? Yet we knew a lot of kids growing up with us that just hated it when their grandparents were going to be at their house."

"Well, we would have been one of them."

"How are your parents about your baby? If you don't mind me asking."

"They don't know about the baby."

"Oh! Are you not going to tell them?"

"I am sooner or later. It just won't be a nice when I do so. I am trying to put it off as long as I can."

"Sorry to hear that. That is ironic. My mother wanted nothing more than to be a grandmother, and here you are, scared to tell your mother she is going to be a grandmother."

"I'm not scared to tell her. She just won't be happy about it. That is why it was nice to have your mother because she just filled that void, and I didn't have to think about it."

"I know how excited Mom was about you and the baby. That was all she talked about. I feel like I have known you forever, and so do the other boys."

"Thank you, James. That's very nice of you to say."

"I think that what you and Sam are going to do is a good thing." The look on my face must have said it all.

"What Sam and I are going to do?"

"Yeah. You, moving in with Sam and him helping you with the baby and all. Mom would be so happy for you, knowing you don't have to go through all this on your own. I think it is good for Sam as well to take responsibly for someone as he has always had Mom to take care of him. He might be the youngest, but it is time for him to grow up."

"I'm sorry, James, but I have no idea what you are talking about. For one thing, I am not moving in with Sam. I live in the basement suite, and that's where I plan on staying. My baby is just that, my baby, and there is no one going to be responsible for it or myself. I can take care of us just fine, thank you very much. So I don't know who or why you were told such a thing, but it is not true!"

"But I thought."

"I don't care what the hell you thought, it's not happening. I don't really know Sam. And what I do know of him I wouldn't want him responsible for myself or my baby."

"Now wait. I don't think he is that bad!"

"Maybe you don't, and for a brother, he may be great, but I will not have anyone pushing me or my baby around."

Now James gets a little testy.

"What the hell is that suppose to mean?"

"I have seen him when he has been drinking and how he treats Mary, and I won't be treated that way, and I sure the hell won't put my baby at risk."

"What has he done to mother that you think is so bad?"

"He is mean, and he pushes her around, really pushes her around."

"Bullshit." He sits there for a bit thinking. "Are you sure about this?"

"Yes, I have seen it, and when I talk to Mary about it, she says he only does it when he is drinking."

"Mom never told any of us about the abuse that Sam was giving her."

"Of course not, because there was always a good reason. Booze. She always covered up for him. Now I don't know if he ever apologized to her or not, she never said."

"I really can't believe this. Our father never showed us any kind of meanness towards mother, so why would Sam?"

"Are you saying you don't believe me?"

"No. Then whose idea was it for you to move in with Sam."

"I don't know, but it sure wasn't mine. But I'm betting your mother was behind it. She thinks she was doing us both a favor by arranging this setup. I wouldn't be alone to have my baby, and I would be there to look after Sam once she is gone. I know she was just trying to be helpful, bless her heart, but James, there is no way I am moving in with your brother, so please would you talk to him about this."

"Sure, I will. I got the feeling that he was OK with all of this, and when we saw you two together at the café, we just took for granted that you were all for it as well. I am very sorry that we jumped to the wrong conclusion. I have seen Sam look at you, and I really think he has something for you."

"I can't help that. And he best get over it. It is something you will have to tell him to get over because I am not interested in starting anything with him now or later. I have seen him in action, so no, thank you."

"Wow, you really don't like him, do you?"

"I wouldn't say we can't be friends, but I have a baby to think about, and I don't want to get us into a bad situation. Seeing it firsthand, I would be really stupid to jump into that."

"I can see why Mom really likes you. You're very strong willed and minded. I don't think you and your baby will have much to worry about. I will talk to Sam. What if he says he wouldn't be like that with you? Would you think about it then?"

"No! I am not taking that kind of a risk. I have known women who have lived like that, and their lives were hell all the time, and every day, it got worse. So no, thanks. I will just stay down below."

"None of us knew he was like that. But then when we have all been around drinking, he wouldn't dare take on one of us, and he sure the hell wouldn't be pushing Mom around with us there. This has been a very well-kept secret. It makes me wonder when it all started. I will have to ask him."

"Oh please! I don't want to cause any trouble between you boys. I just wanted you to understand why I wasn't interested in moving in with him."

"I do understand, and thank you for telling me. Do you plan on staying in the basement long?"

"Why do I have to move out now?"

"No, I don't think so. I am sure whatever deal you have made with mother, Sam will stand behind. I think I will go back to the room now before they think we ran away together. Are you coming back to the room?"

"I will be there in a few minutes."

"All right, I will see you then." He winks at me then leaves. I just wanted a few minutes to take in some of the things we were talking about. How do I face Sam now that I know what he and his mother were planning? It will be awkward for me, and I only hope James doesn't say anything until after this is all over with.

Will he be pissed enough to tell me I have to move out. Maybe things will stay the way they were. His mother won't know, and that will take the pressure off Sam as far as any promises he had made to his mother goes. I wouldn't mind helping Sam out now and then when it came to housekeeping. Perhaps preparing meals as a friend would do at a time like this. But that would be the only arrangement I would be interested in. Thinking that when the time is right, I will talk to Sam about this and see how he feels about it.

I walked slowly back to Mary's room. I found the boys all standing around her bed so I just slipped in and stood off to the side.

"I think one of use should go get Charlene, or she maybe to late if we wait," says Sam.

"I can do that," said James, and he turns around just as I stepped forward.

"Oh, I was just going to come and get you."

"How's your mom?" I asked James.

"She hasn't long. The doctor has just been in, and he told us it will be any time now. We were worried that you wouldn't be here with her. We don't know if she knows we are here or not, but we can only hope she does. I could see the way Mary was breathing. It was like she only needed a breath once in a while. I did not time it, but it was a long time in between breath, and I guess the doctor had told the boys that was her body shutting down. Once all her organs had finally quit, then her heart would just quit as well. All anyone could do was wait, and it seem like no one had anything to say. If someone did say something, it was answered with a nod.

At one point, I had seen the boys were breathing with their mother, and none of them even knew they were.

James had said to the boys, "I think we should pray for Mom. You know she would want us to."

Sam looked at James and said, "Is she gone?"

"Yes," the others said in unison.

They took each other's hand to hold in a circle, and James turned to me and said, "Would you like to join us?"

"If you don't mind? Thank you," I say as I take his hand and Sam's hand.

"The circle is now complete," Sam says as he looks at me. James starts the pray off, "Our Father in heaven we would like to thank you for such a great lady that we knew as our mother. Not only was she our mother but our doctor, nurse, and teacher. Mom was kind to all she knew, young or old, and never missed a chance to help someone out at least once a week. This seemed to be a goal she had set for herself especially since you took our father. We ask you to please take good care of her and please see that she is rejoined with our father so when we come home, they will both be there to greet us. Thank you. In Christ name we pray. Amen."

We all just stood around, and no one seem to know what to do or say. There were tears on everyone's face except Sam's. He was the first to leave the room, and I just couldn't believe that after all his mother had done for him, all this time he didn't have a tear to shed for her. *What a coldhearted son of a bitch* is what was going through my mind. I will sure as hell tell him so.

"Come, Charlene," James said as he takes me by the arm.

"I will take you home before we go down to the funeral home."

"I would appreciate that, James, thank you." When we got into the car, one of the other boys had asked James if he knew where Sam might have gone.

"I have no idea."

"What about you, Charlene, do you have a guess?"

"I am afraid not. I don't know Sam that well to know where he would have gone."

"Really" is all I heard from the backseat.

"I will explain later," James tells them.

Sam did come home much later. I could hear all of the boys upstairs. They were pretty upset with him as he never showed up at the funeral home like he was supposed to. He was fairly hammered by the sounds of it. I could hear one of the boys yelling at him.

"Couldn't you leave the damn booze alone just for a while?"

"You handle it your way. I will handle it mine, all right! I don't need anyone to tell me when I should drink or not." Next I heard the door slamming shut, and I could her Sam coming down the stairs. Oh shit, this is not what I need. Maybe I won't answer the door. I will let him think I'm in bed. He doesn't just knock; he bangs and bangs on the door. Next thing, he is yelling at me, "Charlene, I know you're in there, so open this goddamned door or I will kick it in. Come on, open the damn door now. PLEASE!" I heard him say, and now he sounded like a little boy pleading with his mother. I was just going to open the door when I heard someone else outside my door, so I looked through the peephole, and I saw it was James.

"Hey, little brother, why don't you come back upstairs. Don't bother Charlene. She needs her rest remember. She was good enough to sit with you all this time. Now why don't you let her rest?"

"Guess you're right, do you think I woke her up?"

"I think you're safe. She was pretty tired. Otherwise what I know of Charlene she would have been out here and kicking your ass." With that, I saw them turn around and head back upstairs. James looks over his shoulder and nods. That bugger knew I was at the door.

CHAPTER THIRTEEN

This was a busy week for the boys. Mary had a lot of family from the old country, and I did see one lady that I thought might be her sister. She looked a lot like Mary. I couldn't believe there would be that many people and to be in her little house. But then I guess if you're just sitting around talking about the dead, you don't need much room. The coming and going of people made me restless, and I was worried about who would all know about the deal Mary and I had and what people might be saying about it. I stayed in as much as possible just so no one would notice me and maybe point, saying something like "There she is. Someone should go tell her she has to pay rent or move out." I can't see the boys letting me stay too long without paying anything, but guess, time will tell. For now, I will just finish reading the book Mary had given to me so I can return it to the boys. I guess it was a good thing I never got to read it in the hospital because now I have something to do. So that's just what I was doing when a soft knock came to my door. Frowning, I got up to answer it and was surprised to see Sam.

"Sam! Are you all right?"

"May I come in?"

"Oh sure, come on in. What can I do for you, Sam?" He looked so sad, and I had no words to say to him. I know he will be missing Mary because she still took care of him. Now he will have to do it all himself, and I know some guys just don't do well at that. Sam seems like he could be one of them.

"How are the arrangements coming for your mom?"

"Not bad, but we need your help."

"Mine, Sam? How?"

"We need to pick flowers for Mom, and we don't know what were her favorite ones, and I know Mom talked to you about her flowers, or I should say used to." And a tear rolled down his cheeks.

"I'm sorry, Sam."

"No, I'm sorry. I came down here to get your help not to go on a pity trip."

"That's all right. It has only been a week, so it should still be a little hard to talk about."

"I will miss my mom a lot." Then he paused for a few minutes, and he got such a shameful look on his face. I didn't know what the hell he was thinking, and he started to make me nervous.

"I didn't always treat my mom very nice," he said as he looked down to the floor. "But I did love my mom very much. She took very good care of us boys after our father died. We never needed for anything. Mom worked hard to provide for us and seen to it that we got what schooling we needed to go somewhere in life. I think we all made a point of doing something great with our lives just to show her we were grateful for all she had done for us. Mom always put us boys first no matter what. I know when I was drinking, I used to push her around, and I don't know why I would get rough on her. I never wanted to hurt her, and I don't think I did, not physically anyway. I would always tell her I was sorry in the morning and hug her and give her a kiss on her cheek. She seemed to be OK with that. But God knows I would do anything for her, and I would do anything to have her back.

"My brothers think I don't care that Mom is gone. When I told them that wasn't true, James had said to me, 'Why? Do you miss having someone to push around?' and I just looked at him then left the house. I don't know how he knew. Mom must have told him at one time. But what could I say? I was guilty of exactly that, so there was no denying it." Now his tears are really flowing, and I'm not sure what I'm supposed to say or do. I did get the box of tissue paper for him. What do I say that would make him feel better and to let him know that I know how much he is hurting without him thinking more of it than it is. After the plans that him and Mary had made, I just wanted to stay far away from him so he wouldn't think maybe I was OK with those plans now. I felt like I had to get him out of here.

"Sam, you said you needed my help. Can you tell me with what?"

"Oh yeah, the flowers what were Mom's favorite flowers?"

"I will think about it and let you know because right now my mind is drawing a blank."

"Can you please let me know in the morning before we head down to the funeral home?"

"Yes, what time will you be leaving?"

"We will be leaving sometime around nine thirty."

"All right, I have to go downtown, and I will let you know what I come up with before I leave."

"That would be great. Do you need a ride downtown tomorrow?"

"No, my brother is going to pick me up. But thank you."

"If you ever need a ride and I'm at home, please just ask and I will take you down."

"Thank you, I will." And while we were talking, I was walking to the door, so he would leave; at least I was hoping he was going to. Then he said to me, "Char, can I ask you something?"

"Yeah, sure, Sam, what is it?"

"Have you thought anymore about what Mom wanted for us?"

"Us?"

"Yeah, you and me."

"No, Sam. I never did."

"Are you going to?"

"No, Sam. I'm not."

"Why not?"

"Those are not the kind of arrangements you go into just because—"

"Is the baby's father going to take care of you?"

"No, Sam. He's not, but I don't need anyone taking care of me."

"I would take real good care of you and the baby."

"I believe you would, Sam, but we are not your responsibly, and like I said, I don't need someone to take care of me."

"Is it because of how I was with my mother when I was drinking?"

"Sam, I don't really know you, and the fact that you do get that way when you're drinking definitely would be something to think about because I would not want to put myself and my baby into a bad situation."

"I see, well, will you think about it? Because I can leave the booze alone. If you change your mind, you know where to find me." He reaches out and rubs his hand down my arm. I think it was meant in a friendly way, but it did nothing for me but make me a little more apprehensive. Showing him to the door was the only way for me to answer him.

"Sam, I will let you know about the flowers first thing in the morning. Good night now." I was already closing the door when he said good night back. Turning and leaning on the door, I thought, *What now?* I thought that was all over with. It wasn't really late, but I felt drained more mentally than physically, so I decided to have a bath and then I would read awhile.

My bath must have been more relaxing than I thought because I woke up to my book lying on the bed beside me. I don't even remember what I had read about or if I had read anything; maybe I was just lying there thinking and fell asleep. I was feeling pretty good and thought I might as well get up and make myself some coffee. It was so quiet and peaceful; no one must be up yet upstairs. I can usually hear shuffling and mumbling going on upstairs; it is not loud but I can hear it. Oh, peaceful, maybe I will just lie here a little longer. Yes, then it hit me. Peaceful, the blue ones. So I hurried and got dressed so I could catch Sam before he left. I can always come back for my coffee. I will just get it going, so once that was done, I went upstairs. I debated whether I should knock or wait awhile. I still could not hear anyone, and if the boys finally got to sleep in one morning, I didn't want to be the one to wake them. They have had a hard week, and tomorrow will even be worse as Mary's service is tomorrow. Pulling my hand down and I was just turning around when the outside door opened, and there was James. I don't know who got frightened the most.

"Good morning, James."

"Good morning, Charlene."

"I was just leaving. I thought maybe you all got to sleep in today, so I didn't want to be the one to spoil that chance."

"No, Sam had to go to work this morning, and he told me you would be by, so I wanted to be up, so I was outside having a smoke. Mom never did allow us to smoke in the house."

"It is nice to see you still won't even if she's not here."

"She earned the respect."

"You're right about that."

"I have coffee brewing. In fact, it should be ready. Would you have a cup with me while you tell me about the flowers?"

"All right, that would be nice, thanks. I have my coffee brewing as well, but I thought I had better catch Sam before he left. He told me he had to be at the funeral home by nine thirty."

"Yes, we do, but Sam won't be as he got called to the office."

"That's too bad."

"Sam didn't want to have to deal with this anyways. I guess once a baby always a baby, and I'm not saying that in a derogatory way. There are just a lot of things that he can't handle, and I guess it comes from him having Mom to do it all the time. What do you take in your coffee?"

"Just milk or cream, which ever you have handy."

"What did you come up with as far as flowers?"

"Blue roses were your mom's favorite ones."

"Did she tell you why?"

"Yes, the aroma from two of them were nicer than a bouquet of any other flowers. Your mom had told me that each color of rose stands for something special."

"So what does the blue one stand for, sadness?"

"No, it stands for tranquility although sadness does seem to fit with the blue."

"Tranquility! What?"

"It means calm, peaceful, which I would hope your mother is at peace now."

"Yes, I would think so. Is that what the blue rose really means?"

"That's what your mom told me."

"Then blue roses it is. What else would we put with them?"

"I would put lots of small baby's breath in it, along with some flowing satin ribbons to break up the blue, and it will also make it very elegant. Your Mother had very nice taste in the things she bought or planted."

"Also in her taste as friends, Charlene." With this, he reaches over and takes my hand. "How are you doing with all of this?"

I didn't know if I should pull my hand away or wait until he did.

"I'm not really sure. It is hard to believe that your mom has passed away. Some morning when I wake up, I think I'll go up and have coffee with Mary. Then it hits me. I miss her already as a friend, but I miss her more as the mother type. I could talk to her about anything. At first because she went to church, I was scared that she would ask me to move out when she found out I was having a baby, but she just did the total opposite, and she made me feel strong and not ashamed of myself.

"When she asked if she could be my baby's adoptive grandmother and my adoptive mother, I didn't really know what to say. But she had convinced me that God and/or her husband had sent me to her. She said we needed each other, and it would be good for both of us. Oh, how she wanted to babysit for me so I could go back to work."

"Yes, she was very excited about that, and she had told me she hoped you would have a girl. All she ever wanted was a daughter. You were going to be the closest person to fill her dream."

"Your mom had told me about the girl they were to adopt."

"She did? She was really depressed for a long time after, and us boys, we never felt like she loved us any less because she was always loving and caring and always there for us. Mom went the extra mile for us no matter the cost. Our father left us well provided for, so Mom never had to go to work, but she did once we were all in school but was always home when we got home. We would ask her why she would work, and she said that she would just shrivel up if she couldn't keep busy, so we said no more."

"Yeah, she would still get very upset over that, but she had lost two in a short time, so it hurt her very deeply."

"With none of us boys taking wives and giving her grandchildren, we sort of let her down. But I guess we all felt we had lots of time yet. It is funny because if you look at our ages, we should all have a wife and at least two kids by now. But oh no, we have dragged our feet, and now, our children won't get a chance to know any of our grandparents."

"I'm sorry, James."

"Why would you be sorry for us? You're the one having a baby on her own. That deal Mom and Sam were putting together, have you thought about it anymore?"

"It is funny you should ask. Sam asked me the same question last night, and no, I haven't thought about it anymore."

"Why not?"

"I will be fine, and I will do it on my own."

"You're a pretty stubborn person."

"I don't think I'm being stubborn. But this isn't anyone else's responsibility but mine."

"But couldn't you use the help?"

"Perhaps, but not that way. I will not use Sam or anyone else."

"I have to say, I admire you for taking this big undertaking on all alone. It can't be easy to raise a child by yourself."

"I don't know. I have never done it before. But I can let you know a few years down the road." He had taken his hand away to reach into his pocket, and we had forgotten that he had had a hold of my hand while we were talking.

"Here, Char. This is my business card, and I want you to promise me that if ever you have trouble of any kind, you will call me."

"No, that's OK, James. I will be OK."

"It's just a damn business card, Char. I am nothing like Sam. I do not need a woman to take care of me. But I do like what I know of you, and my mom has told me a lot about you and what you are trying to accomplish. I think if you would just give it a chance, we could get to mean something to each other."

"Please, James, I am having another man's baby."

"So is he in the picture at all?"

"No, he's not."

"So the baby could be anyone's."

"No, James, he can't be anyone's. He is mine. End of story. I am not ready for any of this."

"How about friends then? Can we start there? Mom would want us to watch over you. So please, for Mom, take it and promise me that you will call."

"OK, James, and thank you, and thank you for the coffee. Now I must go. I've got a few things to do downtown."

"Thank you for knowing about the flowers that Mom liked and the chat, and we'll see you later at the viewing."

"I forgot that was tonight. But no, I won't be there."

"You won't be? Why not?"

"I believe that this should just be for close family. After all, it is your last evening with your mother. I don't feel that everyone should be there taking your time away from her."

"That is nice of you to think that way, but it is for the public."

"I know, but it is not for me. I'm sorry, James."

"No need to be sorry. Everyone handles death differently."

"We will see you at the service, right?"

"Oh yeah! I will be at the service, so bye for now."

"Bye."

I left and was going uptown as I needed some black panty hose and a card. I was glad that Sam had gone to work, seeing how I had told him my brother was giving me a ride, which he wasn't. Stupid me as if he couldn't see out the window if I was walking or catching a ride.

The weather was nice for a walk, something I haven't done in a while, so I will just take it easy. There were birds singing everywhere, and you could hear the odd lawn mowers running, so you could also smell the fresh cut grass. People were out in their yards doing one thing or another; some look like they were getting their garden spots ready for planting, and others look like they were just giving their yards a good cleaning. Any way you looked at it, it was a very nice day to be outside. I did not see any action at Louise's when I walked by, so I will check on the way back.

I thought I might as well go into the drugstore as they will have both. That way, if I want to, I could walk down to the shop at lunchtime and see Beth, and my shopping would be done. The drugstore had some nice baby books in, and they were on sale for twelve dollars, so I thought I would pick one up; it is the ones where you kept all the records of anything that had to do with the baby as it is growing, and there were a couple of pages that were on the family history, which I think is a good idea to keep; then one will always know where they came from except for I couldn't fill out anything on the father's side. I wouldn't have any information on them at all. Maybe someday, that would change.

I was just going through the till when I felt a hand on my shoulder.

"Hey, what's with the blue." It was James.

"Hi, James, that's all there was, and will it really matter? It is just to keep records in. I can always buy a pink one later if need be."

"You sound sure that you're having a boy."

"I feel that way, and I don't know why, but they say most women if they're turned in to their bodies, they will know what they're having before anyone."

"Is that what you want, a boy?"

"I think so. I think a boy would be easier to raise on my own."

"Then I hope you're right. Now can I buy you lunch?"

"I'm sorry, James, but I am having lunch with a girlfriend from work, but thank you just the same."

"Maybe I will be able to buy you lunch before I leave to go home." I just started to protest, "James."

"As friends! You know friends do buy lunch for each other now and again."

"You're right. I am sorry."

"So what do you say? Will you have lunch with me one day next week?"

"All right, James. I would like that."

"I'll leave you now, and we will talk later."

"Yeah, I better get going. Beth will be waiting for me."

I got to the shop five minutes before she was done, and she was somewhat surprised when she saw me come through the door.

"Hey, Char, what are you doing here?"

"I was hoping to have lunch with a friend today."

"Oh, who?"

"You! You fool, unless you're booked up through lunch."

"No, I am not, and yes, I would love to go for lunch. We haven't been in touch for a while, so we have some catching up to do. Just give me one minute, and we can go. I have an hour and a half today, so you're lucky."

"Right on." We went to the little corner café; we knew it would be quiet compared to the others at this time of day. It is still busy, but not run-you-over busy as it is of the main track, and the food is good. It is a small German establishment, so they also carried some pastry that you can't just buy anywhere. Some of this I knew because my first real job away from home was working in a German bakery and café, so it was a little bit like home for me.

"So tell me, Char. What have you been up to?"

"Not much. Tomorrow is Mary's funeral."

"That's right. I did hear about that, and I am sorry. What does this mean for your living arrangements, Char?"

"I can't really say right now. No one is saying anything different, so I am assuming that all is well. I have had long talks with two of the boys, and they didn't say I couldn't stay with the arrangement Mary and I made.

But you know what Beth, Mary and her son Sam were setting up some kind of a deal that I could move in with him, and he would take care of me and the baby."

"You're kidding!!"

"No, I'm not. This was sweet on Mary's part even on her deathbed she was worried about me and the baby, and she had promised to be there for me, and I guess this was the only way she felt she could keep her end of the deal."

"So are you?"

"Am I what?"

"Are you moving in with her son?"

"No, Beth. I am not. He seemed to be upset about it when I told him no. But I think he was just wanting someone to take Mary's place in taking care of him. I told him I was not interested.

How do you just move in with someone you don't even know. Besides, I saw what he is like when he is drinking and that alone scares me."

"I have heard the same from some people who know him well, and they say that's why he has no women in his life now. Guess he had a very nice girl once, but he couldn't leave the booze alone, so she left him."

"He told me he would leave the booze alone if that's what was stopping me."

"He said that to you?"

"Yes, he did because he was telling me that when he was drinking he wasn't very nice to his mother. He said he never hurt her as far as he knew. He said he never meant to if he did, and she never told him any different."

"I don't think I would want to move into something like that and take a child into it as well. Talk about making a deal with the devil himself."

"Besides not knowing him and I have seen what kind of a problem he has with his booze, that's exactly why I'm not interested."

"Good for you, Char." Our lunch came, and we were having a great time just sitting and catching up.

"Char, don't turn right now and look, but about five minutes ago, this man came in, and he looked twice at you, and now he just sits there watching you."

"Where is he?"

"At the counter by the door."

"What does he look like?"

"He is a nice-looking man, very tall well-built, and he's not really dark but maybe a little darker than me." Beth looks like she had a tan all year round; she was a lucky one.

"What is he wearing?"

"He has on a white dress shirt, and they look like a black or very dark jeans but new jeans. He looks like he could be in his early thirties. He is carrying some kind of brown leather bag."

"You have to be kidding! Is he following me?"

"I don't know who is he?"

"It sounds like Mary's oldest son. I just saw him at the drugstore. He was going to the funeral home. I told him I was having lunch with a friend from work."

"So why would he be following you?"

"I really don't know."

"Come on, Char. What is going on?"

"Nothing really. He thinks maybe he and I could, what did he say, 'get to mean something to each other.' He says he likes what he sees in me and wants to get to know me better."

"Lucky you, Char."

"No, Beth. This is not how I want it to be. I don't want some man feeling sorry for me or maybe they think I am just easy, so they could have their way with me. They make me feel cheap. If he keeps this up, I will have to confront him about it. I already told him I was not interested. The fact that I am having another man's baby doesn't seem to bother them. But it sure the hell is bothering me."

"Calm down, Char. He's getting up."

"Oh shit."

"It's OK. He's paying for his drink. Now he is leaving." So when she said that I turned around to see if I was right."

"Is that who it is?"

"Yes, that's him."

"I think I would get to know him, Char."

"He has asked me if we could start as friends."

"What did you say?"

"I told him yes, that we could do that."

"Attagirl."

"Beth!!"

"Well, I'm just wanting you to keep all your options open."

"Beth, I am not ready for a man in my life. I will have to have time to adjust to a baby, never mind a man, and one that is not the father of the baby's taboot."

"So because you're having a baby by someone that means there's no room in your life for anyone else?"

"I just think it would make thinks a little awkward when you try to mix one man's child to another man. You know they won't treat the child very lovingly, how can they?"

"A lot of that, Char, will depend on you and how you raise your child and how old the child is when you meet someone. Like now, if you were to take up with someone that doesn't have children and love you, they will love the baby as if the baby were theirs. The men that can't do that would not want you now."

"You believe that, Beth?"

"Yes, Char, I do. I have seen it done, and no one would know but the two of you that the baby is not his. It has been known that babies have taken on traits of the man that raises it. I think that you should think a little more about this guy. What is his name by the way?"

"His name is James."

"That sounds young yet firm."

"Oh, aren't you the funny one."

"Come on, Char. It's not an old man's name like Donald." We both started to laugh, and it felt good to laugh. It seemed to be a long time since I had anything to laugh about. So we carried on our lunch and had talked about her boys and how work was going, and she told me that most of the women I used to do have gone somewhere else. We all think they have gone to get Elaine to do their hair because she had put a big ad in the paper when she moved to the other shop.

"She told Liz she would lose a lot of women when both she and I were gone."

"Well, she did. It is a good thing the rest of us had a good clientele. Otherwise, she would have been real sorry for the crap she pulled. I'm still thinking of moving to another shop. It just isn't the same now knowing what she will do to someone. Speaking of that, I had better get back. You know the saying about how fast time goes by when you're enjoying yourself."

"It seemed like we have just sat down, but we have covered a lot of ground."

"Yeah, Char. Looks like we are caught up on everything. Let me know what happens, and I think you should give Mr. Sexy a chance."

"Beth!"

"I know, I know, but you could keep in touch with him and see what happens after you have the baby. After all, Char, if he is willing to take on that responsibly, he can't be all bad. He knows you're pregnant now and is interested, so don't shut him out. After all, his mother wasn't making a deal with him. He is interested because he wants to be. I think you could use a good man in your life right about now. Even as a friend."

"I have a good friend in you. I don't need a man, thank you very much."

"That's true, but having to go out with me for suppers or lunch is not what I would call very interesting or exciting. Not to mention the cuddling in front of the fire at night."

"Oh you are too." And we both laughed as we left the café. I carried on my way home and would check to see if Louise was home; it was so nice out I didn't want to hurry home just to sit in the basement. The sun felt so nice on me. I would have liked to have a chair and just sit outside and soak it up. Everything was so green; it is funny there are so many different shades of green this time the year, and I bet most people don't even realize it. There were more flowers now, and with all the birds singing, it made you forget winter was even here.

There still was no one home at Louise's, which was strange, because she should have had today off. I could see she had been out in her yard as well, and it was looking very neat and clean. I wonder why the yards become so messy over the winter. People spend all fall raking and cleaning and putting things away for the winter, but still in the spring, it seems like we have to start all over.

Once at home, I decided to lie down for a while; the walking and fresh air had made me a little tired. I had slept for only an hour but got up feeling great. I made myself an iced tea and decided to go out and sit in the sun. Mary had a small table in among her rosebushes, so today would be a nice day to sit there and remember Mary. I could almost see her walking around, talking to her plants. I wonder what will become of all her work as I never saw anyone but Mary in her flowers. I got up and started to wander around and smelling and just taking in the flowers that she was so proud of.

"I don't know what will become of all of you now that Mary is gone. You are going to be some lonely." What was this? I was talking to the plants.

"Is that for the plants or are you talking about you?"

Jumping back and taking in a deep breath, I say, "Oh, James, you scared me half to death."

"I am sorry, Char. And I guess that is something one should not do to a lady who is pregnant." I know I blushed, so I turn away so he couldn't see my face.

"Guess not, it is a good thing I am not due anytime. You could have scared me into labor."

"I wish you were closer and that would have happened."

"James, what an awful thing to say."

"I didn't mean for it to sound like that. I just mean, then I would have been here for you now that Mom isn't. I would get to see this little man before anyone else. That is if you are right! But it might be a girl. It has been a very long time since I have seen or had anything to do with a newborn baby. It would be exciting to see such a wonder and a miracle. Do you ever just think about how they can become a fully developed person. To be so perfect in every way right from the start and so delicate and precious very much like Mom's flowers." I hadn't realized that I had a tear running down my cheek. James reaches over and wipes it away.

"I am sorry to have upset you, Char."

"You didn't upset me. That was so kind of you to say. It was very touching and sweet. I guess I just never thought that you would give such deep thought into a baby."

"Why because I'm a man and the fact that at my age I don't have any children?"

"I suppose that's it. That is something maybe a man that has already had experienced the birth of a baby would say."

"So you think that for men to think about babies they have to have had one?"

"I guess so, I don't know."

"Well, you're wrong. I will have you know I have thought about it a lot lately."

"Oh, I'm sorry" was all I could say.

"Yes, Charlene. I think about your baby and you."

"Please don't go there." I turned and was walking away when he grabbed me by the arm, and it was a firm hold he had on me. I just looked at him and said, "Let me go, James!"

"Please stay and talk to me."

"Talk to you about what? Which one of Mary's boys will be the father of my baby? Do I have a sign hanging out anywhere that says I'm looking for a father? And while we're having this talk, why the hell did you follow me today?

"First of all, calm down, secondly, I did not follow you today."

"So what were you doing at the café?"

"Is that café just for you and your friends? If so, no one had told me, and I'm sorry for trespassing."

"No, of course not. I'm sorry, it's just that—"

"You had just seen me, and you had told me you were going for lunch, but you did not tell me where you were going."

"You're right. Please, I'm sorry."

"I used to take Mom to that little café whenever I came home. With her being from the old country, it always made her feel like she was going back home. I thought I would go in there today and maybe feel like I was with her. But it wasn't the same. In fact, I found it too upsetting that's why I left. I had thought of coming over and meeting your friend, but you two looked like you were having a very serious talk.

"The other boys didn't like the little café, but then they were never over in Mom's country, and I had taken her home a couple of times after our father passed away, and I knew how much she like her hometown."

"So how come she never went back home after your dad passed away?"

"Because of us boys. We all have real good jobs here."

"She never said anything to me about it. We used to go to the other one that is all done in antiques. But then she knew I am an antique lover."

"Mother also liked antiques as you can see by what she has around the house. I think you and Mom would have liked a lot of the same things. That's why she took such a liking to you. When she would call me, you were all she ever talked about. When I saw you at the restaurant when we first came here, it was like I had known you for a very long time already.

"Why are you fighting this can't you feel anything when were together?"

"I don't feel anything but fear, James."

"I don't want to hurt you, but I would like to get to know you."

"You have already said that."

"You keep running away from me. Why?"

"James, I'm not looking for anything or anyone right now. Don't you understand? I just want to be left alone to have my baby. I don't want to have to depend on anyone or expect anything from anyone."

"Wow, that guy has done a number on you. Do you love the baby's father?"

"Love! No. I sure don't."

"Do you still have feelings for him?"

"No, I don't."

"So why are you always ready to bite and run whenever I try to talk to you?"

"Once again, I'm sorry if that's how it seems to you, but that isn't it really."

"Then why don't you talk to me? Come on, Char, sit back down, and we'll talk. I'm a good listener." He takes my hand in his and walks me back to the little table that is among Mary's roses.

"Now promise me you won't disappear on me, Char. I am just going to go get us some iced tea."

"All right."

"Promise me!"

"I promise I will wait for you."

"All right then." He hurried off like it was life or death. I don't have anything to talk to him about, so I don't understand what he's making such a big deal out of it for. Why can't he see I just want to be left alone and have my baby? *It will be just fine, deary,* and the hair on the back of my neck stood up, and I was looking around. "Mary," I whispered.

"Here, Char, is your iced tea. Char, what is it? You look like you have seen a ghost?"

"Oh, nothing." I reached out to take the iced tea. "Thank you."

"Here's to a new friendship," he says as he tips his glass to mine and takes a drink, so I do the same thing.

"Can I ask you something, Char? It is personal, so you don't have to answer me if you don't want to."

"All right, what is it that you want to know?"

"Why is the baby's father not involved?"

"To make a long story short, by the time I knew I was pregnant, he was with someone else."

"What did he say when you told him?"

"I haven't told him, but I think he knows about it."

"Why haven't you told him about the baby?"

"Because he had already moved on, and if he didn't want me before there was a baby, I didn't want him because there was a baby. I have seen that a lot, and it just doesn't work out in the end. It may take a few years, but what a waste of time. It hurt enough to be let down once that it is not something I want to do again anytime soon."

"I see, so that's why you won't give me a chance? You think I will let you down as well!"

"I didn't know I was expected to give you a chance, James. Like I said, I'm not looking for anyone right now."

"Do you have to be looking? Can't it just happen? You think because you are pregnant by some other man no one else will find you attractive and enjoy your company."

"I can't say I have thought about it."

"So tell me just what do you think about then."

"James, don't do this."

"Come on, Char. What do you think about being single and waiting for a baby? What makes you happy?"

"Right now, what makes me happy is knowing everything with my baby is OK and that we have a nice place to live thanks to your mom. After the baby comes, I don't know what will happen then because I will have to go back to work, and I will have to find someone to take care of my baby. That in itself scares the hell out of me. I know I have a year before they will make me go back to work, but that year will go by so fast."

"So tell me what are you so afraid of that you won't let anyone help you?"

"James, you don't understand."

"Yes, you're right. I don't understand, so please make me. Come on, Char. Tell me."

"I made my bed, now I must lie in it. I'm also afraid of losing my baby."

"Losing your baby, but you just said all was OK with the baby!"

"That way, yes."

"Then what the hell are you talking about?"

"They have money, and if he really wanted to, he could take the baby away from me."

"Why would he be able to do that? You're not an unfit mother."

"He and his family could give the baby more than I could."

"Do you really think that is why someone would take a baby away from its own mother? You look like you take very good care of yourself, and I mean real good care that you have me looking."

"James."

"No, I mean it, and I know what all you have done in the basement and how much time you have put into the room for the baby. No one could love this baby more than you do." And with that, he had placed his hand on my stomach. I then put my hand on top of his. "No one is going to be able to take your baby away. I want you to quit thinking like that and relax more and really enjoy this time with your baby. It will all be over soon, and everyone will see how much this baby means to you and to all your friends. As far as you making your bed, it is not one you have to lie in alone. Who told you that anyways?"

"Thank you, James. It doesn't matter."

"I mean it. If anyone tells you any different, call me. You have my number."

"That is very kind of you, James, but none of this is any concern of yours."

"Listen to me when I say I am making it my concern, do you understand?"

"But, James."

"No, buts. I mean what I say, and I say what I mean, and I also want you to remember that I am not Sam, and my mother has nothing to do with me wanting to be involved with you and your baby. Yes, maybe if you weren't living here, I would not have met you. I believe in the fact that things happen for a reason. I also believe in fate and so should you. One thing we all should have is faith. My mom always told us if you have faith, you can do anything and handle anything that comes your way."

"I know she had her faith and she believed that either God or your father had sent me to meet your mom."

"That's right, and by doing so, it gave me the chance to also meet you. So please quit fighting me so much." He leans over and kisses me on the cheek, and I know I turn ten shades of red and wanting to get back to something I felt comfortable talking about I said to him, "James, how did you make out with the flowers?"

"Great, they had all we needed in stock, and she said it would look very elegant, and it would surpass all others in any ability. So she said she wasn't going to change anything I had ordered because she couldn't offer better than that. So thank you. You were right on the money. I guess I had better go in and get ready for the viewing."

"Yes, it is getting on that time."

"Did you want to come with me?"

"No, thanks, James. I am not going to the viewing."

"Oh, that's right. You had told me that already. Why not, if you don't mind me asking?"

"I feel that it's for close family, your last night with your loved one."

"But to Mom, you were part of her family, and we sure won't complain."

"Thank you, but no. I want to leave it as it is."

"All right then. I will talk to you tomorrow some time." And he gets up and walks away. He seems like a very sincere man and a very sweet man. He isn't like Sam, but yet in some ways, I can sure tell they're brothers. Getting up, I decided to go in and have a bath and turn in early. I will just read for a while and try to empty my head as it seemed to be going in circles. All the "Should I's" and "Shouldn't I's" were starting to confuse me totally. Tomorrow was going to be a trying day and a long one.

CHAPTER FOURTEEN

I woke to a lot of commotion upstairs. I guess it was understandable, for there was a lot of people for a small house, and today was a very somber day for all involved. I got up so I could have a shower to wash my hair as I had been doing it by bending over the sink, but it is not very comfortable doing that way anymore. I am not a shower person as it always leaves me feeling cold.

I was drying off and blow-drying my hair and thinking about what I should wear today. I remember having bought a navy blue uniform that had what they called an empire waistline with a white collar and white sleeve cuffs; it would be perfect. Hope I can find it in time to iron it because it would be packed in one of these boxes in the closet.

I finished drying my hair and went and opened the first box, and there it was right on top. The hair on the back of my neck stood up, so I just slowly turned around as I felt I was not in the room by myself.

"Mary, are you here with me today? If you are, thank you," I say as I lift the dress out of the box. "I want you to know how much I miss you. I am so sorry you had to leave us." I sat down hard on the bed.

"Why, Mary, did the good Lord take you away? You had me believing that he had brought us together but then to turn it around in such a short time and take you away. Is it because I am without a husband and having a baby? Oh, Mary, what am I going to do?"

"I know what you and Sam wanted me to do, but that just is not right. I cannot and will not live like that, and I am sorry if that lets you down. You probably know what James has asked of me as well, and again I can't. I don't want some man feeling sorry for me and later throwing it in my face if things don't turn out as they should. I think he is a very nice man, your son James. But to be a friend is fine and the same with Sam. But I can't give more right now. I just want it to be the baby and me. I hope you understand. I hope you will guide them and make them see that I am not what either one of them really want. They see a pitiful girl who is having a baby on her own and that is no way to start any relationship. You and I both know that, and if you were still here, this would not be happening. Perhaps I would have met James sometime down the road but not like this." The tears are flowing, and I don't think I have really cried for Mary, but that is what is happening now, so I just let it flow.

After about twenty minutes, I heard "You're going to be just fine, deary."

Wiping my eyes and blowing my noise, I decided to go and put on a pot of coffee so it would be done after I iron my dress.

"You're right, Mary. I am going to be OK. I know now that I will have you with me always. In my heart, you will always be." I believe in the hereafter and the fact that you can communicate with the dead, if you are really tuned into them and not be afraid of the unknown.

I remember having a conversation with my little brother after he was killed, and after that, I was at ease with his death. He stood in front of me as plain as day and talked to me; he knew I was troubled by his death, and he came to assure me he was very happy and not to worry about him. So there was nothing to be afraid of and most of all him.

The ironing was done, and I was dressed and was just about to pin up my hair when someone knocked on the door.

"Hi! What are you doing here?"

"Better yet why aren't you using your peep hole?"

"I always forget I have it."

"You best start using it, Char. You don't know who is on the other side of this door."

"You're right. I will have to make myself a sign and hang on my door."

"You haven't answered me."

"I came to go to Mary's service with you. I knew you would be going alone and thought you might like to have someone to go with."

"Are you sure?"

"I am here, am I not?"

"Yes, and thank you. How did you get the day off?"

"I worked yesterday so I could have today off to be with you."

"Oh, that's why you weren't at home yesterday."

"You were down?"

"Yes, I had to go downtown, and I had checked on the way downtown and back. Why don't you get us a coffee while I finish my hair. I will only be a couple of minutes."

"I can do that. I like your dress. It is really cute. You look good pregnant."

"Oh, thanks, but I'm not going to set no trend, I can tell you that." I went back to the bathroom to finish my hair, and I could hear Louise out in the kitchen. The doors and draws were being opened and closed. Now what is she up to?

"Coffee is poured, Char."

"All right, I will be right out."

I heard her saying, "Char is getting dressed," so I peeked out to see who she was talking to.

"Hi, Charlene. I was just going to ask if you needed a ride today."

"No, thanks, James. My sister is taking me."

"I will talk to you at the church then. You look very nice by the way. You look good pregnant." He says as he runs his hand down the side of my arm. He made the hair on the back of my neck stand up.

"I'll see you there then."

"You bet and thank you."

"Who was that hunk, Char?"

"That is Mary's oldest son James."

"He is quite the looker."

"Not bad."

"Yeah like you haven't noticed. Is he married?"

"No, none of them are married, and Mary never even talked about their girlfriends."

"Oh, really, I wonder what's wrong with them. Are they all gay boys?"

"No, they're not gay."

"You know this, how?"

"Well, Sam thought I should move in with him. It was something he and Mary were setting up, and James wants to be more than friends."

"Boy, what have you been up to since I seen you last."

"Not a damn thing, staying down here and minding my own business. I think it is just about taking pity on a girl who is pregnant and on her own. It's probably just the way they were raised. I had a deal with their mother, and now she is gone, they feel it's up to them to watch out over me."

"That one could watch out over me anytime."

"Louise!"

"Well, it's true. So are you two friends now or what?"

"I don't know. I don't really know him, and he says he wants us to start being friends, then the next time, he talks like it should be more, and I'm not ready to have anyone in my life like that. I have a baby to think about."

"That's all fine, Char. But you need a life as well."

"I will have one with my baby."

"Char, it is not the same. You try having a real conversation with a baby for any length of time and you will become brain dead. Trust me, I know. I have tried it."

"He tells me the baby has nothing to do with it, and if the baby's father is not in the picture, then he doesn't understand why I have a problem with going out to lunch or anything else he might ask."

"I agree with him. Seeing how he knows you're pregnant and he's still interested and he's not embarrassed to be seen with you, and he thinks you look good pregnant should tell you something. It's not like he is just a man of twenty or younger, so he should be over the mucho thing by now. To get together with a man before the baby is born if you can fine a man that wants to do that makes you lucky because they are ready to take on that responsibility. Who can't love a newborn baby, and the baby would know no other man. It can work, Char."

"Maybe, but it scares the hell out of me. I don't want to be used again and tossed aside like I never meant anything. I trusted once and look where it has gotten me." I rub my stomach and raise an eyebrow to her.

"But you know what, Char. When you have this baby, you will never regret the time you were used and tossed aside because you will have the best of that time spent. In the end, you will almost forget how this baby came about. The joy and the happiness it will bring you will erase everything else. Don't get me wrong. You will have some rough days, nights, and maybe even years, but over all, you must remember you have someone who will love you unconditionally. But it is even better if you have someone else to share all this with. Just because you are having one man's child doesn't mean you quit looking, living, or loving. Most of all, you have to love yourself to be able to give love. Being ashamed of yourself is not loving yourself.

"Remember I have been there, and I do know how you feel, and I know you are ashamed of yourself, and that is why you hide away like you do. Not wanting anything to do with other men, this is not healthy for you. Just because you're pregnant doesn't mean you can't go out."

"I know that, Louise."

"Do you, Char? Tell me how much and where have you gone since you got pregnant."

"I have been out."

"I know you went out for lunch with Beth and myself. You went out to supper with Jacob. Boy, that is a busy schedule now, isn't it?"

"I just haven't felt like going out."

"That is bullshit, and both you and I know it. You're hiding away, Char. Who are you hiding from?"

"His family has a lot more money than I do, and what if he decides he wants the baby after it is born? I can't afford to fight him."

"Have you told any of them about the baby?"

"No, I have not, and I am not going to."

"You told me that right at the beginning, so if you don't tell him, how would he know?" If he sees you with another man while you are pregnant, he would just think that you and that man were going to have a baby, end of story. I also think it would even be safer as far as not having to worry about anyone wanting to take the baby away if you have a life with someone else."

"You really think so?"

"Of course, I do. I also think if this James guy is on the up-and-up, you should give him a chance. What can lunch hurt?"

"I guess, eh."

"Tell me you will think about it, and about him, I get good vibes from him."

"He just makes me nervous and hot all over."

"Lucky you! No really, Char. I don't mean for you to jump into his bed or start to live with him, but at least, get to know him, give him a chance to prove himself and don't be so afraid. You can call it quits at any time. After a couple of times out to a meal or a show, you will know whether you want it to go any further. Just tell him straight out that it is only a trial thing, that you will not make him any promises. He seems like a pretty understanding man. In a way, I am sorry I came today."

"Why?"

"Because now you would have been going with him instead of me."

"No, I would not have. I would have gone alone."

"Char."

"Well, I would have."

"Speaking of that, we best get going. I think I have given you the mother-daughter talk long enough."

"Thank goodness!! Just kidding, Louise. I am glad you came and that you care."

We drove to the church, and we were going to have to park three blocks away. "I will drop you off at the door and then go park."

"I will wait outside for you."

"All right, I won't be long." It looked like we could get wet later on if we're lucky.

I found a bench just outside the door and sat down to wait for Louise.

"Glad to see you made it."

"Oh yeah, no problem. My chauffer is just parking the car."

"Some people are lucky to have such luxuries at hand." We both laughed.

"You are coming to sit up front with us, right?"

"No, James. I want to sit right at the back, so I can leave if I have to."

"Why? Aren't you feeling all right?"

"No, I'm not so. In case, I don't want to disturb anyone."

"Well, maybe I should sit with you?"

"No, James. You have to be with your brothers. My sister is here with me, so I will be looked after."

"All right," he says as he gets up to leave.

"Char, are you ready to go inside?"

"Yes."

"Good day, ladies, are you friends or family?"

"Friends."

"Then come this way please."

"Please!" I say as I take his arm, "we just want to sit right here inside the door, just in case I have to leave. I don't feel well," and I rub my stomach, and he says, "Oh, I understand, miss," and he seats us right at the door.

The casket was beautiful; it was a deep red mahogany with big brass handles. It seems to be such a waste that all that beauty was going into the ground, and no one else would ever know how beautiful it is. The flowers were just as tasteful as they told James they would be. They also had a picture of Mary and her husband together on a stand with the same flowers. There was something written beside them, but I would not know what it was as I was not going that far in. For the amount of people, it could take all afternoon to go by that coffin to say good-bye. There was a lot of up again down again, and most of the people knew what it was all about, but not me. I just stayed seated, and I looked at my hands. The service was long, and when they got down to playing the hymns, then it chocked me up. It wasn't because of Mary but because I remembered the songs from when by little brother had died and the songs took me back to that darken day. That whole day came back to me as if we were reliving it. I looked at Louise, and she was watching me; she reached over and took my hand. I had whispered, "Please, let's get out of here." Louise nodded, and we got up and left.

"Are you all right, Char?" she asked as we sat on the bench outside that I had sat on earlier.

"Yeah, I feel awful, but it wasn't Mary I was crying for. It was Mickey. It was like we were back in the summer of 1970. Everything came back so vividly. I don't think I had thought about any of this, for all these years now, today I just relived that terrible day sitting in there when I was supposed to be saying good-bye to a friend. What kind of friend does that?"

"Who says what or how you are supposed to feel when you go to funerals. It hits everyone else differently. How many of these have you been to since Mickey?"

"This is the first one."

"Then of course, everything would be about him. There hasn't been anyone else for you to have memories about. The pain you carry for Mickey is still very much there. You just didn't know it.

"But this should have been about Mary."

"Mary will know."

"Boy, am I glad this week is over. I bet the boys will be glad to be able to move on. I wonder why that is that all is on hold until you have buried the dead. It seems like the whole week was blank. You don't do anything until this day is over."

"I don't know, Char. But it is the same every time. Now if you are going to be OK, I am heading for home."

"Thank you for coming with me, and yes, I will be just fine," I said, giving her a big hug and seeing her to the door. As I shut the door, I let out a big sigh. I was so glad to be home and have all this behind me. I think I will change my clothes and maybe lie down for a while.

Lying there, I wondered what was going to happen now. Will I get to stay here? Or will I have to move on? Who will watch my baby when I go back to work? The money I get each month won't cover a big rent bill plus living; it will only be more when the baby comes along. I was surprised that with so much going through my head I did drift off to sleep. It was a soft tapping that I could hear that finally woke me right up. I laid there for a moment, not knowing where this tapping was coming from. Then I heard it again, and I realized that it was someone at my door.

Going to the door to open it, I had spotted the sign that Louise had made for me that read Look First. I had to laugh to myself, but I did look and saw it was James, and he had turned around and was headed back upstairs. I thought, *Do I or don't I?* Maybe this wasn't a good day not to answer the door to them, so I opened it up and said, "James, I am home. Can I help you?"

"Sorry, I don't want to bother you. I gathered you weren't feeling well, seeing how you left the service so soon. I just thought I would check and make sure you were all right. I wanted to give you this." He hands me one of the blue roses off of Mary's casket.

"Thank you, and I am feeling a little better. I was just taking a nap."

"I'm really sorry to have woken you."

"It is OK really. Too much longer and it would have spoiled my night sleep anyways. Would you like to come in for tea?"

"If you don't mind, sure!"

"So what brings you here when there are people upstairs that you should be with?"

"Enough is enough. I just want to move on, and I really need to go home, and that is why I wanted to see you."

"Me, why?"

"Because I am going home tonight, and I won't be able to take you out for lunch like I had asked. I am sorry."

"Don't worry about it. It's not a big deal. Here's your tea."

"It is a big deal to me, I will have you know. I don't like making dates then not being able to follow through. But I do have to go home sooner than planned, but I will be back at which time I hope you will be able to have dinner with me then. I have to come back and help Sam settle some of Mom's affairs. I just don't know when for sure."

"That's fine, and how are your brothers now that the service is over?"

"I think no one wanted to say it out loud, but if you go by how I feel, I think we're all so damn glad that it is over. It has been a long dragged-out few days, or at least it feels like it. Please don't get me wrong. We loved our mom. But all this stuff you have to deal with, they make you feel like until you do all these things that just cost money, your mother won't rest. Yet we know she went to heaven as soon as she took her last breath. The rest of it is just a real moneymaker, and I think Mom would have been tick at us for spending what we did. But we felt she was worth the extra. We wanted to send her out in style. All the time we were growing up, Mom always taught us to spend wisely, and she seem to be able to make a dollar go a long way."

"I thought everything looked beautiful, and you're right, you did send her out in style. She would have been proud to see her sons had done such a fine job on the choices that they had made."

"That was only because we had you to turn to, and thank you for that."

"You're welcome for what little I've really done."

"You knew our mother and what she liked, and that was more than her boys knew."

"Glad to be able to help."

"What's wrong, Char?"

"Why do you ask me that?"

"I know you said you were napping when you came to the door, but I sense that something is not quite right with you today. Is it the baby?"

Oh damn, how do I tell him how I feel or why? Taking a deep breath, I say, "No, it's not the baby, although I do feel very heavy today. James, I don't know how to explain what is wrong in a way that you would understand."

"So why don't you try me. I am a good listener."

"OK then. My youngest brother was killed when he was fourteen, which made me fifteen. It was the first time I had to deal with death, and it was with someone so close to me. There are a lot of blank spaces in those days that followed the shooting as well as his funeral service. But today, sitting there at your mom's service, when they played some songs, they were the same songs that had been played at my brothers, and it brought it all back to me. So in the end, I was sitting at my brother's service and not your mom's. I'm so sorry, James. I felt so bad about that as well. I just couldn't stay for any more.

"That day five years ago was what I was reliving. It was like all this was bottled up inside me, and I had not let it go until today.

"Please understand that when my brother died, it seemed like we lost our parents the same day. We didn't have Mom or Dad to take us and hold us or even talk to us about any of it. So we went on living the best we could, trying to move on with no answers and no one to talk to. Sure we had each other, but no one was asking, but then again, no one knew what to ask. At first, we were so busy taking care of our parents and living in the tomb that we almost forgot what it was like to live.

"We were not allowed to speak of our brother, and the last thing we wanted to do was forget him. I remember one day, we needed wood as we still had the wood cook stove and that was always Mick's job, and my dad had called me Mick and asked me to get some wood. The look on his face when he realized what he had said almost tore me to pieces. It was like he had spoken the unforgivable, and all he said was "I'm sorry" and walked away. I said that's OK and went and got the wood. I never heard them speak his name again. We also were scared to. I think it was because we were afraid to bring them more pain or bring the pain back to them. So in the end, no one said anything. We just found it easier to move out. Our parents weren't our parents anymore. They had become distant from us, or I felt they had towards me anyways. I just didn't feel like I belonged or that they cared what happened to me after that.

"In my mind, I had put it off to the fact that if they kept us at arm's distance, it wouldn't hurt so much next time.

"Now after all these years, I don't think that was it, but I still don't have any answers." As I said this, I was pouring us more tea; my hands were shaking so much it was hard to pour the tea into our cups.

"Wow!" is all James could say at first.

"I'm sorry, James. I should not have said anything to you."

"Hey, I asked, and I am the one who is sorry. This must have been hard on you all this week, with Mom and all?"

"No, James. It was just the service. Nothing else was the same, so I guess that's why I was fine up till now. I've never been to another funeral since my brother's so I guess that's why today it came out like it did. So I feel very mentally exhausted."

"I can sure understand why, Char, you know. Just because I am going home it doesn't mean we can't talk. I gave you my business card. You can call me anytime you feel like talking. I am home most evening around seven."

"You work that late all the time?"

"Yes, I don't have too much else on the go right now as I found my age has changed a lot of my ways and the things I want to do. I am not sure what I want right now, or if I even know what I am looking for. I have lost contact with most of my friends, so I just keep myself busy at work until I am tired enough to go home."

"Boy, that sounds about as interesting as my life. Why have you lost contact with your friends?"

"You are waiting for a baby, that has to be exciting in itself. As far as my friends, they have all married and started to have their families, and I began feeling like the odd man out, so I just started to decline when they would ask me over to dinner or whatever they had in mind. When I would go over, their discussions were about their upcoming weddings or about the baby that was due or about the child they already had and I had nothing to offer to the conversation. This made me feel very uncomfortable. So going head down and ass up in work kept me away from all that.

"That seems like a lonely way to live."

"Yes, it is, and that is why with Mom going so fast, I have decided to change some things in my life. I told you I didn't know what I wanted or what I am looking for, but that is not true. Mom has opened my eyes."

"How is that, James?"

"Charlene, when I first met you, I got such a warm feeling from you, one that made me want to reach out and hold you. You are what I am looking for. Can't you feel it too?"

"Please, James, we have talked about this already."

"You're right. We did to some extent, but you don't understand. I would really like to share this birth with you. I watch you, and how you are with everything, and I dream of being part of this with you. It is more than just the baby. It is you. I would love to be there with you, help you, and know that the baby and you are being taken care of."

"James, I have told you I don't need someone to take care of me. You are just feeling this way because all your friends are parents."

"No, that is not so. I just didn't know that it was something I wanted until I met you. You are having a baby alone. Why can't I be there for you and the baby?"

"It doesn't work that way, James."

"I had asked if we could start as friends. You said yes. Is that still a go?"

"Oh James, I don't know. Now I will be worried about saying all the wrong things. Knowing what you want is going to make me very uncomfortable."

"I am sorry. I will back up, but I would really like for you to think about giving us a chance. I do want to be a friend, and I do want to be with you when you have the baby."

"I don't know if that is a good idea, James!"

"Why not? Are you hoping that the father will be there?"

"No, I am not."

"Do you want him there?"

"No, James. I do not want him now or then!"

"Then why don't you just let things happen instead of fighting everything?"

"Listen, James. I have been on my own now for some time, and I really don't see the rush for any of this."

"It will be a lot of special moments missed, and they should be enjoyed to the fullest."

"I am sorry, but I don't plan on missing anything when it comes to my baby!"

"No, you won't, but I will if you keep shutting me out. Wouldn't it be nice to share all the special moments with someone? To laugh and cry together with someone. You are having a miracle. That is what a baby is all about, and I would very much like for you to share that with me, Char. Are you not scared of doing this on your own?"

"I would be a fool to say I'm not. But if that is how it has to be, so be it."

"But it doesn't have to be that way, Char. Please."

"Well, I will tell you what. If you and I are still friends by the time the baby decides to come, I will let you be with me so long as the doctors say you can."

"Do you mean that?"

"Yes, I do. It might be kinda nice to have someone else go through the pain with me."

"Oh, is there lots of pain?"

"I understand there is, but I won't be able to answer you until it happens, seeing this is my first time."

"I guess so, eh."

"Are you good with pain, James?"

"I don't know. I haven't had to deal with any as of yet. I guess I should have been listening when my friends were talking about their babies being born. I know some of them had stories to tell, but I just shut most of it out. Now I wish I had listened. Maybe I could have more good to you then."

"I have lots of books to read, and some of it I wished I hadn't read. I think sometimes not knowing is the better way of going into something."

"Maybe I should take some of your books home to read."

I just laughed and said, "I don't think you are that bored that you would want to read them."

"Yes, Char. If you have some that you could give to me, I would very much like to read about it. That way, I would know what you and the doctors are talking about. No one would have to know that I am almost a stranger standing in. I remember one of my friends saying he was his wife's coach. Whatever that meant. He would talk her through her breathing and help keep her calm when need be during labor. You see there are good things for me to learn so I can be with you."

"All right, if you're sure." And with that, I got up to get him a couple of books. When I came back, he was putting our teacups in the sink.

"Thank you for tea and the chat," he says as he walks towards the door.

"Thank you as well, and here are your books."

"I am calling on you when I come back, you can bank on that. I just don't know when for sure, but I don't think it will be too long. Sam will want to get everything done so he can move on with his life as well, which brings me to another question. Would you please check in on Sam a couple of times a week just to see how he's making out? I am worried about him and his booze."

"I don't want to be a spy."

"No, not like that, but if he seems like he isn't leaving the house and maybe missing a lot of days work, you could call me."

"OK."

"Thank you." He pulls me into his arms and gives me a hug, kissing the top of my head. "I will be calling you as well, so till then, you take care of yourself and baby." And he pats my stomach. I know I went red, and he just laughed at me. "Bye for now, Char."

"Bye, James. I hope you have a good trip home." I closed the door and just stood there for a moment. I felt a little light-headed, and I wasn't quite sure why. Was it because he did make me feel alive? It was nice talking to him about things that were important to me, and he seemed to care.

Could this be something or could he be just telling me things he thinks I would want to hear, like the baby's father did. He said he was going out of town to work and that never happened. So will James really call and will he come and see me when he comes back to deal with all this with Sam? Am I being a fool to think maybe he would mean what he says and really show up? Am I looking to be let down once again by trusting what a man has said? Damn him.

I washed up the teacups and then went and climbed into the bath. A warm bath always makes a person feel better.

Sleep never came easy that night or the next; it seemed like I couldn't empty my mind.

So by night number 3, I was so dog tired that I had finally fallen asleep, and I felt great when I got up. I had decided to go downtown today to the secondhand store to see what they might have in baby furniture. I thought I should get these while I can as far as having money goes. Besides that, maybe they will need painting, and now that the weather is so nice would be the perfect time to do them. This would also get me outside and keep me busy; not working has given me a whole lot of time to kill. If I find something, I would have to see if Louise would have time to pick it up for me. She is working today so I could swing by to see her at lunchtime.

This place is so quiet now that Mary is not out messing around in her flower beds. Oh, her flowers. I wonder if Sam will keep them up as nice as Mary did. Perhaps I should ask him if he needs some help with them. This would also help keep me busy and outside more as Mary had a lot of flowers to take care of. I could sure use the sun and all the vitamin D we are suppose to need. I must check with Sam tonight when he gets home.

I was going to enjoy today, and it has been a long time coming. I like shopping alone; this way I can take all the time I want to look at whatever I want. Having lunch with someone is great, but after, I do prefer to be alone. That way, I don't have to worry about anyone, and I have no one to answer to. I don't even like talking on the phone unless I really have to. I find I have become a real loner.

Walking along slowly as I find I'm feeling heavy to walk and at times it is also painful if I push it, I have learned to take it easy. People have been telling me that I waddle like a duck. Most of the time when I walk, I hold under my stomach and lift it up; this takes some of the pain away, making it a little easier for me to walk. But overall, I'm enjoying being pregnant. I think about having a little one that will always be mine and always be there for me as I will him. There can be no greater love than a mother and her child.

I know I don't want to be tied to a man but a child. I have always been crazy over babies and small children. They are the most fascinating little creatures that God could have put on this earth. It has always amazed me how much these little people learn in one year. If our learning capacity stayed so great for a few more years, there would be nothing we couldn't do. I do think it works this way, or we would all have brain burnout. We all start with the basic quick start that we need in the very beginning, then we shift into the slower mode of learning. I have heard it said that you are never too old for learning. Yet on the other hand, I have also heard that you can't teach an old dog new tricks. So I guess all these things I will find out as life goes on. I know for me having a baby is going to be one of the biggest learning experiences in my life. I'm also hoping it is going to be the best. I rub my stomach a lot as this seems to soothe him, and I also hope he can tell how much I want him.

I know I keep referring to the baby as him; it is funny because I don't ever think of it being a girl. I have never even looked at girls' names. Names—now that is something again. How are we supposed to know what name is going to fit the baby? I have thought about waiting until I see the baby and seeing if his name would just pop into my head. A name is something you have to carry for the rest of your life, and I sure don't want to bring my child any heartache by giving him a totally wrong name. A name should show strength and pride. I remember in school some of the children had really terrible names, and I wouldn't use their names because I felt sorry for them. I had often wondered who in their right mind would give a child a name like that. Other kids would laugh at them and make fun of their name and make up rhyming songs to go along with their name. Kids can be mean at a very early age. So I want to make sure I don't make such a terrible mistake. Sure the child can change their name when they get older, but it doesn't help while you're in the most vulnerable time of your life.

I can't say I was really happy with my name. I always felt it was too long. I had thought at one time that was why I didn't have a middle name. I had found out many years later that it was to be Charlene Ann. My dad at the time of registering me had forgotten about it. I'm more than OK with that.

The secondhand store that I had entered was jammed right full; you could hardly move around in there. They had a very large selection of baby things. It was going to take me some time to look at it all because of the shortage of space to move around in. Things were piled on top of each other, and some were still in boxes. So it meant you would have to take your time if you really wanted to see what all was there. But then I have nothing but time, so I started to pick my way though. Some of the things were pretty dirty, and I didn't think there was much chance of getting it cleaned. Those I was just going to skip over.

After an hour and a half, I had found a crib, change table, and a matching dresser. The set was supposed to be white, but over the years, it had yellowed a lot. It was a very nice set in its time. The spindle work was something to admire although it needed some sanding and refinishing. I was thinking I could redo it with the crackle paint, and this would surely pass some time, and I wouldn't have to rush. I could take my time and do a real good job of it. I could see where it could be a beautiful set once again. I could make it look like an antique.

The store owner had told me I could have all three pieces for seventy-five dollars. I had asked him why. There must be something wrong with them. Oh no, he assured me; it was only because he was so overstocked he had to let things go cheap to clear them out for new stuff he had coming in. I would have been a fool not to take them right then.

"Let me put them in your truck."

"Truck?"

"Yeah, don't you have one?"

"No, I don't."

"Then how were you going to take this home?"

"My brother or sister will be picking it up. I'm not sure which one it will be or which day for sure. If it is OK, I will pay for them now, sir."

"That won't be a problem, little lady. I will just have it all moved to the back door for them. You just come over here and put your name on this paper, and I will stick it to them when I move them."

"All right, thank you. Would you have a washroom I could use?"

"Yes, just to the right of you. I'm sorry it won't be overly clean right now. My wife is away, and I don't clean very well."

"I'm sure it will be fine, thank you." I found my way to the bathroom, and he was right about it not being clean. I was so glad I just wanted to wash the dirt off my hands. I know I can use the washroom just around the corner when I stop to eat. It was now after lunch, so there would be no one to have lunch with as it took me longer than I thought it would. I do need to have a sandwich and a glass of milk. When I entered the café, I was surprised to see Jacob sitting there.

"Hi, what are you doing here?"

"I'm going to the washroom first, then I will come back and talk to you."

"Oh, all right, be that way." This washroom even smelled clean, never mind looking at it. Holding it in for so long made it almost impossible to go. But once I started, there was no holding back. I thought I would never be done.

"Oh man, does that ever feel better," I said to Jacob as I came back to the table.

"I was thinking you went out the back door or something."

"I really had to go."

"No kidding. Are you going to have something to eat?"

"Yes, I am. I worked up an appetite."

"What were you doing?"

"I was over in the secondhand store getting baby furniture."

"Were you able to get all you needed?"

"Yes, I did."

"How are you taking it home?"

"That's your job."

"Oh right. I forgot about that." We both laughed.

"It is paid for, so whenever you have time, the guy was putting it at the back door with my name on it."

"Why don't we do that after we have had our lunch?"

"Thanks, that will work for me."

"What have you been up to? I haven't seen you around, so I took it that you had gone back to the bush?"

"I went and met Elise's family. We ended up staying there for a week. They are very nice people. They make you feel right at home. You would have thought I'd had known them all my life."

"How big a family does she have?"

"She has two brothers, one is older than her. They don't speak English very well yet."

"Oh, so you don't know what they really said about you! Just kidding."

"So how are you liking the basement suite?"

"I love it, sure does beat the attic. I'm very happy in my new home, especially having a bathroom."

"Yeah, Char, I don't know how you did it in the attic. It might not have been the greatest place in Louise's basement, but it did beat the attic."

"The attic was fine for just me. You learn to do with what little you may have and make the best of it."

"I guess, eh. How is the old lady to get along with?"

"She was great. I miss her a lot."

"Why? Where did she go?"

"Mary passed away."

"Oh, I'm sorry to hear that. I didn't know. Now what happens to the house? Will they be selling it?"

"I don't think so. Her youngest son lives there, and I haven't heard any talk about selling."

"That's good for you then."

"I just don't know how long they will let me live there rent-free."

"Rent-free?"

"Yeah, it was a deal Mary and I had made. As long as I would let her be part of our lives and let her babysit once I went back to work, we could live there rent-free. That was all she talked about."

"Didn't you have some kind of paper with all this written on?"

"No, we just agreed between ourselves. Who knew she would get sick so fast?"

"Well, I sure hope you get to stay after all the work you have put into that place. But it does look like you will be looking for a sitter."

"I have a year, so hopefully, someone will come to mind or I find someone I will feel comfortable leaving my baby with."

"Good luck with that. I will keep an ear open, and I will also mention it to Elise. Maybe she will know someone who would be interested."

"I appreciate that, thank you."

"I'll buy lunch. Now let's go pick up your furniture."

"I would like to stop and buy some paint, if you have time."

"Sure, not a problem. What are you painting now?"

"The baby furniture needs some work. So I would like to get started on it while the weather is nice so I can do it outside."

"I see. Would you like some help sanding it down first?"

"No, thanks. I want to do it myself. It will give me something to do. The days are long now that I'm not working. I was also thinking of asking Mary's son if I could do some of the yard work. It would get me outside more and sure would kill time."

"Yeah, I guess time is something you have a lot of right now."

"More than anyone should have, and it is starting to get me down. I can only read so much."

"It might help if you would read something besides those damn hairdressing books."

"I am. I will have you know. Mary had given me a book, which I've enjoyed reading, and it has a second part to it, so I will go looking for it so I can see how this story ends.

After Jacob got the furniture unloaded, I had asked him.

"Jacob, are you going to come in for coffee?"

"Thanks, Char. But I promised Elise I would pick her up from work."

"Don't say I didn't offer. You were going to bring Elise over so I could meet her. What happened?"

"I will on the weekend, if that is OK with you."

"Sure. I'm looking forward to it. Thank you for your help today."

"Don't mention it. See you on the weekend then."

"See ya Jacob. He was gone like the wind. Jacob was never one to stay anywhere for too long. I guess he was afraid of wearing out his welcome. He always had some place he had to be.

I went inside and made myself a cup of tea. Thinking I'm going to wash all this furniture down so I can really see what it looks like. Maybe I won't want to see it, but that is the gamble you take by buying secondhand. This will kill some time waiting for Sam to come home so I can see about the yard work. Sam has been very quiet while coming and going I haven't heard him nor have I seen him.

Washing down the crib and dresser were harder than I thought they would be. With all the wood carving on them, it was harder getting the dirt out so I had to go dig my old toothbrush out from under my bathroom sink, which I use to clean around the toilet seat and taps. This made cleaning them somewhat easier. Now that I had the crib clean, I could see where I had to use some wood filler and do some small repairs before I could paint. I was having fun doing this. This is the kind of work I really enjoyed doing. The style of the crib and dresser were just what I was looking for. The change table is somewhat plainer. It has the same style of legs on it, but there was no wood carving on it. There really isn't anywhere to have the carving on it as it has a top to lay the baby on for changing, and it has two shelves for storing diapers and whatever else you might need to use on a baby. I guess that's why the legs look like they do. It sort of blends them together. I'm not sure if it belonged to this set or not, but once I paint them all, you won't be able to tell.

Suppertime had come and gone, and Sam still hadn't come home. So I decided to write him a short note just to let him know what I would like to do. I will go tape it to his door.

Hi Sam:

I was wondering if I could help out with the yard work? I could clean around the flowers and mow the lawn if you don't mind. It would get me out of the house and would also give me something to do with my time.

Thank you!

Charlene

CHAPTER FIFTEEN

I was sticking it on the door when the phone started to ring. It doesn't ring often because I didn't give my number to many people. Mary was good enough to hock me up so I could get help if need be, and I didn't want to take advantage of her kindness. It would ring twice when it was someone calling me. Something like the party lines were like when phones first came out while we were living on the farm. Mary had insisted that I have this, so some of it was to make her happy. It also made me feel better knowing that I could get help if necessary. I had finally got to it on the fourth ring.

"Hello."

"Hello, Char. Is that you?"

"Yes, it is."

"How are you doing?"

"I'm doing fine." I had no idea who was on the other end; names were running through my head, but the voice didn't belong to any of them. Guess he must have sensed that I was troubled by who was calling.

"Char, this is James calling."

"James! Oh, hi! I had no idea who was calling."

"I thought so. That's why I figured I best tell you before you hung up on me."

"I would have done that all right. How are you, James?"

"I am fine. I thought I would have been back out to Mom's by now. But I got sent away, so it will be a couple more weeks before I get out there to see you."

"You got sent away? Where are you?"

"Believe it or not, but I'm in Australia."

"You're where?"

"Australia."

"Are you shitting me?

"No!"

"I'm supposed to believe you're calling me from Australia."

"Yes! I didn't want you to think I had forgotten about you. In fact it has been totally the opposite. I think about you every day. I wonder how you are. I thought you might have called me by now. But seeing how you didn't, I thought I would be the one to break the ice and call first."

"You thought I would call you? Why would I do that?"

"Don't friends call each other from time to time?"

"I guess so. I'm not a phone person, and I don't want to tie up your mom's phone."

"Char, Moms not there anymore, even if she were, she wouldn't mind you using the phone. So tell me how are you keeping busy these days?"

"I haven't been doing too much until today."

"What have you been doing today?"

"I went shopping today at the secondhand store and bought a crib, dresser, and change table. The three pieces cost me seventy-five dollars."

"It sounds like you got one hell of a deal."

"I think so. I was just washing them up so I can repair them and then I want to repaint them. They are already antique white and have a lot of carving on them. There is some repairing that has to be done, but that won't take long. I will lightly sand them down and then I want to put crackle paint on them."

"Sounds very interesting, but what the hell is crackle paint?"

"It is a spray that you put over your paint that makes them look well worn and cracked just as antiques do over time."

"Oh, I thought the reason you would paint them is to make them look new."

"They will look new yet old. Remember I like old things."

"Well, I'm glad to hear that."

"Why would you say that?"

"Then I know that you will like me as well."

"You're not old."

"I am probably older than anyone else you have ever gone out with."

"I'm not going out with you."

"Not yet. But you're going to when I get home. You said you would or have you changed your mind?"

"We were just going out for dinner. You can't really call that going out."

"I can call it anything I want to, and you can believe it to be whatever you want."

"Oh, so that is how it is, is it?"

"Hey, Char. Have you talked to Sam since I left there?"

"No, James. I haven't. I was just putting a note on his door when you phoned."

"A note on his door, why?"

"I want to know if I could help with the yard work. It would get me out of the house and give me something to kill time at."

"I think that is a good idea so long as you take it easy and don't overdo it and hurt yourself."

"How can I hurt myself by pulling weeds and mowing the lawn?"

"People have been hurt doing less, and remember you're the pregnant one."

"I might be pregnant, that doesn't make me a cripple."

"Please just be careful and take it easy while doing the yard work, enjoy it but don't overdo it. *Please* promise me that much."

"James, I will be just fine."

"*Please* promise me you'll be careful!" I could tell by the sound of his voice he was very concerned and sincere.

"James, I promise I won't do anything foolish."

"That's my girl."

"James!"

"So you said you never talk to Sam." I knew he was changing the subject. So I thought I might as well join him.

"No, I haven't seen or talked to him since you left."

"You haven't."

"No! He must be leaving very early and coming home very late."

"Has the yard been done at all since Mom passed away?"

"No, James. It hasn't been touched. That is what made me think that maybe I could do it. Perhaps Sam just isn't up to facing that just yet. I really wouldn't' mind helping out."

"Maybe I should call him on his cell and see what's up with him. I won't be leaving here for another two weeks at least. That's if everything goes as planned. I didn't get a chance to call him once I went home. It just got so crazy with work, but I do like the fact that I'm busy. Or at least I did until I met you. Now I wouldn't mind some free time so I could come and see you like I promised. We are still going out to dinner, that much I promise, and I booked two weeks off around the time you are to have the baby, so I can be there with you."

"James! You didn't have to do that. Taking time from work because I'm having a baby. I mean."

"Char, you told me if I were around, then I could be with you when you had the baby. I want to make sure I'm there at the right time."

"That's very nice of you, James, but not necessary. I just meant that if you were around at the time, it would be OK to be there with me."

"That's right, and I'm making sure that I will be around. By the way I finished those baby birthing books, I had to go out and buy a couple of more."

"You did?"

"Yes!! My friend's sister-in-law told me where I could get some real great ones. Boy, have they been interesting reading. The pictures are as if you're right there watching." I knew my face was beat red, and I was so glad that he was on the phone so he couldn't see me. "I want to make sure I can help you at the time. I don't want to be there and just be in the way or more of a nuisance than help."

"Didn't your friends want to know why you were so interested in birthing?"

"Yeah, they asked. I told them a friend of mine was having a baby on her own, and I wanted to be there for her. They never asked for any more details, and I didn't offer anymore."

"Thank you."

"You're welcome. You know, Char. You're not the first one to have a baby out of wedlock. It is happening more and more all the time. There are a lot of girls out there that want to have a baby but don't want to be tied to a man."

"That may be so, but I wasn't one of them. I had no plans on having children right now. I wanted to finish my hairdressing."

"You know what? Shit happens, and sometimes, we just don't have control. You have to take it one day at a time and deal with whatever is thrown in your path. Just keep your head held high and don't be ashamed of having a baby. I can tell it really bothers you. But don't let it. The one who should be ashamed is the man who got you pregnant in the first place. Then he walks away like he has no obligations."

"I never told him about the baby. So don't go putting all the blame on him."

"Are you kidding me? He has to know that every time you have sex with someone there is that chance. Did he ever come back to find out?"

"No!"

"So he does deserve to take some of the blame."

"It takes two to tango. My mom would tell me I've made my bed, now I must lie in it."

"There is some truth to that. Just remember, Char, having this baby is going to make you a much stronger person."

"Your mom used to tell me that. I was so afraid to tell your mom that I was pregnant. She made it easy in the end. She was the one who made me want to really enjoy being pregnant. Mary use to tell me to enjoy it because it doesn't last long. It will just seem that way as I get closer to the end."

"That is right. You are going to forget all the pain and negative thoughts once you have the baby. So I have read in one of these books."

"Sounds like you have had some very interesting reading."

"I have learned a lot. Maybe you should ask me some questions. I could take the place of your doctor." We both laughed at that idea.

"I wouldn't be able to tell whether you were telling me the truth seeing how I haven't read those books."

"Why would I want to lie to you about something as serious as having a baby? I wouldn't lead you on."

"You wouldn't, eh?"

"No way. I say what I mean, and I back it 100 percent." I didn't know what to say, but I had the feeling it was time to say good-bye.

"Char, are you still there?"

"Oh yeah, I'm still here."

"Sorry, I didn't mean to scare you off. I just want you to understand how sincere I am about you and the baby. I don't want to put pressure on you. I just want you to relax and let me be there for you. You and the baby. I wish I wasn't so far away. It makes me feel like I have already let you down."

"No, you haven't, James. You told me you would see me when you came back to your mom's, and that has not happened yet. So, no, you haven't let me down. I think you are a very sincere friend, and I thank you for that. I haven't had a man that would just be friends. There always had to be more, so I tend to push away.

"The baby is my responsibly and I *won't* ask anyone for help."

"I know you won't, but I am offering, and it is because I really want to, not because I see you as a charity case. I see a very proud woman when I look at you. You can tell it in the way you dress and the way you carry yourself. This baby doesn't know how lucky he is to have you as his mother. I know you would go to the end of the earth and back for this child.

"I have read that not all mothers-to-be love their baby before it is born. They hadn't wanted to be pregnant in the first place and didn't like anything about being pregnant. Having a baby to please their husbands doesn't always work out in the end. A lot of those women don't love their babies even after they're born. Having a child to save a marriage is so wrong. What a responsibility you have put on that baby. One thing that shows on you is how much you love this little person that hasn't name or face."

"Oh, but you're wrong about that. This little man," I say as I rub my tummy, "has a name, so he also has a face."

"Here you go saying 'he' again. What is going to happen when you end up having a girl? Then what?"

"I'm not having a girl this time."

"You're really sure of that, aren't you?"

"Yes, I am! And no one is going to make me second-guess myself."

"You want a boy that bad that you're willing to stake all your money on him."

"Why, are you betting me now?"

"Yes, I am."

"I don't have much money, but I will bet you what I have in my pocket." So I dig out what I had, which turns out to be just over ten dollars. You still in?"

"Of course, what are you naming this boy of ours?"

"JAMES!

"Come on now, tell me. You're so sure it is a boy."

"You will know when the time is right."

"How will I know you haven't changed your mind a hundred time by the time *he* is born?"

"When you do get to come back to your mom's I will have it written on a piece of paper and in a sealed envelope. The day the baby is born, you will be able to open it, so he will know his name, and you will know who to say hi to. Deal?"

"Deal!! This is getting to be more fun by the month. After the baby is here, will you have a problem if I go shopping for the things you will be needing for the baby?"

"Like what?"

"I don't know. Let me know what you have. Make a list of the things you will need. Or I could just ask my friends what they had to buy. Maybe they can tell me what really works and what doesn't."

"James, you're crazy, you know that."

"Yeah! You make me crazy, and waiting for this baby is making me even crazier. I didn't think I could be so excited over a birth of a baby."

"You mean over the birth of another man's baby."

"No! I don't mean that at all. I don't even think about him when I think of you and the baby. I have never heard his name nor seen his face, so it is just you and the baby I see when I think of you."

"James, how are you going to handle it when and if he wants to come see for himself when he finds out?"

"I thought you said you weren't telling him."

"I'm not."

"Then how will he know?"

"His mother used to come into the shop where I worked. The best kept secrets always get out. They always come back and bite you in the ass. So it will be a matter of time. On the other hand, once he knows, he maybe one of these guys that never give a damn."

"Then I guess I will have to deal with it when it happens. Until then, we will enjoy this baby as much as possible. You know I never notice pregnant women and babies. Now they seem to be everywhere I am. There are a lot out there. I don't know how I couldn't have seen them before now."

"You know the saying "People can't see the forest for the trees." Besides that, it is something you have had your mind blocked from for years. This was something you just weren't ready for yet."

"I think I was running scared. Then when I met you and found out you were having a baby on your own, it made me think. If she can have a baby on her own, what the hell am I so afraid of? Watching you and getting to know you made me want to be a part of this baby's life, and yours. Like I said, I am very excited about the birth of the baby, and I think about the two of you all the time."

"Like I said you're crazy. You never did tell me why you went to Australia." The subject was getting a little too deep; it was time to change it.

"I came over here as a troubleshooter. I don't know if the guy is going to listen to anything I have told him. It is hard getting it through to people who don't speak our language very well."

"That sounds like fun."

"I find it frustrating most of the time. I feel like I'm wasting my time and theirs. Seeing how they can't get me out of here for two weeks, I hope that in that time I have some kind of an understanding with this man.

"Other than that, the trip itself was great. The country over here is so different than at home. To see a kangaroo up close like this makes the trip worth it. Some of these beasts are huge. Sure is funny to see their baby in those pouches. They look cute and cuddly, yet the parents look like very mean animals. Their tails look deadly. I must read up on these babies so I will put my baby books away until I get home."

"You do that. I would like to hear more about them when you get back."

"It is their winter months over here, so it is only going to get colder. I sure hope I am out of here by then."

"It must feel strange to you knowing it is summer here, and you're in snow."

"It was strange getting off the plan to it, that is for sure. Now I must go, Char, and it has been really nice talking to you. If I get a chance, I will call again."

"You don't have to worry about calling me again. We can always talk when you get back home. This must be costing you a lot."

"Now who's worrying when she doesn't have to? It is just money, nothing that another day's wages won't cover."

"Are you for real? It is going to take a day's wages to pay for this call?"

"Oh, I don't know what it will cost for sure. The point was it is just money, something I make every day, so don't sweat it."

"James!"

"I know I'm crazy. You have already told me that a few times. I guess Sam is not home yet."

"What makes you think that?"

"You said you had left him a note. I would have thought that if he was home, he would have come and talk to you by now."

"You're right. I wasn't thinking about the note. I haven't heard anything moving upstairs."

"Is it real noise living in someone else basement Char.?"

"It's not too bad most of the time. We are in different parts of the house at different times. The chairs are the loudest when they are being moved."

"Maybe we had better look into making it more sound-proof down there."

"You don't have to do that for me. I'm fine with the way it is."

"You want a bunch of noise when you are wanting your baby to sleep? This is one thing I do hear my friends all complaining about. 'We just get our baby to sleep, and someone will phone or ring the doorbell.'"

"I have been around a lot of babies, and if you do it right, they will sleep through a lot. Keeping it completely quiet while they're sleeping is not the way to go. After all, they hear all the time we are carrying them. My girlfriend does her vacuuming and her laundry and the dishes while her baby slept, and she was not a quiet person. Sometimes this is the only time you will have to get these things done, so they best get used to the sounds as soon as possible."

"See you are teaching more things that I don't know. Too bad my friends didn't know you before they went ahead and spoiled their sleep. I wonder if it would be too late to change things."

"That I cannot help you with. I'm sorry to say. Char, this has been nice, and I don't want to say good-bye. But I'm afraid I have to go. I have to go to work and make some money so I can go shopping soon. I will go and say so long for now and whatever you do be careful. I hope to talk to you soon."

"Thank you for calling, James. It was sure nice talking to you too. Take care." I hung up the phone, and glancing at the clock, I saw that we had been on the phone for an hour. It sure didn't seem that long. He best work for a few days to pay for that call, and I hope he thinks before he calls again. I must admit I really enjoyed talking to him. Sometimes talking to the same people all the time becomes boring.

I also can't believe he bought books on birthing. He must be out of his mind. I guess he really must be interested after all. I wonder for how long after will he still be interested. Will this be some kind of a game with him until he gets tired of it? After all, he is just a friend, and that is a nice thing about being a friend to someone who has a baby; you can just get up and leave whenever it suits you. Whereas a parent, you're there through thick or thin, sleep or no sleep, which reminds me I think I will go have my bath and turn in early. It doesn't seem like Sam will be home early tonight either. Maybe I will hear him in the morning, and I can catch him then.

James has given me a lot to think about. I won't be able to go to sleep with such a head full of thoughts. My bath must come first, and with any luck, it will help me fall off to sleep. I will just have to empty my brain while sitting in the tub. I think I should use my lavender bath wash; it is said to help calm and aid you into slumber. I find it does help a lot if you really empty your mind while sitting in it, so here goes while I slip into the tub. I think I got a little carried away as the bubbles are almost over my head. It smells so refreshing you would wonder why it would put you to sleep instead of giving you energy to keep going with the aroma that it has.

Sitting back in the tub and taking several deep breaths, I was doing a very good job of emptying my head. About a half hour in the tub, I started to fall asleep. I better get out of here before I'm drained too much to make it to my bed. Getting into my pj's and climbing into bed, I don't think it took more than five minutes, and I was out like a light.

The sun was shining so bright when I woke up I was sure I had slept until noon. Rolling over to check the time, I was shocked to see it was only seven bells. I felt wide awake and decided to get up.

I think after breakfast I will start to work on the furniture. There wasn't much filling to do, and as warm as it already was, it wasn't going to take long for it to dry, so I can do the sanding and start on the painting. While the furniture is drying, I will start pulling weeds from around Mary's roses. If Sam doesn't like it, he will just have to get over it.

Putting on a sundress so I won't get heat stroke and eating my breakfast of toast and a banana with a cup of coffee got me started. My second cup of coffee I took outside with me not wanting to waste any time once I had decided to do the job. Finding a couple of old tables behind the greenhouse, I brought them out so I could lay the crib pieces on them. That way I wouldn't have to be down on my knees. This alone would make my work easier. Mary must have used these tables when working on her flowerpots.

Going to town on the dresser and change table I had found they both had broken pieces. They were in areas that once filled and painted no one would know. A couple places on the crib were harder, and it was going to be tough to do it right; too much sanding will spoil the look of the crib, so I must be extra careful there. I'm going to have to make the filler a little more watery and work it in to place with my fingers instead of a putty knife. That way, I shouldn't have to sand too much. Once my filler was all on, I went to get a drink of water as I sure had worked up a thirst, hoping to start on the flower beds and get some of them done before Sam got home. After all what was the worst he could do? Tell me he didn't want the yard work done. Then maybe he just doesn't care one way or another.

Deciding to start in the flower bed that was more in the shade, thinking I've had a lot of sun already today, it's only going to get hotter as the day goes on.

Being down on your knees like this for any length of time starts cramping them. I could also feel it in my thighs as well. When your belly sticks out, it does make it more of a challenge. After my second bed, I decided to go in for some lunch. I was needing a break by then. I can go out after lunch and start doing some sanding on the pieces that were dry enough.

The flower beds I got done were looking very nice once again. They were on the front side of the house. So people walking by would see Mary's beautiful flowers once again. Finishing my egg salad sandwich, I thought I would just lie on the sofa and put my feet up a few minutes. I wanted to see if that would take the Charlie horse out of my thighs. It did take the pain away, and I also dozed off for about one hour. Waking up, I felt great again; now I can get back at it. The sun was still bright and hot. There wasn't much of a breeze today, so this will probably bring us a storm sometime tonight. Best get the sanding and painting done before that happens.

Working steady all afternoon on them and they were looking great. I was so pleased at how they were turning out. Jacob will be surprised when he sees them again. He said he thought it was a good buy, but he also thought it was going to be too much work. It wasn't a lot of work for anyone who knows how to go about it. It didn't need a lot of heavy sanding, just enough to make the new paint stick. When the sanding was done I had found a snow brush lying beside the greenhouse. I used it to sweep all the sanding dust off. The painting didn't take long either. I did what is called dry brushing. The paint looks more like a stain than paint, and it is not on thick, so it dries very fast. By dry brushing it, you won't fill all the carving in. The crackle paint is a spray, so it also dries very fast. As it dries, it will create a cracked look in the wood. I have seen a lot of dishes in secondhand stores that look like this. Most of these places want a lot of money for those dishes. I would buy those dishes just to use on my walls. With them being crackled like that, it is showing me that the finished glaze on them no longer has a seal. It is now just a place for bacteria to form. A person could get very sick eating off of them. So for me, those beautiful old dishes would just be strictly to look at.

Everything went fast. I didn't have to do the backs of the dresser or change table. The sides needed a little sanding and no filling. Over all, they were not in bad shape at all, but being so dirty, it was hard to tell. I don't think they had been used for a very long time. I know they will look great in my baby room.

I might have to see if Jacob will come help me set it all up. If not, it will just be one more thing I'll learn how to do on my own.

While it was all drying, I figured I might as well start on another flower bed. Mary only has four, but they're big. She also has some planters, but I won't know what is what. So I think if the plant looks nice, I will just leave it, weed or not. I like doing the roses; there was no guessing with them.

I was getting to the end of the bed when that damn pain came back high into my thighs and into my butt. I wish I had paid more attention to how I was kneeling again. I wouldn't have the pain now. I was glad to be done even though I didn't need to do these until tomorrow. It wasn't like they needed to be done today. Oh well, they're done now, and it will be a lot easier keeping them done up from now on. I was just getting up on my feet when I heard.

"What the hell is all this?" Oh! Sam is home, so I hurried around back to see what his problem was.

"Hi, Sam!"

"What the hell is all this?"

"It's my baby furniture. It needed to be painted, now it's drying."

"Looks like it's all cracked. You can't be putting a baby in something that is all falling apart. I can buy you a new one.

"Thanks, Sam, that is sweet of you, but it is supposed to look like this."

"It is?"

"Yeah! I used the crackle paint to make it look antique."

"It does look really old all right."

"That's what I want."

"So it won't all fall apart when you put your baby into it?"

"No, it won't." Sam walks around and looks a little closer at it all and then says to me.

"You know, Char. I think I like the way this looks. When will it be dry enough to put it all together?"

"It can be put together any time now."

"Would you like me to do that for you?"

"Sam! You really want to do that?"

"Sure, why not? I think it could be fun."

"All right then, sure." It had been a busy day for me, and I felt I had gotten a lot accomplished. I was very tired so help would be great. Sam got busy and hauled it all downstairs, and in no time at all, he had it all set up. It was so very suitable for the baby's room.

CHAPTER SIXTEEN

"**H**ey, this looks great, Char. It looks like very expensive furniture you have here."

"Thank you, Sam. I am very pleased with the way it all turned out."

"What would you have to pay at an antique store for something like this now?"

"It would cost a thousand dollars easy."

"You did this for how much?"

"I paid seventy-five dollars for the three pieces and about twenty-five for the paint and filler and sandpaper."

"That's incredible, and look at what you have. You sure do nice work, Char."

"Thank you, Sam!" I turned and gave him a hug just because he was being so kind and he had helped me. But he takes this opportunity to put his hand on my shoulder and run his hand down my arm, saying to me, "Does every pregnant woman have such soft skin?" Backing away, I said, "I don't know. I am really tired after today, so I think I will have a bath and put my feet up."

"By the way, Char, did you see which one of Mom's friends done her flower beds?"

"Yes, I did."

"I must go to the church and see who I should pay."

"Oh, there is no need to pay. That was of my choice while my paint was drying."

"You've done the flower beds too?"

"Yes, is that OK?"

"I don't know how much you are supposed to do, Char. You're the pregnant one not me."

"Exactly. I am pregnant, not a cripple."

"OK, OK. I was just asking. So I would think after all that, you should go put your feet up. I have some paperwork to get done for tomorrow, so I best go do that."

"Thanks again for the help." I shut the door a little faster than I needed to, but there is just something about Sam that disturbs me. I wish I knew what it was.

I decided to make myself a cup of tea while my bath was running. I might just have to break down and take a painkiller. The pain in my thighs and butt was not letting up, and it was starting to wear me down.

Reaching for the teacup, I felt water running down my leg. Shit, I knew I had to pee but not that bad. So I hurried to the bathroom, and taking a look as I went to sit on the toilet, what I saw scared the hell out of me. There was blood, and it was very red and a fare amount. *Oh god, what is happening? I have to phone some body. I will try Louise first.* But to no avail; after six rings, it went to her answering machine. Great! Today she would have to be at work.

Thinking who else should I call, *Who can I call?* I think I will go have a quick wash in the tub seeing how the water is already there, and it won't be too warm. I know when there's blood, you don't use hot water. Once I was washed up and I put on a clean sundress, and this time I put on a pad; I don't know how much more I will bleed. But I think I had best go to the hospital.

I will try Louise one more time; still no answer. *Damn it! Anyways now what do I do? I guess I could walk. I know I am not far, but when this is happening, just how far is too far.* Then I heard Sam push his chair across the floor. Of course, Sam is home, and I hurried upstairs in case he was getting ready to leave again.

I was knocking, what I thought, pretty loud, but it seemed to take him a while to come to the door.

"Hey, Char. What's wrong?" Guess he could tell by the look on my face that I hadn't come for a visit.

"Sam, could I get you to take me to the hospital?"

"Sure, what's up?"

Without going into the finer details, I just said, "I think I could be having the baby."

"Now!"

"Yeah!"

"Isn't this a little early, Char," he says as he runs around to find his keys. "Shit, oh shit, what the hell did I do with my keys?"

"Sam, calm down a minute and just think. When you came in, where did you go?"

"I went . . . I went to the fridge to get a beer."

"OK, let's track your trail." We go to the fridge. "Where did you go from here?"

He reaches out to lean on the fridge and knocks the keys on to the floor.

"Great, let's go."

"I'm right behind you, Char." I think if there were any cops around, he surely would have gotten pulled over. I was almost too scared to say anything. I was glad we didn't have far to go. Once we were at the hospital, Sam says to me, "Char, wait here I will go get you some help."

"Sam, I can walk."

"No, damn it, will you stay put? I will be right back." He was gone no more than a couple of minutes when he came back with a nurse and a wheelchair.

"Sam, I can walk."

"If what your husband is telling me, I think you best just sit and let us push you in."

"All right, but he's not my husband."

"Sorry, I still want you in the wheelchair. How long have you been having pain?"

"Pain!"

"Yes, pain! Are you not having pain?"

"Well, sort of."

"What do you mean sort of?"

"I have pain high in my thighs and into my butt."

"Well, any pain while you're pregnant shouldn't be taken lightly."

"It was the bleeding that scared me into coming here."

"You're bleeding as well?" I heard Sam take in a deep breath, and I knew at that time my face went red.

"Yes."

"When did that start?"

"About half an hour ago now."

"Char, you didn't tell me that!

"That's OK. You got her here now. Let's see what all is happening with you. The doctor is on his way. But if you are bleeding and with pain, there is a good chance we can't stop your labor. Please climb into bed so I can do an exam on you. Would you please step outside, sir, for a few minutes."

"Oh yeah, of course."

"All right, Char. Just lie back and relax." I wonder if they really think just because they tell you to lie back and relax you can actually do that.

Once she was done her internal exam, she left the room, and the doctor came in, and he had my files in his hands.

"All right, miss, by the looks of this, this is not your first time around."

"No, it is not."

"Is it worse than the last time?"

"I didn't have the pain last time."

"I'm going to give you a needle to try and stop things. In the next hour, if things haven't changed, we will be airlifting you out to the neonatal unit in the city because we do not have the equipment here to handle preemies like this. But we should be able to tell more even in a half hour. I will go talk to your husband, I saw him just outside the door."

"That's my friend, not my husband."

"Do you have a husband we should call?"

"No, I don't."

"Have you someone else we should call?"

"Please call my oldest sister."

"I will send the nurse in, and you can give her the information she will need."

"Thank you."

"In the mean time, I don't want you up and about. You are to stay right in bed other than the washroom. So the nurse will also arrange for you to have a lot of reading material. You could be in for a long haul."

"How long is that?"

"One week for starters and we will see what happens after that. That will also depend on whether or not we can get you stabilized. So for now we will have to wait and see. I will send the nurse in, and I will go phone the city to make sure they will have room for you if need be." He was gone and in came Sam.

"How are you feeling now?"

"It seems like the pain is easing up."

"Well, that's a good thing, right?"

"I think so."

"You know what I think?"

"What do you think, Sam?"

"I think we should get married. It sure would solve the confusion around here."

"You are very funny, Sam."

"I am not trying to be funny right now. They see a man with a pregnant woman, and they just can't get it through their heads that we are friends. Even the doctor figures were married. Or maybe they just think we should be. Maybe they know more than we do." At this time, a nurse came in with my needle and says to me, "Which cheek do you want this in."

"It doesn't matter to me so long as it works." Sam turns a little white and says, "I think I will leave now."

"Sam, I would like you to bring some things from home for me."

"I could see the nurse looking at me with a frown."

"OK. Make me a list when the nurse is done. I will just wait out in the hallway."

"Great, thanks."

"So roll over there, miss, and let's get this into you so it can start doing its job."

"What is it that you are giving me?"

"It is a steroid. It is used often to stop labor."

"I hope it works."

"Me too. So you say Sam is a friend."

"Well, he's more like my landlord now."

"Why is that?" I knew she was still fishing.

"I was renting off his mother and she passed away. So now it is him I rent off of. I am glad he was home tonight. I guess it is a good thing I live in the basement. It didn't take long to get help."

"That is handy all right." I couldn't help think she thought in more ways than one. "The doctor told me to get a number of your sister so we could call her for you." I told her, her name and number, and she told me she would go call her right away in case they have to ship me out. Sam had come back in to get the list of things to bring back for me.

"I think there is a notepad and pen in the top drawer of that night table. Would you get it for me, Sam, please, and I will make you that list."

"Sure." It didn't take long to make a list, and I had written down where he would also find the things he would be looking for.

"Do you need my key?"

"Yeah, Char. I have no idea where Mom had her keys or which key goes to what."

"Maybe while I am in here, you should get another key cut so you will have one just in case you need it."

"I won't be going into your place if you're not home."

"Something could happen, Sam, with the water or something like that to where you would have to get in downstairs. You should have a key."

"Maybe you're right." Then I got to thinking. Maybe that was dumb on my part. Maybe I could be sorry that Sam has a key, and he could come in at any given time. Whether I am home or not. Too late now to think about that you dumb ass.

"Sam, you don't have to bring my things back tonight. There is no rush."

"OK. Maybe I can drop them off in the morning on my way to work and that way I can get the paperwork finished that I started for tomorrow."

"I'm sorry, Sam. I took you away from your work."

"No, don't you even think about that. I am glad I was home tonight. I had thought about staying at the office again. I really don't know why I came home."

"You know, Sam, they say everything happens for a reason. Sam, why haven't you been coming home? I haven't seen you much around since your mother passed away."

"I just can't stand the empty house. It is too quiet without Mom. Not that she was noisy, but she always had something new to tell me when I got home. Most of the time, it was about the church, but it was still something. It was uplifting most of the time as it was always something simple, which was a relief compared to what I have to deal with at work."

"When James called, he was asking if I had talked to you since he had left. I told him I hadn't. So he said he was going to call you."

"I guess I best listen to my messages when I go home. Did he say what he was wanting?"

"No, I think he might have been lonely."

"James, lonely. No way. He has more friends than anyone I know."

"Maybe so, but not where he is."

"Why? Where is he?"

"James is in Australia."

"Australia? What the hell is he doing there?"

"Something to do with work."

"He called you from there?"

"Yeah, like I said he was lonely."

"Really, that's it."

"That's it."

"Well then, maybe I best go home and see if he left me a number, and if so, I best call him back." As Sam was leaving, the nurse came back in.

"I called your sister, and there was no answer, so I left a message. I told her what was going on and to call first in case we have sent you out by the time she gets the message."

"Thank you."

"You're welcome, Charlene."

"What is your name?" She reaches down to where her name pin should be.

"Oh, it seems I am whoever you wish me to be tonight. I have lost my name." We both laugh at her.

"My name is Lillian."

"For sure, or is that who you just wish to be tonight?"

"No, that is my name. I will be back in a little later to check and see how the bleeding is doing, and if we are keeping you here. I will help you get ready for bed if that will be OK with you. I know washing up in the sink isn't as nice as having a bath, but you know the rule on that."

"I will be OK with that thank you." Lillian left, and I just lay back, and I dozed off. It was dark now when I woke up to some voices out in the hall. I couldn't make them out at first. Then I heard Louise ask, "How long would she be off her feet?"

"The doctor figures she will have to basically stay in bed from now until she has the baby.

"Wow, that's a while yet."

"Yes, it is, but she seems to be prone to hemorrhaging, and it is the only way to see that doesn't happen. He has ordered ultrasound to be done tomorrow."

"Does she know yet?"

"No, I was just about to go in and tell her, so it is a good thing you have come along because this is going to be some upsetting for her. We don't want her to be upset because that doesn't help the cause."

"I'm glad I came up now. I was going to wait until tomorrow morning."

"If the pain hadn't quieted, we would have shipped her to the city. The bleeding is lessened, so we hope we are on top of that as well. We have given her the same steroids as they did when she was in Calgary, and it worked for her then, so we figured we had a good chance of it working again."

"Is there not some danger to her having these steroids while pregnant?"

"No, it is in such small dosages. That is one thing about steroids. It doesn't take much to help. A little will go a long ways."

"How long does Char have to stay in here?"

"The doctor wants her to stay for a week, and he says he will see how things go after that."

"I didn't have any of these problems when I was carrying my twin."

"For some reason, pregnancy for some people is very hard on them." Louise and the nurse came in, and the nurse didn't beat around the bush. She just jumped right into telling me everything she had just told Louise in the hall. I didn't want to say "Yeah, I heard" as I had hoped maybe I hadn't heard it all and somewhere in all this there was good news. Then again if they weren't sending me out to the city, that was the good news. So long as everything keeps going the way it is at this moment.

"I'm sorry, Char. I wasn't home when you called?"

"Hey, not to worry. I got here, didn't I?"

"Who brought you in?"

"Sam was home tonight, so I went up and asked him if he could give me a ride."

"Char, should I go and bring you some things from home?"

"Sam was going to bring the basics but would you please go and get me some clean underwear!"

"What you don't like ours?" Lillian asked.

"I can't say I like the granny pannies you gave me no."

"I didn't know what else would fit over your tummy."

"They have done in a pinch, but if I can get my own, that would be great."

"Are there any certain ones you want, Char?"

"In my second draw, there are my maternity ones. They feel the best."

"All right, I can do that." She turns around to leave.

"Hey, where you going?"

"I'm going to go get your underwear."

"You don't have to do that until tomorrow."

"Are you sure?"

"Of course, I'm sure. These granny pannies will keep me till then."

"Char, I want you to get washed up while your sister is here. That way I don't have to worry about you overstaying on your feet. Right, sis?"

"That's right. I will keep her in check. Just let me know what she can and can't do. I will be all over it."

"She has to use the sink or a basin to wash in as she is not allowed to use the tub or shower as of yet. So whichever she prefers. We would sooner see her stay in bed as much as possible with her feet up."

"So bed it will be. I will bring her, her water and anything else she might need."

"Thank you."

"Hey, what about me? Don't I get some say in this?"

"Sorry, Char. But I know you, and you would want to be up at the sink, but you heard the lady. They want you off your feet as much as possible, so what is the problem. The more your off your feet right now, the sooner you could be back up even if it is for just a little while."

"Yeah, you're right, thanks for coming."

"You're welcome, how are you handling the news about being off your feet so long?"

"I can't say it thrills me, but if I want to have this baby closer to the due date, I guess that's what I have to do."

"You best make sure when this baby is old enough to understand, you best tell him how much you had to go through and how much you had to give up for him."

"I will. He will know how much he owes me for his life." We both laugh at that.

"Char, you are going to have to rethink your living arrangements."

"How do you mean?"

"You should be moving upstairs with Sam like he asked."

"Are you out of your mind?"

"You need someone around all the time if you have to be in bed from now till the baby is born."

"Sam is not home all the time, and that is not an option even if he were home."

"But, Char, you can't be alone anymore."

"I will figure something out. But it won't be with Sam, thank you very much."

"I just thought that if he was a friend like he wants to be, it would work out."

"Then in that case I can stay right where I am. He is just upstairs if I need anything."

"Char, what about your meals and shopping and doctor's appointments and everything else."

"Well, Sam, isn't about to be doing that."

"I'm not about to be doing what?"

Shit this is just what I need now. "Nothing, Sam."

"I was just saying to Char that if your offer was still open, perhaps she should take you up on it seeing how she can't be left alone."

"Louise!"

"Well, it's true, and you are going to need help."

"Why? What's up?"

"The doctor says Char has to stay off her feet now until she has the baby. She is to do nothing short of going to the bathroom."

"So you want to move upstairs now with me!" I could tell he wasn't impressed with that idea now that I was the one who would need the help.

"No, Sam. I don't. It wouldn't work anyways because you have to work, and I will still be alone until you come home. That's why I said I would stay right where I am."

"Yeah, I could make sure I checked on you every night when I got home. I would give you my cell number so that if I am out and you need help, you could just call me."

"That sounds like a better plan to me, Sam."

"Char!"

"I will be fine, Louise."

"I wish I had room for you at my place."

"You also work, so why would I move from a place I love, and it is all ready for the baby, to crowd someone else out of their own place. It sounds pretty ridiculous to me. So I am staying put. Thank you just the same. If the only time I can be up is to go to the bathroom, I think I can do that on my own."

"Don't be so stubborn, Char."

"I'm not, but I am not going to put someone else out."

"You know, Char, I could find out from Mom's friends of the church if there is someone free to pop in and out during the day. I know there are a lot of older ladies who like being nursemaids."

"No, Sam."

"Yes, Char. I think that is a great idea, Sam, thank you. There are a lot of women of the church who do voluntary work, and they love it. It makes them feel useful again."

"All right, all right, you win. But I stay where I am."

"For now, so long as things stay well with you."

"Now can we move on to something different to talk about?"

"Oh, I almost forgot to give you your things," Sam says as he hands me a bag.

"Thank you, Sam, but you didn't have to bring it tonight."

"That's OK. I promised James I would come back tonight and check on you."

"James!"

"Yeah, I finally got a hold of him."

"How is he?"

"He's fine. Can't wait to get home, he says. But he had asked me to come down, and I am to call him back now that I know a little more of what is what with you. So I will say good night, ladies. Char, I hope you get some rest. They always say to rest while you're in the hospital, but I always found it too noisy to sleep or a nurse is always in poking you for one thing or another."

"That's the truth. Please say hi to James for me."

"I will. Maybe I will stop in tomorrow." He was gone.

"Louise, I can't believe you would put him on the spot like that. Besides you know how uncomfortable I am around him."

"I'm sorry. I was just trying to help."

"I know you were, but shit, Sam as a nursemaid." We both laughed at that idea.

"Would have been something. Now how about you getting washed up for bed. Then I will leave so you can sleep.

"Sure." Louise brings me the basin with water and soap. "I also need to brush my teeth."

"That's fine just spit in the basin I have to rinse it out anyways." She hands me my toothbrush and paste. "Do you feel human again?"

"Half maybe. I had a quick bath before I came here, so it's not like I am really dirty or sweaty."

"Char, you know you shouldn't be bathing when you are bleeding."

"I already had it ran, and it was just warm as I was getting washed up from being outside, and I already was too hot, so the bath would have cooled me down. Besides that, I was a mess from the blood, and it was the fastest way to clean up. I was in and out in a couple of minutes."

"I don't know what I am going to do with you?"

"Just love me and be here for me, that is all I ask."

"Char, you know I love you as if you were my daughter. After all, you are the same age. I just wish I had room for you."

"Please don't go there again. I will be just fine. OK. Please!"

"All right. Now I will go, and I will come check on you tomorrow and see what the ultrasound shows. You be good and do as they say."

"Yeah, I will."

"Everything they say, Char. This is serious. You could still lose your baby."

"I know, Louise, and that scares me to death, but I don't want anyone having to take care of me." The tears are rolling slowly down my cheeks.

"Oh Char, I guess you're scared, I would be too," she says as she comes over and sits on the side of the bed and pulls me into her embrace, holding me and rocking back and forth as if she were my mother. "It might be tough going, Char. But you will be just fine and so will your baby. The doctors do know what they are doing. But you have to also remember that if you lose the baby, it is God's way of taking an unhealthy child back. Somewhere in the mix, something goes wrong, and he feels better by taking the baby back than to give you a gift that is only half there. I pray that this is not the case, but I do want you to be prepared for it as well."

"How do you prepare for something like that? Right now, I feel like I am being punished for having a baby out of wedlock."

"Oh god, Char, no! The good Lord would not use a child or anyone's life to punish someone. He knows we all make mistakes, and he will guide us through them if you let him. A baby is a miracle and is a gift given to us by the good Lord. So don't you be thinking anything else. You stay thinking positive and upbeat. Your baby feels all your emotions so keep up the chin, and I am sorry for bringing you down."

"Mary told me that the baby was a gift from God as well."

"Of course, it is, so he won't let anything happen that is not supposed to. Everything happens for a reason. Sometimes it will take us a while to figure out the reason. Some people never get an answer because they are so busy blaming someone or themselves for what has happened. Please don't let this be you. You have done nothing wrong, and like I said before, you don't have anything to be ashamed of either. So just lie back, relax, and hum a nice song to your baby. You know they can hear you."

"I read about that. They even talk about reading stories to them while you are pregnant."

"There you go now see. You will have a lot of time to do good for your baby. Right now, the best thing you could do is sleep. So I am going to go." She pulls the covers up and tucks me in and kisses me on my tear-stained cheek.

"I love you, Char. I will see you tomorrow."

"I love you too. Thank you for coming, good night."

"Good night." And she slipped out the door as quietly as possible as it was way past visiting hours. But they had told her she could stay as long as she felt she needed to, to help me calm down.

The talk she gave me was actually working, and I felt relieved now and tired, so I did as she said and lay back, and before I knew it, I was sound asleep.

It seemed like I had just fallen asleep when the nurse was in, telling me it was time to go for my ultrasound.

"Already, don't I get to brush my teeth?"

"Sorry, you have to do that when you come back. You were on the list for the first to be done, so away we go." She helps me into the wheelchair, and we head on down to x-ray department.

"You do know I really have to go pee."

"That will also have to wait because they need your bladder full for the ultrasound."

"My, they don't ask for much first thing in the morning, do they? Bad breath and a full bladder sounds like a winning combination to me. What do you think?"

"I think they get what they ask for."

"You got that right."

"Here we are. Now I will just help you up onto the table, then I will let the tech know you're here. Hopefully she won't take too long so we can get you to a bathroom."

"That would be great, thank you." The nurse left, and it wasn't even a minute when the tech came in.

"Good morning, Charlene."

"Good morning."

"Are you ready for this?"

"I have to pee bad if that's a good sign."

"It is, that is, what we need is a full bladder. Now this gel will be cool, so hang in there with me please."

"Oh, it's cool all right."

"Well, we use to warm it up, but some ladies ended up wetting themselves once the warm gel was put on their stomach."

"I could see me doing that. It would be easy to lose control right now."

"Please hang on a little longer." She pushed the ball-shaped wand around and back and forth applying pressure where she needed it. At these times, she made it hard for me not to pee myself. Sometimes there was even pain when she pushed down. I didn't want to seem like a baby, so I didn't say anything, but she must have been able to see it on my face.

"I am sorry if I am hurting you, but they want a real good look at what is going on inside here, and I don't want to miss anything. I know the pressure can be painful. Believe it or not, I have been where you are now."

"You have?"

"Yes, I had a lot of trouble carrying my second child and had a few of these done."

"What was your problem?"

"My placenta wanted to come before the baby."

"That doesn't sound like fun."

"No, it wasn't. I ended up having a caesarean."

"Was your baby OK?"

"Yes, he was. I had to have him a little early, but all worked out fine in the end."

"How much too early did you have him?"

"Two months, which wasn't too bad, and some ways, I was glad it was over. I had gotten so damn big and uncomfortable."

"The doctors all tell me I'm bigger than I should be. Maybe I am having a big baby. Was your baby big?"

"No, he was not, and neither is yours. You have a lot of fluid but not a big baby."

"So what is happening to me?"

"I am sorry, I can't say. That is up to the doctor to tell you."

"OK.

"Do you want to know what it is?"

"No, that will spoil it."

"Makes shopping easier."

"It might do that, but to me, to know ahead is like knowing what you are getting for Christmas, so why get up Christmas morning. I will wait and find out when I am supposed to."

"What do you want, boy or girl?"

"A boy, I like the idea of a bigger brother to a little girl someday."

"Maybe if you pray hard enough, you will get your wish."

"I will just take whatever the good Lord thinks I can handle."

"That is the best way to be. OK. Now we are done. I will help you up to a washroom."

"That didn't take long."

I find if I can talk to my patients, then they don't think so much about the fact that they have to pee so bad. It makes it easier, I hope."

"It did, thank you." Sitting on the toilet, I thought I would never be done. It just seemed to go on and on. The nurse finally came back to ask me if I were OK, which of course, I was but it was also hard to start to pee after having to hold it for so long. I guess my muscles didn't want to relax enough. I must have sat there ten minutes.

"Are you sure you're OK in there?"

"Yes, I am." I had also noticed that there was just a spot of blood, nothing alarming, so this was good to see. Maybe they will let me have a shower this morning.

"All right, I am ready to come out."

"That's fine. I have the wheelchair ready for you." So sitting in the chair, she said she would take me back to my room instead of calling the nurse that brought me as my breakfast should be waiting for me.

"I do feel hungry."

"I hope it won't be too cold as the food here is not great to start with."

"Why is that?"

"I don't know. I guess they think people will get better faster so they can go home to good food. So they keep hospital food just above tasteless."

"Sounds like a good reason to me. I thought maybe they had this thing that everyone had to be on a diet while in the hospital."

"I know some sure need to be, and this would be a good place to eat if that was the case, but not you. If you get hungry before we serve meals, you ask for something. After all, you have a baby to feed as well."

"I will be fine, I'm sure."

"I mean it, Char. I know what the food is like, and it doesn't always fill you up. We do have extra good things in the little kitchenette, so just ask. That is why we are here."

"I will then, thanks." She gets me back to my room and into bed. I sit up and pull my breakfast try up to me and lift the lid. There were two hard-boiled eggs and two slices of toast and orange juice, a cup of coffee, and a small bowl of fruit. The only thing that wasn't real good at room temperature was the coffee, but I still drank it anyways. If the truth be known, coffee most likely wasn't good for the baby. I should quit drinking it as well. I quit smoking when I found out I was having a baby. Actually, it was before that because they were making me sick anyways, and I quit drinking alcohol. Not that I drank much, but I wanted to have a healthy baby.

The medical staff really pushed the fact that whatever I took in, the baby would also get, which only stands to reason seeing how it all goes through the mother's blood.

After my breakfast was done, I picked up a book I had seen lying there, but it didn't take long before I dozed off again. I think it must be something in the air of the hospitals because they all seem to make me sleepy. Perhaps it is the way to make time go by faster.

"Good morning, Char. Can we get you up so we can make your bed? Here is a clean gown so you can wash up while we are doing your bed."

"Oh, all right. What time is it?"

Looking at her upside down watch, she says to me, "It is 9:30."

"That's all?"

"Yes, that's all. Why, what time did you want it to be?"

"No time really. I guess going for ultrasound so early has made me feel like it should be a lot later."

"Yes, those girls start early around here. They woke you up, didn't they?"

"Yes, and it felt like I had just gotten to sleep."

"Are you having trouble sleeping, Char?"

"No, I went to sleep right after my sister left. It just felt like I hadn't slept long before they woke me up."

"Well, seeing how you are on bed rest, we will straighten out your bed. You get washed up and then we will let you sleep until noon. How does that sound?"

"I am not going anywhere any time soon, so I guess that's fine." I took what they handed me and went to the bathroom to brush my teeth and wash up and change my gown. Now doesn't that seem silly because I am getting right back into bed? I had no more bleeding, so it wasn't like I got dirty overnight. But whatever makes them happy.

After washing up and the nurses fussing over my bed and checking me out for bleeding and pain, once they were satisfied, they left me alone and I did fall right back to sleep. Some of it, I think, was the fact that I was relaxed more now that the pain and bleeding had stopped. I wonder how many women have this problem. It is going to make for what time I have left in my pregnancy seem like forever as it will drag on so, if I am going to have to stay off my feet, and I would think I should get a little on the heavy side with very little exercise. That won't be healthy for me or the baby and very hard to get rid of after the baby is born. I know I don't have a choice in the matter right now; it means putting on weight versus losing the baby. This is no contest.

CHAPTER SEVENTEEN

The muffled sounds of a voice woke me up, and the sun was shining so bright I don't know how long I had slept.

"Hey, sleepyhead, don't you think it is about time to wake up?"

"Hey, I have been awake already. I will have you know. Besides, what else would you suggest I do while lying here all day?"

"I got your things you were wanting, Char. Now tell me you're not a neat freak."

"What is that supposed to mean?"

"Well, who and the hell rolls their panties up and puts them inside a toilet paper roll and stands them up in a shoe box, not only that, but all in colored rolls."

"I like things neat and easy to get at, and I also believe that everything should have its place."

"No kidding, but really, Char. Who has time for that?"

"I do."

"I guess you do, but you won't soon."

"The baby's room will be all organized as well. I don't like having things just tucked in wherever. I feel like my place is clean inside and out when things are all in order."

"I have to hand it to you, Char. your place is very clean inside and out as you put it. But after the baby comes, you won't be keeping it all like that, trust me."

"How much work can a little baby make?"

"You will see. I will come check you out a few months down the road, and we will see who is right."

"That's a deal."

"Now did you get any sleep last night?"

"Yeah, Louise, I did."

"How is the pain and the bleeding?"

"It had all stopped last night. I think that is why I could sleep. I didn't lie here and worry all night long."

"That is good news, eh. I wondered this morning when I got up if you were still here or if they had sent you to the city."

"I would have had them call you if they were sending me out."

"What have they found out about your ultrasound?"

"I have not seen the doctor yet today. But the tex didn't seem too anxious at the time. So I am taking that as a good sign."

"I sure hope you're right. What time does your doctor come in?"

"I would think anytime now."

"Good. Maybe I will still be here when he does come in. How about I go to the cafeteria and get us some coffee?"

"Sounds good to me. Would you make mine a large please?"

"Sure can do. I will be right back." While she was gone, I decided to dig through my bag of goodies to see what she had bought me. A hair brush was on top and that was great because I sure needed to do my hair as I was starting to feel like a bush ape. Brushing my hair and getting it pulled back out of my face was a good feeling. I also found my makeup, not that I used much, but I did like to do a little with my eyes as my lashes are blonde, so it makes it look like I don't have any, and I always find that when I do my eyes, it makes them look so big and alive. This is just what I need right now so the little mirror on my bed table worked great.

"Here you go, Char. And it is fresh and hot."

"That is great, thank you."

"By the way, I thought I had seen everything, but I have to tell you, I have never seen anyone who has such an organized underwear drawer. Where did you get the idea with the toilet paper rolls?"

"In a magazine that was showing how to make more space."

"But takes more time."

"Not really, you fold them anyways, so I just roll them instead of folding."

"Who the hell folds their underwear? Don't people just throw them in their drawer?"

"I guess some do, but I like to be able to find what I need right away."

"Having them color coordinated like you do must really cut down on your searching time!"

"Are you being nasty now or are you jealous because yours is so messy?"

"Well, mine sure doesn't look like yours, and that is for sure. But it doesn't make any difference to me because I buy nothing but white and the same ones all the time."

"Well, there you go. You should put some spice and color in your life."

"And what? Liven up my underwear drawer." We were both laughing at that when the door popped open, and all we could see was the biggest bunch of flowers coming in. I could see men's shoes, but no face; the bouquet was so large. Then he stuck his head around the side, saying, "Did I get the wrong room?"

"James! Hi, what are you doing here?"

"Looking to deliver these flowers to a very pretty pregnant lady."

"But why?"

"Usually when someone is in the hospital flowers cheer them up, but with you, they just make you ask a lot of questions," he says as he bends over and kisses my forehead.

"Oh, I'm sorry. Thank you so very much. They are beautiful and so many I don't know where they will put them."

"Not to worry, the nurse is already on it."

"They are?"

"Yes, they are, so for now, I will sit them on the floor over here until they bring the stand."

"Why, James, did you bring so many?"

"I hear you are going to be laid up a while, and I know you like to be outside. Seeing how you can't go out, I will bring the outside to you."

"That's very sweet of you, but—" He cut me off right now with "No buts. That is what friends do, right?" he says as he turns to nod at Louise.

"Yeah, I don't have friends like this so, Char. If you don't want the flowers just says so, and I will take them home. If nothing else, they might open my husband's eyes that seem to have forgotten what a bouquet of flowers look like." We all laugh as James goes to put them down on the floor. God, they stood way out in the corner. I couldn't see them finding any stand that big in the hospital.

"Now tell me what the hell you were doing to get yourself in here like this."

"Nothing really, just working on the baby furniture and cleaning your mom's flower beds."

"I had asked you if you should be doing all of that, and I also asked you to be careful not to overdo it."

"I was being careful, and I didn't think I was overdoing anything."

"That's the trouble with you, Char. You don't realize how hard you go at the projects that you are working on. Even the carrying of the crib even though it is all apart is still putting strain on the baby and your body."

"Your sister is right. You have to stop and think a little more and start asking for more help." I was surprised that he remembered who Louise was as he had met her briefly at Mary's funeral.

"How many times do I have to remind you people that I am pregnant, not a cripple?"

"Yeah, and who is the one stuck in bed?"

"You have a point, James, sorry. How come you are here anyways? I thought you were stuck in Australia till who knew when."

"I had told you I wanted to be here for you."

"You had said when the baby was to be born."

"Well, Char, I see James here has it all under control. I think I will go now and come back later."

"I don't want to scare you away."

"That is fine, James. I can see her anytime, but you are on a certain time off."

"Thank you. I appreciate that."

Bending over the side of the bed to hug and kiss me, Louise says in my ear softly, "Listen to the man would you. I will check on you later."

"OK. See you later and thanks for the goodies."

"It was my pleasure. Like they say 'You learn something new every day.'"

"Oh, get out of here!" She chuckles on her way out the door, and as she was leaving, the nurse was coming in.

"Well, Char. Your flowers are the buzz of the hospital." I knew I had turned red.

"Oh really."

"I don't think there has ever been such a bouquet brought in here like this, and I have been here thirty years."

"Here, let me help you with these," James says to the nurse who was going to pick up the flowers or attempt to anyways.

"I think they look very nice on that TV stand," the nurse says as she stands back to admire the flowers. Somewhere they had found a crocheted doily big enough to cover the top of the stand; it was a pale green, so it fit in just right.

"Yes, they do, and thank you for the stand, miss."

"My name is Shirley."

"Hi, I'm James."

"I will leave the two of you alone with your beautiful flowers."

"Thank you," I say to her, not knowing what else to say.

"Did I embarrass you by bringing you flowers?"

"Yes and no."

"Why, because the bouquet is so big?"

"Well, it is a little much, I think. It is beautiful. Don't get me wrong, and I think it was very sweet of you to do that, but you really shouldn't have, and in fact, you shouldn't even be here."

"I don't want to be sweet, and who says I shouldn't be here?"

"James, your job is important to you."

"So are you, and when Sam told me what had happened and you were in here, I was sick to think you were here going through this by yourself. I knew I had to be here because I couldn't think straight on the other side of the country knowing you were in here. For some reason, the day you ended up coming in here, you were on my mind all that day, so when Sam called me, I knew it was about you as soon as the phone rang."

"Sam called you? Why?"

"Because I had asked him to keep an eye on you and call me if he thought he had to."

"James, I wish you wouldn't get so involved."

"Why not? I thought we had this talk already."

"We did, and we also agreed that you could be with me at the time of birth if you were around."

"There are no ifs. I will be there. I already told you that I have booked that time off."

"I wish you hadn't."

"Do you always find it hard to except something nice being done for you or given to you? What has happened to you that has been so bad that you don't want to trust in anyone?"

Now he has my tears flowing, so I just turn my head away and weep in silence.

"I did not want to upset you, Char. I want to make you happy. I want to help you have a good pregnancy what is left of it, and I also want to share in the birth of this miracle. What I don't understand is why you won't let me get close. I thought we could talk to each other easily. That is one thing that has attracted me to you. I felt I could just be me, and I didn't have to worry whether I had a lot of money or not because you don't care about things like that. It has been so refreshing meeting someone so down to earth. I know you have both feet on the ground, and you know what you want, and I do admire you for that. When Mom first started to talk about you, I thought it was someone she dreamed up because she wanted the perfect daughter. But you are not a dream, which I had learn as soon as I met you, nor are you a user looking for easy money, which I have to say, I was worried about Mom and who she was putting so much faith in. But you made her very happy for the short time you two had, and I know she would have continued being happy to have you so close and being involved in your and your baby's life.

"But she is not here, and I see what she saw, and now, I would like to be involved as much as possible in your lives. Please, Char. what is wrong with it? What is wrong with me that you won't let me in? I don't mean into your bed either although I wouldn't mind that either.

"I will show you the respect you deserve, and if it is because you are carrying another man's child, who cares? You could have gotten rid of the baby, but you choose to go through this alone, which in my eyes makes you a very special person, but you seem to be so down on yourself and hard on yourself. There is no reason for that. I have told you before the one who should keep his head hung low and be ashamed is the guy who got you this way and then to move on like he did. He used you for his own satisfaction with no regards to the consequences. You cannot go on carrying all the shame for the two of you when there is no shame to be had.

"You are going to have a baby, end of story. I only want to see that it is a happy ending to this story and to be involved in it. Am I asking too much of you?

"Char, there is chemistry between us, and you know there is. I feel the pull and so do you, and it happened the minute I saw you."

"James, please."

"Please what?" I just shook my head and wiped at the tears. I will be right back. "I had no idea what that man was up to now. I wish it was as easy for me as it seems to be for him. I have heard of men taking women on that were pregnant with other men's babies and the outcome was not good at all. How can it work they will always have the baby's face to look at reminding them that the baby is not theirs. I have heard that some men have gotten very cruel to the child and I don't want that. I am not having a baby to put in harm's way just so I can be happy. Besides how could I be happy if that is how it turned out? In the end I would have been better off alone then to bring that on to us.

Sure I want the whole family setting, who doesn't but to what expense do you get it. I got myself into this mess I sure don't want to get into a bigger one. James comes across as very sincere and caring, but what happens after the catch. With that thought James comes back in pushing a wheel chair.

"Now what are you up to?"

"It is a beautiful Day I am taking you outside."

"James I can't go outside."

"OH yes you can I already ok it with head quarters and you will be off your feet and that's all they are worried about. I had to sign a paper stating I would hog tie you down if necessary."

"OH, aren't you the funny one."

"Come on now let's get going before dark."

"Are you trying to say I am slow?"

"No, I might just walk slow, that's all."

"One thing first, before we leave."

"Anything, just name it."

"I need to use the bathroom."

"Hop in."

"I am aloud to walk that far."

"I could use the practice in pushing."

"I think you will do just fine with the pushing." I went by him slowly so I wouldn't get shit for doing it at a fast pas as well. James reaches out and touches my arm, so I turn and look at him.

"You OK now?" Taking in a deep breath I say, "Yeah, I'm OK."

"Good. We're good?"

"Yeah, James. We're good. I will be right out."

"Take your time."

"I thought you were afraid it was going to be dark soon."

"Give me a break here, will you? Now hurry up."

"There is no pleasing you."

"Just go do your thing, will you? I will get your slippers for you." When I came out, he had my slippers and a blue rose from the bouquet he had brought me. Taking my hand, he sits me in the chair and hands me the blue rose.

"What is this for?"

"Did you not say that a blue rose was to calm and soothe a person?"

"Yeah, something like that. Thank you, it smells great."

"See it is already working."

"How do you figure?"

"You think something is great, and you have that beautiful smile of yours on."

"James." I know I was red in the face as we headed for the door.

"There are two things I know about you for sure."

"What's that James?"

"Number one, you know my name as you use it a lot, and number two, you're embarrassed easily. There is nothing wrong with either one, but I find it to be an entertaining quality about you." He bends over and kisses the top of my head and taking a peek down to see how red I was once again.

"Well, I happen to think James is a very nice sounding name."

"So you really like my name?"

"Yes, James. I really like your name."

"Um."

"What is the *um* about."

"Do you think if you had a son, you would think about calling him James?"

"What? Are you asking me to name my son after you?"

"Would that be so bad?"

"No, James. That is not bad at all. In fact I find it very touching, but I told you, I already have his name picked out."

"You were serious about that."

"Yes, I was, and I also have it written down and in a sealed envelope just for you."

"Hey, where are we going?"

"For lunch or whatever we want."

CHAPTER EIGHTEEN

———◆———

"I can't go anywhere dressed like this!"

"Why can't you? You are on an outing from the hospital, which people can tell by the bands they have on your arm along with the needle thing you have happening there, which by the way I was going to ask you about. What is that for?"

"This is so if they need to give me more shots for anything, they don't have to keep poking me and bruising me. If it was a short time, they wouldn't have bothered, but they said this could be a ongoing thing for a while."

"I see. So all these needles they give you won't hurt the baby?"

"They say not, and I can only pray they're right."

"I guess you are sort of in their hands sort to speak."

"Yes, I am, and I have to hope they know what they are doing."

"Would you feel better if you had a doctor in the city?"

"Maybe, but I have no way in there nor can I afford it."

"Maybe you can't, but I can. I also could make arrangement for you to get there and back."

"That is so nice of you to offer, but no, James, I will see what happens here."

"If things don't seem right or for some reason you change your mind, call me right away. Please don't take any more chances."

"I will and thank you."

"I wish you weren't so stubborn."

"I'm not. I'm just taking care of myself."

"Yeah, yeah, I know. And there is nothing wrong with that, but sometimes you need a helping hand from a friend."

"Well, when that time comes, I will be sure to call you."

"Promise?" he asks as he bends over and kisses the top of my head.

"I promise. Now where are we going?"

"There is this little hamburger place just down the street, and it makes the best mushroom cheese burgers I have ever had, and the bad thing about it, they're only open in the summer."

"I have seen it and was always going to go there."

"Well, today is your lucky day, and seeing how they have drive-through, that's what we will do if they will consider the wheelchair as our wheels and then we will go sit in the park and have our dinner. How does that sound to you?"

"Sounds good to me, and like fun."

"That's good because I think it has been a while since you have been out and have had any fun." I didn't say anything, but I was thinking how right he was. It has been quite some time. So we did go through the drive-through with the wheelchair, and people smiled as they looked at us, but James didn't seem to care what anyone would say or think. He seemed like he was having a blast pushing me around. The way I was sitting in the chair, you couldn't really tell I was pregnant, so that made me feel a little easier about being with him out in public. I didn't have to worry about anyone asking questions about the baby and putting us on the spot.

We found a very nice place at the park that had these huge trees on it; they must be a hundred years old. They hung over us like an umbrella not that I minded the sun because it can never be too hot for me.

Sitting there talking about whatever came up, it was easy; there was no pressure about anything. We just talked, and I was enjoying that as well as being outside. Then we heard someone calling.

"Hi James. I can't believe it's you! God, it must be three years since I saw you last. How are you?" Not once did she look my way. She was a very pretty blonde, and she knew it to.

"Hi, Alice. I've been great."

"What brings you back here these days?"

"Alice, I would like you to meet a friend of mine." He reaches over and picks up my hand.

"This is Charlene."

"Hi, sick, are you?" You could tell just the way she wasn't interested in who I was nor the fact that I might be sick.

"I—" James cut me off and said.

"No, actually we're having a baby, and she had a little bit of trouble, so she has to be off her feet."

"James!"

"It's OK, Char."

"Oh, I'm sorry to hear that. I must be going now take care," and she was gone as fast as she had come.

"What was that all about?"

"She is one of those blondes that make all the blonde jokes true."

"Oh really?"

"Yes, really, and she really thought that I wanted her at one time, and she was not good at taking any hints then. It didn't seem to matter how rude you would be with her, she would just laugh it off and hang all over me. I hated it."

"Why did you tell her we were having a baby?"

"She doesn't like kids, period, and there is no way I wanted her to think I was still single."

"So you used me!"

"Yes! Do you mind?"

"No, and it was kind of funny to see the look on her face."

"Yeah, it was. Sorry about that, she spoiled a nice outing."

"No, she didn't, she added to it."

"How do you figure?"

"It was cheap park entertainment. I thought maybe she would trip on her high heels when she left in such a hurry."

"Now that would have been entertainment worth watching."

"You got that right." For the rest of the day, we sat in the park and watched people come and go with dogs, kids, and just couples out walking. It seemed like everyone just had nothing but time on their hands and all decided to come to the park. We had made our comments on some of the people and some of the dogs. For a while, it seemed like we were having a dog show, for there were so many different kinds of dogs coming through the park today. But like all good things, it must come to an end.

"Well, miss, I best get you back before they think I kidnapped you and send out the posses. It is time for you to have a rest. All this fresh air will make you sleep good."

"I dread going back there. But you're right, the fresh air will help me sleep."

"Are you having trouble sleeping?"

"Just because I sleep off and on all day, so it is hard to sleep all night. Then you have the nurses coming in and out all night long."

"I know, they say stay in the hospital to rest, but the nurses don't let you."

"They're just doing their job, I know, but it is irritating. I had thought that once I got stable that they wouldn't be in as much, but that hasn't happened."

"They told me they were keeping a very close eye on you. Doctor's orders."

"They should all be going crazy seeing that we have been gone this long."

"I told them what we were doing, and they said so long as I kept you in the chair, we should be OK."

"I really didn't have any reasons to get out of the chair, thanks to you."

"Hey, don't thank me. That was their orders. Besides why would you want to give up the best seat in the park?" We both laughed, and he hurried along now so we wouldn't be much later. It had been such a nice day, and to be able to spend it out side was even better. But knowing I had to go back and stay in bed was not very appealing to me.

"Don't think so hard about it, Char. Just take it one day at a time. Remember, it is for a good reason that you do as you're told here. I could see your wheels turning," James says as I turned around and looked up at him.

"I know, and thank you for today." Rubbing my stomach, I could feel the baby moving. I think he was tired of the same position all day.

"Is someone else complaining as well?"

"I think he is feeling squished with me sitting like this all day."

"It is surprising that they can withstand all they go through now and at birthing. No wonder it is considered a miracle."

"That is so true."

"Well, here we are. I will get you to your room and set you up so you won't have to get out of bed."

"Thank you, but you don't have to go farther than the door."

"I always return my dates to where I picked them up at."

"You're so funny."

"Don't mean to be."

"Well, hi there, we thought maybe you weren't coming back. We were about to rent out your room."

"Sorry! I know I had her out a little longer than I had told you, but the weather is so nice, and we got lost in the park."

"Hey, no harm done. The main thing is that Charlene had a relaxing day, and she stayed off her feet."

"That she did. I would have tied her in the chair if need be."

"Good for you."

"I would like to be able to take her out again and so I made sure she's done what she was supposed to do."

"Hey, you two, I am right here, do you mind?"

"Not at all."

"James."

"OK. OK. You don't have to get grumpy now."

"I'm not."

"I must go now as I do have an appointment with Sam tonight."

"Sam, how is he?"

"I am not sure. He said he had something to tell me, so we were going for supper tonight. He is so hard to track down."

"Say hi to him for me, will you?"

"I will. Now you get some rest, and I will see you tomorrow."

"James, you have other things to worry about. I am fine here by myself."

"What? Are you telling me you didn't enjoy today, or is it my company?"

"That is not it at all. I did enjoy today and the company. But that is not why you're here!"

"It sure the hell is. I told you Sam called me to tell me you were in here, and I took the next flight out. I promised you, you wouldn't have to go through this alone."

"I don't know how long I will be laid up, and you have to get back to work."

"Who says? When the doctors say you are totally stable, then I will go back to work. Otherwise you're stuck with me as a nursemaid. So you might as well accept it and enjoy it." He kisses me on the forehead and says, "Bye for now, sweet dreams. I will see you tomorrow."

"Thank you, James, and good night." When he left, I climbed out of bed as I really had to go to the bathroom. But I didn't want to say anything while he was here. I wanted to wash up after being out in the hot sun and sweaty all day. It will be nice when I can have a shower, which should be in a day or so, seeing how everything is staying stable. When I came out of the bathroom, the nurse was waiting for me.

"Now that you have washed up, I thought I would give you some good news."

"What is it? Can I go home?"

"Sorry, not that kind of good news. But you can have a shower. Just don't make it a very hot one."

"Great, and I don't care if I just washed up. I am still going for a shower."

"I thought so. Here is a clean gown and some towels. Do you need help?"

"No, thank you. I should be fine."

"Just take it slow and easy. If you feel anything strange, ring the bell right away."

"I will, thank you."

Oh, standing under the shower felt so great it was like having a Christmas present in July. I did not stay in it long, just enough to really shampoo my hair and get a good body wash. Washing in the sink just doesn't cut it. Once I was back in bed, the nurse had brought in the evening snack before everyone turns in for the night.

Falling asleep was easy that night whether it was from the shower or being outside all day or both, I don't know, but I did not wake up until the nurse came in with my breakfast, and it was even late.

"We thought we would let you sleep a little longer today. We know you haven't been sleeping well, and there was really no need to wake you early."

"Thank you. I had a very good sleep."

"Your doctor is coming in around ten. He said he wants to talk to you."

"Tell him he knows where I will be."

"I just thought I would let you know in case your friend wants to take you out today. He will just have to wait until after ten."

"Don't worry. I will be waiting. Is something wrong? Is that why the doctor wants to see me?"

"Nothing that I have heard about. I'm sure he is just checking up on you today to make sure we all have been doing what he has ordered us to do when it comes to you."

"All right then. I guess I will just have to wait and see." I picked up the book I had started and was well into it when my doctor showed up.

"Good morning, miss, and how do you feel this morning?"

"I feel well enough to go home."

"All right then, that is why I am here. There is no need for you to have to stay in the hospital."

"Oh right on. I can go home today?"

"Now hold on a minute. I am not done with you. You may go home under a couple of conditions."

"What are they?"

"You are to stay off your feet as much as you can. I would sooner have you lying down more than sitting. I also don't want you to be alone. Can you arrange that?"

"I think so."

"That wasn't the answer I was wanting to hear. Do you have someone you can stay with until you have the baby or perhaps get someone to stay with you."

"Yes, I can do that." I didn't know of anywhere or anyone, but if it meant getting out of here. I can lay around home by myself just as easy as doing it with someone else. After all, Louise is not that far away. I do have a phone.

"All right then. I will give the girls at the desk your discharge orders. But you have to promise me that any signs of a problem, you get right back here. You are not out of the woods as far as being able to carry this baby full term. Anything can still happen, and you have to understand how delicate you are right now even if you feel great. You're body is telling us different."

"Why is this happing?"

"It is almost like your body is rejecting the pregnancy."

"Doesn't that mean there is something wrong with the baby?"

"No, for some reason, your body thinks the baby is a foreign object, and it wants to get rid of it. By the ultrasounds you have had, the baby is fine."

"So I can go home today?"

"I will want to talk to the person who is going to be there with you."

"Why?"

"I want them to understand how serious this is and how careful you have to be."

"How serious is what?" James asked as he comes through the door.

"This lady's condition. Are you going to be taking care of her?"

"Yes, sir." James made it sound like he was taking an order from someone from further up the line.

"Well, I have told this young lady she can go home, but she is to stay lying down as much as possible. If she doesn't, she will be back in here by tomorrow."

"You can come home," James says as he takes my hand in his.

"This is great news."

"Only if she is going to obey the rules. I will write them out for her on her discharge papers."

"Oh, believe me she will."

"James!"

"Well, you are. Just think how much better you will like being at home."

"All right, sir. I will go tell the head nurse that you are to go home today."

"Thank you, doctor."

"You're welcome, and I really hope we don't have to see you in this way again."

"I hope not too."

"That makes three off us," James says as he begins to lift me from the side of the bed."

"I can stand on my own and get dressed."

"Sorry, I just want to help."

"I know you do, but there is helping and then there is smothering. Please just give me a little space and room to move."

"What can I do to help you?"

"You may get my bags from the closet." It didn't take long before James had me back home and lying on my bed. He had me all propped up both head and feet. It was sort of nice that he would take the time to do all this. He didn't act like he was in any hurry, but I felt like I was in his way even though I was in my own place.

"Is there anything else I can get for you, Charlene?" James climbs on the bed beside me as if he had done it a hundred times. He looked quite at home.

"No, I think I will be good now. In fact I know I will be great just being home.

"By the way, how was your supper with Sam last night?"

"I got stood up. Sam had to go to a meeting, so we are meeting tonight."

"So you will get to go out for supper again tonight."

"No, we are meeting upstairs."

"Here you mean, at home?"

"Yes."

"Do you know what it is about yet?"

"No, he isn't saying much other than 'I will tell you when we are together.'"

"Sounds a little mysterious."

"Yeah, I don't know what he is up to these days, he hasn't talked much since Mom passed away. It is like he has become someone I never knew."

"Has he been drinking a lot?"

"That is the funny thing about all this. He hasn't, and that makes me wonder even more. What would keep him from the bottle? He always seemed like he needed it before. I was scared that with Mom's passing that he would go off the deep end and lose control of his drinking. It had started out that way, but somewhere along the way, he has done a real about-face, which I'm grateful for, but I can't help but wonder why."

"I can understand the concern, but I think you will find that now that your mother is not here to baby him, he has found out that he had to grow up and become responsible as a man."

"I sure hope you're right. Whatever it is, I am glad it has taken him away from the bottle."

"Me too. He wasn't a nice person when he had had too many drinks."

"He would get hard to take, all right." Not too sure what James was thinking about because he became awfully quiet, and I wasn't saying anything either, and before we knew it, we had both dozed off to sleep. It was an hour and a half later when I opened my eyes to see him staring back at me.

"I wondered if you were going to wake up before I left."

"How long have you been awake?"

"Long enough to watch a sleeping beauty." I knew I was beet red by now.

"Aren't you a funny one."

"You know, I read in one of those baby books how mothers-to-be get a glow to their skin. You have one most of the time. That is when you're not blushing. It is so easy to make you blush. For someone who was raised on a farm, you sure do blush easy."

"What does being raised on a farm got to do with anything?"

"Most farm girls have heard and seen almost anything you can imagine."

"Oh really!"

"What? You telling me you're from the old school?"

"I'm not sure what you mean."

"Well, you seem a little shy whenever I speak of your looks or about sex, why is that?"

"I don't know. Guess it is because sex was never talked about at home. It was a no-no."

"Don't you think you're pretty? Now don't turn away and hide your beautiful eyes. You are very pretty with the blond red hair and those big blue eyes. You know your eyes talk for you? It is so easy to see when you're sad or when you are happy. Even when you like to try and throw me off, I know what you're feeling, your eyes tell all. They also tell me how insecure you are. I don't know why you are so insecure, but you shouldn't be. You know what you want and don't want, and you can make good out of anything. I have seen what you have done down here, and I have seen what you have done with secondhand furniture. You, my dear girl, can do anything you set your mind out to do. You are very strong minded, and your willpower outshines anything that is putting you down. So I don't understand where the insecurity comes from?"

"It isn't with everything. I know what I can and can't do as far as working with my hands."

"So the insecurity is only with the heart. Why? You have so much to offer. Who wouldn't want you and take care of you and your baby? You have to be the most honest person I have met in years. Any man would be crazy not to want to hang on to you."

"I have already proven that theory wrong now, haven't I?" I say as I rub my stomach.

"I am talking about a real man not some fly-by-night goof. Have you ever had time spent on you by a real man?"

"How do you mean a real man? What are you calling a real man?"

"A man who can think with more than the head between his legs." Now I know I am fifty shades of red.

"Guess I can't say I have. It always seems to be the only thing they are after and then you don't see them again. Even during sex, they say all those sweet things and even say how much they love you. But they don't come back."

"Is that what has you so distant from me. Is that why you won't let me be close? You think I won't be back?"

"No, I never ever thought you would be back. Why would you be? You don't know me, and you sure don't owe me anything."

"I have come back because I do want to know you." He lifts my chin up so he can see my eyes. "I don't care you are carrying another man's child, don't you get that? I want to know you, and if it means getting a baby somewhere along the way, then I guess I have been double blessed. Wouldn't you say?"

"You have no idea how hard it is for me."

"Hard it is for you?"

"Yes, when I see you like this, I want to take you in my arms and hold you. I want to be able to share your baby every step of the way. I want it to be us. I also know you're scared, and I don't blame you. But please give me a chance to show you that I can think with the head on my shoulders." I turn away. "Don't turn away. Look at me, can't you tell how serious I am about all this? About you?" The baby is moving a lot, so I rub my stomach and shift on the bed.

"Is the baby moving?"

"Yes."

"Would it be OK if I felt him?" he asks and lifts his hand up to put on my stomach. I take his hand and put it on the spot that I can feel the baby move the most. The look on his face was somewhere between awe and shock.

"My god, he's really moving! Does it hurt when he moves like this?"

"Sometimes, it gets uncomfortable, but not painful. It is such a joy to know he's moving that what discomfort he causes is nothing compared to the joy that it brings."

"This is awesome. Do you think they can really hear us like it says in the books?"

"I can't see why not. After all, we can hear underwater, maybe not perfect but we can still hear. That is why you're not to tap on fish tanks, it is loud to them."

"Have you been playing music or reading to him like they suggest in the books?"

"The music I have on most of the time very softly."

"I noticed if you weren't paying attention you wouldn't know it was even on."

"I don't like it to be the main attraction in my home, but I do like it better than dead silence. This way it drowns out any noise that may spook me."

"Do you spook easy?"

"Only at night, it bothers me. I like to know what or who is around. So I am a very light sleeper."

"But you don't get a good night's sleep if you don't let your mind close down totally."

"That maybe, but it will come in handy once the baby is here."

"See if you were with me, then we could take turns with the baby and at least get a good night's sleep every second night."

"That is true, but I won't mind being awake with the baby. He will only be a baby once, and after all, what else will I have to do but to take care of him?"

"You're right to a point, but remember you need a life as well."

"There will be lots of time for that once the baby is older."

"What? You plan on becoming a hermit once you have the baby?"

"No. I will take him out walking and downtown."

"And?"

"And what?"

"Oh please, tell me you will have more of a life than that."

"I will do what I want to do."

"Well, I can see that I had best be close by or you will lose all communication skills with the real world."

"Aren't you the funny one. It won't be that bad."

"I will see to it that it isn't. What is that?" James asked as he cocks his head to one side to listen. I strain to listen as well.

"I would say Sam is home."

"Oh, it is that time already," he says as he looks at his watch. "I will go see what is on his mind, and I will check back with you in a while."

"I will be OK. I won't go anywhere except to the bathroom. I will even do that slowly."

"You promise me that."

"Yes, I do. I don't want to be back in the hospital."

"Good girl. You were listening to the doctor."

"Of course, I was."

"I will tell you what. I will bring supper back went I come, OK? You like Chinese food?"

"You don't need to do that. I can have a bowl of soup."

"I know I don't have to. Now do you like Chinese food?"

"Yes, I do."

"Good. I will see you in a little while now. How about reading to that little boy in there so he can be as smart as his mom." He leans over and kisses me very lightly on the lips. I'm not sure who was more surprised him or me.

"I would say I'm sorry for doing, that but I'm not." Then he gets up off the bed and leaves. I lay there in some disbelief or maybe even stunned. But I also have to admit it was sweet as

well as exciting at least; my heart rate was up. I also know I can't
let it happen again. I must remember I will have a baby to think
about no matter how good his intentions are; this is still someone
else's baby. The ringing of the phone brought me back to the real
world.

CHAPTER NINETEEN

"Hello."

"Hi, Char. I was up at the hospital, and the nurse told me you went home."

"Hi, Louise. Yes, and it is so nice to be home in my own bed."

"I hear you have a pretty good-looking caretaker."

"You do, do you?"

"That is why I didn't come over. I thought you would be fine in his hands."

"Well, he is gone now, and I will be just fine."

"The nurse told me the doctor said you had to stay in bed most of the time or at least off your feet. How are you going to do that?"

"Well, what do I really have to do other than feed myself and go to the bathroom?"

"Yeah, but we both know you, Char, and that is not going to be enough for you."

"How long is the gentleman around for?"

"His name is James, and he should be leaving in the next couple of days."

"I will come then, and we will make plans for me to come do your house cleaning and laundry, plus I will bring your meals."

"That is so nice of you, but you have enough to do without doing my work and cooking for me as well."

"Char, we won't discuss it right now. Like I said, I will be over in the next day or two. If you need anything before that, call me, don't hesitate."

"Thank you, but you don't have to wait until James leaves to come over."

"You're right. Maybe I should come over and see what his plans are so I will know just how much time you are going to be alone. The nurse told me the doctor doesn't want you to be alone."

"I should be fine, and Sam lives just upstairs."

"Yes, he does, but we also know he's not home much, and when he does come home, it is usually very late and that could end up being too late for you, Char, if something happens again. Last time, your timing was right, or his timing. However it happened, he was there for you, but you can't bank on Sam to be there when need be. You already know that, and this is nothing you want to take chances on. So I will be over tomorrow, and we will all sit down and make sure we have a bomb-proof plan in place."

"Louise."

"I don't want to hear any excuses, so please just do as you're told."

"All right, all right. So you will be over tomorrow?'

"Yes. It will be later in the morning around ten thirty. That should give you plenty of time to be able to get up and tend to yourself without rushing."

"That's sounds great to me. Thank you for calling, and I will talk to you tomorrow." After we hung up, I laid there thinking about how we could arrange things so that it would be easy for Louise to do so much; after all, she has already got a big family to take care of. If I know her, she will do way more than she has to just because she is old enough to be my mother, seeing how her oldest daughter is six months older than myself. Louise will be in the mother mode not sister mode.

It is funny because I don't ever think of the age difference when we are together. I just think of her as my oldest sister, and it is something that I am proud of. She has never given me a reason to feel anything different than pride in the fact that she is my sister. I know she will have sound advice and tell me the way it is going to be.

I also know she will ask if I have told our parents yet. I don't know why I keep putting it off, but I guess someday they should be told. I guess after all this time, I could wait now until I have the baby. Then call them to let them know they are grandparents again. Really what is going to be the big difference? Telling them now or later is not going to change a thing. I'm still pregnant and still on my own, and that is the way it is going to be. Neither one of these conditions will please our mother, so why hurry with the news; it's how I see it. Louise will see it totally different but then she is already a mother, and she's probably putting herself in our mother's shoes, and she would want to know what was going on with her daughter. Although, I don't feel that would be the case with myself and my mother. Oh, I'm sure my mother loves me as she does all her children but just differently. I guess out of respect for them as my parents, I should have called them a long time ago. Now the guilt feelings start to come to the surface and I hate it when that happens because then I feel like I have let them down so many other times and this will just be another as well as a disappointment to them.

Not only that but when I start to think about Mom and Dad, I get really homesick, and I want so much for her to be here for me and tell me everything will be fine as she hands me a bowl of hot home-made soup. Now the tears are coming, and I curse myself for going down this road. It never gets any easier, and I always end up in the same place. Alone and homesick with these words going through my head, *You made your bed, now you will have to lie in it.* God, I hate those words. They seem to be there haunting me all the time. I think the worst is the fact that I know she is right.

I did make my bed, and this is my problem, no one else's, and I will have to deal with it on my own. Whatever the outcome will have to be of my own doing. I can't sit around and wait for things to happen because someone else says so. Nor can I expect anyone to take care of me; they didn't put me here. I did by making a bad choice.

God knows I'm sorry for the choice I made, but seeing how I have chosen to have this baby on my own, I would hope he could see his way clear to see me through this without having to burden anyone else.

With this thought in mind, I went back to thinking of a way to make it easier on Louise. But my thoughts were disturbed from loud voices coming from upstairs, and I mean real loud. What is going on up there? I could tell it was a very heated conversation going on and then I heard the door slam shut. I waited to see if anyone was coming downstairs, but everything became very quiet. It was an eerie quiet. It did not sit well in the pit of my stomach. I had to get up and get a glass of water. I got this real gut feeling that something was wrong. Now I wish James would hurry back so I would know what was happening. There wasn't going to be any sleeping right now, I can tell you that much. I wasn't hungry but, watching the clock, knowing James was coming back with supper was putting me in an antsy-type mood. I also couldn't get the fact that something was wrong out of my head after hearing such commotion upstairs. You know what it is like when you get that feeling in the pit of your stomach, and it doesn't go away until you have an answer, be it good or bad, but then you move on.

Not knowing for sure what time James planned supper for, I didn't know how long a wait I was going to have. I tried reading, but I couldn't get my mind back into it, so I just tossed my book aside. Maybe I should have a warm bath that would use up some time and keep me busy for a while.

Sitting in the tub was relaxing even if it was warm as I always like my baths fairly hot. I think this comes from having to share our bathwater on the farm while we were kids. By the time our turn came around, we usually had lukewarm water, and you couldn't stay in it long because there was always someone else needing a bath. Plus bath day was on Sunday evening in time to get ready for school. This I also take advantage of now and bath every night. I know I won't make up for all those lukewarm once a week baths, but I really enjoy knowing at the end of the day I can end it by soaking in the tub and take as long as I want. I found myself dozing off when I heard someone in the kitchen. Who the hell is in here? I got a little nervous as I climbed out of the tub and wrapped myself in a towel. Whoever it was wasn't being quiet, so whoever it was didn't care if I knew they were there.

I opened the door just so I could peek out.

"Hello, who's there? Hello."

"Hey, it is just me. I brought supper. I was trying to be quiet. I thought you might be sleeping, but I can see you were elsewhere. Looks good that towel. I think they are in fashion this year."

"Aren't you the funny one."

"Have you looked in the mirror? If not, do so, then tell me who is the funny one." I know I went red.

"Sorry, I will go get dressed, and I will be right out."

"No," James says as he grabs my hand. "I was just kidding. You look sexy, so if you want to stay wrapped up in the towel, that's fine with me."

"No, that's OK. I will dress to eat, thank you anyways."

"No problem, need help?" I looked back over my shoulder and gave him a what-with look as I carried on my way. I dried myself and then just climbed into some pj's and put my house coat back on. What really was the purpose of dressing? I was just getting back into bed after I ate.

"Oh well, that is nice too, come sit down and let's eat. I wasn't sure what you liked, so I got a few different dishes."

"So I see, looks like you're going to feed an army."

YOU MADE YOUR BED   313

"Nope, just us and you tomorrow. That is one thing about Chinese food. You don't have to do anything with it the next day. You can eat most of it cold."

He wasn't acting too upset now, so maybe there was nothing wrong.

"Are you OK?"

"Yeah! Just hungry, so come now and let's eat."

"OK." James had put the dishes we would need out on to the table, and it looked like he had everything covered right down to the iced tea for drinking.

"I was going to bring some Chinese tea but didn't know if you liked it. Some people find it too bitter."

"I don't think I have ever had Chinese tea. If it was too bitter, I do have honey."

"Sorry, I never thought about honey. So next time, we will have Chinese tea, for tonight it is iced tea."

"That is OK too." We carried on with our supper, and the suspense of what happened upstairs earlier had me only half listening to what James was talking about, which was about his trip to China a couple of years ago. I know he was talking about what he had to eat then and how different their food over there is and how a lot of people wouldn't be eating what they cook over in China.

It seems to me he was doing a lot of talking. Not really eating.

"You said you bought this supper for the two of us, but you don't seem to be eating anything." He just sort of sloughed me off and kept on yapping away. I also noticed he wasn't looking me in the eye when he was talking.

"OK," I said as I laid my fork down, "spill it James. Something is on your mind, and we might as well discuss it before it takes up all our suppertime. I am not enjoying this at all. You are like a babbling fool. Something is wrong. I can feel it so come clean."

He pushes his chair away from the table and starts to pace the floor. He was quiet for a long time. I could tell he was going over something in his head, and I'm sure it was something about me.

"James, have I said or done something wrong? Are you upset with me?"

He comes right over and takes by hand.

"Oh no, it's not you. You haven't done anything, but my dumb brother has."

"Really! What has he done now?" James lets go of my hand and starts to pace the floor again.

"Please stop that. You are going to make me dizzy."

He throws his hands up in the air and says, "Whatever possessed him to do such a thing. He didn't even talk to any of us to see if we would mind or maybe we would have bought it. Oh no, he just takes it upon himself to do what suited him and the hell with everyone else. I know it was left to him that was Mom's wishes as the rest of us got money, but for all tense and purposes, he should have talked to us first. What about you? Did he not think what stress this was going to put on you? Of course not, because that means he would have to think of someone else besides himself."

James runs his fingers through his hair, and he seems to be in a real state over something I couldn't make head or tail out of.

"Oh shit, what was he thinking?"

"James, are you going to tell me what it is you are talking about and what it has to do with me?"

"The house."

"What about the house?"

"Sam sold the house, Char?" I was sick to the stomach as soon as he said it. I know I must have turned as white as a sheet because James was over there in a flash.

"Oh god, what have I done? You want to lie down to take this all in?"

"No, my supper doesn't feel like it is going to stay down, please excuse me." I got up and went to the bathroom. After running cold water to splash on my face, I took a face cloth and just sat on the toilet and held it over my face. Now what? What if these new people don't want me here, and if they do, how much rent will they want? Where will I go? Who has room for me and a baby? My EI check is not that big. Maybe I will have to go to social services after all.

"Char, are you all right, Char?"

"Yeah, just give me a minute. I will be right out." I wiped my face although it didn't make me feel any better. I had this awful sick feeling in the pit of my stomach, and the baby was moving like crazy so that wasn't helping any.

"Hey, I'm sorry about this. I should have told you in a different way not like that. What a blow. Here come lie down. I will bring your ice tea."

"Thank you. I think I will do just that." I went over and climbed up on to my bed.

"Here take a drink, maybe it will help. I will go put supper away. Unless you want something to eat in here?"

"No, thanks. I don't feel hungry right now."

"That makes two of us. I will be back in once I put everything away."

All I could think was "What now?" Maybe James could change Sam's mind once they both cool down and think it over. Maybe James and the other boys could buy the house. Then they could rent out the top as well. Maybe I don't have to worry. Sam never came to tell me any difference. Just because he sold the house doesn't mean I have to move. Surely he would have told me. Could James just be jumping the gun, or is that what the fight I heard upstairs was over?

"Here, Char, your tea." He hands it to me and climbs up on the bed with his in his hand. We lie there for a good half hour, no one saying a word.

"James."

"Yeah, Char."

"Who bought the house?"

"A couple."

"So I might be able to stay?"

"I don't know yet. Sam didn't say one way or the other."

"Does this couple have children?"

"I think he said they had older children."

"Oh."

"When were they to take over the house?"

"At the end of next month."

"When did Sam sell the house?"

"Two weeks after Mom passed away."

"And he wasn't going to say anything to me?"

"I guess he was going to wait until the last minute. That is what we had the fight over. I told him he should have at least told you. But he didn't seem to think he had to because you just rented. He owns the house, and he wasn't going to ask any one's permission to sell it."

"He didn't have to ask my permission, but it sure would have been nice to have a heads-up before I had to move out."

"He didn't say anything about you moving out. Not yet anyways."

"Do you think he knows if I have to or not? Or is this going to be just dropped in passing?"

"I really don't know. But I will find out in the next day or two. He tells me the people will be here to have a better look at the house on the weekend. Perhaps then, you and I can talk to them ourselves and see what they have planned. They might be very nice people and will love you like I do and want you to stay. I hope it is someone who will help take care of you when I have to leave."

"When is that? Do you know?"

"The boss wants me back by midweek. I told him if you were good, I would be back to work by then."

"James, you don't have to wait around for me. My sister is coming over tomorrow. She says she is going to make a bomb-proof plan as far as taking care of me goes, so you don't have to worry about me. Thank you anyways."

"That's good. At least I will know she is around, seeing how I can't count on Sam."

"Now, James, don't be so hard on Sam. Maybe he finds it hard to live in the house without your mom."

"That is what he said. But he also got a transfer, and he felt the move would do him good."

"Oh, where is he moving to?"

"Calgary."

"Sam is going to a big city. He should find that a whole lot different."

"I just hope he stays out of the bottle."

"I thought he was doing OK with that."

"He has been. That was all part of him working at getting this transfer. He had to be drug- and alcohol-free when tested."

"It must be something he has wanted pretty bad to stay with it like he has."

"I just hope he stays with it once he is moved and has what he wants."

"He would be losing a lot if he turns back to his old ways."

"I know this could all be for the best for him, but it bothers me that he didn't even think about you. About the condition that you're in."

"James, my condition is not Sam's or your problem."

"Our mother started to take care of you, and she had asked us to do it for her when she got sick. I have to admit, I wasn't to keen on the thought at first. I didn't want the responsibility of a pregnant young girl. But when I met you, everything changed, and I didn't feel that way anymore. You weren't just some dumb young girl who got herself into trouble and was out to take whatever she could get from anyone.

"I knew as soon as we met, that I did want to be part of all this come hell or high water, and let me tell you, you're not making it easy on me. You could just agree to move in to my place, and my worries and yours would be over. I have a great housekeeper who would love to be a nanny as well. We have already talked about it, and she is more than willing and able to help you, help us.

"If it turns out that you do have to move out of here, would you just think about my offer? You can have your own room, and we would start from there. But we would all be close, and I could help you with the baby and be a part of it all. It would be stress free for you, and you could just enjoy being pregnant and planning on the baby instead of all this. How do you go on each day with all the uncertainty? That alone has to be more stress than your doctor wants you to be under. I could make you happy if you would just give me a chance."

"It's not about giving you a chance. It is about what is right, for myself as well as the baby."

"By giving the baby a father, that's not right in your books?"

"My baby has a father!"

"He sure has, and what has this father done for you so far?"

"James, you're not being fair, nor are you thinking straight."

"My thinking is just fine. It is you who has to think in a different direction. You're right your baby has a father, but what about a dad? A dad who will do things with him and be there for him and love him no matter what else happens. Someone he can count on all the time."

"He will have me!"

"That's right, he will have his mother, and he is going to be one lucky little boy to be on the receiving end of all that love that you carry for him. But why can't he have both."

"He will have both someday, when it's right."

"OK, I give up for now. I will go now so you can wrap your pretty little head around what is what and what is right. I will talk to you tomorrow. I hope you have a good sleep," James says as he kisses me on the forehead and climbs off the bed to leave. "I will lock the door on my way out."

"Thank you, James," I called to him as he was going through the bedroom door.

Stopping in midstride and looking over his shoulder at me, I could see the hurt in his eyes.

"Yeah, Char."

"I'm sorry, James, and thank you for everything. I know you care, and I will think about what you said and your offer."

"It's not just an offer, it is how I feel. I wish you could see that." He leaves before I could say any more. Besides what was I going to say? I'm scared you won't like my baby after you see him. Maybe he will be a crier, and some people just can't handle that, and seeing how it is not his, it would be easier to take a dislike to a bad baby versus a good baby.

It would be a good place for me. I can see he cares, but I don't really know what I feel for him. I like it when he comes around. He makes me kind of giddy, and my heart does these funny little jumps, but what all does that mean? Some of this I have not felt with anyone else, but does it mean I could have feelings for him? Even if I do, it doesn't mean you move in with them. Maybe these feeling are just because I don't really know him. He seems to be sincere and kind and caring. Why else would he bother with us? He sure doesn't have to. With this thought in mind, I had drifted off to sleep. The night seemed like it was a short one. I woke to Louise knocking at the door.

"Hey, Char, are you awake in there?"

"Coming." I was still in my house coat from the night before, so it didn't take me long to get to the door even at moving like a turtle. Opening the door to see Louise's smiling face was a good way to wake up.

"Hi, kiddo, how are you this morning?" she asked as she came in and hugged me.

"Not so bad. If you want to go put on coffee while I go wash up, that would be great."

"I sure can do that. I thought you would have been awake by now."

"Why? What time is it."

"Ten bells."

"Really?"

"Yes, it is."

"Guess I was sleeping better than I thought."

"Looks that way. I will make the coffee."

"Good. I will just be a few minutes."

"Take your time. I'm not in a hurry today."

I'm not sure why I feel so tired. I went to sleep with no trouble, and I don't remember dreaming, so I slept all night long. Maybe just being emotionally drained tires a person out.

Washing my face with cool water seems to bring a little more life to me.

"Good thing for these Tim Horton's coffee pots, eh."

"Yeah, it's like having coffee on demand." We both laughed.

"So, Char, anything new?" Louise asked as she poured the coffee.

"Oh yeah!"

"That doesn't sound good."

"I don't know how good it is yet."

"What's up, Char?"

"Sam sold the house."

"And what does that mean?"

"I don't know for sure whether I can stay here or if I will have to move."

"You're joking, right?"

"No, I am not."

"That will suck after all the work you have done here. Then you won't get to stay. When will you know?"

"James hopes to find out this weekend. The people are coming to look at the house again."

"Oh god, Char, what will you do if you have to move? Where will you go?"

"I really don't know at this very moment. James said I could live at his place in the city, but I don't like the idea."

"Why not? Don't you like him?

"Sure, I like him, but that's not reason enough to move into some man's place."

"Now you're right. What else does he say about it?"

"He says I would have my own room for starters."

"For starters, what does that mean?"

"He wants it to be more than that with us, but I'm not ready, and he thinks I'm being too hardheaded about it all."

"So what is holding you back if you have nowhere else to go?"

"What if he doesn't like the baby after it's born, then what? What if the baby cries too much, or if there is something wrong with the baby and he finds it embarrassing to be with us then?"

"Char, your mind is on overdrive. I would not have thought of those things. They are reason of concern, I must admit, but what other choices have you got?"

"I guess I will have to call Mom and Dad and ask if I can go home just until the baby is born. I don't have any friends here that would have room. They're like you, there full up."

"Did you ever call Mother to tell her the good news?"

"No, but now it looks like I won't have a choice."

"Oh Char, I am sorry. Maybe we could put you in the living room."

"No, that would not work. You have a family that likes to watch TV and wouldn't they just love to know their aunt is sleeping in their space of relaxing."

"I guess you're right. I just don't know what else to do. Here when I came today, it was to tell you of our bomb-proof plan to take care of you, and now we can't."

"I would like to hear about it anyways just in case I can stay."

"Well, a couple friends of mine just live a block from here, one east of you and the other one north a block, so between the three of us, you you're never going to be alone. We were even doing the sleepover duties."

"No WAY!"

"Yes! And if you stay here, that will be the plan. It is not up for negotiation, so don't even try. These ladies helped me when I had my baby on my own, and they have been friends ever since, and now, we are going to do the same for you. It will be like having three mothers and three grandmothers looking out over you. You will be well taken care if this is the road we go down."

"But, Louise, that is a lot to ask of people who don't know me."

"They know me, and that is all they needed to know. In fact when I was telling them about the shape you were in, they came up with the idea. They have no one at home anymore, and they would like to share their time with you. They even talked about babysitting for you when you go back to work. That is if you like them and want them to take care of your baby."

"Wow! You have been busy since I saw you at the hospital."

"Not really. I was just having lunch with friends, and they had asked how you were doing. Hope you don't mind me telling them about your life."

"No, of course not. It's not a big secret anymore."

"If I have to go to Mom and Dad's, I will have to store my things until I come back."

"You think you would come back here."

"Oh yeah, I won't be staying out there. There are more opportunities here for me. If I don't get to go back hairdressing, there are other things I can do here. I like it here because I can get around on my own by walking where anywhere else I have to drive, and buying a car right now is not up on the top of my list. This town is big enough for me. I don't like the cities, and where Mom and Dad are, there is nothing to look forward to. It is pretty to live there if you are retired but not for young people."

I get up to make myself some toast and refill our coffee cups.

"What are you doing?"

"Getting myself something to eat and getting us some more coffee."

"You just have to ask, now off your feet. What do you want to eat?"

"I was just going to make some toast."

"That works for me."

"You never ate yet either?"

"No. I hurry around home to get what had to be done so I could get out of there before the phone started to ring. So I didn't take time to eat. So I guess we will have breakfast together."

"That sounds great to me. I could get used to this. James brought supper, and now, you're making breakfast."

"You better enjoy this attention because it won't last long. You will be very busy once the baby comes, so sit back and enjoy."

"All right then. I will do just that." Louise went ahead and got us our breakfast, and we talked a little about everything but nothing really important. I think she was just trying to keep my mind off the fact that I may have to move and maybe to Mom and Dad's. We make it sound so bad, but it really would be nice to spend some time with them now that they are retired. We only see them once a year now as they make their yearly trip to Alberta. More if we get to go home for any of the special holidays that come up.

CHAPTER TWENTY

If any of us are going out to Mom and Dad's, we let the others know, and there usually ends up being a crowd. Most times, it becomes very enjoyable.

This is probably hard on Mom and Dad as they don't see any of us, then we all show up and leave again at the same time. I would think they must get lonely from time to time.

Perhaps if I have to go home, it will be good for them. That is if Mom says it is OK.

Louise and I went ahead and had our breakfast, and she cleaned everything up.

"Char, can I throw in a load of laundry while we have the next cup of coffee?"

"Yes, that would be great. I don't have much that is dirty, but I do like to stay on top of it."

"The towels I will put on the sofa, and you can fold them. I will put them away."

"Sounds good to me."

"I will also do the vacuuming today while I am here."

"But—"

"No buts. I will get it done. That way I know you are not doing it."

"All right, you win."

Louise had done everything you could think of doing, and she moved along at a pretty good speed, and we were able to talk the whole time, except while she's doing the vacuuming. She had just sat down when someone was knocking at the door. Louise goes and answers it. I could tell who it was as soon as he said, "Hi, Char. Home?"

"Yes, she is, come on in."

"Hi, James."

"Hey, how are you today?"

"I'm great, how about you?"

"So-so."

"James, do you remember my oldest sister Louise?"

"Yes, I do, and it is nice to see you again."

"You might not think so after I tell you what I have to tell you."

"Oh! And what is that?"

"Those people will be here tonight to see the place and not on the weekend."

"Oh!" Louise says, and she turns and looks at me. I just raised my eyebrows and said, "Well, it is all clean and ready, thanks to Louise."

"There was nothing wrong with it in the first place. I just freshened it all up for you, that is all."

"So I guess I am as ready as I will ever be. So bring them down whenever you need to."

"I won't be here, Char. Sam will be bringing them down."

"That is OK too."

"I have to leave here by seven tonight. I have to be at work tomorrow morning, but I would like to have supper with you before I leave. I would like to take you out for supper while those people are here looking at the house. I think it would be easier on you if you weren't here."

"I will be OK, that isn't necessary, James."

"Yes, Char. It is. I'm leaving, and I would like to treat you to a nice meal before I leave."

"You just did that. Remember the Chinese food we had for supper?"

"That fiasco! Who wouldn't remember? But this is to be a better meal plus a better evening than what we had then. How about it?"

"Yes, she will go with you. It will do her good!"

"I need time to get ready."

"All right then, how much time do you need to get ready?"

"Give me a half hour."

"You got it. That's all I need. I will see you in a half hour, and it was nice seeing you again, Louise. You're going to be Char's babysitter while I'm gone?"

"Myself and a couple of my friends are going to take turns, but she won't be alone not even at night."

"I am so glad to hear that. Now I can go to work and not worry, but I won't be gone long. You can call me any time you need to. Char has my numbers."

"Thank you, and I will if I need to."

"Now I will go have my shower while you get ready. See you in a bit, Char," James says as he brushes his hand down my arm, sending shivers right down to my toes.

"Char, are you out of your ever-loving mind? I think this man has it bad for you, and you just keep pushing him away."

"You think so, do you?"

"Yeah, I do, and I also think you would be a fool not to let him in."

"Do we have to go there?"

"Yes, Char, we do. You don't think I can see the wall you have around you. How long do you think this man is going to keep beating his head against it if you don't cut him some slack? Please tell me you're not waiting for the baby's father to show up."

"No, I promise you I'm not. I'm just not comfortable having another man take over my baby when the baby isn't his."

"This is the best time. He is coming into this eyes wide open, and he will know the baby from day 1, which makes things so much easier all around. You'll see I'm right. The younger the child, the better."

"You keep saying that, but every time he looks at the baby, he will see someone else, not himself."

"I have heard it said that babies born out of wedlock look like their mothers. It is God's way of protecting them. The way he looks at you is pretty obvious what he feels, and he will be the same about the baby. He didn't ever have to show his face around here, but from the first time he met you, he hasn't turned away just because you are pregnant with another man's child. I think he deserves some credit for that. I also think he deserves a chance to prove himself."

"Yeah, and what if it doesn't work out and he turns on us, then what?"

"Char, there are no guarantees. Where is the father? Does that not prove to you what I'm saying?"

"I guess you're right."

"Now go and get ready, or he'll think you didn't want to go for supper. I am going to finish up here in the kitchen, and when you're ready to leave, so will I be." Louise cleaned up our teacups and put a few more things into place for me as well as she got the laundry all done and put away. I should be good now for another week.

It had been nice spending the day with her even if she spent most of it chasing after my house. One thing about it, women can talk and work at the same time; otherwise nothing would get done.

James was right on time; it was a half hour since he had left, and one thing about it, I don't have much to do to get ready these days. I don't do anything to get dirty or messy. So I brushed my hair and pulled it back because I wear it long; sometimes I pin it up but not to day. I don't have many clothes to choose from that fit once again. So today, I chose a blue-and-white sundress to wear over a long sleeve blouse.

"Hi, Char. You look very nice."

"Thank you, James." He lifts my chin up and repeats himself.

"You look very nice, and I am proud to take you for supper."

"I'm leaving now, Char. I will see you tomorrow. You guys have a good evening."

"Thank you, Louise, we will," James says to her as we are all stepping outside. I was glad I had put on the long sleeves; it is a little windy today, and the restaurants are usually cooler than need be. James opens the door to his truck and helps me in it because it is one of these high off the ground trucks. I guess he has it this way because he is so tall it makes it easier for him to get into. Or at least he didn't seem to have the trouble I would have had. But then I just had to get up on his running board and I would have been OK.

We made it to the steak house and had a very nice meal; we even had a glass of wine, which I found myself really enjoying. I found that at the end of it all, I was sorry to have to say good-bye to James.

"You know I am going to miss you badly this time. I thought last time was bad, but I know I don't want to go and leave you so far away."

"That is a nice thing to say, James. I will miss you too and all your help."

"Your sister won't be far away, and she will do all that has to be done. So I don't want to hear about you ending up back in the hospital because you were doing something you were not supposed to be doing."

"Oh, I won't. That is the last place I want to spend a lot of time at."

"Char, have you thought about where you will go if the people Sam sold the house to need the basement?"

"I think I might see if I can go out to BC."

"Go home! As in your parents' place?"

"Yeah, it would be nice to spend some time with them. I wasn't able to go there for Christmas last year. My job just didn't give me enough time off. Seeing how the baby is due around that time, it might be a good Christmas to be there. I don't know for sure. They don't even know I'm pregnant, so it could be hell to pay yet."

"I will ask you one more time before I leave. Will you move into my place? After the baby is born, I would be pleased to take you and the baby to see your parents, Char. That way you are not under any stress that should bring harm to you or the baby."

"James, that is really nice of you to ask. But I cannot at this time. I wish I could make you all understand why I can't."

"Would you have a different answer if I were to ask you to marry me?"

My mouth must have hit the floor, and I had to shake my head. I must have heard him wrong.

"Well, would it be?"

"Are you serious, James?"

"I couldn't be more serious if I tried."

"Wow!"

"Is that all you can say?"

"Yes."

"You will!"

"Oh no! I mean, wow!!

"Would you make up your mind?"

"James, this is something I would really have to think about."

"That's all you do is think about things. Don't you ever take chances? Do you have to know how everything is going to turn out before you can just say yes or no?"

"James, I'm not pregnant because I never took a chance. This is exactly what happens when you do just take chances."

"I'm sorry. I shouldn't have said it that way. I do know why you're hesitant about making these choices, but go with your heart. I can see it in your eyes that you care for me or at least like me. You always get so shy and nervous when you're around me, and I know you're not scared of me. We do have good times together even if all we do is talk and eat. Am I wrong, Char? Am I reading something that is not there? If so, please tell me so I don't go on making a real fool of myself."

"James, you're not making a fool of yourself, and yeah, I can feel the pull to you, but the baby . . ."

"But the baby what? I can love the two of you as easy as loving one."

"James, you have become a very close friend to me, and you have done things for me that only a true friend would do. You have never really asked for more than I can give although I know you want more, but I feel I have to do the right thing here and have my baby first. Then we can see how things go after that."

"Am I still on for being with you when the baby is due," he asks as he reaches over and takes me by the hand and pulls me close enough to him I couldn't get away if I tried, putting my hands up on his chest, which sent shivers down my spine, and he could feel it too.

"I hope you are with me, James. You have already shared more of this baby with me than anyone else, and it will be great to have you beside me when the time comes." He pulls me closer into a hug as if he wasn't going to let me go, then pushing me back just enough so he could lightly kiss my lips, saying, "Thank you, I will be there."

"Oh, James, I'm sorry to put you through this, but I have to be sure."

"That's all right. I'm not going anywhere. I will be ready whenever you are. I would like to be this little boy's daddy," he says as he rubs his hand ever so gently over my stomach.

We stood there, embracing in each other's arms for what was not long enough because I knew that when he was gone, I wouldn't be seeing him again for some time, and he had become such good company. His work would take him away, and no one knew where I would end up. I really didn't want to be taken home to find out I don't have a home. This thought made me sick to the stomach, and I shifted my stances.

"Are you all right?"

"Yeah, but I best get off my feet."

"I will get you inside and settled before I leave, and maybe we can talk to Sam as well before I leave so we all know what has to be done."

"That scares me."

"I guess it does, and I am sorry this is happening to you."

"Don't you worry about it. Sam has to be able to go on with his life too."

"I know he does, but I would have bought the damn house from him if he would have let me know that's what he wanted to do. Then you wouldn't have to go anywhere. Not unless you choose to."

"That would have been great," I said as I climbed up into my bed, and even though supper was great and the company was super, I was glad to be back in my bed. I can only hope the baby will settle down as he has been moving around like he was looking for a way out. He puts pressure on places you don't want.

"I didn't see Sam's truck out front when we pulled in. I will check the back and see what I can find out. You wait right here." He kisses the top of my head and the top of my stomach and leaves.

Lying back, I got to thinking about how nice he is and caring. I know he has money and a very good job, a nice place of his own, plus a housekeeper. How could I go wrong? But is all that worth the chance I would be taking with a baby?

I don't want people to think that is what I went for because I know they would. I haven't known him very long. Plus a baby. There is no doubt that he would handle whatever came our way. That too wouldn't be fair to someone who is so sweet. Why can't things stay the way they are for four more months and that will give us more time to get to know one another? Maybe by the time the baby comes, it will be able to all fall into place without having to work at it. Maybe, in the end, it will be so natural that we will know it is to be.

"Hey! What are you thinking so hard about? You didn't even hear me knock."

"Everything and nothing."

"Well, Sam is not around, but I do have to get going, and I will keep trying to get a hold of him while I'm driving, and I will also call you often, so here is the phone." He places it beside me on the bed.

"Thank you."

"Char, I would like you to give my proposal a thought while I'm gone. I know it wasn't very romantic, but I would like you to marry me." He leans over and seals it with a sweet kiss.

"I promise I will give it serious thought. I want you to be sure that you really want me and a baby. A baby that is not yours!"

"He could be mine. All we would have to do is get married before he is born, and I could give him my name from birth. Char, he would never have to know any different unless you plan on giving him his father's name."

"No, that will never happen as long as I can help it."

"You really mean that, don't you?"

"Yes! Neither he nor his family will know about my baby."

"I did not mean to upset you, Char. Now calm down. I am sorry that bothers you so much."

"I'm fine, and I will think about it all."

"Good, I will call you in a bit. Now no getting up except to pee. Remember your sister will be back in the morning."

"I think I am going to have a snooze right away."

"All right then. I will talk to you later." He kisses me lightly on the lips and leaves. I know he must be thinking about my reaction to telling the baby's father or his family about him. I can't take that chance; after all they have more money than me, and if they wanted to, they could probably take my baby away. I know it has happened to some girls because his parents thought they could do a better job of raising the baby than the girl could. I will run before that happens to me. Until I can be sure he doesn't want anything to do with the baby, I will stay hidden away. I know going out for supper was a risk, but he would not have known the baby wasn't James.

I did doze off and slept for quite a while. It was dark when I woke up and thought, *Gee James hasn't called yet.* I got up and went to the bathroom. I got myself a glass of milk. Looking over, I see the phone was knocked off the hook. Of course, it was. I didn't move it after James had put it on the bed, and I must have knocked it off while I was sleeping.

I checked the time; it is now midnight, so I didn't think James would call me this late. I will go have a fast bath and put on my pj's and see if I can go back to sleep. I was digging for my pj's when the phone rang scaring me out of my pants.

"Hello."

"HI! I guess you can't sleep with the phone in bed with you."

"Hi, James. No, I can't. Why, do you?"

"Yes, I do."

"I guess it takes practice."

"I guess so. I haven't talked to Sam yet, so no news is good news, I assume."

"I guess that could be so."

"I won't keep you up any longer. I just wanted you to know and to be able to say good night."

"Thank you and good night, James."

I went and had a quick bath and was back in bed when I heard Sam come home. I guess I will know more tomorrow. I was more tired than I thought because I fell right back to sleep.

The night was either shorter than usual or I never fell into a deep sleep because I was woken up to someone knocking at the door. Rolling over to see what time it was, I was surprised to see that it was only 7:00 AM. So who would be at my door this early? The light knocking came again.

"I'm coming, just give me a minute." Grabbing my house coat and stumbling to the door still half asleep, I decided to peek in the peephole. Sam? Opening the door to Sam at seven in the morning couldn't be good.

"Hi, Sam."

"Sorry to wake you, but this was going to be the only free time I would have to talk to you."

"That's OK, Sam, come on in and tell me what's up."

"Well, Char. This is a shitty way to have to start your day. But the people who bought the house want the basement suite empty as well. I'm sorry about this after all the work you have done here to make a nice home for you and the baby. I had hoped they would have rented it to you."

"They don't want to rent it out?"

"That isn't it. They have a granddaughter who has just become a single mom, and she will be living in the basement, and Grandma's going to babysit. They really liked the way you have done the basement especially the baby's room. I know that sucks now that you won't be using it, and again, I'm so sorry, Char."

"Yeah, sure."

"Char, I had to do something different. I stayed here because of Mom. Now she is gone I have to move on with my life." Feeling numb was an understatement, but I felt like my brain was also frozen in time.

"I know, Sam, and I'm OK with it all."

"You are?"

"We have to do whatever, and if this is what you have to do, who are we to say it is right or wrong? I really hope it works for you, Sam."

"But what are you going to do? Where are you going to go?" With all you have to deal with as far as being pregnant goes, now you have to move as well."

"I'm not sure, but something will come up. How long do I have before I have to be out?"

"They want to be able to move in about three weeks from now."

"That is fast, isn't it?"

"Yeah, it is, but their granddaughter is a teacher, and they want to be all settled in before school starts."

"I see. Well, thank you for letting me know."

"James is really mad at me. He doesn't want to talk to me right now."

"I know. He was waiting to find out more before he left. I will talk to him. He won't stay mad very long. That isn't in his nature."

"Thank you. He is taking this very personal because of you. He would not have cared if I sold the house if you were not living here."

"I know, Sam, and I promise I will talk to him as soon as I can. Moving is not a big deal. Yeah, it upsets me that the work is going to be enjoyed by someone else. But wherever I go, I can do the same. Home is what you make of it."

"Thank you for understanding, Char." I was crumbling inside, and I really wanted to sit and cry, but I wasn't going to let Sam know that.

"We all come to crossroads in our lives, and it is hard to know which one we are to take. Most of us take the path of the least resistance, but that doesn't make it the right choice for us. It just means that you have pleased everyone else but yourself. I wish you luck, and I hope you don't ever have to look back with any regrets. I hope you find what you are looking for, and your future is a bright one, Sam." Sam comes over and hugs me, and it wasn't just a quick hug because he felt he had to. It was a very sincere hug; as he steps back, I could see the tears in his eyes.

"Char, I wished things would have been different for you and I. You are a very kind person, and James is lucky to have you in his life. You two will be just fine, and he is so excited about the baby."

"Sam, James and I are just friends."

"I know that is what you want, but James wants more. Most of the time, James gets what he wants. He has the money to make anything happen."

"Oh really?"

"Yeah, Char, he does. You and the baby would be very well cared for, and he thinks a lot of you. You must be something because it has been a very long time since he has been interested in a woman. A woman with a child is even more of a surprise. But he is so very happy with it all and seems to think that all is going to work out just fine. So I hope it works out the way he wants and the way you want. This must be one of those crossroads in your life that you were talking about. Will you take the road of least resistance? I don't think you will. You seem to be pretty strong minded and know what you want. I do wish you the very best in whatever you choose to do."

"Thank you, Sam. The same to you."

"Bye for now, Char."

"Bye, Sam." Once Sam was gone, I just went over and sat on the sofa. Putting my head in my hands I looked around at what I had, and I just let it; come there was no more holding it back anymore. I sat there and cried until I couldn't cry anymore. Oh Mary, if only you hadn't gotten sick, everything would be great right now, and things would be the way they were supposed to be. Oh God, I don't want to sound so selfish, but this isn't how it was supposed to turn out.

I'm sure I heard Mary say, "Oh deary, you will be fine, and everything will work out. You are strong, and you will have guidance." It was a funny feeling I had, but it was like Mary was there with me. Or was it because in my mind, I knew what she would be saying to me. So I could bring her back whenever I needed her for the strength I needed to get by. She always had the answers and she could make you feel good about anything. God knows I miss her and her wisdom.

At eight thirty, Louise came in looking like she was ready for another long busy day.

"Good morning, Char. And how are you today?" She dragged it out not really knowing if she should be asking the question.

"As good as I can be. I guess."

"What is that supposed to mean?" Louise came over and took a better look at me. "Hey, Char, why have you been crying?"

"I have three weeks to find someplace else to live." Blowing my nose, I look up at her. "Where am I going to move to? I have no one here that can give me a room."

"When did you find this out? Have you been up all night?"

"No. Sam just left before you came. He said the people need the basement suite as well. Their granddaughter is also a single mother, and they are helping her out."

"Well, isn't that just dandy. After all the work you have done here, now you don't even get to use it." That started the tears to flow again. "Hey, Char. I'm sorry. I guess I don't have to point out the obvious."

"It's not your fault.

"Have you any other ideas of where you might go?"

"I guess I don't have a choice but to call Mom and Dad."

"Char, did you ever call them and tell them you were pregnant?"

"No, I never did."

"Oh Char."

"I know, I know. This isn't going to be easy."

"That isn't the word I would be using."

"Well, we will start with that. I can't say I'm looking forward to this call."

"Do you want me to go get some boxes?"

"Might as well have to start sooner or later."

"You're not doing any of the packing. If it takes me the three weeks, so be it."

"You can't do it alone."

"Why not? It won't be the first time."

"I can just do the light stuff."

"No, you're not, Char. Remember you are to stay off your feet. You just have to let me know what you want where. I will put us on a pot of coffee and then I will go get us some boxes. I want you to go lie down and wait until I come back."

"I will."

"I mean now, Char. Come on, I will see you to your bed, and you stay there until I come back." Louise helped me back to my room, and getting back on to the bed, I grabbed the phone. " I will be back as quick as I can."

"You know where I will be."

"Good girl." Louise was gone for about twenty minutes when I thought no time like now to call Mom. My heart started to pound so loud I could hear it in my ears. I hate when that happens. It used to happen a lot to me with all the ear infections I have had over the years. As I was dialing the phone, my hands got sweaty. Boy, this is so stupid. I was calling my mom and dad, why should I react this way? I sure hope my children never feel like this whenever they need me.

CHAPTER TWENTY-ONE

The phone was ringing just then I remembered there was a time difference. Oh god, this could be way too early. But Mom picked it up on the first ring, and she didn't sound like she had just been woken up.

"Hi, Mom!"

"Hi."

"How are you and Dad doing?"

"We're fine."

"What is your weather like?"

"It's still hot. So what's up? Why are you calling so early? Something wrong?"

"Well, I was wondering if I could come home for a while?"

"Really, what about your hairdressing?"

"I'm not doing that right now."

"Why doesn't that surprise me?"

"I'm going back to it after."

"What do you mean by after? Why aren't you finishing it now?" Oh god, this is hard. But I have no choice but just to lay it on the line.

"Mom, I'm pregnant." I heard her take a deep breath in, and there was silence on the other end. "Mom, Mom, are you still there?"

"Of course, I'm still here. When is the kid due?"

"Around Christmastime."

"Oh great. So why do you have to come home? People work right up until the baby is born."

"Mom, things aren't going well with my pregnancy and so I have to stay off my feet. I basically have to stay in bed."

"Really."

"Yes, and where I'm living has just been sold. So I have to move out, and I have no place else I can go right now."

"What have you been doing up until now?"

"Louise has been coming over and doing whatever had to be done. But she doesn't have room for me. So I had hoped that when Louise has done the packing, Dad could come pick me up."

"I guess you can come until you have the kid. But you will have to find your own way, and we don't have room for any of your things."

"Why can't Dad come and get me?'

"Because it is too far for him to drive."

"But you come this way every year for holidays, and Dad drives."

"That's different."

"But—"

"There are no buts, Charlene. You can come home. But you store your belongings and find a way to get here. You're lucky we have room for you."

"All right. Thank you."

"When will you be coming?"

"Probably within the week."

"OK. We will talk to you then. Bye." She had hung up the phone, and I was still sitting there holding it in my hand when Louise came through the door with her arms full of boxes.

"Hey, Char. What's wrong?" Louise asked as she puts the boxes down that she was carrying and came over to sit on the side of the bed.

"I called Mom and Dad."

"Didn't go well, I gather."

"Mom is Mom."

"Did you get the third degree?"

"No, but she said Dad couldn't' come and get me."

"Why can't Dad come and get you?"

"She said it was too far for him to drive."

"What? They come this way once a year, and Dad drives."

"That's what I said, but she said I had to find my own way home, and I couldn't take my belongings."

"She is not going to make this easy for you."

"I'm used to it."

"Oh Char, I wish I had room for you. I know it wouldn't be for long, and I also know you wouldn't like it in my living room."

"Neither would your family."

"You're probably right."

"Did you get many boxes?"

"I got a lot. I will pour us a coffee and make some toast before I start to pack for you."

"All right. I think I will put on some clothes today. Maybe it will make me feel better." Hugging me, she says, "Keep your chin up, Char. You will get through this."

"Thanks, I know I will." As I was dressing, I could hear Louise in the kitchen getting our toast and coffee. I was going to miss not having her around even if it is going to be for a short time. We might not have really known each other when I came to live here being such an age difference between us. Louise had left home and was married and had three kids already by the time I had gotten to the age where I knew who she was. In fact she was pregnant with her twins. This is a very vivid picture I have of her in my mind. I had thought it was very exciting. She was having twins. I remember lying on the floor, and as she would walk by, I could see her tummy and wondering how those babies fit in there. Now I get to find out for myself. I'm not having twins, but it still makes you wonder how a baby really fits.

"Char, coffee and toast are ready."

"OK, I will be right there." It smelled good. But coffee first thing in the morning always smells good.

"Are you hungry this morning, Char?"

"Not really."

"Come on now. Don't let Mother get you down. You have to eat."

"I know I do, but I just don't feel very hungry."

"Being upset will do that to you. I wish I could find someplace else for you to stay. My friends have all moved into smaller places since their kids have all moved away."

"Speaking of friends, you best let them know I won't be needing their help and watchful eyes. Once I am at Mom and Dad's, I will be OK. After all, they are both at home and not that far from the hospital."

"If you say so. Remember I have been down that road with them. Mind you, I didn't have to stay in bed. Char, what are you going to find to do all day that will keep you out of Mother's way?"

"I don't know for sure, but I have always wanted to write a book. Maybe this would be a good time to start that."

"What do you want to write about?"

"I have a few ideas. I will have to give it more thought."

"Well, after breakfast, you can give it more thought while I start the packing. Where are we to store your belongings?"

"That is something I can do after breakfast. I will make a couple of calls and see who has room and won't mind for a few months."

"Sounds like we have a plan in motion. If we had a shed out at the acreage, we could store it all out there. We will be moved out there by next summer, and you wouldn't' have to worry about anything. But the only thing out there is an old log house, and it is so full now we can't get in the door without falling over something."

"You're moving?"

"Yeah, didn't I tell you?"

"No!"

"We are building a house. It will be nice to be out of town. Now the kids are all grown up, we won't have all those trips to make back and forth to town. I don't know how some of these women get anything done. They're always taking a kid here or there. Just to know I will be able to sit in the nude if I want to and have coffee with my curtains open without having someone looking in on me will be great."

"Sorry, I was one of those people."

"I don't mean you, silly."

"I know you don't." While Louise cleaned up our breakfast mess and started in on the packing, I went to my room and started to call around to the people I knew who might have room. I was starting to get a little worried because no one I called had room.

The knocking at the door had Louise and I looking at each other. Raising my shoulders and saying, "I have no idea."

"You want me to answer the door?"

"If you don't mind, please."

"Well, hello there. What brings you this way?" I heard Louise ask.

"I thought I would come take Char for a coffee."

"Come on in, she is in her room." I could hear it was Jacob, and thinking it was a nice surprise, I started to get up when he came in.

"What's with all the boxes?"

"Char has to move out."

"Oh, why?"

"The house has been sold. Sam is moving away."

"After all the work you have done down here, couldn't they at least rent it to you?"

"The people have a granddaughter who has a baby, so they are letting her live here so they can babysit for her while she works."

"Lucky her, but it sucks for you. Where are you moving to?"

"I'm going out to Mom and Dad's until I have the baby."

"Who is moving you out there?"

"No one. I will take the bus out there, and I have to store my stuff somewhere until I come back. But I haven't been able to find anyone who has room. What about you? Do you know anyone?"

"Pour me a coffee, and I will make a call, see what I can come up with."

"Deal." With that I got up again and poured him a coffee and waited while he made his calls. The couple he was working for had a large shed that their daughter had used so they said I could use it if only they got a notice of when I had the baby. I could handle that.

So over the next couple of weeks while Louise packed on this end, Jacob took it and unloaded it at the other end. I was glad that he had time off work because this would have been a lot of work for Louise.

On my last day, there I had another surprise. Anna and her two children came to spend the day with Louise and I. Louise had thought to call and let Anna know that I was having to go to Mom and Dad's.

"I wish I didn't live so far from the hospital, Char. You sure could come and stay with us. I just don't think it is worth taking the chance with you being the way you are. Things seem to be working out just fine for you. How things can change overnight, eh."

"You got that right."

"When you come back, you come see us, and I will help you find another place that you can make into a nice home. You won't have to rush or worry then because you will have had your baby, and there won't be any need to worry so much."

"That would be great. I plan on coming back as soon as I have the baby."

Both Anna and Louise laugh about that.

"We believe you, Char," Louise says as she hugs me. We had spent a very nice day even though my place was somewhat empty.

The living room furniture was still there as well as the kitchen table seeing how it belonged to Mary.

Louise had brought down an extra coffee pot, and she had made sandwiches for us to get through the day with. There wasn't any cleaning up to do at the end.

Anna's kids were very well behaved, seeing how there wasn't much for them to do. I hope my baby will grow up to be as good. Anna and her kids left so they would be home in time to make her husband supper.

Louise made sure I had everything I needed, and she was coming back to take me to the bus later that night. My bags that I was taking with me were already in her car. All I had was a carry-on bag to worry about, and she wanted me to make sure and keep it as light as possible. She was going home to make supper for her family, and I was just going to lie down and sleep until she comes back for me.

I was excited to be going to see Mom and Dad, but it also upset me to know what all I was losing and leaving behind for now.

Perhaps I should have taken James up on his offer. It will be only a few months, and I will be back, and maybe then, we can see if anything can become of him and myself. Once he sees the baby and maybe once he holds him, he won't have the same feelings that he thinks he has now.

I wonder if I should call him. Maybe I will wait until I am at Mom and Dad's. That way, he will know I am safe, and I am with someone all the time, so he won't have to worry anymore. Perhaps this will give him his freedom, and he won't feel like he still has to do right for his mom. He never had to, but for some reason, he felt since Mary was gone, it was up to him to see that the baby and I are taken care of.

This distance between us will most likely put things more into perspective for him. James is way too nice a man to be saddled with someone else's problems.

I have to say I have missed his company since he's been gone. I know he will be upset that I didn't call him to let him know my plans, but then, it's not his problem.

I think he could be a very possessive man. Maybe even a little overprotective over anyone whom he thinks is his responsibility with some of his action when I didn't say the things he thought I would or do what he thought I should do. This and we hardly know each other. Sometimes this can be a bad thing. I have seen it where the woman can't even have friends come over nor can she go anywhere with them. That is not the kind of life I would want to live.

I wonder if deep down inside me, this feeling is what has kept me from letting James get too close. Oh well, I guess we will have time to figure this all out. Falling asleep with that in mind brought on a very restless sleep, and I was glad that at three thirty, Louise was waking me up to take me to the bus.

Getting my bus ticket and bags tagged wasn't a long process, seeing how there were only five people getting on. Four of them were headed to Vancouver.

"Char, I'm going to call you off and on just to keep check and make sure your OK. Health wise as well as mentally. I know this is going to be a very trying time for you. I hope it goes by fast for you, and we will have you back with us. With a little one for all of us to spoil."

"I will be fine. I have no choices left, and I am glad to be going to spend time with Mom and Dad even if it doesn't turn out to be the greatest time. Who knows, maybe this will help turn Mom around. I know she has a heart and is there for us. We just have to learn how to bring it out."

"You are a better person than me, Char. And you have a lot more patience," she says as she hugs me good bye. "Take care and remember, I love you."

"I love you too, and thank you for all your help. I don't know what I would have done if you wouldn't have been here for me."

"That's what sisters are for. I hope you have a safe trip."

"I will call you when I get to Mom and Dad's."

"That would be great. I will talk to you then." Climbing up on to the bus gave me a sinking feeling in my stomach. When I turn around and saw Louise walking away, I was almost tempted to change my mind, thinking where would I go. So I just took a seat three back from the driver. Looking out the window, I saw Louise smiling and waving to me, so I smiled and waved back. She probably knows how I'm feeling right now, but what could she do to change anything. We had used up all our resources.

I can't wait to be back. I have never felt at home living in British Columbia. Perhaps it was because the brothers and sisters I remember being raised with were living in Alberta. After all, there were three of us living just in Stony Creek. So that had become home to me.

It is funny because we say we're going out to Mom and Dad's, but it's not home to us anymore. They bought a new mobile home since they retired, and none of us have lived there and so there are no memories of our lives there, so to all of us, it is Mom and Dad's. We have been back to visit them on special holidays, but it just never feels like home.

To me the only special memory of that place will be this stay and the birth of my baby. I can only hope it will be a special one. I would like it to be one I can tell my baby about with love. After all, he will have spent his first few days at his grandparents' home. I also would hope there will be many more times for him to go to Grandma's and Grandpa's.

The bus driver said that we would be stopping in Jasper for about a half hour, so I knew I had about two and a half hours, so I curled up on the seat and would try to just rest. The evening was very warm yet, and the view I knew would be breathtaking coming this way. One thing about riding the bus, you get to just look while someone else drives. It has always been a beautiful trip. The mountains are very nice to look at, but I don't like the closed-in feeling I get being there.

I have two older brothers who have lived there since they were in their early twenties. So to them, it is home. I know I will get to see them while I'm at Mom and Dad's. At least I would hope so.

When our parents had the small country store, my two brothers would come for Christmas and bring their guitars as they both played, and they would play for us. It was always a great time. We also had a young neighbor who played, so he would join us as well. Those days are long gone, and we won't see them again, I am sorry to say.

Getting into Jasper is always a pleasant sight. You get to see the bighorn sheep and bears up close. There are a lot of elk wandering around most of the time. These animals, I'm sure, know that they are protected here.

The lakes around Jasper have a real greenish color to them. Most bodies of waters are blue or close to it.

I have also seen a lake just out of Calgary that has the green colors instead of blue. My sister Marie and I had taken a drive out towards Canmore, and we saw some nice views on our travel, which I was able to take pictures of. Someday I hope to frame them.

With it being a warm evening, I would get out and take a slow walk around the bus whenever it was stopped long enough to do so. The driver knew something wasn't quite right.

"Miss, are you OK?"

"Yes, I'm fine, just having to stretch my legs a little." Reassuring him, I got back on the bus and read for what time I had left before we would get rolling again. I couldn't read while the bus was moving; otherwise, I would be sick as hell. I wished I could be one of those people who could read while traveling.

After ten hours on the bus, we pulled into Kamloops. Here I find out that I had to do a bus transfer. I also find out that the bus doesn't leave here until 7:00 AM. It is now 1:30 AM.

"You're kidding, right?" I say to the driver.

"No, miss, I am not kidding." I saw a payphone, so I had gone over to call Mom and Dad. Surely Dad would come and pick me up; after all, it is only two hours to Mom and Dad's from here. I don't like calling anyone at this time of the morning, but I'm sure Mom will understand. What other choices did I have?

"Hi, Mom, sorry to wake you up."

"What do you want at this hour?"

"I'm in Kamloops, but the bus doesn't leave until seven thirty. So will Dad come and get me?"

"I'm not waking him up at this hour and expecting him to drive that far this time of night."

"But—"

"You will just have to wait."

"The bus depot is closed until seven AM."

"There must be something close by that you can go to until then."

"But, Mom—"

"I'm sorry, Charlene. I'm not waking your father." The line went dead; she had hung up. I stand there looking at the phone, and the tears are rolling down my cheeks, and I had not even realized they were flowing. I turned around, and everyone else was gone, and my bags were just set off to the side. So here I am in the dark, in a city I don't know, and no one around to help me with my bags. What was I to do? I was scared out of my mind. What if something happens to me now? No one will know about it in time to help me.

Looking around, I saw an alcove in the wall of the bus depot. I pulled my bags over into it, setting them up so I could sort of hide down inside of them a little bit, I checked to see if I had enough change that I could call 911 if I had to. I hoped I was far enough back that no one could see me.

The evening wasn't as warm now as it had been earlier when we had stopped along the way. I had some pain starting from pulling on the bags and that was worrying me now because with pain always came blood. I also knew that I wouldn't be waiting too long before I call for help. I wish I were back in Mary's attic where I was safe and warm, and life was simple then.

Every time I heard a noise I would get all uptight, not knowing who or what might be coming my way. I can't believe that a bus depot is run like this. Where did everyone else go? I know there were more people who got off here besides me. Sitting here quietly in the dark and cold, I had noticed the pain was going away. Thank god for that.

Then I heard these voices of men coming my way, and my heart was beating a hundred miles an hour. I was sure anyone within a ten-foot radius would here. The two men then came into view, and stopping damn near right in front of me, the taller one was taking something out of his pocket. All I could think was a knife. Now my heart was pounding so hard I could feel it in my head. I knew there was no way they wouldn't hear me if I made any sound at all. Oh god, what now? Watching what seemed to be a long time to see what they were going to do was making me wish more and more that I was back in Mary's attic.

Then they were lighting up their smokes and chatting and laughing. I don't think they were drinking. The taller one of the two had turned a little to the side.

"What the hell?" he says to his friend as he touches his arm making him turn around. They stand there looking at each other, so I wasn't sure if it was me he was referring to or not.

Then they started to walk my way. Now my heart is jumping out of my chest. What was I to do? I couldn't go anywhere as I had myself back in the corner pretty good so I could keep warm. There was only one way out, and it was through them. Like that was going to happen.

"Miss! Miss!" the taller one was calling.

"Are you all right?" the shorter one asked as they came closer. Holding my breath, I hoped that if I didn't answer, they would just go away.

"Miss, you can't stay there."

"Yes, I'm just fine," I answered in hopes that they would just leave me alone.

"Why are you sitting out here? The bus is not due for a very long time."

"I know. I was on the bus, and no one told me there wasn't going to be a bus to transfer to when I got this far."

"Where are you headed?" the shorter man asked.

"I'm going to my mom and dad's in Red River. I have called them to tell them I was this far." I thought I best let them know that someone does know I'm here.

"Are they coming to get you? Red River is not that far away," the taller man asked.

"No, my dad can't make the trip," I said that before I could stop myself and thinking that was a stupid move.

"So you're just going to sit here and wait?"

"Yes." I was feeling uncomfortable, so I stood up and came out into the light a little more. The look on their faces when they saw I was pregnant was somewhere between shock and disbelief.

"You're pregnant!" the taller one said as if he had a hard time with the words.

"Yes, I am."

"For sure you're dad's not coming for you?"

"No, my mom said she wouldn't wake him."

"What?" the shorter man said. "Is she out of her mind? You can't stay out here all night being pregnant and all."

"I will be fine. I will just sit back in the corner. No one will know I'm there."

"Are you crazy? We knew you were there, and it didn't take much looking, so if we can see you, so could someone else that won't be so nice. There are a lot of nuts out here at night. You can't stay here."

"I have no place else to go."

"Were you not told about the all-night café two blocks from here? It stays open all night just for the bus people."

"No one told me. But then I was on the phone to my parents." The taller man was on his phone while I was talking to his friend, and when he hung up, he said, "We have a friend that drives a cab here, and he is on his way to take you to the café."

"Oh, you don't have to do that."

They both answered, "Yes, we do! We can't just leave now knowing you're out here and the shape you're in. If something were to happen to you, then it would be our faults, and we're not about to take blame for something we can prevent."

Their friend pulled up with the cab, and they did their chatting while loading my bags. I hear them ask the driver to make sure he brought me back in time for the bus. The cab driver had promised them he would. I saw them shake hands, and the cab driver then put his hand into his pocket.

"Now, miss, we hope you have a safe stay and a good trip to your folks."

"Thank you for your help."

"It was our pleasure, miss." And they turn and walk away.

The driver was kind and caring. He made sure I got inside the café, and he set my bags over the window seat I had picked to sit at. He then went over to talk to the waitress and handed her something and smiled, and nodding her head, she came over to greet me.

"Good evening, miss. My name is Mary, and what can I get for you tonight?"

"I would really like a mint tea please."

"Sure thing, anything to eat?"

"A piece of apple pie would be nice."

"Coming right up. The washrooms are over there to the left if you need to freshen up while I get your order."

"Thank you. I think I will do just that." Getting into the washroom, I then realized how badly I was shaking. I am cold, but I didn't think I was that cold. It must be from being scared.

Mary brought me my order.

"I'm not busy right now. Would you mind if I sat and chatted with you a while?"

"Not at all. I would love that. The trip has been a long one."

"Where are you headed?"

I told her, and I also told her I had called home, and she was horrified that my dad wouldn't come and get me.

"You being pregnant and all, I would have thought he wouldn't have wasted any time getting here."

"He wouldn't have if my mother would have wakened him and told him I needed a ride."

"You and your mother don't get along?"

"Not the greatest."

"And you're going there for how long?"

"I have to stay until I have the baby. I have to stay off my feet, or I may lose my baby." I had gone ahead and told her of all that had been happening along the way. I had also told her how it came about that I now had to go to Mom and Dad's.

"You had nowhere else you could have stayed?"

"No." Then I thought of James. I wondered if I should have called him. Would it have been better than going to Mom and Dad's? I had not told her anything about James and his offer. I know already she would have told me I was out of my mind for not taking him up on it. At this moment, I think I was stupid and out of my mind for not taking him up on his offer.

"Well, I sure wish you luck, girl." Then we went on to talking about her job and why she works such a late shift. She told me it was for people like myself that need the safe warm place to wait for the bus. There aren't always people on the bus that need to stay and wait, so those evening, she said, she would get caught up in her reading.

She had given me her address and phone number so that when I go back home, I could call her when I came through. I was to send her a notice when I had the baby.

She had made the evening go by very quickly, and it was very pleasant to talk to someone after that long ride alone.

The cab driver came back as he had promised his friends he would. He loaded my bags back into the cab while I went to pay my bill.

"Oh, miss, it was all paid for."

"Pardon me!"

"It's been paid for."

"But by who?"

"Those two men that sent you here. They sent money with Harry to see that you had something to eat and drink."

"Well, I need to give it back. They don't owe me anything."

"They wouldn't take it back, and they don't look at it as if they owe anyone anything. They used it as a guarantee that you would be taken care of even though they know I would have done so."

"But . . . I don't know what to say."

"Listen. Those two men are what we consider our own walking angels. They walk the streets at night just to keep an eye on people who are in need of a helping hand. They have sent a lot of people this way. But I must say you are the first pregnant one. Those two men have kind souls and do a lot of good for a lot of people. You're lucky they came along instead of someone else. So now go and have a safe trip, and I wish you luck with your parents and your baby. Maybe I will see you again."

"I hope to see you again, Mary, and thank you for the evening. Would you please let those two men know how much I appreciated their help?"

"I sure will, miss." I wounded if all the ladies that have the name Mary are just nice people.

Once I was back on the bus, I then realized just how tired I was, sitting back and thinking. If I have a daughter, there is no way I would put her through what I have just been through. With that thought in mind, I fell asleep.

Sleeping made the last two hours fly by. In fact it was about three by the time they had done there other stops along the way.

Dad was waiting at the bus stop when we pulled in. This made me glad to be here. Seeing Dad again was great. As always, Dad had a big hug and kiss for me.

"Hi, Dad, how are you?"

"Good, good. How about yourself?"

"Not bad, thanks for picking me up."

"Yeah, yeah," he says as he goes and gets my bags and put them in the back of the truck.

"Mother was making coffee when I left."

"That sounds good to me." Then we rode in silence. I didn't really know how to talk to Dad about being pregnant. It wasn't because he couldn't tell. But guess we will have lots of time to talk.

CHAPTER TWENTY-TWO

We didn't have more than a mile to go before we were at Mom and Dad's trailer. They have a beautiful place right alongside a creek. Dad has worked his wonder with all his flowers along the creek bed, and all his flower boxes he has built up on the top rail of his fence. Everything is still in full bloom.

"Dad, your place looks great. I didn't know you were so into flowers. I never saw you do anything like this before."

"I never had the time or as nice a place to do it with. Your mother always done the gardening on the farm, and it was always for food, not to look at."

"I guess that's true. Mom always had a huge garden on the farm, I remember."

"The food had to do us through the winter, so she worked hard to provide us with that as well as all the berry picking she did."

"Does Mom not help you with the flowers?"

"No. She sits out on the step with her teapot and watches me. I think she has had enough with gardening."

"But this would be so different. It should bring her peace and pleasure."

"Perhaps at one time, it would have. Now she says she just likes to sit in the sun. You have to remember the ten years we had the store, she was inside most of the time. The store was open seven days a week, and she worked most of them herself."

"You're right, Dad."

"Let's get your bags inside now. Mother will be waiting with the coffee."

"Sure thing." I went to grab a bag.

"No! No! I will get them, you shouldn't be lifting heavy things. You go inside now and see your mother."

"Thanks, Dad." Taking a deep breath, I went on up the steps into the porch. Just as I was reaching for the doorknob, the door opens up.

"Hi, Mom." Stepping in, thinking I was going to give her a hug, she stepped back and said,

"Hi, did you have a good trip?"

"Yeah, I did, thank you."

"That's good. Now go sit down. I will get you a coffee."

"I would really like that. Thank you."

"I will get this one for you, but after that, you will have to get what you want yourself."

"No problem, Mom. Thank you. Dad's flowers sure are looking nice out there." I didn't really know what else to say. I felt like I was facing a stranger.

"They should, he is out there all day long with them. I have to take his tea outside to him all the time."

"I guess he really likes it outside then."

"Maybe he should try sleeping out there." Now I really didn't know what to say, and I was thankful Dad came through the door.

"Charlene, where do you want your bags put?"

"Mom, what room do you want me in?"

"The first room."

"That's a real small room," Dad says.

"She can take it or leave it," Mom says.

"That's fine, Dad. I don't need a big room." He raises his eyebrows and turns and takes my bags down the hall. I follow with the small handbag that I had been carrying and my purse. Dad was right; it was a very small room. It had a single bed and a built in closet with two drawers on the bottom. There was just enough room to stand beside the bed. There was not enough room for two people in there at one time. I had to wait for Dad to get out before I could go in and put the bags away that I was carrying. A person could get closetphobic staying in here. Having no other choice, I wasn't about to complain. Putting my bags down, I decide to go back out to visit with Mom and Dad while our coffee was still hot. I'll have lots of time to unpack my bags later.

"Do you want something to eat?" Dad asked as I came down the hallway.

"No, Dad, thank you. Perhaps I will feel more like eating at lunchtime."

"You have to eat now, you know, for two."

I chuckle at this and say, "Yeah, Dad, I know, but I'm more tired than hungry."

"Maybe you should lie down for a while."

"I will, Dad, right after my coffee." That was like Dad to be like an old mother hen. Mom was being very quiet at the moment. I knew I didn't want to get her started because I know there should be quite a lecture coming from her yet.

We sat and drank our coffee in silence for what seemed to be forever, but in reality, it was more like maybe ten minutes. I could see some white netting behind Mom, and there was a container of beads on the table, so I thought it would be a great icebreaker.

"Mom, what are you doing with the white netting?"

"I'm making Marie's headpiece."

"Oh, right on. Is it going to be a long one?"

"No, she is having a three-layer full one."

"Oh, nice. Did she give you a picture of her dress so you could match it all up?"

"I also made her dress. This is the easy part."

"I didn't know you took up sewing?"

"There's a lot of things you don't know." Then Dad saw where this was going, so he was very quick to intervene.

"The wedding is going to be here alongside the creek. We hope the weather is still nice for that day."

"Oh, it should be, Dad. Now I know why all the work that has gone into the flowers. I think it will be beautiful. Marie should be impressed when she sees what you have done."

"Well, I guess! Your father knows what he is doing when it comes to flowers." I wasn't suggesting that he didn't, but there was no need to try and explain it wasn't going to get me anywhere.

"The lady I was renting from had a real touch for flowers. Hers were very nice as well."

"Which ones did she grow the most of?" Dad asked.

"She grew a lot of roses. I don't think I have seen so many different colors in one yard before."

"Does she have a big yard?"

"No, she didn't have a huge yard, but she did have a lot of flowers in a smaller space than what you have here. But it was beautiful when she was able to take care of it. She also sold flowers right from her yard. She had a lot of people who shopped there for their wives."

"She doesn't do that anymore?"

"No, Dad. She passed away, and her son sold her house."

"Oh, that is too bad. I would have liked to see it."

"You would have liked it, Dad. What are your favorite flowers?"

"I like the sweet william. They have a beautiful smell and come in all colors. I will take you out for a walk after, and you can smell them."

"I'd love to Dad."

"I thought you were to stay off your feet? Isn't that why you're here?"

"Yes, it is, but I don't think Dad has miles for me to walk."

"Oh no! No, it's not far at all. But maybe you shouldn't." Dad sounded so disappointed.

"I will tell you what, Dad. I'm going to lie down for a while because it has been a long night. Give my body a chance to rest, then we can take a small walk. OK?"

"All right. I have some more to work on in my little shop, so when you get up, you can come and get me."

"I will do that, Dad." Getting up, I went into my small room and just moved my things aside, enough so I could lie down on the bed. I was thinking how nice it would be to be back in the attic. I had more room there than I do in here, and I was happy there. With that thought in mind, I fell asleep, which didn't surprise me. I knew I was wiped out.

Hearing voices woke me up. I had no idea how long I had slept nor did I know what time it was. I did not get up right away. I lie there, listening to the voices and trying to figure out who would be there. It was a woman's voice. I could not hear Dad at all. He must be out in his shop. I should go find him because I know he will be waiting.

I just wasn't sure how Mom was going to react with someone here, and I didn't want to be embarrassed. Maybe I should wait until her company has left. Then I heard the door shut.

"Charlene still sleeping?" Dad had asked Mom.

"I guess so. She isn't out here."

"Charlene is here?" the other lady asked. So it was somebody who knew me.

"Yeah, Henry picked her up this morning."

"How long is she here for?"

"We're not sure," Mom answered as I came down the hall. Dad was just pouring himself some tea.

"I'll have one of them, Dad. I reached out and touched his arm, and poor Dad damn near dropped his cup.

"Oh! You are up."

"Sorry, I didn't mean to scare you."

"Hi, Char. It has been a long time," Linda said as she stuck her head between the counter and the cupboard. Linda is Ron's sister-in-law.

"Hi yourself. It has been a long time. I've been gone from here now two years."

"Yeah, and Ron has been back here for about a year."

"How is he?" I asked as I came around the counter. I thought her eyes were going to pop out of her head.

"Betty and Henry didn't tell me you were pregnant."

"Good news is always better kept as a surprise."

"I guess so. When is the baby due?"

"To wards the end of December."

"Oh nice, a Christmas baby. What a gift to receive. I must tell Ron that you are here. How long are you here for?"

"I'm here until the baby is born."

"Oh really."

"Yeah, I can't be on my feet a lot. I've been in the hospital twice already, and I can't be alone. The lady I was renting from was going to help me but then she passed away, so it sort of left me with no one but Mom and Dad."

"I bet you were happy, eh, Betty, that Char was coming home to have the baby with it being so close to Christmas."

"We sure are," Mom answers as she gets up to go to the washroom; that way Linda wouldn't see her face. She was happy all right.

"My little sister Shelly is going to have a baby too."

"Oh right on."

"They're going to get married next summer. How about you? Are you getting married?"

"Not that I'm aware of."

"The baby's father doesn't want to?"

"The baby's father isn't even in the picture. Hasn't been since day 1."

"I'm sorry to hear that. He didn't want the baby?"

"No, he didn't want me. So he doesn't know about the baby."

"Aren't you going to tell him?"

"What for? He didn't want me without a baby. I don't want him because there is a baby."

"It's going to be tough on your own."

"Perhaps, but at least, I know I have no one to count on right from the beginning. My oldest sister will help me when I get to go back."

"You're going back to Alberta."

"As soon as I can after I have the baby."

"Aren't you scared?"

"I don't really have a choice." Just then I thought of James. I guess I did have a choice, but I wasn't comfortable with it. "I will take it one day at a time and see what happens."

"You're braver than I would be, that is for sure."

"It's not been brave, it's been stupid," Mom answers as she comes back into the kitchen. The look on Lind's face was of total shock.

"You're going to come see what I have been working on, Charlene," Dad asked as he got up from the table. I knew he was trying to keep me from Mom.

"Yes, Dad, I would love to. Linda, I will talk to you later."

"You bet. I just live right there." She points over her shoulder to the mobile home next store to Mom and Dad's. There wasn't even twelve feet between the two places on that side.

"I guess I can see you later then. I won't have to go too far."

"Come for tea."

"I will do that, thank you." I got up and went outside to see what it was that Dad was so busy working on.

"Dad, are you sorry I came? Does it embarrass you that I'm pregnant and not married?"

"No, it don't matter none to me. You're not the only one having a baby by yourself these days. Look at Lind's sister."

"But they're getting married next summer."

"Anything can happen between now and then."

"That's true. I didn't want to cause any trouble between you and Mom by coming."

"She'll come around, don't worry about her."

"She seems to be really pissed at me."

"She is always like that. She has been worse since we sold the store. I think it is because she doesn't have anything to do now."

"So why did you sell the store?"

"Mother said none of you kids wanted it so she wasn't keeping it any longer. She said she was tired."

"I was never asked if I was interested in the store. I would have loved to be able to keep it going."

"I guess she thought that with all you moving back to Alberta that none of you were interested in it."

"I didn't think she was ready to give it up yet. She seem to be very happy in the store."

"She has never been the same since—" Dad just stopped right there, and the pain that came across his face told me all I needed to know.

"Since Mickey was killed, right, Dad?"

"Yeah, she couldn't wait to get out of there. I think she tried really hard to be able to come to terms with it all. But it just kept eating away at her, and with the rest of you gone, she had nothing else to keep her mind busy."

"She had you and the store. Besides Mom always had someone stopping in for tea, she was never alone."

"Things just weren't the same."

"We know that, Dad. Why do you think we left? It was like living in a tomb. No one was talking. No one was laughing anymore, Dad, and we wanted to live. Mickey wouldn't have wanted us to keep living that way. It was so nice to be around laughter and happy people again. Most of all, we could talk about Mickey if we wanted to. There was no one getting upset at the mention of his name. We have a lot of good memories about him, and we wanted to share them with each other. Staying home, we couldn't. He died, but that didn't mean the rest of us had to.

"Dad!" I took him by the arm and turned him around to face me. He had tears rolling down his face.

"I'm sorry, Dad, if I upset you."

"That's really why you all left?"

"Yes, Dad. We couldn't stand it anymore."

"It was a bad time."

"It was bad for everyone, Dad, and we needed you and Mom to talk to us. We didn't want to be made to feel bad because we wanted to talk about our brother who we all loved and were missing. Are you OK with it now? Mickey's death, I mean."

"Yeah, I'm OK. It has been a long time. But your mother, she not right yet."

"Dad, has she ever tried going for counseling or getting help from a doctor?"

"She got some pills from the doctor. I don't think they do her much good 'cause she's still not happy."

"Me coming here is not going to help, that I'm afraid."

"I think it is good for her. She will be OK with it by the time you have the baby."

"Oh Dad! I hope you are right. Otherwise this is going to be a very long stay." We said no more; we just continued walking to his little shop. I had my arm tucked through his, and it was a warm feeling to be walking like this with my dad and not having to feel ashamed of being pregnant. I have seen Dad with babies and small children since we moved out to BC, and he loves every minute he spends with them. I don't remember the way Dad was with us while we were growing up. But I also don't remember my dad ever laying a hand on me. He yelled at us when we needed it, but that was just the way it was. It sure didn't do any mental damage. I think my dad is a little-people's person.

I hope my baby gets to know him. My dad is also quite the joker, or at least he use to be. I'm hoping that I see more of the old Dad this stay.

Maybe Mom will see in the end that it's not all that bad me being pregnant. Things happen for a reason, and just maybe, this baby will help put some life back into them. Perhaps that is why I have had to come back here. This is all part of God's plan to help heal Mom and Dad.

"Oh Dad, that is beautiful."

"You think Marie will like it?"

"Oh yeah, she sure will."

"It has taken some days to get things to fit the way I wanted."

"I guess so." Dad had built a beautiful trellis for Marie's wedding. He had put it up on wheels so he could roll it into place. There were flower boxes built on both sides, and he had painted it all white. The flowers he had climbing up were all different colors of yellow, orange, reds, and some were burnt colors or more of the fall colors. It was so breathtaking.

"It must have taken you a long time to get the flowers to grow like that?"

"I started them in small pots and transplanted them once I got the sides up. I had it down by the creek until two days ago, and I don't want the wind or anything to wreck it now it is so close to the wedding day."

"I guess not, Dad, but the flowers are so thick that the wind probably couldn't get through any ways."

"Maybe not, but I don't want them ripped off either. So I will keep it in here and just keep deadheading them so they will keep growing until Marie needs it."

"Has she seen this?"

"No. She doesn't know I made it for her. I think it will be a nice wedding gift."

"Are you kidding, Dad? It's the best." I leaned over and kissed him on the cheek.

"You think so?"

"Yeah, I do, Dad." He had a grin from ear to ear.

"You think we should go see if your mother has lunch ready?"

"Isn't it a bit early for lunch?"

"Maybe a little, but your mother likes to take the dog for a soft ice cream after lunch."

"You're kidding, right?"

"No, and Toosie really likes her ice cream." Toosie was a very small mixed breed. Mom and Dad have had her now for many years. She had started out belonging to our little sister, but as everything else, once she had her, she didn't want her and she was left to Mom and Dad. I think in the long run, it turned out to be good for them to have her to take care of. It sounds like she is very spoiled.

"Where has she been? I haven't heard her or seen her since I got here."

"She sleeps beside our bed. She is there most of the day. But she knows when it is time to go for ice cream. She'll be out waiting at the door. She is deaf now and going blind, so she doesn't go far."

"That's why she didn't bark at me this morning."

"She doesn't get up until around noon to go outside."

"She doesn't mess in the house?"

"Never has yet."

"Oh. Then I guess she deserves an ice cream for lunch."

"Well, she doesn't eat much all day long. I don't think she will be with us come spring."

"Do you think she is sick? Why don't you take her to the vet?"

"We have taken her. She's not sick just getting old. We have had her for a lot of years."

"I know you have, Dad. You will miss her when she's gone."

"I think your mother will more than me. She will do anything for that dog. Your mother even bathes her twice a week."

"You shitting me, Dad?"

"No, I'm not. It is like the dog has become her baby."

"That's all right. Isn't it, Dad?"

"Sure it is. Anyways let's go see about lunch."

"All right." I was feeling like I had been on my feet to long today, so I was moving very slow.

"Are you OK?" Dad asks as he looks at me with a frown.

"Yeah, I am. I just need to get off my feet."

"Yeah, yeah, I forgot. I shouldn't have had you come out here."

"I'll be OK after I sit for a while." There was nothing more said as we walked back to the trailer, and he helped me up the stairs.

Going inside, we could smell lunch being cooked.

"Something smells good in here, Mom."

"Everything I make is good."

"You're right about that." But I wasn't going to say "Except for pea soup." God, I hated it when she made pea soup. It was one of Dad's favorite soups. I would try so hard to eat it, but I always went outside and threw it up. The smell alone would get me to heaving. So on the days we had pea soup, I knew I would be going hungry. The rule was you ate whatever was put on the table whether you liked it or not. There was no replacing it with anything else. Sometimes we were lucky and would have bread with it but then we could only have two slices. I would eat my bread slowly so she wouldn't catch on that I wasn't eating the soup. Mickey often would take my bowl when he was finished his. We would just wait until Mom had to get up from the table for something, and we would switch our bowls. Now whether she ever knew we were doing that, she never said.

"The trellis Dad made sure is nice."

"I know. Lunch is going on the table."

"I will go wash up then." God, this is going to be hard if she doesn't let up. Biting my tongue is going to get harder to do with each passing day. I know I need to stay here. I have no choice, but how does one do it and stay sane?

Going to the washroom, I noticed I had some bleeding happening. Shit, this is all I need. This isn't as bad as I have had it, so maybe I will be OK if I just lie down after supper. I have been up too much, and perhaps the stress I feel with Mom isn't helping either.

I went back out to the kitchen to find Mom and Dad already eating.

"Sorry, I took so long in the bathroom."

"It's OK. We have a bathroom in our room. Your mother washes up in the kitchen anyways," he said passing me the plate that looks to be pork chops in mushroom gravy. I thought, *Right on, one of my favorites.* I didn't know if Mom knew that or not, but I wasn't about to say anything because, sure as shit, she wouldn't make it again while I'm here.

Lunch was very good, and I ate my fill. Dad and I chatted through lunch. Mom put a word in now and again. Most of the time, it was in disagreement with something I had said. I would just carry on talking with Dad like I hadn't heard what she said. I could see the looks Dad kept giving her whenever she would speak up. When he would look my way, I would just raise an eyebrow and smile. So he would smile back and go on eating.

I had gotten up to help Mom with the dishes, and Dad stepped up to the sink.

"You better go sit down. Remember you've been on your feet to much today. You told me."

"Thank you, Dad, I will." I saw he had plugged the teakettle in, thinking I could use a cup of tea.

I sat there and watched as Mom and Dad did the dishes, and I was surprised that Mom didn't say something about me not helping. They didn't talk much. Mom had asked if they were still taking Toosie for her ice cream. Dad said, "Sure we are." Then he turns to me and asks, "Are you coming with us?"

"Thanks, Dad. But I'm just going to have a cup of tea, and I think I will call it a day if you don't mind. I'm tired."

"I guess it has been a long day for you."

"Yes, and I do need to put my feet up."

"We go to Richards after we go for ice cream, so if you need us, you can call us there. Your mother has the number there by the phone."

"OK. Thanks. They finished up what they were doing and left. I had noticed that Linda was home, so I thought if I needed help, I would just get her instead of pissing Mom off.

I took another trip to the bathroom to check things out, and it was no worse. I had given thought to a bath but decided not to just in case. I got into my pj's and climbed into bed. Dozing off and on, I did hear Mom and Dad come home. I had no idea what time it was, and that was something I was going to have to buy. If I'm going to be in this room for any length of time, I want to know what time it was.

I never got back up. It was a restless night for me because I kept getting up to see if I was bleeding more than before, and it seemed like it was stopping. But I was scared of falling asleep and not knowing if things changed until it was too late. So the next day, I was dog tired. I told Mom and Dad it was just from the bus ride, and I stayed most of the day in bed. By that night, the bleeding had stopped. When I went to bed that night, I slept like a log. I had had no pain with the bleeding this time, so that is properly why it stopped on its own. I was thankful I didn't have to tell Mom about it. She would have made me wait it out anyways.

By the time I had gotten up, Mom was back working on Marie's veil, and Dad was out in the work shed.

"Good morning, Mom."

"I guess it is."

"The sun is shining."

"Anybody can see that. There is coffee made. If you want one, help yourself."

"I will, thank you. Is Dad just outside?"

"Yeah, somewhere."

"I think I will take my coffee outside and sit in the sun. Care to join me?"

"Maybe later."

"All right." I go outside and find a place to sit in the sun. I didn't want to do a lot of walking today, so I was content to sit on the step off the back side of the deck. The view of the creek with all the flowers Dad has planted was almost picture perfect. I suppose even with the neighbor's fallen-down fence, it will still make a beautiful picture. I knew Dad would be along sooner or later. He is probably ready for a coffee break pretty soon.

I can sure see why he would spend so much time outside or in his little shop. I'm hoping that I am still on speaking terms with my mother by the time I leave. But then, am I really missing anything if we're not?

CHAPTER TWENTY-THREE

"Hi! Good morning, Char. Thought maybe I would find you out here."

"Good morning, Linda. It's a beautiful place to sit and have coffee. Listening to the birds, you could sit here and dream all day long."

"Yeah, your mom and dad were lucky to get this spot. It is the only one in this whole trailer court that has any kind of a yard. Your dad has turned it into a park. So the rest of us can enjoy it as well. We were all so grateful when he built all those tables and benches and put them around through the yard like he did." As she was saying this, she waves her arm around in show of what Dad has done.

"Dad built all those tables and benches for the trailer court?"

"Yes, he did. Even though all this land is what they pay rent on, they let all of us use it. Your dad is very gifted when it comes to his woodworking skills. He has even made me some plant stands."

"That was nice of him." I wasn't going to tell her I knew Dad was good at building. He has made tables and plant stands for some of us but not me. I haven't gotten anything that Dad has built, but I'm not telling her that. I think some of the reason is that I don't have my own place.

Even at Mary's, where would I have put them?

"Char, are you OK? You look upset."

I could feel the tears right on the edge, so I had to recover fast.

"No, I'm fine. Still a little tired."

"I don't think that is it at all. I wasn't born last night. Your mom is giving you a hard time right."

"Not really."

"Come on, Char. She didn't even tell me you were coming home nor did she say you were pregnant."

"She didn't know for very long."

"Char, I have tea with her twice sometimes three times a day. I hear all about Marie but not one word about you."

"Mom and I have never been close. I have never been able to please her no matter what I did, and she was always quick to blame me for some things I didn't do. She never has believed in me or trusted me."

"She seems to be close to your little sister."

"I don't think they're close, but Mom allows herself to be used by her all the time. I don't really want to talk about them."

"I understand. So, Char, have you been well with your pregnancy?"

"No, that is why I had to come to Mom and Dad's. I can't be on my feet long before I start to bleed and go into labor. I have been in the hospital a couple of times now. Once when I was down visiting Marie. I'm glad I was down there when it happened. It gave her and I time together like we have had for a while. She was funny about the whole thing. She started out being a hardnose like Mom, but before an hour was up, she was OK with it all. So I'm hoping Mom will come around. Everything started out good. I had a very nice place to live. I had fixed it all up. The old lady that I was renting from had become my mother and wanted so much to be my baby's grandmother. She had no grandchildren of her own. She was going to babysit so I could finish my hairdressing." At this moment, I thought about James. I have to admit I miss him big-time.

"Will you be able to rent from her when you go back?"

"No, I'm afraid. Mary passed away. Her son sold the house and moved away. That is why I am back here."

"Oh. That sucks. I'm sorry to hear about that."

"You got that right."

"So coming back to your Mom and Dad's wasn't of choice."

"Not really. I had no other choice. Believe me when I say if I had, I would have taken it."

"Well, Char, you can come over any time you need to. Don't let your mom get to you. I know it is easier said than done but try to. The stress won't be good for you or the baby."

"Thank you. I might have to take you up on that now and again."

"I talked to Ron last night. I told him you were here. He said he was coming to see you in a couple of days. He will be off work then."

"Oh, you shouldn't have."

"Why not? Because you're pregnant with another man's baby. It doesn't mean you can't see old friends."

"It was more than that at one point."

"He still cares a lot about you, Char. He just is not the settling down type, but he is still your friend. I think you need all the friends you have right now to stand by you and help see you through the days ahead. You don't have to be alone."

"I won't be. My dad is OK with the baby."

"He's a very good person. So is your mom. Just give her time, Char. She will come around."

"I know she will." I wanted to say I doubt it. It has been twenty years already, and she still has not come around.

"I thought I heard voices over here."

"Good morning, Henry."

"Good morning, Linda." Dad looked at me with concern in his eyes.

"Good morning, Dad."

"Good morning. Are you OK?" I reach out and take his hand.

"Yeah, Dad, I'm just fine. I had a very good sleep."

"All that walking played you out."

"It sure did."

"I'm going to get myself a coffee. I will be right back."

"All right, Dad. We're not going anywhere."

"Your Dad looks tired, Char."

"I don't think he sleeps too much, and he does love working out in his little shed that he calls his workshop. I will keep an eye on him the next little while and see if there's something else. But he could just be overdoing it with Marie's wedding."

"That's right around the corner."

"You should see the trellis Dad has made for her. It is so breathtaking."

"I told you he does good work."

"This is beyond that."

"Your mom is busy with her dress and veil. She was having her cake done in Calgary and brought out."

"Hope it makes it all in one piece or three whichever way they decide to transport it. That seems like a real risk. I wonder why she didn't get it done here."

"Your mom said some friend of her future sister-in-law was making it for nothing and something about a fountain in it."

"Great, we will have the cake with a fountain. Should be a pretty wet wedding." We were both laughing when Dad and Mom came with their coffee.

"Hey, are you having a party without us?" Dad asked.

"No, that is in two weeks," Linda told him. Mom and Dad come and join us, and the three of them talked on nonstop. They had a lot to say for first thing in the morning, and Dad had told Linda he would show her what he was working on. She let on like she knew nothing about it.

Mom seemed like she was enjoying the talk they were having and the company. But then when I think about it, this is what she is like with everyone but me.

Linda did try bringing up the baby, but that went over like a lead balloon, and she caught on right away and moved on to something else. This pleased me, never mind Mom. If there is going to be any talk about the baby, I want it to be just Mom and I. Dad too if he dares sit in on such a conversation.

Dad did take Linda and show her his work in progress, and Mom said she was going in to make breakfast. So I just sat in the sun and thought about how nice it will be to go home. It hasn't been one week yet, and I'm homesick.

"Charlene," Mom called.

"Yeah, Mom."

"You're wanted on the phone."

"OK. I will be right there." Who would be calling me at Mom's? Whoever it was will break up my day and maybe have some good news for me.

"Hello."

"Hi, Char."

"Hi! What's up?"

"I thought I would call and make sure you made the trip and see if everything is OK."

"The trip was fine, and yeah, everything is good."

"With that, I take it that Mother is right there, and I can tell you're very sad, Char."

"Yeah! But it is a beautiful day."

"Char, Crystal and I are coming for a visit."

"Oh! Just you and Crystal. When?"

"Yes, it will be just the two of us. The men have gone on their big hunting trip, so we thought it would be a good time to come check up on you. We hope to make it for next week."

"Why not the week after? That's when Marie is getting married here at Mom and Dad's. You could be here for it."

"We were not invited. Besides we wanted to come see you."

"That will be great."

"Is there anything I can bring you?"

"No, I have everything I'm going to need."

"All right then, we will talk to you next week. By the way, tell Mother we have rented a hotel room so she does not have to worry about us.'

"I will do that, and we will talk to you then. Bye." Hanging up the phone made me so homesick I could have just sat there and cried.

"So is Louise coming?"

"Oh, yes, Mom. She and Crystal are making the trip."

"Really? Why is that?"

"Their men have gone on a hunting trip."

"I don't know where I will put them to sleep?"

"You don't have to worry about that. Louise said they have booked a hotel room."

"That's good. It makes things easier for everyone."

"That it does. I think when people are away they like to sleep in longer than they would at home. Besides with the two of them, they might just stay up all night because they can."

"That would be a stupid thing to do."

"Some people may think so. But for a lot of people staying in a motel or hotel is a real treat, and they will take full advantage of it. I for one."

"I myself would sooner be at home." I wanted to yell at her they won't be at home. But what was the point. I was saved by the ringing of the phone. I could tell it was Marie on the other end just by the way Mom was answering on this end.

I had gathered that it was up to Mom to take care of the flowers. I'm hoping for the bouquets because Dad has put a lot of time into the rest.

Then she went on to talk about the supper and had told Marie who was cooking what and who was delivering everything and at what time. Mom sounded like she had everything under control. It also sounded like there was a lot left up to her to do all alone.

Besides all this, I know she's done her dress and veil. I don't care how simple anything looks it is still a lot of work, and I don't know how all this worked out with Marie in Calgary. Mom should be downright worn out by now. Perhaps this is the reason she is been the way she is with me. I will have to see if I can help with something to take some of the load off.

I don't understand why Marie would do this. Her wedding, you would think she would want more hands on. How the hell do you do that from six hours away unless she was making trips back and forth? But neither Mom nor Dad said anything about that.

As Mom was getting ready to hang up, I had heard her tell Marie that I was here, which surprised me.

"I will tell her," Mom said just as she hung up. She sat there for about five minutes and wasn't saying anything, so I finally asked. "Is everything OK with Marie?"

"Yeah, she will be down this weekend. She wants to see the lady that is cooking her supper."

"Oh, there is something you're not doing."

"I wanted to cook her supper, but she wouldn't let me."

"Well, it sounds like you have had a lot to do already. She's lucky it hasn't given you a heart attack."

"This has all been easy. Raising my kids should have given me a heart attack."

"Oh come on now, we were not that bad."

"Not all, but some of you have been very trying." Now do I say like who or do I do the wiser thing and let it go? Of course, I choose the wiser because having a confutation with my mother this early is not how I want to start the day.

"Well, Mom if there is anything I can do to help you, please just let me know."

"If you're not to be on your feet, just how do you think you can do anything?"

"Come on, Mom. I can stand for short times, and besides, there must be something I can help you with sitting down."

"I can't think of anything."

"What about the veil. Why don't you show me what you want? I can sit and sew them beads on. If you have a pattern you're following, show me. So you can be free to do something else."

"I guess you could do that. There are a lot of beads to sew on. There is somewhat of a pattern but nothing hard. But the veil is three layers. It is simple but beautiful."

"What about the dress? Are you done it?"

"Yeah. It also was simple, but it is Marie. She never did like frills and big puffy anything. If it wasn't for her Dad doing the yard the way he has, she would be having a pretty plain wedding. I really don't know why they just didn't go to the JP in Calgary and get it over with."

"Mom, are you and Dad all right with Marie marrying Gary."

"Why shouldn't we be?"

"Were you just a little surprised?"

"Surprised maybe, but she thinks this is what she wants."

"I know but—" Mom cut me off before I could go any further.

"Listen! Like you, she has made her bed, now she must lie in it."

"I suppose that is true."

"Besides we can't pick your partners for you. That never works."

I knew where she was going with that. Mom had told us once about her arranged marriage that her parents had done to her. The man was a lot older than she was, and he was very abusive. She told us that she didn't get the balls to leave until she had had a baby. When she did finally run away, even her parents wouldn't talk to her or help her because the guy had money and they thought no matter what she should have stayed with him.

She had it hard for some time, and she had told her son that his father had died. They never had any contact with him from the time she left. When she told her parents she would not go back, then they told her. Remember then that you have made your bed, and you must lie in it. So I guess that is where that saying came from in our family, and like I said before, *I hate it.*

I also know that many years later, her lie came back to haunt her. Thanks to my grandmother, the grandmother from hell, her mother who no one liked. Our loving grandmother who liked to see the pot stirring all the time had told Mom's son that his father was not dead.

You can just imagine how that went over and what it did to the mother-and-son relationship. Needless to say, all hell broke loose, and Mom's son moved away and didn't have anything to do with her for a lot of years.

This on top of losing my little brother has played a big part in who Mom is today. I don't know the whole story behind it, and I probably never will, but it does make me try and be more forgiving of my mother's ways towards me. Someday I will have grown children of my own, and time will tell what kind of hoops they will put me through because of the choices I have made in regards to their lives even though everything you do as a parent is done out of love and safety for our children.

I think being honest with your children about everything from an early age should help all transitions that they might have to go through sometime in their lives.

To live with a ghost in your closet is not healthy or wise. They seem to be able to get out when you least expect and turns your life upside down. I know there are a lot of people with ghosts in their closets. This is where they should stay until you yourself have released them. Not someone who thinks it's right for them to play God. Usually it is not in the best interest of any one party; it is just someone being resentful. There is no thought given to anyone and how it might all play out.

I guess it would be easier if you don't keep ghosts in the closet.

Myself I will have one for a while. I don't know what I'm going to tell my baby about his father and why he is not with us or why he never sees him. Maybe telling him that his father died is the way to go. No one but me knows who his father is, so I could tell whatever I want to. Who out there is going to second-guess it. His name never once has been spoken to anyone.

I will have plenty of time to think about what to do.

"So if you really want to take over the veil, then I can get it out and show you."

"Yes, I would like to do that for you." When Mom brought out the veil, all I could say was

"Wow!"

"Do you still think you can do it?"

"Let me have a better look at it please." So she laid it on my lap. The work Mom was doing was so amazingly beautiful.

"When the hell did you start this?

"I'm not quite sure, but I have been at it for a while."

"I should say. Do you think we will have it done in time?"

"Sure with the two of us working on it, we will.

"If not, I guess you could always cut it off at wherever you were done to."

"There's a thought. So now if you want to help, I won't be the only one to blame if it's not right."

"I thought you said this was simple."

"Her veil is simple. I was just making it, so it wouldn't be so plain. I've done the same to her dress but only the top."

"Show me how to do this then, and I will sure be glad to help." Mom got us a coffee and then got into showing me how to do her handy work. It was going to take me a few tries to get this right, and we were laughing at my creation. At one point, we were laughing so hard we had tears in our eyes, and it felt so damn good to be doing something with Mom and having fun doing it. I was scared at first when I messed up, and I thought maybe she would just throw it in my face, that it was something else I couldn't do. But instead, she was encouraging me to try and try again.

"You know nothing good comes easy."

"I will have to agree with you there, Mom."

"Well at least there is something we can agree on." I wanted to get back on to a topic that wouldn't bring the bitch back as I was really enjoying *my* mom at this time.

"Mom, what was your dress like?"

"Mine?"

"Yeah."

"Well, the first time I had a real wedding dress. It was off white and some lace overlay. My veil was three layers of lace. It was fairly simple, yet back then, it cost a lot. Remember I was marrying money, so it all had to look good." She became quiet and was off in her own world as she continued to work on Marie's veil. I started to study my mother. I mean really look at her, something I had not done for a long, long time. Mom was still a very pretty lady for her age. I remember her wearing lipstick and mascara the times she and Dad went out. She never really needed too much makeup to look good. She did have some deep lines starting, which I was always told was from smoking. We had asked her many times to quit smoking, but her answer was always the same. "When you start buying my smokes, then you can complain about it. Until then, I will do as I damn please." The subject would be dropped.

"Mom, would you have any pictures of you and Dad when you were our ages or when you first got married?"

"Why do you ask?"

"It would be nice to see them. I would like to know what my parents looked like when they were younger. As far as I can remember, Dad still looks the same. Not having any teeth when we were kids has not made him old. It does to people who get their teeth pulled out at his age now, but not Dad. It hasn't changed him.

"I would also like to see your wedding dress."

"I never had a wedding dress when your dad and I got married."

"Oh. You didn't? How come?"

"I met your father in a logging camp, and when we got married, we were just married by what they called the JP. And I only wore a suit coat and skirt."

"That was too bad."

"Not really. Both your father and I had our big wedding the first time around, and it done neither one of us any good. So why spend all that money. It won't make a marriage last any longer. Besides we were out in the bush. We made do with what we had. We had each other, and that's all we cared about."

"Did you have a honeymoon when you went back home?"

"No, our honeymoon was our time spent in camp. Once we were home, then we were busy getting the kids all back together."

"Was that hard to do?"

"Yeah, it took some time." I got the feeling that she didn't really want to talk about that part of her life, so I just left it.

"Well, anyways, I sure would like to see some pictures someday."

"I will see what I can do."

"Sounds good to me."

"Now are you going to try your hand at this sewing again or do I have to do it all?"

"Oh, you still want me to put my mark on it, do you?" We were both laughing at the thought of that. When Dad came in, I could tell as he looked around with the frown on his face that he was thinking he was in the wrong place. He closed the door ever so slow and wasn't sure if he should come in or not.

"What's going on in here?"

"I'm teaching Charlene how to do some sewing. Now that she has a kid on the way, it might come in handy someday for her." She was very snappy at Dad. The bitch was back, and I just wanted to say "I'm sorry, Dad, for being here."

Was I the reason she treated Dad so badly? But then she's never been any different with me. So I don't understand.

"Are you just going to stand there, you old goat? Or are you having some tea with us?"

"I'll have tea." Mom gets up and pours Dad a cup of tea, then she leaves.

"I got the dance floor done. Now I just have to put up the walls."

"Dance floor! They're having an outside dance?"

"Marie didn't want a dance, but we figured if it is nice out and everyone is outside why not."

"That sounds cool."

"It isn't a big one, but they can still have fun on it."

"What kind of walls are you putting on it?"

"I'm going only four feet with the white lattice, and I will have clear lights all around."

"That sounds very nice, Dad. I'm sure Marie will be OK with it."

"That's why I want as much done so when she comes home, we will have time to change things if need be. Think you will have that done in time?" Dad asked about the veil on my lap.

"I had told Mom that we could always cut it off at wherever we are finished at the time."

"That would be OK too. Where did your mother go?"

"To the bathroom, I think."

"Maybe you guys want to come see the dance floor. I will have it ready with the lights by tonight."

"I will see what Mom says when she comes back."

"I'm going to go back out and get busy on it."

"All right, Dad." One thing about Dad, he never sits still very long. When he has something to do, he keeps at it until he has it finished. I guess it is one way of him killing time. Now that he is retired, it is a good thing he has his woodworking to keep him busy.

Mom had been gone for some time now, so I walked down the hallway and knocked on the bathroom door.

"Mom, Mom, are you all right?" There was no answer, which made my heart start to race.

"Mom!" I called a little louder. Then I heard a noise that was coming from their bedroom. Going to the door, I knocked lightly just in case she had decided to lie down.

"Yeah." I open the door a little and peek in.

"Mom, are you OK?"

"Yeah, I was just getting out those pictures you wanted to see."

"Oh, I didn't mean it had to be right now."

"I know, but seeing how you are sewing on the veil, I have some time to look for these now. I should have them in albums but just never got around to it. So shoe boxes have come in handy."

"One thing about a shoe box, it has a lid, and they are made of pretty strong cardboard."

"That they are." By this time, I had gone in and sat on the edge of the bed. This alone was a very strange feeling. All the time we were growing up, we were never allowed in Mom and Dad's room. I don't ever recall a time even sick was I ever taken into bed and cuddled. I don't ever remember going in and talking to them while they were in bed. To us, it was a very forbidden place. I saw an album lying off to the side.

"Oh, what's this one, Mom?"

"Nothing you have to see."

"Oh." I could see it had cloth sticking out of the ends. Why would there be cloth in an album? I knew I wasn't to ask. We have gotten this far, and I sure didn't want to blow it. I was still waiting for her to tell me to get out of their room.

"I think I got them all so we can go out into the other room where the light is better for seeing."

"Sure." I picked up the one box, and Mom brought the other. I was excited to be able to look at pictures that we never ever done before. This was something out of Mom's norm. She was doing it with me. Now perhaps the other kids have gotten to see the pictures when I wasn't around, which was very possible.

We sat at the table, and she let me go through the box I had, and if there was someone I wanted to know about, she would tell me. For the most part, I recognize most of the people in the pictures.

"Hey, Mom. Who is this on Grandma's knee?"

"Let me see. That is you."

"Really, what is wrong with my head?"

"There's nothing with your head."

"It looks deformed to me."

"Well, it wasn't."

"Who is this sitting on the step beside us?"

"That is Marie." I had thought maybe it was Marie if that was me in Grandmother's arms. But I'm sure my head was deformed. Yet I remember it being talked about how our little sister's head and face were out of shape, and Mom had to wrap her to form them properly. Either way, I guess it doesn't much matter as we both have normal heads today. So long as it wasn't something that could be passed down to our children, then we should know about it. Going through the pictures really didn't tell me a lot of anything as most of them were from a distance, and you couldn't say who looked like who. I had hoped that there would have been a picture somewhere that showed that I looked like Mom. Thinking about it, I guess none of the kids really looked like either Mom or Dad until they got much older. Yet it is strange how Dad's kids from his first marriage look like their mother and dad. There was no denying who the father was or their mother.

Yet when you look at the last six of us, we resemble Mom and Dad very little. Were we all adopted? Is that why we are all strange? I don't think so, but who knows, right?

Mom couldn't show me pictures of all the kids when they were babies; she said she didn't know where they were. The only baby pictures were of myself and of Jacob. This I found to be strange as well. So in the end, looking at the pictures made me feel uneasy instead of good.

There were some things she was good about answering and then there were things that you didn't dare ask. When we went through the boxes, I let on that I was pleased with what I saw and what she told me.

"Here, Mom. I can put them back in your room. I have to go to the bathroom anyways."

"All right. I'm going to make your father some tea and take it outside."

"OK. I will join you there." I took her pictures back to her room, and I just put them on top of her dresser. I spotted the album still out, and it made me jumpy to do it, but I lean over the bed and opened it at one of the cloth pages.

Oh! This must be Mom and her first husband. She looked beautiful, and he looked mean. He was also much older than she was. Her dress and veil were beautiful. I wonder if she has these packed away somewhere. I would wear them on my wedding day. I wish she would share more of these details so we could ask more question. Maybe even where her dress is. I hurried up and got to the bathroom in case she came back in. I will have to see if there is a way that we can get her to show us those pictures.

Besides, there were other pictures in there besides her wedding pictures.

CHAPTER TWENTY-FOUR

Going outside I found Mom over at the dance floor that Dad was so busy with. They were both sitting there with their feet handing over the edge. I noticed Mom had kicked off her shoes.

"What is this? You're ready to dance already, Mom. I see you kicked off your shoes."

"You bet. I'm ready to dance." With that said, Dad just laughed at her.

"Why you laughing, old man?"

"You? Dance? In a pig's eye you will."

"We used to dance a lot, so what are you talking about."

"We used to. But we haven't in years."

"Well, maybe it's time we did again." Dad just nods his head and laughs.

"This looks pretty good, Dad. You think it is strong enough to hold up drunks." I ask him as I shake the lattice he has put all around three sides.

"Oh, I think it will. There won't be that many here anyways."

"No, but it only takes one."

"It only takes one what, Char?" Linda asked as she came around the corner.

"One drunk to knock Dad's wall over."

"Oh, I think it would have to be more than one drunk," she says as she shakes the wall as well.

"I know. I'm just giving Dad a bad time."

"This looks good, Henry, you sure have been busy."

"I don't have much time left."

"Linda, would you like a cup of tea?"

"Sure, Betty, that would be nice." So Mom got up and went to get Linda her tea.

"Char, Ron is coming out today, and he wanted to know if you would come over when he's here."

"I don't know."

"Come on, Char. We already had this talk. There's no reason you can't be friends." Maybe to her there wasn't, but I'm the one who he just up and left and I cared very much for him and I'm not sure how I feel about him now. After all, he was my first love, and they say you never get over your first. I guess just because he wasn't really ready to play house is no reason not to see him.

"All right. What time?"

"He'll be here around four thirty."

I saw the look my dad was giving me. Dad is a man of a few words until he is mad.

"You mean he's around again, thought he was in jail."

"No, Henry. He paid his fine and didn't have to go to jail."

Oh was all Dad had to say. Linda looked at me as if to say "What the hell was that all about?" and all I could do was raise my eyebrow.

I knew neither Mom or Dad had approved of Ron when I was dating him. He drank too much. He never kept a job very long. He lived for today. He wasn't the man for me. In their eyes, he wasn't even a man. But I thought he was great.

Mom came back with the tea. The three of us sat there and watch Dad work for a while anyways; then I had asked to be excused. I was feeling tired and wanted to go lie down for a while.

"I'll do more on the veil when I get up OK, Mom?"

"Yeah sure, go ahead."

Sleeping once I lay down didn't come easy because then I started to think about James. I wonder if he's been back around. I should have called him to let him know where I was. I had told him I thought I would be coming to Mom and Dad's but never gave him a phone number or address. But then he never asked. Maybe that was his way of disappearing. Or maybe he thought he had more time. I should get Louise to get in touch with him when she goes back. I will see what she has to say.

The day had gone by fast after I lay down. Dad was calling me for supper. I was totally lost on what day it was. I couldn't believe I had slept so long. Once I was washed up, I had gone out to the supper table. Mom and Dad were chatting up a storm, and I didn't really want to enter because I don't think they do this often. They always seem to be off on their own planets.

"Boy, you must have been tired."

"I guess, Mom, all that beadwork is heavy duty." She and Dad laughed at me.

"Linda came over earlier to see if you were up." Then it hit me.

"Shit."

"What's up?" Mom asked.

"Nothing really. She had invited me over today. Ron was going to be there around four or so, and I said I would go have tea with them. No big deal. There is always another day."

"Ron! You were going to go see Ron?"

"Yes, Mom. I was."

"Don't tell me you're going to take up with him again. Remember your carrying another man's baby."

"You don't have to remind me. Trust me, I haven't forgotten. And no, I'm not taking up with Ron again. But we are still friends, and you better get used to it because we will always be friends."

"Thank God. For a moment, I thought you had lost your marbles. I don't think he would make good father material."

"I don't think so either, Mom." I also wanted to say, "But then neither would the baby's father."

"We are going over to Richards's after we go for ice cream. Did you want to come?"

"No, thanks. A little of her goes a long ways." I had just been over there with them a couple nights ago, and Richards's wife isn't one that you could stand too much off. But guess she does whatever it takes to keep him happy.

"Yeah, well, you just have to learn to tune her out or only believe half of what she says."

"That's OK, Mom. I will just do some more sewing for you so I can sit with my feet up."

"Suit yourself." After supper, they did go for their evening ice cream with their dog. It was funny because the dog knows right away when they're headed out the door for their ice cream. She goes half crazy until they tell her. "Yes, you're coming." They had been gone almost three quarters of an hour when I heard the motor outside. Not thinking anything of it until a knock came to the door.

"Just a minute, I'm coming." Opening the door as I said, "Did you forget your . . . Oh! Hi."

"Hi, how are you?"

"Pregnant," I say as I rub my hand down over the baby. I was too surprised to say anything else.

"I see that."

"What brings you here?"

"Well, seeing how you didn't come for tea today, I thought I would come take you out for tea."

"Oh, I don't think so."

"Why not? It can't hurt to go for tea, can it? Come on, Char, as friends."

"Oh, all right just let me leave Mom and Dad a note so they don't worry."

"That should go over well. Unless they have decided to like me."

"I wouldn't hold my breath if I were you."

"I didn't think so. And I'm not even the one who got you pregnant." We both laughed on our way out.

We went down to the highway café where everybody knows everybody including me.

"Are you sure you want to do this, Ron?"

"Why not?"

"This will get everyone's tongue a flapping."

"So let them flap all they want."

"You're OK with that. It won't be embarrassing for you?"

"Why? Because you're pregnant? Char, you're not the first, and you won't be the last.

"Oh, you have had a lot of pregnant women on your arm, have you?"

"No, you are the first, and it is just fine with me. Now let's go inside."

"All right then, but don't say I didn't warn you." As I thought, everyone was surprised that Ron and I were together, and me being pregnant got some whispering going right away.

"Let's sit here by the window."

"Anywhere you want, Char."

"Hi, may I help you?"

"Bring us two teas, would you please." The girl just stood there looking at me like I had two heads.

"Is something wrong, Brenda?"

"No." But she didn't take her eyes off of me while she answered Ron.

"Then we'll have our teas now, thank you."

"I got it." She turned around with such fire in her eyes it was quite obvious that she had been on Ron's arm at one time or another.

"You two still dating?"

"How you know we've ever had?"

"By the darts she was throwing at me."

"No, we are not dating and haven't been for some time."

"What happened?"

"Just that. I could never talk to any other girl I knew."

"Oh, that would be hard for you."

"It didn't last more than about four days, and she has tried to get me to take her out many times since, and that just isn't going to happen."

"I would say I feel for you, but it is your own fault. You shouldn't love them and leave them the way you do." The look on his face was as if I had just slapped it.

"Oh, I'm sorry, Ron. I didn't mean it like that."

"It's OK. You're right, and I shouldn't have done that to you. But I thought we were still friends."

"We are, or I wouldn't be here with you now."

"You mean that, Char?"

"I sure do."

He reaches across the table and takes my hand.

"You know, Char, it would be the saddest day in my life if you ever told me we weren't friends anymore."

"For me too."

"I'm sorry. I did leave you the way I did."

"No need to be sorry. All has worked out. I knew you wouldn't stay."

"You did?"

"Yeah, I did. You wouldn't stay in Alberta any more than I'll stay in BC. So we had this against us right from the start. But what time we had was special, and no one will take that away from me. We have both grown up a lot since then."

"Well, I don't know about grown up, but some of us have grown outward."

"Oh, aren't you the funny one." After that, he had asked me about the baby's father and what we were doing. He wanted to know how long I was going to be at Mom and Dad's. So I told him, I had nothing to hide, and I wasn't going to pretend like I had some great guy waiting for the baby and me.

"That sucks now that you are pregnant and to be left on your own."

"It will be tough for just a little while. Once I have my hairdressing ticket, we'll be OK."

"You sure about this, Char. I could help you with money."

"That is sweet of you, but it is not your responsibility."

"Friends help friends, don't they?"

"Sometimes."

"Well, this will be one of those sometimes."

"We'll see, OK?"

"All you have to do is call, no questions asked, and the help will be there."

"Thank you." After three hours of talking, I had mentioned that I should get back home.

"Why? What is the hurry? It's not like you're going to get into trouble."

"A little late for that." So we sat and talked about an hour more, then I was ready to go back to Mom and Dad's. Ron walked me to the door, and as I was saying good night, he asked, "Char, Moose Mouse Days are coming up. Will you come with me?"

"I don't know. I will have to see how I feel at the time."

"Fair enough. I will remind you as it gets closer."

"Thank you for taking me out for tea, it was a nice break."

"I've missed you, Char. And we will do this more."

"Ron, I don't think we should be."

"Why not?

"I'm not staying, Ron. Once the baby comes, I'm out of here."

"So why can't we spend the time together? Who knows when the next time will be?"

"You could come out to Alberta and see us, you know it would be easier for you than it is going to be for me."

"Yeah, you're right, but while you're here, I intend on seeing as much of you as possible."

"Let's just take it one step at a time, could we?"

"Sure, no problem." He bends over and kisses me good night.

"I'll come over in a couple of days." With that said, he turned around and left. It was still nice outside, so I stood there and watched him drive away, thinking it is nice to have a friend like him. It seemed funny to go from friends to lovers to friends and be comfortable with it or at least I am. When he kissed me, there was nothing there anymore. With a sigh of relief, I thought, *My god my heart has healed, it's not pining for him anymore.* Is that why I wouldn't let James get close? Was it because I thought Ron still held my heart and I wasn't going to betray him? Now I'm free. It feels good taking a deep breath. I think. I went into the house to find Mom still up sewing on the veil.

"Hi, you're up late."

"Yeah, couldn't sleep, so thought I would do some more sewing. Long coffee everything OK?"

"Yeah, it's great, Mom. No worries."

"That's good. There's coffee brewing if you want some."

"Sure, that would be nice, but first off, I must go get rid of some tea." While I was doing this, I could hear her up getting a cup. Now did she wait up for me? Is this her way of letting me know she cares? I know it is said that mothers can't sleep while their children aren't home. It doesn't matter if they're in bed. They lie there awake until they hear their child come in and then they fall fast asleep. I guess I will be finding all this out soon enough. I hope she doesn't go on about Ron because there is no need to worry about him in my life other than being a friend. I wish I could get her to believe that.

Being finished in the bathroom, I was a little nervous about the coffee thing. Guess, I will find out what is up.

We sat and drank our coffee and talked about a lot of things that really surprised me. Then I thought this might be a good time to bring up her pictures.

"Mom, do you have any wedding pictures of yourself?"

"Why?"

"'Cause I would like to see your dress. See what they were like back then." Even though I had already seen it and it was beautiful.

"I do, but it's not of when your dad and I got married."

"Oh, you didn't have a wedding then?"

"No, we were married by a JP Then, and it wasn't no dress-up affair."

"That's sad."

"No, it was what we both wanted because we both had had the big wedding thing, and we were happy to do it the way we did." Now I had heard the talk about how Mom was expecting and that was why they got married the way they did, but who are we to criticize? They got married in December, and my brother was born in April. Didn't take much to figure out the math.

"Do you still have your dress from the first time?"

"No, I left that at my mother's when I left. Lord knows what happened to it after that."

"That is too bad. I hope that someday I will have a daughter who would be able to and want to wear my dress. I would have liked to have the choice to wear yours someday."

"No chance of that happening."

"Maybe not, but you know what maybe I could find one like it or have one made. Seeing how you have a picture, we would have something to go on."

"I guess if that is what you wanted."

"We have a lot of time before that will happen, so guess we should just get Marie's out of the way." I know it wouldn't be the same wearing Mom's dress that she wore while marrying another man, but the dress would still have been hers. That alone would have meant a lot to me anyways. Maybe to her it would hold nothing more than a terrible memory. So I guess it is something to really think deeply about and when the time comes get her honest opinion. I wouldn't want to do something that would cause her any undue stress or sad memories. I left that conversation, and somehow, we ended up talking about the baby's father.

"Does the baby's father know about it?"

"No, Mom, he doesn't."

"Why not? He has the right to know?"

"I know he does, but they have money, and I'm afraid that they might take the baby from me."

"You really think they would?"

"His mother is a real bitch, and I don't trust her."

"Financially, he should have to help."

"I know, but then, he will also have a say in the baby, and I don't want that. I don't always want to be looking over my shoulder and worrying whether I'm doing things good enough to suit them. This way, I have to answer to no one but me and by conscience."

"You think that is the better way to go?"

"Yes, I do."

"It won't be an easy road you're headed down. It is one thing when it is just you, but when there's a child in tow, it makes things a little more difficult."

"You did it with David."

"Yes, I did. But things were a lot different back then. Nowadays they don't like you taking your child to work with you. Remember I was cooking in a logging camp. There really wasn't any reason why I couldn't have David with me. You said you want to finish your hairdressing, what do you do with the baby then?"

"I don't know."

"Where do you go for your training?"

"I will be going back to Marvell in the city. It is one of the best. Beside it is where Auntie Lillian works, and I know she will help me out a lot when it comes to the school."

"Lillian works there?"

"Yeah, she has been there now for some time. When I went in for my six-week basic, she was there. It was great having her there to help me. Besides that I stayed with them."

"I never knew that."

"That will be great when it comes to your hairdressing, but what about the baby?"

"I don't know, Mom, guess I will have to wait and see. I have a long time to figure something out."

"The time will go by quickly, mark my words on that." I wish I knew she was hinting around for me to ask her if they would think about babysitting. But I can almost hear her say, "I raised my kids now you have to do the same." I know she does babysit for other people, but never for any length of time. I never did know whether it was because they didn't need her anymore or if it was because she couldn't handle it anymore.

Raising six kids of your own and six stepchildren has to make you a expert at child raising, I would think. I can't think of anything that could be more rewarding than knowing I raised all those children and saw them go out on their own and make it in this world.

If the rest are like me, all I ever wanted was to make Mom and Dad proud of me and what I accomplish. Right now I haven't accomplished much other than getting pregnant, but that is just another stepping stone in life. I have tried to do whatever I can on my own. Yes, I have had help from my sisters, but this too is also a way of life. I know that somewhere down the road, I will be able to return the favor.

"Well, Mom, I think I'm going to bed. After all, it is one o'clock."

"It is?"—Looking at her watch—"You're right. Where did the time go?"

"They say time goes by fast when you're having a good time." Getting up, I walked over and kissed Mom on the cheek. "I have to say I had a very nice evening, thank you. I will see you later this morning." I left before she could object or say anything that would spoil our evening. We have never had any time spent together that was like this evening. I think I will hold it dear to my heart as a special time spent with my mother.

After washing up, I climbed into bed feeling great, and I must have fallen asleep instantly 'cause next thing I knew I woke up to voices. I laid there for a while trying to figure out who they were. Then one of them laughs, and I knew right away who was there. Pulling on the oversize house coat and running the brush through my hair, I went out to say my hellos. They were all in the kitchen, so none of them saw me coming.

"You can always tell who is on holidays, they don't know how to sleep in." I reach over and put my hand on to Louise's shoulder.

"Good morning, Char," she says as she gets up to hug me.

"How you been?"

"Pretty good so far."

"I see you are taking to sleeping in."

"Hey, Mom and I were up until one, so I didn't really sleep in."

"Any other time you would still have been up before everyone else."

"That would have to be really early to beat Mom. I think she sleeps less than I do."

"Hi, Crystal."

"Hi, boy, are you getting huge!"

"I noticed I'm not getting any smaller, that is for sure."

"Can you get much bigger before you pop?"

"Plus my wardrobe doesn't do much for the slimming effect."

"I thought it was quite becoming of you."

"Thanks, Louise." Getting myself a cup of coffee and listening to their talk made me think of the times when some of us would come to Mom and Dad's for Christmas or Easter and how all the chatter would carry on. You never knew if anyone had heard a word you said because everyone is talking all at the same time. Both Louise and Crystal are load talkers. Their laughs are ones that can be heard over everything else. They both laugh from the bottom of their souls, and it is sort of catchy. They both have very sincere laughs. You know when they are in a room. I always thought Crystal put light into a room of gloom. I think I have only seen her down a couple of times in my life. But then again I also know that we can always put on a happy front when need be. But hell, we're young, yet there is no reason why we should have downer days. Well, maybe one or two.

"What time did you guys get in?"

"We got in at twelve o'clock last night," Crystal tells me.

"You should have called. Mom and I were up until after one."

"We were pretty tired from the long drive, Char. I just wanted to climb into bed," Louise tells me.

"Yeah, it is a long drive. You should try it on the bus. One thing about the bus, you can sleep a little. I just don't like the bathrooms on them. For some reason, I find it hard to pee and ride at the same time." Everyone laughs.

"Trust you, Char, to come up with that."

"Well, Louise, it's true. Have you ever tried it?"

"No, Char. I can't say I have. I'll take your word on it."

"Mom, is Dad up yet?"

"Oh hell, he's been up for hours. He is already outside. Christ, he has been to the hardware store already."

"What was he buying today?"

"He's going to paint the lattice white now that he has that all up."

"Crystal, we'll have to go out back so you can see what Dad has done."

"I'd love to see what Grandpa is building."

"It is to be the dance floor for Marie's wedding."

"Mom was telling me on the way down that she was getting married. It sounded a little strange."

She got by the look on my face that we would talk about it later.

"I guess if she is happy that is all we have to know."

"That is so true." We sat and chatted some more and had our morning toast and coffee. All this time, I wanted to ask Louise so bad if she had seen anything of James. I didn't want to bring him up in front of Mom as I have never said a word to her about him. I can't say I really know why I haven't other than I don't find my mother easy to talk to. But if things keep going on as last night, then perhaps I will feel like I can tell her about James and maybe she would give me some sound advice on what maybe I should do. But for now, he will still be my mystery man and just be between Louise and myself. She must not have said too much to Crystal; otherwise, I'm sure she would have been all over it by now. She wouldn't have been meaning any harm either. I'm sure Louise and I will get some alone time at one point so I can ask her. If she doesn't bring him up first and that could be a mistake right now.

"Well, guys, I think I will go and get dressed. So we can go out and see Dad."

"Good idea, Char. Crystal and I would both like to go see this masterpiece of Dad's."

"All right then. I won't be long." Leaving them and going to get dressed, I could hear some of their conversation, Louise telling Mom what a rough break I had with Mary dying and how everything before that was working out so well for me. She had also told her about the basement suite and how nicely I had fixed it up. Louise had also told Mom about the furniture and how I had redone it all and how beautiful it was and how nice everything looked in the basement suite.

"Really!" I heard Mom say. "She never said anything about any of it. She had told me the lady was renting from had passed away, but she didn't say anything about the rest of it. Where is all her stuff?"

"We hauled it over to another friend of hers that had an empty shed. They were keeping it for Char until she comes back."

"At least, it is somewhere, so she can get it back."

"Oh yeah, that won't be a problem." Louise knew that Mom had told me I couldn't bring anything with me because they didn't have room. In fact they barely had room for me. Louise kept the conversation light as there was no need in making waves. After all, I still had a few months to go. Then I heard the dishes being done, and the subject had been changed to Marie's wedding. I was thankful for that. Mom was telling them what all she had gotten done and what she had left to do.

"This has been all up to you to get done?" Louise asked Mom.

"Yeah, but I started doing things as soon as Marie told us what she wanted. So over a few months, things were stretched out a bit, and now we are down to the final little things. Dad has done more than he had to, but he has enjoyed it, and it has given him something to wake up for."

CHAPTER TWENTY-FIVE

———◆———

"I guess that is a good thing."

"I will get some tea made so that when Charlene is ready we can take it out to him."

"That sounds like a plan. But I think I should go get rid of some of this coffee first."

"The last door on the right."

"Thank you." I hear Louise going down the hall. I couldn't hear Crystal. Maybe she had gone outside already. So I found some clothes that fit not too bad. Dad had given me some of his dress shirts. He said they were too big for him, and I had gotten a couple pair of sweatpants that had the zipper on the leg so I could make them into shorts as the day got hotter and put my legs back on in the evening when it started to cool off. This I found very handy. Dad's shirts were great as well. I didn't go anywhere that I needed good maternity clothes. So I was happy. As I was coming out, I bumped into Louise.

"Hey! We are going outside now, you coming?"

"Yeah, I am. Where is Crystal?"

"Out for a smoke."

"I forgot that she had that bad habit still."

"Well, I hope she doesn't think she has to be like you and get pregnant to quit."

"Why not, it was a good reason to quit."

"So is your own health a good reason."

"You're right. I will go out and give her a bad time about it."

"Mother and I will be right out."

"See you then." Going outside, I found Crystal, talking away to Dad, and he's looking like the paintbrush has had a run away, and he was the target except for his hair as it was already white. The lattice that he had done was looking fantastic, and he had done a lot already. That is one thing I will say about Dad. When he has something to do, he stays on it until he is finished. Now I don't know if he has always been like this but has been since they had bought the store. Mind you, on the farm, I remember him going pretty steady. I only remember him going into the house for meals and bed.

"Hey, Char, you finally decided to join us?"

"Yeah, and I'm glad to see you don't have to be washed down with paint thinner like Dad does."

"Hey, that is why I wear these." And he pulls at his overalls that he has on, which when you look at them, they have seen more than this white paint.

"Good thing or Mom would be making you undress outside." Going around and sitting up on the dance floor on the end where the steps are, Crystal comes around and joins me.

"Your mom told me you had come out for a smoke."

"Yeah, I did. I thought Grandpa smoked."

"He used to. Or I should say his ears did the smoking for him."

"His ears?"

"Yeah, Dad always rolled his smokes, and he would puff on it until it went out then he would tuck it behind his ear until he wanted it again. Sometimes he just had it hanging out of his mouth. He wasn't a heavy smoker. But I'm glad he quit."

"You quit too?"

"Having a baby helped with that. I also wasn't a heavy smoker. I could go all day without. It wasn't anything I missed at any one time. Beside I can't afford to smoke and feed a baby."

"I guess not, eh, Char. How are you going to do that?"

"If I have to, I will go to social services until I go back to work."

"You would do that?"

"I sure will. That is what they are there for. I might be going while I'm here, so I can pay Mom and Dad some rent money."

"Grandma and Grandpa are charging you rent?"

"They will. That is just the way it is. You don't leave home then think you're coming back to live for nothing. Not with Mom, you don't."

"This is different. You can't work."

"Not their problem."

"Mom would never do that to one of us."

"Maybe not, but your mom is not Grandma. Grandma is very much from the old school. Once you are out of school, you are on your own. There is no going back. I'm lucky to be able to be staying here right now. So I won't look no gift horse in the mouth."

"God, this has to be hard on you. I don't think I could do it."

"If you had no choice, you could. Besides it isn't for a real long time, and it is just another lesson to be learned in life. You learn to appreciate things big or small. And right now, I'm doing just that with the little time Mom and I are getting to spend together. Just maybe, we will get to know each other a little better."

"Has it been hard, Char? I know Grandma has never been really nice to you."

"It has been trying. But it always is between Mom and I."

"Why is that?"

"I don't know. The more I try to please her and make her proud of me, it seems it always backfires somehow. Like now. I had my own place, I had a good job that I would be able to make something out of it, and then I go and get pregnant."

"You can always go back to it."

"Yes, I can, but right now, in Mother's eyes, that doesn't mean anything."

"I'm single and pregnant, no job, and nowhere to live. Now that is a lot to be proud of, wouldn't you say? So hearing it said, I could see why she would be the way she is. It would have to be embarrassing as hell when she is asked any of those questions from any of her friends."

"Maybe so, Char. But you're not the first, and you sure the hell won't be the last. After all, my mom had me on her own. My dad wasn't in the picture either."

"That is right and just ask her how Grandma was with her. It will be somewhat different with Grandma being your mom's stepmom, but I bet it wasn't all roses."

"What isn't all roses?" Mom asked as she and Louise came around the corner.

"Marie's bouquet," I said and looked at Crystal with raised eyebrows so she knew enough to go with me on this.

"I was just wondering what Marie was having for flowers, and Char didn't think it would be all roses."

"She is having some roses with a mixture of sweet william instead of the white baby's breath everyone else has. The sweet william looks almost like small carnations. She will be using the white ones."

"That sounds very pretty."

"It will smell heavenly if nothing else."

"Hey, Char. I like to go walking in the morning. Are you up to it?"

"I'm supposed to stay off my feet as much as possible. So this is about as far as I walk."

"That has to suck."

"It does, but it won't be for long now. I haven't had any bleeding since I came, and I would sure like to keep it that way."

"So what do you do all day?"

"I've been helping Mom sew beads on Marie's veil. Other than that nothing."

"Knowing you, this must be driving you crazy. I have never known you to sit around so much."

"Sometimes we do what we have to, and in this case, I don't have a choice or I will lose my baby."

"It's that bad I didn't realize that. Mom never said anything about it."

"I have come close a couple of times already so I have to be careful of how much I do."

"I don't think I want to have a baby if it is going to tie me down that much."

"This won't happen every time or to everybody. For some reason, this time, I'm having a hard time carrying the baby to term."

"Did you ask the doctor why?"

"Yeah, they tell you all their medical reason, which to you and I don't make sense, and they leave it at that."

"Char, do you ever think of it any other way?"

"Like how."

"You know."

"You mean like God is punishing me for being a single mom. I have thought about it. But then, I wonder if that's been the case why wouldn't he have just taken the baby completely away from me the very first time I started having trouble."

"I guess. I never thought about it that way."

"Do you think he has control of us to that point?"

"I don't really know. I do wonder about God and the things that happen and why he lets them happen if he is so mighty. I also have to say it scares me to second-guess him because we don't know. So I can only pray that he sees me fit to be a mother and that he will let me have a healthy baby."

"Aren't you scared of having the baby on your own? Don't you worry about all the things that could go wrong?"

"Good lord, no. You would drive yourself crazy if you worried like that. I know I can work after and be able to house us and feed us. It is to find someone I trust to take care of my baby while I work."

"Well, if you are coming back to Stony Creek, why don't you get the baby's grandmother there to watch him?"

"No damn way. I don't want them to even know about the baby."

"Why not?"

"'Cause what if they think I'm not a good-enough mother or I'm not providing good enough for him, then what? They just step in and take him away from me."

"Char, you really think they would do that?"

"They have money, I don't. I'm not willing to take the risk, and besides, that he didn't want anything to do with me in the end."

"But now, there is a baby."

"Yes, there is, and he didn't want me without, so he doesn't get with."

"You sure you want it to be this way? Couldn't it be easier if he helped you out?"

"Sure, it could be easier, but then, I'd have to answer to him on where I wanted to live and how I'm going to raise the baby. So don't think so. I like it this way so far."

"Mom had told me about the good-looking man that was hanging around and how he wanted to be involved in the baby's life and yours. What happened to him?"

"It's one of those things that to me seem to be too good to be true. I will wait and see what happens when I come back."

"Mom was saying he wanted to be with you when you had the baby, like right there with you!"

"That is what he said, but I'm not in Stony Creek anymore now, am I?"

"You don't think he would come this far to be with you if he was really sincere?"

"I guess, I'll never know now, will I?"

"Why did you not tell him where you are?"

"I told him I would probably be coming to Mom and Dad's."

"Did he at least get a phone number?"

"No, I had not talked to him again before I left, things happened to fast."

"Oh Char! Wouldn't you like someone with you when you have the baby? Aren't you scared?"

"Yeah, I am scared, but I have been alone right from the start, so I guess I will finish alone."

"That is the point, Char. You don't have to be alone. Mom said that this guy seemed very sincere, and she also said he looked at you with nothing but love and admiration."

"This guy as you keep calling him has a name, and it is James."

"Do you at least like him?"

"Yeah, I like him."

"Like in like him or really like him?"

"I guess, you could say I really like him. He was so sweet, and he did seem to care about us. The baby and me. He even bought books on birthing, he told me, so he would not be coming into the delivery room blinded. He wanted to be there to help, not be in the way."

"Oh Char, you're kidding, right? And you haven't been in touch with him since you came to Grandma and Grandpas?"

"Well, no."

"Are you out of your tree or just plain stupid? I mean there are not a lot of men around that want anything to do with another man's baby, and here you have one falling at your feet and you just walk away. Good lord, being pregnant has eaten away at your brain, girl.

"You know you could still call him. It's not too late to let him know where you are. You do have a phone number, don't you?"

"Yeah, I do. He gave me his card and told me to call him any time."

"Well then, what the hell are you waiting for?"

"I don't want someone feeling sorry for me and then been sorry for it later. There won't just be me to think about."

"I can see you thinking that way. But, Char, you deserve something good in your life and some happiness even if it is for a short time. There are no guarantees."

I rub my stomach and say, "I have something good in my life, and we will be happy."

"Come on, Char. You know what I mean."

"Yeah, I do. I'm also telling you that I couldn't be happier."

"I call bullshit. You can always be happier."

"Time will tell."

"I hope you don't wait too long to call that prince of yours. You could give me his number, I will call him."

"I will not give you his number."

"Then promise me you will call him, Char, before you have the baby."

"I will think about it."

"Not near good enough, promise, Char. Come on, this could be the best thing that ever happened to you."

"No, this is." I tell her as I rub on my stomach again. "Oh, he liked that what a kick I just got."

"Does it hurt when they kick?"

"Sometimes. I have one real sore spot just under my rib that the baby seems to hit all the time, and it makes me sit up and take notice."

"Have you told your doctor about it?"

"No. I will when I go back and see him next week."

"Hey, you two you coming in for lunch?"

"It's lunchtime already? Yeah, Dad, we will be right there."

"All right. I will let Mother know."

"Thanks, Dad."

"How is Grandpa taking this?"

"He's been good. Or at least, he hasn't made me feel bad about it."

"But Grandma isn't so easy going, is she?"

"She's not as bad now as she was when I first came. Maybe this will be as good as it gets with her. I would like to talk to her more about the baby and life in general, but she is not that easy to talk to."

"Grandma seems to be mad all the time. Like someone has pissed in her cornflakes every morning. I don't know how you handle that every day?"

"Some days are worse than others. But right now, she is busy with Marie's wedding, so she hasn't been too bad to deal with. She is even letting me help."

"I hope you don't try and do too much."

"I can't do too much but sit, so I've been helping her sew beads on the veil. Mom has done everything else."

"This is a strange wedding, is it not?"

"Yeah, it is. I tried to talk to Marie about it when I was in Calgary, but she wouldn't listen."

"I know, isn't she marrying his brother?"

"Yeah, I'm not sure what is up with that. She wouldn't say too much about it. But I'm sure that is why it is such a small wedding. She talks like there are going to be more at her wedding then what she wanted. He has a lot of natives in his side of the family, and we have some in ours, so it should be one rip snorting party."

"Maybe that is what she is afraid of."

"It could be. I know I would be a little worried. I know some of our families are very prejudiced, and it could be a disaster."

"Hey, Grandma, it sure smells good in here."

"Hope it tastes as good as it smells."

"I'm sure it will, Grandma." We go down to wash up for lunch.

"Char, is Grandma and Grandpa OK with Marie's wedding?"

"They seem to be. After all, they do know him from having the store. Him and his ex lived right across the road from us. He used to spend more time at our place than he did at home. His woman was a drunk, and I think, he found it easier to stay away."

"Were they married?"

"No, they weren't."

"So why did he stay with her?"

"They had a little girl, and I don't know if she was his or not."

"Where are they now if he's marrying Marie?"

"The mother died. I don't know whatever became of the little girl. I will have to try and remember to ask Marie next week when she comes."

"You think he has had his eye on Marie all this time? Even while she dated his brother?"

"Looks like it." Then we went to join Mom and Dad and Louise for lunch. It was nice talking with Crystal. It made me feel like I was back home. I have gotten very lonely being here at Mom and Dad's. Going for tea with Ron was nice too, but all our friends are different, and we really do live a different kind of life in Alberta than they do here in BC.

I feel life in BC is very laid back where in Alberta life is so serious. This could just be me growing up and moving on from the partying.

In BC it seems like the party goes on and on. I feel it is because there are so many tourists the summer more so than the winter months. But you have tourists all winter long. So it just never stops. I think one could get tired of it over a period of time.

People must want to sit down and just put their feet up and not have to worry that someone else is hanging around their place as well. I like my alone time. Oh, I like to visit and shop, but I do very much like my space. Besides, there will be one more to share my space with soon. I will start out with someone small and see if I will be able to handle having someone else in my space all the time.

At this point, I thought about James. I did enjoy his company when he was taking me from the hospital and popping in now and again. But was that the trick because it was now and again? When he told me I could move in with him, I hadn't thought about our space. He talked like he had a big place and even a lady to do all the housework. Now that for me would be a drag. I like cleaning my place. Once again you would have someone else in your home all the time. When would you ever have privacy or your time alone? Just maybe I will be to set in my ways to take up with a man or roommate. A baby will learn and grow accustomed to the way you are without knowing any difference, whereas moving in with someone, you have to live with how they already are. That could be terrifying.

I wonder if that is why so many marriages don't work. People are not able to accept the other's way of living. To me the answer would be to continue dating. You keep your own place and just spent time together when it is really something you want to do. Otherwise you have to be in each other's face day in and day out. This does not sound so appealing to me at this point. Either that or I'm really missing something here.

I guess one never knows until you try it. So I guess the living together is a good thing before marring so you can see if the two of you can work things out and enjoy each other 24-7.

Living together would take all the excitement out of getting married. After all, what would be the reason. Getting married was just a legal way of having sex, so no one would bitch about what you were doing. Now who cares? There are a lot of people living together. I have seen older people as well. They call them their companions.

In the end, I guess it all boils down to what you, as the individual, want to do with your life.

When I think about the time Ron and I spent together, it was changing us a little every day. Making you more aware that there was more to life than partying. I thought at the time I was ready for that, playing house, but he wasn't, and I'm glad he left when he did because if we were meant to be together forever. His kiss should have had more of a punch than it did after all our time apart. This way, we are still good friends. At least, we are not on some battlefield with our hearts and minds.

I wonder if Ron has thought of any of this. Maybe guys don't think that deep. It would be interesting to hear how he feels about us. I will have to ask him some time, if the time is ever right for such a talk between us. With lunch done, everyone was going back outside, but I had said I would like to lie down for an hour or so.

"Char, are you all right?"

"Yeah, Louise, I'm fine. I just find if I lie down it seems to give my stomach a chance to rest. As well, I don't feel like I'm being stretched a mile. It takes away the burning pain I get after being up on my feet."

"Are you sure?"

"Yeah, I am."

"I will check on you in an hour or so then, all right?"

"Sounds good." Leaving them, I went to my room. I know they're not going to be here long, but it does feel so much better when I can lie down. I have rolled up a quilt Mom had on the foot of the bed, and I put it under my knees. This helps take all the pressure off all the right spots.

It is funny when you walk around carrying this extra weight how it makes you tired. I don't know how those people who are really overweight do it. Some of them look like they must have the weight of two or three babies in them. That's men and women. That can't be good on the rest of your body. It is one thing to be pregnant because you are going to lose most of what you have gained when you have the baby. But the people who are just that much overweight must struggle every day to get anything done.

With that in mind, I had fallen asleep, and all I did was dream of big people, and I mean, real big people. Some of them were so big they ended up having two heads and four hands. This had gone from being a dream to a nightmare. I was pregnant but still not as big as all of them, so I was being squished by them every time I tried to go anywhere. You know when you have those damn dreams where you're trying to run, but you're not moving; well this was the same way. I could not for the life of me get out from between these big people. The worst of it was they didn't even know I was there. I just sort of disappeared in their rolls. Trying to push them away and yelling at them to please let me through, I had to get through. I couldn't hardly breathe anymore. Trying to keep my hands in front of my face so I could get some air was starting to feel like a losing battle.

Where did all these big people come from? Am I going to become one of them if I don't get out of here? I start to push harder and harder. Oh god, please help me get out. Even the faces that I know like Louise and Crystal even Mom and Dad were there, but they were all so big. I yell at them. "What happened to all of you?" But no one seems to hear me. "Please, I'm down here just look down you will see me." I wave my hands back and forth and start to jump up and down. Then I remember I can't jump up and down that could make me lose my baby. I continue to push and wave my arms around, but I'm not getting anywhere but tired. I feel like I'm going under this big blanket, and it is heavy.

"Char, Char, wake up! Come on, Char. Wake up!" I could hear her, but no way would my eyes open. When I did wake up, the sweat was just running off of me.

"Oh god!" I was shaking so bad, and I felt cold.

"What is the matter? Are you going to be OK? Here keep the wrap on until you quite shivering."

"I'll be OK. I just had a horrible dream."

"No kidding! Are you sure it wasn't a nightmare? Come now, Mother has tea made. I should have come and woke you sooner, but I thought you were having a good rest."

"Thanks, Louise."

"Being pregnant can bring on some pretty stupid dreams or nightmares. I remember when I was pregnant with the twins. I had terrible ones. Sometimes I couldn't go back to sleep. My doctor told me it was due to the big change in my hormones."

"I know what you mean."

"Here, let me help you."

"I will be OK."

"You're still shivering, Char. I will help you get out to the table. Once you get some tea into you, you will be fine."

"I feel like a real idiot."

"Hey, we have all been there, so don't worry about it. Just be glad that's it's just a dream."

"You can say that again." Louise helped me up and out to the table as Mom was turning around with the teapot.

"What the hell?" She almost dropped the teapot on the floor. She came over to me faster than I had ever thought Mom would.

"What happened? Should I call your father to take you to the doctor? You are so pale. Are you bleeding again?"

"No, Mom. I was having a horrible dream, and Louise woke me up out of it. I will be OK."

"Are you sure you don't need a doctor?"

"I'm sure, Mom, thank you. But I sure could use a cup of your good tea."

"That I can get for you right away. Just sit, don't go anywhere."

"I'm not going anywhere, Mom." I watched her pour the tea, and her hands were shaking about as bad as I was. I had almost thought maybe I would end up wearing my tea instead of drinking it.

I couldn't help think. She does care. She cares a lot more than she wants me to believe. Why?

CHAPTER TWENTY-SIX

L ouise was right once I had some tea into me, I started to
feel a lot better, and the worried look finally left Mom's
face.

"Char, when we are finished our tea, I think we should go sit
outside in the sun. What do you think?"

"I think that sounds like a great idea, Louise. Perhaps it will
really warm me up."

"Are you still shivering?"

"A little bit, but it is getting a lot better. The sun will take
what is left away, I'm sure." So that was what we did, and we
all sat around outside talking about Marie's wedding and all the
things that go with it. If Louise was very upset because they were
not invited, she didn't let on to Mother. Louise had asked about
Marie's choice in the man that she was about to marry, and all
mother said was "She's making her bed, she will have to lie in it."
This does seem to apply to this one circumstance even if it is a line
Mother uses that I have come to detest. No one is going to know
why she has chosen to marry the brother of whom she was dating
after all this time.

While I was with her, I got that it was for revenge although
I told her I thought she was playing a dangerous game. But we
cannot stop her from making this choice. It is something she
will have to live with, and we can only pray that it works out
for her.

I will make sure she knows that my door is always open for however long it is needed, when I get a door, that is.

The rest of the time that Louise and Crystal were there, it was so very enjoyable. Louise helped sew on the veil, and before we knew it, we had it finished. There was always one of us sewing on the veil. I must say it gave us a reason to all be together, and we were able to talk about a lot of things.

"You know, Char. I saw James just before we left. He said to say hi and wants you to call him. He was a little upset that you left like you did and didn't call him. He said you could have gone and lived with him. He had lots of room, and you already knew that."

"I know. He had asked me a couple of times, but I just wasn't ready for that kind of a move at the time."

"So are you going to check him out when you come back?"

"Maybe. I'll think about it."

"He said he still wanted to be here with you when you have the baby. I could give him the address and number.

"I don't know if that would be a good idea. Him being here."

"He said he was all read up and was more than ready to be with you. He told me you said it would be OK for him to be with you."

"That was when I thought I was having the baby back home, not out here. I don't expect him to travel this far for that."

"James seems to be very excited about being with you when you had the baby. I think you best call and talk to him. This guy seems to be very honest and concerned about you. I think he really cares. Why don't you give him a running chance?"

"I wasn't sure why I kept him at arm's length, but since I've been back here, I think I figured it out, and now, I might be able to work something out with James. I'll see as time goes on what will happen."

"I think you're a fool if you let this man get away. There are not many like him around. I remember how he was while you were in the hospital."

"Yeah, he was sweet, caring, and kind."

"That's just what the doctor order. So be sure to call him."

"I'll think about it. That's all I will say."

"How old is this man you are talking about?"

"Early thirties maybe."

"Has he got a job?"

"Yes, Mom! He does."

"I think this man has money to spend. He seems to want to spend it on Char and the baby."

"So why did you come home?"

"'Cause, Mom, I'm not comfortable having this guy just jump right into the thick of things like it means nothing. I don't feel like I'm ready for a steady man in my life yet."

"Has he been married or have kids?"

"No to both. He's been too busy working and said he just didn't think about that part of his life until he met me. He said he wants the baby and I to live with him. James told me I could even have my own room, and we would see how things worked out from there."

"And you choose to come here, why?"

"For one thing, I wasn't to be alone, and he has to work, and he travels far away with his work."

"Char, I remember him telling you that he has a housekeeper that he would pay to spend more time with you when he had to be away."

"Louise, I know that, but he is still a stranger to me. I know him, but yet I don't. I'm scared to take my baby into something that might not be right."

"I don't know. It sounds like a real winner to me."

"Thanks, Crystal."

"Sorry, but it does."

"Well, you know you can never be too sure of anything as far as knowing someone. You only ever think you do." I got the feeling Mom was talking about someone in her life. Was it Dad or was it her ex-husband? No one was going to ask. We just looked at each other to see what else she was going to say. Nothing more was said; Mom just got up and left the table. Now we did just sit and look at each other.

"What do you think that was all about?"

"I don't know, Louise. Some things she just doesn't talk about."

"Mother has always been like that. I remember asking her questions when I lived at home, and she would never give a straight answer. It was an answer, all right, but you always had to figure out what it meant on your own. I guess that's because there is always two ways of looking at things. The way you want it to be and the way it should be. The choice is hard to make sometimes, but no one else can make it for you."

"Mom's first marriage was an arranged one. I think that alone would have to be a pretty hard thing to except."

"At one time, that is how all marriages were. Fathers looked for a man that could afford his daughter or bring something worthwhile into the family. The girl's feelings had nothing to do with any of it. She was to bear his children and nothing more. Love meant nothing."

"That would suck if that was how things were today. I know. I for one wouldn't go without a fight."

"Don't we know that is true?"

"Then we have Marie making her choices out of brothers. That has to be a hard one to get over once you all become the same family in the end. It has to be very uncomfortable for everyone involved."

"I wonder how often they will all be under one roof. Do you know if they are all coming to the wedding?"

"That is something I don't know. But it could prove to be interesting."

"You will have to let me know how this all turns out. I sure hope for Mother and Dad that nothing terrible happens. They have gone to a lot of work for her wedding. I don't think I have known anyone's wedding that they have done so much for. So I hope they won't be sorry for having it here on their place."

"I can't see Marie doing that to Mom and Dad. That could be why she is having it here. Perhaps she thinks that no one will step out of line with Dad around. After all, he doesn't hide how he feels about people. I don't think he really liked either one of those guys. Being native plays a big part in it for him."

"We all know what he's like after he has had a couple of drinks or so. He is either out for a good time or he can get mean and nasty. Let's hope it's not the later of the two."

The few days that I had to spend with Crystal and Louise went by very fast. The morning they were leaving was the day Marie was to be arriving. I had tried to get them to stay, but they both felt if Marie wanted them there, she would have asked them. So I finally quit trying. I think most off all I didn't want to be left behind. I had heard Mother talking to them about staying for the wedding, but she had no more luck than I did.

"Char, take really good care of yourself. Please give that young man a call."

"I will."

"Char!"

"I promise, Louise, I will."

"If I see him when I go back, I'm sending him your way."

"If Mom doesn't, then I will."

"Not you too, Crystal."

"Yes, me too! You will be a fool not to give him a chance."

"OK. OK. I get the message." With that said, we all hugged and kissed and said our good-byes. Mom and Dad seemed like they were down just as much as I was. The rest of the day went very quietly and slowly. Mom and Dad had gone into town to do their evening trip with the dog, and I think they were going over to one of their friends for an hour. Mom said they wouldn't be long. Marie was due in around 8:00 PM, and they would be home then.

I thought I might as well take a chance and rest as it could be a long evening seeing how Marie would be in, and there would be a lot of catching up to do on everyone's part.

I was more tired than I had thought because I woke to voices and lots of them. That is one thing about these mobile homes. They did not make them soundproof. My head of the bed was right up against the kitchen wall, so it wouldn't matter how quiet Mom thought she was being, it would never be quiet enough. No one could blame her for the way they were built.

I really did not feel like getting up. I just wanted to turn over and go back to sleep, which I was about to do when my door opened slowly. Seeing the light shinning in was hard on the eyes, so I couldn't tell who was at the door.

"Char, are you awake?"

"Yeah, I was just thinking about whether I wanted to get up or go back to sleep."

Marie came over and sat on the edge of the bed.

"Why, you not feeling well?"

"Oh yeah. I'm all right."

"Mom thought you were upset because Louise left today?"

"Some. I wished I was going back home with them."

"It won't be too much longer now, and you will be able to go home."

"Right! I don't have a home to go back to anymore."

"What? I thought you were living at Mary's, and she was going to help you?"

"Well, that's how it started out, and everything was looking good."

"What happened?"

"Mary died."

"What!"

"Yeah, and her son sold the house, and the people needed the basement for their daughter. She was in the same boat as I am except her baby was already born. She is a teacher, and her mother was going to be taking care of the baby, so it set up great for them."

"Well, that sucks for you!"

"Yes, it does, so here I lie."

"Well, don't lie anymore. Get up and visit with us. It will make you feel better."

"Who's us?"

"My future mother-in-law and sister-in-law came with me to help."

"Don't think Mom left too much undone."

"Well, we will see tomorrow, but for now, let's just do some catching up." She takes my hand and helps me up off the bed. Once I was up, she went to give me a hug.

"My, you have grown, my dear."

"I don't think that was part of Red Riding Hood." We both laugh and tried to get through the door at the same time, and we started to laugh all the harder. We finally made it back out to the kitchen.

"What are you girls doing? Partying without us?" the heavyset lady asked.

"Yep, we got into Dad's bottle he thought he had hidden so well."

"You girls stay out of my stash."

"Now, Dad, we came to party."

"No, you came to get married."

"Oh, isn't that the same thing?

"Now, I think you and I will get along just fine," Marie said to the heavyset lady.

"Charlene, I want you to meet my future mother-in-law. Rose, this is Charlene, my younger very pregnant sister."

"It's nice to finally meet you. Marie talks a lot about you."

"Don't believe everything she tells you."

"Oh, it hasn't been anything bad."

"Yeah, right."

"Hey, now why would I tell none truths when there is enough to talk about by telling the truth?"

"My life is not that exciting."

"A hell of a lot than mine. I'm getting married, end of story."

"Well, I'm having a baby, end of story."

"Perhaps you girls could put them both together and make a real good story," Rose said. We all laugh even harder. The rest of the evening went on, and everyone chatted about everything from when we were young kids on the farm until we all left home. Some of them were great memories to bring back, and others were sad ones, but overall, it killed the time, and before we knew it, the sun was starting to peek through.

"I'm sorry people, but I have to go lie down for a while."

"Yeah, me too, Char. Where am I sleeping seeing how they all brought their campers."

"The air mattress is in the closet in Char's room."

"Thanks, Mom."

"The rest of us will get out of here so everyone can have some shut-eye for a couple hours or so."

"All right, Rose. I will call you when I get up."

"OK, Marie, you do that. We probably have a lot to do today." They all headed out, and by the way they were still laughing and carrying on, I didn't think there was going to be much hope in them getting much sleep. I sure was glad I wasn't sleeping out there with them.

Marie came in and got the air mattress and seemed like she was quite content with everything.

"See you in a while, Char. Hope you get to sleep."

"Shouldn't be much trouble in that now that it is quiet."

"Good thing they decided to go to bed as well. Otherwise we would all be hooped."

"I thought the same thing when I said I had to go to bed."

"Didn't take Mom and Dad long to go to sleep. I can hear Dad snoring already."

"I think he does that to chase Mom out."

"Oh really. Where does she sleep?"

"I've seen her on the sofa some mornings. I've never asked her why."

"Do you think Mom is OK?"

"What with the wedding and all?"

"No, with her health. She seems to be very distant most off the time."

"Oh, you noticed. I thought it was just because of me being here."

"I don't think so, Char. There is something she isn't telling us."

"When Louise and Crystal were here, we would be talking, and she would say things that would make us all look at each other and wait for her to carry on, but she wouldn't. She always left things unsaid."

"I will try to talk to her if we get time alone. See what's up."

"You don't want to bring things up not pleasant at this time."

"It might be the only time I have to do it. I know you and her never talk, so I will try."

"We have done some talking not much, but I will take what little I get from her. It has even been very pleasant to talk to her. She has been getting better lately. When I first came, she was terrible. I didn't know how long I would be able to take it. Usually I'm only here for two days and gone again, and all is forgot about until next time."

"Char, why do you keep coming back?"

"Believe it or not, but I miss them. Some days I get so lonely, I sit and cry. I really miss the farm. I know things weren't good there for them. Maybe it wouldn't be like this between Mom and I if we would have stayed on the farm. Maybe Mick would still be alive. Maybe Mom and Dad would still be alive. His death has changed both of them so much. Hell, it changed all our lives who am I kidding?"

"Yeah, it did that all right. For the three of us still left at home anyways."

"I feel like we don't have a home to go back to anymore. We never lived here, so to me, it isn't home. When I tell my friends I'm coming here. I always say I'm going to Mom and Dad's. Not I'm going home."

"Now that you mentioned it, that is what I say too. I never thought about it before."

"We have no memories here in this trailer. I will have now, but nothing of us growing up. When I think about our good times, it is always or most of the time while we were on the farm. To me that was a good life."

"But there was nothing there for us. The city's or even where you live there is more to offer us."

"True, but are we happy? I mean really happy?"

"Sometimes I feel lost, even in the big city."

"That's just it. Most of you don't even know your neighbor. That is sad. On the farm, we knew people who lived miles from us and a lot of them."

"You're right about that. Anyways I'm going to go to sleep talk to you in a while."

"Yeah, you bet." Once she was gone, I lay there thinking about what we had talked about and wondered if she was right and maybe Mom was sick. But why wouldn't she say something to someone. She doesn't look sick to me. But then how do I know what sick people look like? I didn't know Mary was so sick, and christ, she died in such a short time. I still can't get that through my head that she really is gone. Besides, aren't parents supposed to live forever?

The next couple days went fast, and the day of Marie's wedding was beautiful. The light breeze was great; otherwise, I would have find it too hot.

It was not a big wedding by any means but very elegant. That was thanks to Mom and Dad for the way they had set things up.

Mom was smart enough to put an elastic band around the bottom of all table tops, which made them fitted so everything stayed in place.

There were only fifty people there but that was enough. After the meal was done I was helping clean up and had taken some of the food that needed to be put into the fridge inside. I saw someone had spilled a drink. Grabbing a towel, I bent over to wipe the floor when all of a sudden there was blood running faster than I could wipe. My heart was racing, and I started to shake. I was scared. I did not hear anyone come in.

"What the hell!" It was Dad.

"Dad, I have to go to the hospital fast."

"I guess so. I will get your mother," he said as he headed out the door.

"What the hell happened?" Mom was asking as she helped me up.

"On my feet too long today."

"Oh christ! Henry, get the truck. She has to go to the hospital."

"I have it outside the door."

"Here. Put these between your legs when you get into the truck and sit on them."

"Mom, that won't keep the seat clean."

"It's not for that! Use the towels as a pack. Maybe it will slow down the bleeding."

"Oh, OK." Climbing into the truck and getting the towels between my legs and trying to press down as hard as I could kept me from seeing all the faces staring at us.

We had eighteen miles to go to reach the hospital. It seemed to take forever.

"Have you got pain too?" Dad asked.

"No. No pain."

"Guess that's good."

"Hope so. Glad it waited until now instead of in the middle of the wedding. Marie wouldn't have been happy."

"Don't think she would have said anything."

"You're probably right." With that said, we had pulled up to the doors of the hospital. There was a nurse waiting outside with a wheelchair and came rushing over as soon as Dad got parked.

"Is this the pregnant girl that is bleeding heavily?" she asked Dad as he got out of the truck.

"Yes, it is. Let me help her out."

"OK, please just get her in the chair. We can do the rest. The doctor is waiting inside."

Oh was all Dad could say.

"I think it was your wife who called to tell us you were on your way."

I looked up to the sky and said, "Thank you, Mom!" even though I wished she was here with me. I had no idea what was going to happen.

I was put into bed and given a needle right away, and a doctor came in and checked me all out. He wasn't my doctor. Mine was on days off till Monday.

This doctor didn't say much to me. He asked a few questions and then talked to the nurse just off to the side of the door.

"I don't think there is a chance she will keep this baby. Probably a good thing anyways. Keep an eye on her to see if the bleeding stops now that she has had the needle. If it gets worse, then we will have to take the baby anyways, and do a D&C."

"OK, I will let you know."

"A half hour should tell us what we need to know."

"All right, doctor. I will stay with her as much as I can."

"Are her parents here?"

"Just her dad, I think."

"Maybe see if he wants to come sit with her a while."

"All right." The doctor leaves and so does the nurse. What the hell does he mean? A chance I won't keep this baby. Of course, I will keep my baby. Unless Mom told them something different. Why would it be a good thing if I didn't keep it? God, I wish my doctor was here. He would have talked to me. He knows I'm keeping my baby and didn't see anything wrong with that. He told me not to be ashamed it happens a lot of the time and there was nothing wrong with me wanting to keep my baby. He and I had a very long talk when I first started to go to see him, and I told him everything. He just told me to enjoy being pregnant and let him be the mother hen and do the worrying.

Dad came into the room with his cap in his hands and was twisting and untwisting it. He was very nervous about something.

"Dad, you are going to wear your hat out if you keep doing that to the poor thing."

"Oh yeah, yeah," he said as he folds it up and sticks it into his back pocket.

"How you feeling?"

"They gave me a needle to stop the bleeding. Now we have to wait and see if it works."

"I think I should go get your mother."

"No, I don't think so, Dad."

"I think she should be here. It would be better than me."

"I'm fine with you here, Dad."

"Yeah, but I don't know about these things. Your mother should be here."

I could tell Dad was really out of sorts with all of this. He really didn't want to be here. Not this way any ways.

"All right, Dad, if you think that would be best, then you can go bring her."

"Yeah, yeah, I do. I be right back with your mother." He pats me on the arm and almost runs out of the room. I yell behind him.

"Drive safe." I don't think he heard me. I lay back on the pillow, and the nurse came in. She put my bed more in the sitting position and then put more pillows under my legs.

"You must not get up for the next seventy-two hours."

"What about the bathroom?"

"No, you are to use the bedpan."

"Bedpan? Like what we puck into?"

"No! She reaches down and pulls a small silver pan from the cupboard. It didn't look big enough to hold my ass as I have packed on the pounds.

"Be serious! You think I'm going to use that?"

"I think so, and yes, you are or you will be wetting the bed or worse."

"Come on. Look at me, my ass will not fit that small pan."

"A lot bigger people than you have used the bedpan. There is no other options, so zip it." With that said, she tossed the pan on the bed and left.

Oh nice lady. Taking the pan and setting on the nightstand, I laid back and was just about to doze off when the doctor came in with a nurse.

"How is the flow?"

I went to say something, but the nurse did it for me.

"It has slowed down some."

"I want you to give her another shot of the steroids in a half hour."

"All right."

"That won't be too much on the baby?"

"No, but that won't matter as she won't be keeping the baby." With that said, he was leaving.

"What do you mean? I won't be keeping the baby?" Now I was shouting.

"I'm keeping my baby! No one is taking it from me! No one. Do you hear me?"

"Now, Charlene, calm down. That is not good for you or your baby."

"That is the second time he has said that. I don't understand. He won't talk to me. I want my own doctor, Dr. Connors. He talks to me, and he knows I'm not giving up my baby. He told me that was fine. There are a lot of girls keeping their babies, and he didn't have a problem with it."

"Your doctor won't be in until tomorrow."

"I want to see him then."

"Did no one else talk to you before I came in?"

"No. Talk to me about what?"

"Well, someone should have talked to you by now."

"Talk to me about what? Please, will you talk to me!!"

"Listen, I shouldn't, but I can see you don't understand what is happening, and you should be aware."

"Aware of what?"

"There is no easy way of telling you this. You are losing your baby."

"To whom? Did my mom do this? She did, didn't she? That's why she wouldn't come with me tonight. I thought it was because my sister got married today and she still had a lot of people at the house."

"Your mother had nothing to do with it. But Mother Nature has."

"WHAT?"

"You are miscarrying your baby."

"No, I'M NOT."

"Listen, this is Mother Nature's way of stopping women from having children that are deformed or really sick. Now you don't want either of that for your baby, do you?"

"No of course not. But maybe my baby isn't sick. This isn't the first time this has happened to me."

"It's not?"

"No, this has been happening all along, and I'm not to be on my feet, and I guess with my sister's wedding today, I overdone it."

"Dr. Connors knows this?"

"Yes, I see him all the time."

"I will be back in a bit. I want you to lay back and just do some simple deep breathing and get relaxed. That will help a lot, and I will come back and talk to you some more in a little bit."

"OK."

"That's good. You will see you will feel better if you just calm down some more. Close your eyes until I come back." Then she left. I didn't know what she was going to do, but I tried to lie there with my eyes close and relax, but the tears started to flow. I tried so hard to stop them, but it seemed the harder I tried, the harder they came.

Dear God, I don't want to lose my baby. Please make it OK so I don't lose it. I promise I will be a good mom. Please just give me a chance. Give us a chance.

Sitting there rocking back and forth with my arms wrapped around my tummy in a mother's protective way. *Shush now, little one, everything is going to be OK. Just wait and see. We don't have much longer to wait, then you can come see Mommy. Oh baby, please stay safe.*

CHAPTER TWENTY-SEVEN

———◆———

"Why are you crying?" Mom asked as she came through the door, scaring the hell out of me. Dad was coming in behind her again wringing his cap in his hands.

"Oh Mom! They say I won't be keeping my baby." And the tears really start to flow.

"Well, there is no need to cry over it. That would be like crying over spilled milk. Does no good."

"Spilled milk is nothing like losing a baby, Mom!"

"You have to understand that this is God's way of taking care of his own."

"Why would God let me get pregnant then do this?"

"Everything happens for a reason."

"Oh really? Well please tell me what the reason would be for this. I don't want to lose my baby. Please quit talking in circles."

"Maybe your baby is sick or it hasn't grown properly. How the hell do I know?"

"You're the one who always has the answers Mom!"

"Not this time. I'm sorry this is happening to you, but in the end, you will see it was for the best."

"Why, Mom, because I'm not married? Is that what this is all about? Am I being punished? But the baby has done nothing wrong. The baby deserves to have a chance."

"Well, it seems to have been fighting you all the way. Has it not every time the doctors stop what the good lord has tried to end. You may be sorry if they succeed."

"No, I won't be sorry."

"You want to be stuck with a baby that maybe handicap? Are you out of your mind? It will be hard enough for you as a single mother, never mind having a child that will need round-the-clock care for the rest of its life. That, my dear, is no life for the child or you. You are too young to be saddled with such a burden."

"But what if I don't see it as such a burden."

"Maybe you won't in the beginning. As the child gets older, it won't be the same, and you could even get to hate it."

"Mom, how can you say that? What mother would ever hate her child? Is having a baby sick or healthy not like the wedding vows people take? You take that baby in sickness and in health and promise to give it the best care possible and to love it no matter what comes your way. How could that be so wrong?"

"Because maybe you won't be able to give it all that is possible. Have you thought about that? Your father and I can't afford to pay for a sick child, grandchild or not."

"But I would love my baby no matter what."

"That is fine, and I don't doubt for one minute that you wouldn't. But love is not enough when the child is not healthy."

"We don't know if the baby is sick or what is wrong with it?"

"You're right, we don't, but the good Lord does. So you will just have to accept it for what it is, and that is it. Now I don't want anymore crying."

"That's right, crying is not good for you or your baby."

"Dr. Connors! What are you doing here?"

"Well, I heard my little lady was having some troubles and thought I best come see her. Now tell me what brought this on? Have you not been resting like I told you to?"

"My sister got married today, so I was up more than should have been."

"That would do it. I want to check you out. Do you want your mother to stay?"

"No. I will be OK now."

"Would you two please step outside until I have checked Charlene out?" Mom and Dad left without saying a word. I had no idea if they would wait around and come back in after or not.

While Dr. Connors was checking me out, he asked a lot of questions. The one he asked often was "Is there any pain?" I wasn't having any pain at all.

"At no time did you have any pain, a feeling of tearing or stabbing or a burning pain."

"No, the bleeding just started, and that was all that happened."

"That to me is a good sign."

"It is?"

"Oh yes. You haven't gone into labor so the bleeding we can stop with some medication, and we will get you taking more iron pills, and all should be good to go. Plus you are off your feet."

"What about the D&C."

"You don't need that unless you miscarry. Then we do a D&C that helps stop the heavy bleeding. Do you understand?"

"I think so."

"Will I lose my baby?"

"Not if I can help it. But I need for you to calm down, think positive, and let me be the mother hen as I told you I'd be for. I will do the worrying. All right, young lady, I want you to stay and sleep. Stay off your feet as much as you can."

"Does that mean I don't have to use that thing?" I pointed over to the bedpan on my night table. He laughs and says.

"For the next seventy-two hours, yes. Then we will get you up slowly and see how you do from there. Now I will be back in the morning. Unless something changes, the nurses know they are to call me."

"Dr. Connors."

"Yes what is it?"

"I don't like that other doctor. He isn't very nice at all. He wouldn't even talk to me. He acted like I wasn't even here and he didn't care."

"I heard about it, and I'm sorry you were put through that. I'm here now, and there will be no one else taking care of you, that I can promise."

"Thank you!"

"You're welcome, that is what we are here for. Now you get some sleep please."

I could hear voices out in the hall, and I know one of them was Dr. Connors, and I also know he was mighty pissed about something. I heard him say, "We will be seeing about this."

Everything got quiet and then Mom and Dad came back in.

"So how is everything now?"

"Better, Mom, now that Dr. Connors is here."

"You're lucky to have him. He is one of the best baby doctors around these parts."

"He doesn't make me feel like I have done something terrible or I should be ashamed of being pregnant."

"Yeah, well, guess if that makes you feel better about being pregnant."

"No, Mom, it doesn't. There is no one sorrier than me that I am pregnant. It has not been easy, and it probably won't ever be easy again. But like you always said, 'You make your bed you lie in it.' That is just what I am doing. I'm not asking anyone to raise my baby or give me handouts. I just need help until I can be on my feet again and then we will be just fine. I'm sorry I had to come here and bother you and Dad. I tried not to, but some things are out of our control. I was all set up once, and I told you and Dad what happened. This wasn't how I wanted it to be. I will go as soon as the baby is safe to travel." I rolled over to my side away from Mom.

"Now, now," Dad said as he steps up and pats my arm. "There is no need to talk about leaving. You need plenty of time to get better after the baby is born. Your mother knows that better than anyone." The look on her face was washed away with the last few words that he spoke. Dad was not a stupid man, just cautious.

"I think this little lady should go to sleep now." My nurse had been standing over in the corner being busy but listening.

"Yeah, Mother, we should go now. We can come back in the morning, or tomorrow some time."

"We have a lot of cleaning up to do since the wedding and there are still people there."

"It's OK, Mom. You don't have to come back tomorrow. I know you have lots to do. But thank you for coming tonight."

"OK." She turned around and left. Dad pats me on the arm.

"See you tomorrow then, get some sleep. I'm glad everything is going to be OK."

"Thank you, Dad, me too." He left and it made me sad to see how he cared but was scared to really show it.

"Your dad seems like a very nice man."

"He is, I love my dad a lot."

"I can tell."

"Don't get me wrong. I love my mom too. She's just . . ." I paused trying to find the words to describe my mom which was not coming easy.

"Harder to please. She is the hardnosed one of the two. I get that she tells it the way it is whether you like it or not."

"Yes, that is my mom. She has a big heart. It has just gone into hibernation for a while."

"Oh, something terrible has happened then to her?"

"Yes, to all of us. My youngest brother was shot to death."

"How old was he?"

"Fourteen."

"Oh, very young. Does she blame herself?"

"I don't think so. Why would she?"

"Maybe she feels that she should have made your dad put the gun somewhere else."

"Oh no. It didn't happen at home. He was at his friend's house."

"Oh, I see. Well, a death of anyone in the family is hard, and no one feels they should ever have to bury their children."

"That would be an awful thing to have to do." I wrap my arms around my baby and say a prayer to God. "Thank you, God, for being here with me now. I know you will do what is best, and if there is a way that I can keep my baby I beg you to please give us a chance. Thank you. I won't ask for anything more." When I opened my eyes, the nurse had gone. So I just lay back, and within minutes to my surprise, I had fallen asleep.

The clanking of the food cart in the morning woke me up. There were voices all over and nurses rushing here and there.

Cleaning staff coming and going, and it was just one very busy place. The nurse brought me in my breakfast as well as the other in the room. There were three of us sharing this room. I guess no one could get too lonely in here.

After we ate, the nurses came in and changed and made our beds, helped me get washed up as I couldn't go and have a shower or bath so they brought me water to my bed in a pan. Not like I haven't done this before. You just don't get the clean feeling though. My flow was slower, but I could still smell the blood and that always makes me feel dirty. Even when I would get my periods, I would bath twice on the days I was home just to feel clean. If I can smell it so can everyone else. On the box of pads, I think it said something about changing your pad four times a day. Are they crazy? Try every time you go to the washroom and in between.

Lying there watching the other women and I could see one look like she was ready to have her baby any day. She did not look happy about it at all. Later I learned that she had edema, which is a buildup of excess serious fluids between tissue cells. This makes it difficult for women to get around and is dangerous. No wonder she didn't look happy.

The other lady had, had a baby girl and was going home today. The baby was so tiny and looked so cute. I had asked if I could see her when the nurse was taking her away. She looked so perfect and seemed to be so content. I can only hope mine will be just like that. Seeing the baby girl made me think. I don't care if I have a boy or girl so long as everything about it is healthy.

Their husbands came and went and came and went. That made me feel lonely; I don't have anyone to share this with. Then I thought of James. I wonder what he would be doing. I do miss him, and he did offer, but this is not his responsibility, so why would I do that to him? Besides if he were really into this, he would have been here by now. I know Louise has told him everything by now. Deep down inside, I wished he was here. I turn away from all their happiness and stare out the window and go into daydreaming.

Daydreaming had become a way of life for me. I was to stay in the hospital for the next month to be watched very carefully. Dr. Connors had told me that he had talked to a very good baby doctor in Vancouver and was told that I could very easily lose my baby if everyone wasn't careful. I did put on more weight and got me to thinking. How will I ever lose this? My butt got huge and the tops of my legs. One got to be as big around as both together would have been at one time. This is crazy.

Over the next month, I had seen my mother maybe six times. The visits were not long. I don't know sometimes why she came other than I think they were in town for her own doctor's appointments and would pop over because Dad would drag her here. At least that was how she always made me feel.

Today is cold and gloomy outside and didn't seem to be too many people out and about. The nurses were nice enough to move me closer to the window, so I could watch what was happening outside. After all, I didn't have anything but time on my hands. Being able to watch from my bed made it a little easier to take staying in it.

The bedpan and I never did get along so they brought me a potty chair, which was a wheelchair with a pot under the seat; it did work better. Most of the time, I would get them to wheel me into the bathroom. I hated just getting left behind the curtain. You might as well bare your butt to the world when you sit on a bedpan.

With the weather gloomy and me gloomy today, it didn't take much thinking to make me cry. The nurses were good they tried to talk about different things. Most of the time, I couldn't keep focus. Today, the tears flowed easily, and I was feeling a little foolish. I felt a hand on my shoulder, and thinking it was a nurse, I didn't turn over.

"Hey, I didn't come all this way to be put on ignore." My breath caught, and I turned so fast I had a burning pain run up my neck. I reached out and started to cry so hard as Anna took me in her arms.

"Hey, Char. If I knew it would do this to you, I would have stayed away."

"Oh no, I'm glad you came. I'm so lonely, and I can't wait to get out of here."

"Soon! Then it will be all over, but I hear this is better than at Mom and Dad's."

"Only because I'm too far away from the hospital."

"Mom hasn't been that easy on you or understanding, I'm told."

"Mom is Mom, you know that. But she means well."

"That's not what Dad said."

"Well, with Mom, you know her motto on this." Together we said, "You made your bed." Then we laugh so hard I thought I would have the baby right then. Anna knew some of what I was going through. She had had her first baby young and still at home. In the end, she had lost her son. Out of everyone, she totally understood where I was coming from.

"Now I'm going down to get us some coffee, and we will catch up." She went to leave and I did not realize I was hanging on so tight.

"Char. You have to let me go." She says as she pries my hands off her arms." I can't get us a coffee if you don't let me go. I will be right back."

"Sorry." I know I turned red in the face.

"You going to be OK?"

"Yeah, just make sure you come back."

"I will be only minutes." She left, and it almost seemed like I had dreamt she had come. But it wasn't long before she was back with our coffee as promised.

"So tell me what you have been doing with yourself."

"Not much to do but lie here and read."

"Well, tell you what, I thought you would be doing that, so I brought you something." She reaches into this oversize bag and pulls out some wool and knitting needles. "You are going to learn how to knit. Your baby will need winter clothes and seeing how you have more time than money here." She dumps the wool and needles on my bed.

"Oh just like that I'm going to knit."

"Yes, you are. It is easy. I brought you a beginner's book with simple but cute patterns to follow. I will get you started and talk you through it."

"You don't have time for this."

"Who says? Move over." So I moved over and we got to knitting. She was right by supper time I had the hat and booties done. We only had to start over twice so not bad and it wasn't too far into it so it wasn't a big waste of time. This one also had a blanket you could make with it. It was going to make a good outfit to take the baby home in and Anna had bought it in white with a yellow ribbon look running through it.

"See this isn't so hard and it is a good pass time for you."

"No, it's not hard, and I do like doing it. I wished I had been able to do this awhile ago sure would have helped kill some time."

"I can't believe Mom didn't start you. But you can do it now. I'm going back to Mom and Dad's and I will be back tomorrow. I want to see the sweater started at least. That way I can help."

"How long you here for?"

"I am here for a week."

"Really." I felt my body lift with happiness.

"Yes really." She hugs and kisses me and is leaving. "Anna."

"Yeah."

"Thank you so much for this, you have no idea."

"Oh, I think I do. You're welcome. I will see you tomorrow."

When she left I knitted until a nurse came in and told me I should get some sleep or I would end up making mistakes and not knowing I have until it was too late. So I put my knitting away and was feeling happier than I have felt for a long, long time.

Anna came back each day and spent the whole day with me. She crocheted while I knitted. She had made two outfits for the baby. I completed the one full set with the blanket. This made me feel so good I couldn't believe how good this made me.

"I'm sorry to say I'm leaving tomorrow. This has been fun even with you in the hospital. No kids just been able to crochet and not have to worry about anything."

"Where are your kids?"

"Left them with Louise."

"Oh, that was nice of her."

"Sure was, but listen, I have a bag out in the car for you so I will go get it before I forget and leave with it." She left before I could find out what she had brought.

When she came in the door, she looked like Santa Claus with this big bag.

"What the hell have you got there?"

"Wool."

"What?"

"I brought you enough wool and a couple more books you can knit until you go crossed-eyed."

"Oh my god" was all I could say. There were so many different colors of baby wool I wouldn't know which one to choose. But they were all for boy or girl.

"This should keep you busy for a while."

"Yeah, it will. I will pay you back as soon as I can."

"Just make your baby some clothes, and I will make a few more. Just be happy the end is close."

"I know, but I can't wait to go back home. To Alberta, I mean."

"When you can travel, you bring the baby and stay a while. The kids would love to see the baby. So will I."

"I will." Hugging me as hard as she could, making me feel like she didn't want to let go, made me feel loved.

"Everything will be just fine you will see." I was sad to see her go, but now I had my knitting to keep me busy, and I was happy about that.

The nurses got into the knitting as well, and I was getting a nice collection of clothes. This had become quite a contest between the nurses, and it was funny to see them so excited over baby clothes. To see who could make the cutest ones. Either way, it was making my stay a whole lot more pleasant. I was starting to feel like my family had gotten a whole lot bigger in a very short time.

I didn't see much of Mom and Dad. Only on days they had to come into town. Dad was building me a crib. I couldn't believe it. I was happy about that because I knew it would be built strong. Mom said she was making a crib blanket. She even asked what color I wanted it to be. I asked for yellow and white. When she was done, she brought it up for me to see.

"Oh Mom, that is beautiful. I don't want to use it in case I wreck it."

"Don't be silly. How would you wreck this?"

"I don't know, but I don't want to." Dad brought me up pictures of the crib. He even built a music box into the headboard. This was great. Mom seemed to be coming around. I didn't know if maybe Anna talked to her, or if Dad did, or was it just because I had about two weeks to go and Christmas was around the corner. I didn't care I was enjoying Mom anyways. Not seeing her often gave us a little more to talk about.

Linda had come up to see me a few times, to my surprise so did Ron. Of course, it was on the same day Mom and Dad stopped in, so he didn't stay long. It was still nice of him to come. I think him and I will always have a special friendship. One so that I feel that if I ever had no place to go, I could call on him.

The staff had done some Christmas decorating, and everyone was in the Christmas spirit. I heard them talking about what they had bought for their families. And who were staying home and who were leaving.

Here I sit not able to shop, and it wouldn't make any difference as I have no money to shop with anyways.

My baby is all the Christmas I will need. Hope it doesn't wait until too long after to come. Boxing Day would be OK. That is my dad's birthday. I think Dad would really like that.

Watching the snow come down and watching the people walking through it gave me such a warm feeling inside. It was like one of those old pictures of Christmas past. Everyone loaded down with their packages, and everyone seemed to be happy. Or at least it looked like that from where I sat.

Kids throwing snowballs and falling down making snow angels. This made me think of us as kids and all the time we spent outside doing the same things. Funny how not much changes in some ways over all the years. Many things I will pass down to my children. Some things do get forgotten but the basics of life are simple little pleasures.

CHAPTER TWENTY-EIGHT

M y back is aching after supper, so I thought I would put my knitting away and change the way I'm lying and see if that makes it feel better. I toss and turn and the nurse comes in and out asking if I felt OK.

"Yeah, I'm fine."

"Well, let us know if you need anything, you look like you are uncomfortable."

"I have a bit of a backache. Guess I sat the wrong way to long."

"If you want something for the pain, let me know."

"I will thanks, but I will be OK."

Oh god, I didn't know how wrong I was. By one in the morning, I thought I would go mad with the pain. I was actually moaning when the night nurse came in. It was a good thing I was now the only one in the room. They told me there was a lady due in two days, so they were expecting her anytime.

"Char, are you all right."

"No, I have this horrible pain that won't go away. I don't know if I can stand much more of it."

"Oh really! Is this the same pain you told the nurse at suppertime about?"

"Yes."

"Did it ever go away?"

"No just keeps getting worse."

"I think I best go call your doctor."

"All right, thank you." She left and wasn't gone long when she and another nurse came in.

"Char, we are going to be moving you into another room."

"Why?"

"This is not a delivery room, and that is what you will be needing."

"What? You mean I'm having my baby?"

"Looks like it to me, but your doctor will check you out and tell you and us for sure."

"But it's too early. It's not due yet."

"You and the baby will be just fine by having it now. Your due date is not that far away, and this can happen. So don't worry all is well."

"I can't believe it."

"I think you better. We will get you ready for it anyways. I've been a baby nurse for many years, and I would say that is just what is going to happen soon."

"OK. What do you want me to do? This pain is terrible."

"Once your doctor has checked you, he can give you something that will help with the pain."

"I sure hope so, and it won't be soon enough." I held my baby and rocked back and forth. But all I really wanted to do was get up and run. Oh god, if I could just run. I tried to rub my back but couldn't reach to the spot it hurt the most. The top of my thighs ached like I was having my periods and that made me sick to the stomach. How I didn't miss that feeling. As the time went on, the pain got on bearable.

"Good morning, Charlene, and how are you holding up?"

"Good morning, my butt, this hurts."

"You're right, no one ever told you giving birth was painless. But I can make it somewhat tolerable. Let me check you out first, OK?" It took a little bit for him to do a good check up as he tried to do it when the pain wasn't so bad.

"All right, young lady, we are having a baby, sometime today. It is still a ways away, so you have some work to do. You are five centimeters dilated. Do you know how to breathe when the contractions are here?"

"Yeah, I hold my breath."

"Wrong. You want to take deep breaths at that time. One, you have to breathe for the baby and you have to for yourself. It will also help with the pain. I'm sending you in a nurse that will be with you now until you have the baby, and you do whatever she tells you, OK?"

"Yes," I said as I was holding my breath.

"Breathe, Charlene."

"Sorry." I started taking deep breaths. The nurse came in and gave me a needle, and a little while later, I was dozing off. The pain was not gone, but I could tolerate it enough to doze. I had gone all night without sleeping, so I was tired.

I knew the nurse had come in and gave me another needle, but by now, I had lost track of all time.

"Charlene, would you like me to call your mom?"

"Yes, please."

"All right, I will be right back." I had no way of knowing what time she came back, all I could feel was the pain. Later on that evening, rolling over towards the window, I thought I saw Mom there, and she was crying. Why would Mom be crying?

"Please help me, this pain."

"Come on, Charlene, you are going to have to start pushing down when the pain comes. You have rested enough, and now, it is time to do your work. So when the pain comes, push down like you want to poop."

"I don't have to poop. I want to get up and run."

"Charlene, do as I say."

"OK, OK, here comes another pain."

"Push. Breathe. Push. Breathe. Push. Breathe."

"OK, pant like a dog. Dr. Connors and his helper will be in right away, and they are ready to deliver this baby, so you have to push with all you have."

"OK. Oh god, this hurts."

"Push. Breathe. Push. Breathe. Push and push. One more time, Push. Now breathe slow and long."

"How we doing in here?"

"Baby is crowning, so we are moving right along."

"Good, you want to stand here?" Dr. Connors tells his helper. "I will give the baby to you as soon as it is out." His helper nods.

"Push. Push. Push."

"I can't push anymore. I'm beat."

"You can't stop now."

"Oh, Oh, this hurts, and it feels like I have a torch stuck up inside me! Ohhhhh."

"Come on, Charlene. Push. Push. Come on. Push this baby out." The water is just running down my face. I feel like I have been at this for days. In fact, I don't even know what time or day it is. If I push any harder, I feel like the vessels in my face are going to pop.

"Here comes another one, Oh, oh, oh, oh."

"Push, Charlene, with all you have as soon as I tell you to."

"I could feel the doctor working down there but had no idea what he was doing.

"All right, on the next contraction push very hard."

"Here it comes."

"Push. Puuuuush. Come on. You can do it! Oh yeah. Once more should do it."

"OK."

I felt like an animal this time, but I let out a horrible growling sound like some mother bear. After the second time and pushing for all I was worth, I felt the baby leave my body. It was such a relief of joy that I started to cry. Then I heard the baby cry. At that moment, all the pain I had felt seemed to be a long time ago.

"Here would you like to give the baby to its mother?" Dr. Connors was asking his helper. With a nod, he takes the baby and brings it to me. As he leans over to place my baby in my arms, our eyes meet, and I could not believe who I was seeing.

"Congratulations, here is Justin."

"JAMES!"

"I told you I would be here when you had our baby. Here is that piece of paper you gave me."

"Thank you! How did you know?"

"Your mother called me."

"Mom called you. But how?" The tears were rolling down my cheeks so fast James could not wipe fast enough.

"You have great sisters, Char." And with that, he bent over and kissed me on my tear-soaked lips.

EPILOGUE

James had shown up to be with me just as he said he would. He had told me how Mom and Louise had made arrangements to meet with him. Mom wanted to see for herself if this guy was all Louise had said he was.

Mom had told James that if she didn't like what she saw or heard he could just keep right on trucking. There was no way in hell she would let him near her daughter or grandchild. After four hours of asking questions and getting to know James, she finally agreed to telling him what hospital I was in.

"Not that I wouldn't have found you on my own. But I wanted to wait and see what this lady had to say, and I really wanted to meet your mother. You think your mother doesn't care about you. Boy, are you totally wrong. You may feel like the black sheep when it comes to her, and she can come across as a real bitch. But that is just to let people know, that you can't mess with her. She won't take any bull from anyone. I found your mother to be very refreshing."

"You did? How is that so refreshing James?"

"Do you know how many downright honest people there are? Your mother is one of the few. I would take what she has to say all the way to a bank. Just because she tells it the way it is people take her to be a bitch. Believe it or not, I see a lot of her in you."

"You do?

"Yes! You didn't let me push you into anything. I even tried the money approach and you didn't bite. You could have taken me for a real ride and I would have been asking for it if you had. I didn't know you from Adam but I was going on my gut feelings and my mother's feeling. I think we were both right to believe and trust in you.

I'm not going to say I wasn't pisses when you left the way you did knowing how much I wanted to be with you when you had the baby. But you do have my respect at the same time. I just didn't want you to have to go through it all alone. Your sister told me how it has been. I have to agree with your mother when she says 'You made your bed now lie in it.' You didn't have to go through all of that if you would have trusted me enough to give me a chance."

"I'm sorry can you find it in your heart to forgive me?"

"I don't know?" He reaches into his pocket and pulls out a ring. Now that had me sitting up and taking notice

"James!"

"Does this tell you that I willing to forgive you? I want us to get married before you register the baby so he has my last name. I will go find someone tomorrow to marry us.

"But!"

"Listen, I don't want to hear no more buts, OK? When we get home, we will have a proper wedding with all the trimmings. But for now, could you please just do this one thing without having to rethink and rethink it. Don't get me wrong. I'm glad you will be cautious now that we have a son to think about." Now that went right to my heart. He said that about our son without even batting an eye. I knew at that moment that I was head over heels for this man.

"Yes, James. I will marry you." He looked around the room as if it was someone else talking.

"What did you change your mind already?"

"No bloody way. But I thought I would have to do a lot more talking."

"You're right. I think too much." I pull him down and kiss him. Then we both laugh.

The next day, he went and found a JP and two of my nurses stood up for us. Mom and Dad were there. Mom seemed very happy for us, but Dad seemed to be a little down. I will have to get some time and talk to him and see what is bothering him. But for now, I was in seventh heaven.

James stayed with me for the week I was in the hospital. The nurses had fun teaching him how to bathe, dress, and just deal with a baby in general. He seemed to take it all in stride. If I didn't know better, I would have thought he done this a time or two.

The day we got out of the hospital, we went to see Mom and Dad before heading back to Alberta. Oh, that sounded so sweet to my ears. I was going home.

Our visit with Mom and Dad was short but nice. Dad got up and headed outside, so I got up and followed him.

"Dad, wait I will come with you."

"Oh, I didn't hear you come out." I slid my arm through his and pulled him closer to me. I wanted him to feel my love for him.

"Dad, what's wrong? You're not happy for me? Don't you like James?"

"Seems nice enough. But what is he going to be like with the baby?"

"Dad, he loves Justin."

"How can you say that he wasn't here with you?"

"Dad, he would have been if I would have told him where I was."

"Why didn't you?"

"Many reasons, Dad, one been he has a lot of money, and I didn't want him thinking that was all I wanted him for. I also had other things I had to put to rest."

"You mean that guy Ron?

"You're a sly old fox, aren't you, Dad? Yeah it was. Now I know, I feel sure deep down inside and I can move on without any regrets."

"So this man has money?"

"Yeah, Dad, he has a lot of money."

"So I guess you won't be needing this?" he says as he opens his little shop door. There it was the beautiful crib he had made for Justin. With everything going on, I had forgotten about the crib.

"Oh Dad, that is beautiful. Of course, I will be needing it. It is even nicer than the picture you showed me. I will keep it and Justin can use it for his children." Looking over at Dad, I saw a tear roll down his cheek. So I go over to him and say.

"Dad, what's wrong." I take him in my arms and hug him so hard.

"Dad, did you think I wouldn't want the crib because James has money? Oh Dad, you know me better than that. This crib will always be a special part in Justin's birth. The same as the blanket Mom made their beautiful, and you and Mom have put a lot of time into these. They are keepsakes worth more than anything I could buy. You know I love you, Dad."

"Yeah, yeah. We better go see if he wants to put this in his truck. Maybe you're mother has scared him away."

"Don't think so, Dad, I think she really likes James."

"I think she does too." We were all loaded up and gone by two o'clock. The trip home sure was going to be different than the trip coming to Mom and Dad's. There wasn't going to be any waiting outside a bus depot in the wee hours of the morning scared to death. We stopped a lot along the way taking what time we needed to tend to Justin and just taking it easy. We did not have to rush to be anywhere at any given time. We stopped for supper and got a room. James thought maybe it would be too hard on myself and Justin to go all the way in one day. His decision was fine. I was some nervous about our sleeping arrangements, but James was great he made sure Justin and I were comfortable that was all he was concerned about. He said we had lots of time to have a real wedding night. I went to sleep thanking God and Mary for this great man they had sent to Justin and myself. Our trip was very enjoyable.

Once at home, James had another surprise for us. He had bought a big old house in Stony Creek. It was one we had walked by many, many times when he was taking me out of the hospital in the wheelchair. I remember telling him how I wish to own an old house like that someday.

"James, I don't believe my eyes."

"Well, you better. It is your house now."

"You mean, our house." Wrapping his arms around me, he says, "You're right. It is our house. I know what you can do with it, and any money you want is there to do it just as you would like. So whatever your heart desires, go for it. When you are strong and ready."

"Oh, thank you!"

"You're welcome, now let's unpack."

We were married that following summer in our big backyard. James's brother Sam came with his wife and their two girls, and my mom and dad came along with Jacob and Elise and Anna and her kids. Anna had left her husband by now. Louise came with her husband and kids. Marie and her husband came and she was as big as a house with her baby due at anytime.

Beth and Sam stood up for us, it was small and simple. James kept asking if I were sure this was all I wanted. I had told him. James, a big wedding doesn't make your marriage any better.

Everyone liked our old house. Mom and Dad had come and gone a few times. Their last visit was when our daughter was born. They had come to stay with Justin.

James was on cloud nine now that he had a daughter and a son. He said we didn't need to have any more children if I didn't want to. I had told him it would be nice for him to have his own son. Those were the wrong words to have been spoken. I think that was the only time I saw him bad. He was so happy to have Justin and Mary Ann.

The day our daughter was born and I asked if we could call her Mary Ann I thought he had gone into shock.

"My mother would be honored to know we called her Mary."

"She does know."

The years went by fast. Charlene stayed at home until the children were in school full time. Then she resumed her hairdressing. Her sister Anna had moved to Stony Creek by then and opened up her own beauty salon. The dream the two of them had of working together had come true. Charlene had bought into the salon with Anna and the two of them turned it into the place to have your hair done.

After thirty years, it was time to look at taking things a little easier as James Mud Company was also successful. James and Charlene were able to give Justin and Mary Ann all the schooling they wanted. Before they knew it, the children were done all the schooling they needed, and Mary Ann was a nurse and had three children of her own, and Justin, after all his schooling, decided to take over James Mud Company. Justin had five children of his own. He had said it was a good thing Grandpa had made such a strong crib as it has seen many babies. When he wasn't using it, Mary Ann was.

Our children had told us they were scared when they left for college and again when they were moving due to their jobs. They were scared to death when they were getting married and again when they had their first and second babies. In all this time and going down these roads with them, never once did we say to them "Remember you made your bed."

But we did tell them, "Please remember this is your home. If you should stumble and fall once you have left, then you come back and get back on your feet and start all over again. Dad and I will always be here for you no matter what time day or night, and we will always love you.

"Your dreams are just waiting to be lived, so go and be safe and know you are loved."

Through the years, James had shown me that there was a better place to be than in Mary's attic.

Here is a sneak preview of Darleen's new novel
coming in the spring of 2011.

LOVING THEM FROM A DISTANCE

ONE

———◆———

It is a plus thirty day today and I'm out walking in the park. Not seeing too much of what is going on around me as my mind is so consumed with thinking of ways of getting closer. To be able to get almost close enough to touch her. Just so I could smell her perfume. Every time I smell her perfume on some one else it makes me look around for her. My heart quickens with the thought that just maybe she is close by. Then it is always the same let down when you know all the searching for her has come to the end and you no longer can smell her perfume it has been carried away into the air.

There are so many women out there with her build and hair colour that I'm constantly looking and double looking. I spend most of my days watching and praying that just maybe one of them will be her.

It has been three years since I've seen the face of my angel. Or heard the sweet melody of her voice. With each day that passes a little more of me dies. Every day I make a trip to the post office in hopes that perhaps she has dropped me a line. The post office has always been one place I would stay away from I have always dreaded going there and now each morning I can't wait to get there. When ever the phone rings I stand and stare at it to see whose number it might be. Most of the time I don't answer it because I'm so disappointed when I see that it's not her calling.

Up until now I have walk around in limbo since that awful day that she left. It was Mothers Day weekend. There was no happy Mothers Day from her or even a good—bye. She was just gone.

This hasn't stopped me from buying her a Christmas present each year that I put under the tree just in case she comes home Christmas eve. I would never want her to think for one minute that I have forgotten her or quit loving her. I also buy her a special card and birthday present. Her birthday is the third of January. This makes for a double let down when both occasions go buy and I haven't heard from her. The only good thing about both of them been so close together the severe pain is all over at one time. The dull ache returns and takes over my life.

I always felt that we had a very special relationship and new each other inside and out. All the dreams of the future that we had talked about over and over have all since gone with her. wh. Not been able to share in any of them up until now has been tearing the heart right out of me.

For me to go on I am going to have to find her, so I can put my mind at ease and mend a broken heart.

What changes have come into her life? What has she become? These are all unanswered question that I want answers to. When you really think about it time has gone bye fast. But for my heart it has come to a stand still and I know now that I must push on and do what I can to find her. I have known of the last place she was working and I always stayed away. I did not want to cause a scene nor did I want to embarrass her or myself.

Up until now I have left it in Gods hands and every night I prayed that he would help her find her way back to me. I really hoped it would be while I was still in good health and still had my mind. But going this way I won't have my mind much longer and no one can stay in good heath when you are consumed with grieve so I have decided to take action. I have been thinking about this for some time now and making some plans on how I was going to go about this. With her living out of town it will be easier to put my plans into action.

I have wondered if she ever looks for me. While she is walking down the street or even in her place of work. Does she ever see some one who might make her think of me? Does she pass by some one who wears the same perfume as I do? Does it make it hard for her to breath, does it choke her up so that she think she going to pass out right there on the spot? Does she get the terrible pain in the chest that comes after the disappointment of not spotting me in the crowd? Does she even think about those last words she spoke to me as she went out the door that Mothers Day? I think of them often and wonder how anyone could say such a cruel thing to some one who loves her unconditionally.

At this time I'm walking down main street and I've decided to go ahead with my plans. First on my list is to find a hair shop that has an opening. I'm afraid that if I wait and make an appointment I would end up backing out. This way I will just walk in and before I know it. It would be done.

It was beginning to look like it was going to be a no go today. Every shop I went into they were booked up for days.

They tell me it's because of all the weddings. I guess it is that time of year.

The last shop that I entered they had room for me.

"Good morning Dear."

"Good morning. May I help you?

"Yes dear, I would like to have a make over done. Do you do that here?"

"Just what were you thinking of Madam?"

"I want you to do some thing that will make me feel younger and look it."

"OH! It's that time is it? I wondered what she meant at first.

"You need a little lift in your life do you?"

"YES! I sure do. I've gotten myself in a slump and it's time to get out."

"Then come with me and I will see what all we can do for you."

"Thank you." Following her to the back I saw several women in there doing lord only new what to them selves. But probably not one of them were doing it for the same reason as I was.

Once the girl had shampooed my hair, I got seated so the real chore could begin.

"Now do you have any plans? Or did you need a book to look at?" I took a couple of minutes and thought about it.

"You know what? I am giving you the reins. This will be your chance to do what ever you think I need. After all if it doesn't work I can always have it change to some thing I would want. How does that sound to you?"

"Let me get this straight! You want me to make the choices?"

"Yes I do. You have taken training in this and I know you are taught to look at people and be able to put the right cut and colour together to get what you want." I wasn't going to tell her that I am also a hair dresser but I just haven't had to work for years.

"But your hair is so long, and is a beautiful white. Do you know what people pay to get their hair this colour?"

"Yes dear I do. But like I said I need a big change in my life. I don't want to wear it up in a bun any more. I would also love to have some colour for a change."

"Are you really sure about this Madam?"

"YES! Dear I am! Now if you don't want to do it, maybe one of your coworkers will."

"OH! Madam, I will and I know just what I will give you."

"Then what are we waiting for. Let's do it."

"You will be here for a while."

"That's fine with me I have nothing but time."

My husband was use to me just coming and going. I'm pretty sure he new that I left as soon as he had left for work. I didn't always get home before him. He would come and find me sitting in the mall or a park watching people. He never asked. He didn't have to, he new why I would be there. He would just come along and sit down beside me and wrap his arms around me and say.

"Are you ready to come home yet?" He uses to ask me if I thought this was healthy for me. I would just tell him. Why? I'm just on an outing. He nods his head and taking my hand says to me.

"Come on Babe I will buy you a coffee." So we go for our coffee before we go to our home of silence.

Our marriage has paid the price. She consumes my every thought. I go about and do what has to be done on a daily base as far as house keeping goes. But my husband is on the back burner and I have tried so many times to change how I am but something will always take me back to thinking of her. When she first left I spent a lot of days crying and talking with my husband but it got to wear it was all negative talk and it started to make me feel worse. I didn't need to hear any more negative talk, I needed to see her. I need to be able to wrap my arms around her and tell her how special she is to me and how much I love her.

I don't think my husband felt the same as she is his step daughter. He has been a very good step father to her. He always went the extra mile for her no questions asked.

The morning she left our house the way she did and the things she said also hurt him. He also knows that as a Mother I would put my life on the line for her.

The young girl working on me didn't seemed to know what she was doing, at first she made me a little nervous. I was thinking maybe I don't want her cutting my hair. When she took the first cut our eyes met in the mirror. I just smiled.

"See that wasn't so hard now was it?"

"No Madam." She carried on until I had a cut that was shorter in the back then the front. Yet it was full of body.

"I want to put a perm in it and it will be very easy for you to do every day."

"I don't want an old fuzzy perm."

"No Madam, it will be tighter in the back but the front and sides will only give you a very lose curl."

"What about a colour?"

"OH Yes Madam. But not until after I have perm it. The perm would strip some of your colour out and we don't want that."

"Yes, Madam." Jessie was her name and she did as she said and done the perm. I looked at what she was mixing up.

"That's really red."

"Yes Madam, but I want to also do tin foiling as well which will bring this colour to more of a strawberry blonde when I'm finished."

"OH alright that sounds very nice."

"It won't be such a drastic change if we do it this way seeing how your hair is so white. This will also go with your skin colour better then one solid colour."

Sitting there watching her put the foil on my hair I got to thinking about how old she was. She was small and very dark. I could tell by her language she wasn't from here.

"Jessie, how old are you?"

"I'm twenty three Madam."

"Were you born here in Canada?"

"No Madam." That is where she left it. I figured if she wanted me to know where she was from she would have offered the information with out me having to ask. Seeing how she didn't, I wouldn't push it. She did seem to be a very private person. I could hear the other girls talking away to the women they were working on but not Jessie she hardly said anything at all.

I wonder if my daughter is like Jessie. Does she keep all her life a secret or has she told anyone how she left that dread full morning.

"Well Madam. What do you think?" I hadn't realized that I had been off on some trip and hadn't noticed that Jessie was done. When I did finally focus on myself in the mirror. I didn't know who I was looking at.

"WOW! WOW!" was all that would come out. I new when people had make over's it really changed their appearance. Which I understood for people who never done anything as far as doing their hair or putting on make up. But I always do both and always thought I had done a good job of taking care of myself. But this girl has done a miracle. I'll be surprised if my husband doesn't turn around and walk out of the house thinking he's got the wrong place.

"You don't like Madam?"

"Oh no! On the contrary, Jessie you have done a fantastic job. The cut and colour are beautiful. I like the way you work it all in. I would not have asked for this because I wouldn't begin to have dream of it. I think I must have been out of touch with the up to date hairs dues now for some time. Thank you so very much."

"You're welcome Madam. I sure hope this helps you with the change you needed"

"Oh it sure will. I'm glade I found you." Thinking that my daughter won't know me. If I had picked something she would have been able to pick me out of a crowd because she knows me. But this she would never think I would do something so hip. It has taken ten years plus off my face. Paying the young girl and by the look on her face she was very happy with her tip. I really felt she deserved it. It was really a good job well done. I couldn't believe how this made me feel, almost like a new person. I think I will stop one more time on the way home.

Edwards Brothers,Inc!
Thorofare, NJ 08086
07 December, 2010
BA2010341